MONSTEROTICA

Tales of Unusual Courtship and Coupling

Duck Prints Press, LLC
Schenectady, NY

Edited by boneturtle, Rhosyn Goodfellow, Catherine E. Green, Mikki Madison, Alec J. Marsh, and Nina Waters. Significant contributions also made by all the members of the Duck Prints Press advisory staff.

Print manuscript formatting by Hermit Prints.
E-book formatting by Nina Waters.

Published by Duck Prints Press, LLC
Schenectady, New York
duckprintspress.com

ISBN (ePub): 978-1-962488-46-4
ISBN (PDF): 978-1-962488-47-1
ISBN (Trade Paperback): 978-1-962488-45-7

Table of Contents

DISASTERBIRD

MJ Kiwiana

bipoc, bird person, bisexual, family, fantasy, frottage, getting together, half-human, hand job, kissing, m/m, meet cute, octopus person, present tense, self-esteem issues, size kink, tentacles, third person limited (multiple) point of view

"Hāro? Hāro!"

Hāro groans as his mum's piercing squall drags him out of sleep, his eyes blinking against the too-bright sun. Something's digging into the sensitive skin just under his wing, and one of his talons has snagged in the night—it's short and jagged, tugging on Hāro's feathers when he scratches his face.

"Up you get, chicklet. You have a date this morning, remember?"

Fuck. How could he forget? This is basically his life now—a series of first dates, none of them ever materialising a second. And for good reason.

"I'm *up*, Mum!"

"Up means out of the nest, my love."

Hāro almost pulls a face but thinks better of it. He's, like, eighty percent sure she can't see through the bark walls and into his bedroom, but those odds aren't good enough to risk it. He shoves his bedding to the floor before hauling himself out of his nest, his knuckles brushing against the ceiling as he stretches the kink out of his back, wings shooting out on either side of his torso and filling most of the room. He eyes his dresser with trepidation. He still has to figure out what to wear, and eat breakfast, and comb his feathers, and all he *wants* to do is crawl back into his nest and throw the blankets over his head until everyone agrees to never use the word "date" around him ever again.

By the time he makes it down to the lower branches—dressed in his best tunic, the one that his grandmother always said really highlights his wingspan—Hāro's mum has prepared what could more accurately be called a feast than breakfast. The table is almost buckling under the weight of grains, meat, and the fish that always makes Hāro turn up his beak no matter how many times his mum insists it's a vital part of any good Huruhuru diet.

"You didn't need to do all this." He tugs uncomfortably at the collar of his tunic where it suddenly feels too tight. "It's not like today's going to go any better than—"

"Nonsense." His mum's voice is sharp as she cuts him off, her beak audibly clacking in frustration. "You just need the right attitude; well, that and the right partner. And Kata is a lovely girl, isn't she?"

She is a lovely girl. Her loveliness isn't why he's hesitating. But Hāro has been on no fewer than forty-seven first dates this year, and with one glaring exception, they've *all* been lovely girls, or lovely guys, or lovely creatures. Of those forty-seven dates, there have been forty-seven catastrophic failures, forty-six of which have been Hāro's fault—which means that, statistically, he's all but guaranteed to fuck this one up, too.

"Yeah." He picks up a slice of venison, tipping his head back to drop it into his oropharynx before his mum can chide him for his lack of table manners. "Yeah, Kata's cool."

"Well, then." His mum pats him softly on the cheek, smoothing out the feather under her thumb. "Maybe this time will be different, eh? All you need to do is *try*. And don't screech, or get glue in your feathers, or—"

"*Bye*, mum." He blows her a kiss before making his way to the edge of the branch. As he glides to the ground, he tries very hard not to let his mum's well-meaning advice get under his skin.

Maybe she's right. Maybe this time *will* be different.

The sun beats mercilessly down as Hāro strolls into town, and there's enough of a breeze to ruffle his feathers. It feels so nice that, with no one else on the path, he unfurls his wings and lets the air move through them, hopping and gliding every time he catches a current at the right time. Apart from one dryad who rolls his eyes at Hāro's antics, the few creatures he passes either ignore him or give him a small smile, so he doesn't bother re-folding his wings until he reaches the township. Reflexively, he runs his hands over his tunic; it's still clean, barely wrinkled, and not even a little bit on fire. No matter what happens from here, at least it won't be the *worst* date he's ever been on.

Kata is already waiting at the fountain when he arrives. Her plumage is all the colours of a winter sunset, and she has an elegant silver baldric slung over her torso with several small fans tucked into it, the sort of fans Huruhuru use to modulate airflow if they're doing something particularly flashy and complicated during a dive.

Hāro gulps. He's not sure if he's more impressed or intimidated.

"Hāro! Hi!" Kata's smile is wide and bright as she reaches out, her hand gripping his shoulder and her wing wrapping around both of their bodies in a familiar embrace, his forehead pressed to the bottom of her chin. If she's even remotely as nervous as Hāro is, she isn't showing it; then again, why *should* she be? She's not the one approaching fifty fruitless casts of the net.

"Hey." He tries to match her tone, but it comes out more strangled than breezy. He's vaguely aware that a circle is starting to form around them; whether people are taking note of Kata's baldric or Hāro's trepidation, he isn't sure. He sucks in a breath and puts his audience out of his mind. "Are you ready to do this?"

Kata stretches out her wings with a grin. "Absolutely."

Hāro envies her easy confidence. His wings itch as he follows her lead and lets them expand to their full span, the feathertips of one skating

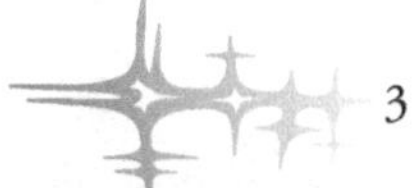

across the water in the pond and doing nothing to distract him from the sharp bundle of nerves in his chest. This is supposed to be easy. It's a gliding ritual, of all the things—compared to the feather displays and the birdsong harmonies, gliding should be simple. Just the two of them, side by side, moving together in perfect harmony.

Kata takes off first, and he only hesitates a moment before following her. She cuts a striking figure against the summer sky, her body twisting gracefully as she catches the air. Hāro does his best to keep up with her, matching her rhythm when he can, trying to complement it when he can't. And it's fun, but it's not…it's not *effortless*. His wings are heavy, as though they're waterlogged rather than aerodynamic, and no matter how hard he tries, he can't seem to subconsciously grasp the currents the way Kata appears to. He glances down, hoping for some sign—a leaf blowing on the wind, maybe, or the direction the trees are bending—that might give him a bit of a hint on how he can actually *do this*.

He doesn't see a leaf, and he doesn't notice the trees. But he does see the river.

It's not like he didn't know the river was there—he's glided over it, walked past it, even waded across it once or twice. There's something about the river today, though, that he can't seem to tear his gaze away from. Sunlight bounces off the surface, a thousand diamonds flickering across a meandering canvas as it winds its way towards the sea, where it empties out into—

The wind current shifts.

Hāro curses, yanking his gaze away from the water, but it's too late. The current should have swept him up and into Kata's airspace, but he met it side-on instead of head-on, and now the air is too thick. He flaps his wings frantically, trying to catch up to her, but he's off-balance and unprepared—he's being dragged downwards as Kata rises higher, the gap between them ever-widening.

Kata turns her head, clearly expecting him to be next to her; when he isn't, she twists her whole body around to face him. She's far, but not so far that Hāro can't read her expression: uncertainty, concern, resignation.

Fuck.

He doesn't bother trying to land gracefully. He staggers when his feet find the earth, and he slumps against the nearest tree without bothering to fold his wings back, letting them flop in the grass as Kata glides down

to meet him.

"Good try, Hāro." Her voice is unbearably gentle, and Hāro wants to scream. It might be easier if she was rude about it. "You almost had it."

He nods, the weight in his chest only getting heavier with how *kind* she's being. He doesn't say anything else, just watches in silence as she walks away.

Forty-eight.

Forty-*eight* catastrophic failures, and forty-seven of them are absolutely, one hundred percent Hāro's fault.

He should go home.

He can't do it. He can't bear to see the look on his mum's face, or listen to her assure him that "it will happen for you any day now, love." He just *can't.*

Instead, he walks. He keeps his head down so that he doesn't meet anyone's eyes, and he doesn't put any thought into where he's going; at least, not until the grass under his feet gives way to dry sand, and then dry sand to wet sand as the sea stretches out before him, over the horizon and out of sight.

He sinks to his knees, burying his talons into the wet grit and letting his wings fall to the ground behind him. A wave creeps in to welcome him, the sand shifting underneath Hāro's palms as the water laps around him then falls back. There's no one around to hear him fighting to catch his breath, or to see how he's trying desperately to blink the sting out of his eyes.

"Forty-eight." He clenches his hands into fists, the sand spilling out from between his talons before being stolen away by another wave. "Forty-*bloody*-eight monumental fuckups, and for what? At this rate, my name's going to become synonymous with species failure. Ten generations from now, they'll be telling stories about Hāro the Failed Huruhuru, and all the kids will think it's a silly made-up legend meant to scare them."

He lets himself slump sideways before rolling onto his back, not caring that one wing is twisted uncomfortably underneath him. It's going to take hours, if not days, to get all the sand out of his feathers.

"'Don't be like Hāro,' they'll say." He's aware that if anyone happens to come along and hears the way he's ranting at the tideline, they're going to be very concerned; he's beyond caring at this point. "'Did you know he once got his tail stuck in a lantern during a candlelit dinner? He had to be cut out. Legend has it that to this day, his tail is still lopsided.'"

Another wave laps at him, almost like it's patting him on the shoulder. It's weirdly comforting, and it takes all the wind out of Hāro's sails.

"I just...fuck. I tried. I really, really tried."

That's when the sea decides to answer back.

"That was rough, I'm not gonna lie." It's a warm voice, low and distinctly amused, but that doesn't make it any less shocking to hear. "But if it helps, I've *definitely* seen worse."

Hāro almost swallows a mouthful of the next wave that rises up to meet him. He launches himself upright, his wings throwing up a spray of sand behind him as he twists around, heart racing as he searches for the mystery speaker.

The beach is empty.

Or, well...yes, the *beach* is empty. But there's a faint ripple just offshore, a hint of something Hāro can't quite see moving below the surface. Before he can say anything, a figure emerges from the shallows, hoisting himself up to lean against a flat rock that sits a few metres back from the shoreline. And, look, Hāro might be having a really shitty day, but he isn't *blind*, he can appreciate the dark skin, the toned body, the hair that tumbles like kelp across the stranger's shoulders. At first, he has the wild thought that the stranger might be *human*, rare though they are around here. But as he lets his gaze wander lower—for...strictly analytical reasons—he notes the lack of a navel, the way slim hips taper off into long, shimmering tentacles that seem to refract the sunlight hitting them through the water. A cecaelia, then. Hāro hasn't actually met one before; the deepwater folks tend to keep to themselves.

"Um." It's not exactly Hāro at his most eloquent. "Hi."

"Hi." The stranger grins, a dimple appearing in one cheek. "Are the dramatic ocean monologues, like, a regular thing? Is there a schedule, or do I have to hang around and hope I might catch an impromptu delivery?"

Hāro splutters out something that isn't really sure if it's a laugh or a wheeze.

"It was a solid performance, I gotta say," he continues. "I mean, if I had to nitpick, the pacing was a little wonky, but that's nothing a good editor can't fix."

Hāro buries his face in his hands. "I didn't realise anyone was listening."

The cecaelia laughs. "A reasonable assumption. Unfortunately for you, I'm a sucker for pretty boys going through emotional crises, so here I am."

That makes Hāro look up again. The stranger is still grinning at him, but it isn't cruel; if anything, it's soft at the edges. "Are you *flirting* with me?"

"Maybe a little." He shrugs. "Maybe a lot. Depends on how receptive you are, I guess."

For a moment, there's no sound except the wind and the tide and, somewhere in the distance, a particularly vocal seagull.

"I'm Hāro," he offers.

"Turana." The cecaelia—Turana, apparently—grins. "Have you *really* been on forty-eight courtship rituals?"

"Okay, in my *defence*—"

"Who said it needed defending?" Turana shrugs, the water rippling around him as one of his tentacles pops up from underneath the water for a moment. "Play the field. Sow your oats. Whatever other odd land idioms apply here. There's no point in settling."

Hāro snorts. "Trust me. I'm not the one deciding it's not a successful courtship."

Turana raises an eyebrow. "Really? You're telling me that all forty-eight times were your fault and yours alone?"

"Well, no."

Turana gestures as if to say, *See?*

One took a stamina-enhancing tonic before our mating dance, but they either fucked up the dose or they had a weird reaction to it. They…threw up on me."

Turana stares at him for a long moment. "In mid-air?"

"In mid-air."

"That's…" He trails off, clearly lost for words.

"Yup." Hāro sighs. "So that one, not my fault. All the others? Definitely my fault. Apparently all I'm good at is making a mess."

Turana tilts his head to the side. "Nothing wrong with a bit of mess."

"There is if it's stopping you from finding a partner."

Turana laces his fingers together, resting them on his stomach. "Okay, but what's more important to you? Finding the right person *for you*, or achieving a successful courtship by an arbitrary, external standard?"

Hāro blinks. "That…is a very deep question for this time of day."

"I'm a cecaelia, darling." Turana smiles sweetly. "'Deep' is something of a requirement. And you're avoiding the question."

"I'm not *avoiding* it." It's a lie; he's absolutely avoiding it. "But…does the distinction really matter?"

"Of course it does." Turana sighs. "Besides, you think you're the only person who's had romantic disasters? I once got my hectocotylus *stuck* in my ex-boyfriend's cloaca."

Hāro barks out a laugh before he can stop himself. "You're *kidding*."

"I promise I'm not. The only difference is that there wasn't a whole societal expectation that we figure that stuff out on day one and in front of a bunch of strangers." Turana smiles at him. "You're not doing anything wrong, Hāro. You just…haven't found the right courtship ritual for *you* yet."

"Forty-eight, remember?" Hāro points out dryly. "Trust me, I've tried them all—several times."

Turana reaches out towards the water, flicking some of it in Hāro's direction with a grin. "Come on, disasterbird. If the courtship rituals aren't working for you, come up with a new one. Make your own happiness."

He says it like it's simple; like it's obvious. But it can't be that easy.

Can it?

They talk for so long, the sun starts casting long shadows, stretching across the sand. Hāro waxes poetic about wind drafts in valleys; Turana gives him a dramatic retelling of a truly disastrous underwater poetry slam that resulted in three injuries and four family feuds. When the tide recedes again, Hāro wanders out to the rock Turana is sitting on, trying and failing to look nonchalant as he tucks himself up on it, Turana laughing at the way his almost-eight-foot frame has to be scrunched up to fit—though he does obligingly slide a little farther into the water so

that Hāro has somewhere for his wings to rest, turning around so that his stomach is pressed against the rocks instead, his tentacles fanning out lazily behind him, bouncing a little in the waves.

He can't remember the last time he was this *comfortable.*

The sun is close to setting, the soft ebb and flow of the tide transformed into a kaleidoscope of pinks and oranges, when Hāro realises how long it's been since they last said anything. The easy rhythm of their conversation slowed without Hāro feeling a need to rush in and fill the gap, letting the hush of wind and water ease the silence instead. Turana has slid farther and farther into the water over the course of the afternoon, his chin resting on the rock's edge, his hair salt-damp above the waterline and trailing like seaweed behind him. Hāro is sprawled across the rock, his legs dangling over the side with the talons of his toes tracing idle patterns in the water as his wings stretch out across the rough surface he's leaning on.

He's tall, even for a Huruhuru; taller still next to Turana, even before considering the cecaelia has spent most of their time together with at least half his body submerged. But right now, it doesn't seem to matter. For once, he doesn't feel too big. Too clumsy. Too *much.*

Turana looks up at him with a lopsided grin, seemingly picking up on Hāro's change in mood. "What are you thinking about, disasterbird?"

Despite himself, Hāro snorts at the nickname. Coming from someone else, he might be offended—but there's so much affection in the way Turana says it, he can't bring himself to mind. It feels like a joke they're sharing, rather than like Turana laughing at him.

"Just...I don't know." He sits up, wrapping his hands around his shins and dropping his chin to his knee, clacking his beak nervously. "Mostly I'm thinking about how I'm more relaxed here, with a stranger, than I have been in months. Maybe years."

One tentacle breaks the surface, flicking with what Hāro can only assume is delight. "The pleasure of my company will do that to you."

Fuck. Hāro's always been weak for confidence. "I bet." He spreads his wings, letting the feathers at the very base of them graze along the top of the water. He loves feeling a bit of water weight in his wings. "But,

like. . . forty-eight failed dates, remember? I know every courtship ritual back to front and inside out, and one of them is supposed to lead to this magical moment, this click where everything falls into place and you feel *whole*." He trails off, throat tight. "But it never happens. And the more I try, the more I think. . . I don't know. That I'm broken?"

Turana frowns, hoisting himself out of the water and onto the rock, twisting gracefully so that he ends up sitting next to Hāro.

"Have you ever considered that there's nothing wrong with *you*? That maybe the problem is a box has been presented to you, and you're so busy trying to contort yourself to fit into it that you haven't stopped to check that the box was the right size in the first place?"

"What do you mean?"

"I mean that I've known you for less than half a day, and I already know that you're funny, and charming, and brilliant. And if none of that matters to your potential partners more than your ability to. . . to fly a particular pattern, or create a particular artwork, or whatever—then they're *missing out*. And that's a 'them' problem, not a 'you' problem. I think you're following a current that was never meant to carry you. Or—" Turana screws up his nose in thought. "Um, you're trying to fly someone else's pattern. And you're never going to be as good at that as you are at your own."

Something cracks open in Hāro's chest, like the ache of a cramped muscle finally starting to loosen. Is that what he's been missing? Do other Huruhuru really not feel like they have to try *so* hard to make it all work?

"I don't think I know how to fly any other way."

Turana shifts closer, his shoulder brushing Hāro's arm. "Maybe that's why you feel so relaxed here. No one expects you to fly any sort of way in the ocean." He tilts his head, considering. "Well, unless you're a seagull. But, you know, maybe don't try to emulate them. Annoying little assholes."

Hāro chokes out a laugh, turning his head to chastise Turana for the comment—but the laughter dies on his tongue when he realises Turana has turned to face him at the same time, their noses barely a couple of centimetres from each other. Something skates across Hāro's mind like wind over feathers: a fleeting idea, impossible to unthink once it's taken root.

He wants…*fuck*, he wants.

"You keep looking at me like you think I'm going to disappear."

Hāro swallows. "Honestly, I'm not totally sure this isn't a super intense dream."

"Well, if it is"—Turana reaches out, one hand brushing across Hāro's cheek before splaying across the back of his neck, possessive and relaxed—"then you might as well enjoy it, don't you think?"

Hāro's wings twitch involuntarily, trying to balance against something that hasn't quite hit him yet. One of Turana's tentacles brushes Hāro's thigh, cautious and curious, cool against the heat gathering under his skin. The contact jolts through him, and he shudders despite himself. His pulse is drumming in his throat, and his stomach is twisting itself in knots—he thinks about all the ways he's gotten this wrong before, all the dates he's floundered through trying to meet some ancient expectation. Whatever this is, it isn't that. It's…uncharted. Wild in a way he doesn't quite have the words for.

"You're serious about this?" Hāro asks, voice thin.

"You're the one with your talons on my rock, sweetheart." Turana's tone is light, but there's a rasp that wasn't there before. "I'm just here. Waiting to see what you want."

What he *wants*?

What Hāro wants is to lean into that smile and see if it tastes like salt. Wants to lose himself in the easy pleasure of heat and body and breath. Wants to be someone who reaches instead of retreats.

So he does.

He closes the distance like a dive: swift, instinctual, inevitable. His beak brushes the corner of Turana's mouth before he finds the right angle, and it's awkward for a moment—he's never kissed someone with such fleshy lips before—but then, suddenly, it isn't. Suddenly it's pressure and warmth and the thud of his heartbeat in his ears, his hand sliding up Turana's chest to find his heart racing just as fast as Hāro's. Turana kisses like he knows exactly what he's doing, that self-assured confidence that attracted Hāro to him in the first place almost overwhelming now as a tentacle wraps lazily around Hāro's ankle. Not tight; just enough to let him know it's there.

And, stars help him, he wants more.

If someone had told Turana when he rolled out of bed and broke for the surface this morning that his day would end with a Huruhuru's wing wrapped around his shoulder, his tentacle hooked around a feathery leg as they awkwardly navigate the give and take of beak and lip until it isn't awkward anymore, Turana would have laughed in their face. But here he is nonetheless, heat pooling in his stomach as he grips the back of Hāro's neck, pulling him closer and startling a moan out of them both at the shift in angle.

He'd seen a little of what Hāro has dismissively deemed his "forty-eighth monumental fuckup" this afternoon. He'd been sunning himself on his favourite rock, eyes closed as he soaked up the heat and tried not to think about the way his siblings always scoffed at how much time he spent "surface-slumming," when a soft trilling sound swept over to him on the wind. He'd watched a pair of Huruhuru—two beautiful creatures, but one breathtakingly so, in Turana's opinion—swoop through the air. The one Turana was most interested in had seemed to be following the currents of the river moreso than the wind.

And then *something* had happened. The Huruhuru had missed a beat, or… Whatever it was, the two of them had soon dipped below the trees and out of sight.

Turana hadn't expected to see him again. Certainly hadn't expected him to turn up on the shore and word-vomit all his despair in Turana's general direction. And he'd been completely unprepared for Hāro to be even more attractive up close, let alone for him to be so clever and funny and *interesting*.

And he absolutely hadn't been prepared to be making out with a Huruhuru in the glow of the setting sun, something hot and hard and enticingly unfamiliar pressing against his stomach.

Hāro seems to realise this at the same time Turana does, because he pulls away with a grimace. "Sorry."

The word lands sharp and unwanted between them, like a stone tossed into a calm tide. For a heartbeat, Turana thinks Hāro is about to fold in on himself entirely; his wings are twitching, beak clacking nervously as his eyes skitter over Turana's face and away again. The kind of retreat that feels rehearsed, like he's had to do it too many times before.

Turana doesn't let him.

"Sorry?" Turana echoes, deliberately incredulous. He tilts his head with a smirk. "What exactly are you apologising for? The kissing? Because if you think that's a problem, disasterbird, feel free to keep right on offending me."

Hāro stammers something, gesturing vaguely downward, as though the awkward swell pressing against his tunic isn't already obvious.

"Oh," Turana drawls, dragging the syllable out like salt sliding back over stone, his grin deepening. "*That*."

The poor creature looks mortified. And beautiful. Kraken's teeth, Hāro's beautiful like this: trembling, awkward, trying so hard to hold himself together while his body betrays every raw, urgent truth. "I just—I know you don't have—and it's not—"

"Sweetheart," Turana cuts off the mortified stammering, finally realising what has Hāro so uncomfortable. "Just because I don't *have* one, doesn't mean I don't know exactly what it's for." Hāro looks up sharply, but it doesn't seem like the time to dwell on the odd sailor who's fallen off their ship in Turana's vicinity and found themselves quite happy to pass the time until rescue. His hand trails down Hāro's chest, stopping just shy of the straining fabric. He can feel the heat radiating off the body underneath his palms, the erratic thrum of Hāro's pulse. "And I know that this is the best compliment I've had in months."

The noise Hāro makes is somewhere between a gasp and a curse, wings twitching wider. "Fuck."

"Exactly." Turana's grin sharpens. "Finally, you're catching on."

He doesn't give Hāro time to retreat again. He pulls him forward, mouth crashing into mouth, and this time, all the tentative exploration is behind them. This kiss is all heat and hunger, gentleness giving way to reckless desperation. Hāro groans into it, his talons scraping rock for purchase before tangling in Turana's hair. He tugs hard, and Turana gasps against his beak, his hectocotylus throbbing in response.

Stars above and currents below, this bird can kiss.

Turana bites, daring him to unravel, and Hāro answers with a groan that vibrates down Turana's spine. The sound is too good, too much, too perfect. He wants to drink it down again and again, wants to see how many different notes he can coax from that sharp beak and those trembling feathers.

He slides a tentacle higher along Hāro's calf, tracing spirals and enjoying Hāro's shivers as his feathers are pushed up. He shudders beautifully, wings flaring wider, and Turana can't help but laugh into the kiss, deliriously giddy with the way Hāro responds to every caress. Another tentacle loops up behind Hāro's thigh, testing the weight of him, the sheer size and strength wrapped up in this awkward, beautiful creature.

"Fuck," Hāro says again, his voice breaking, and Turana feels it vibrate against his mouth.

"I'll take that as a compliment."

He uses his own body to press Hāro back against the rock. The sharp ridge of heat grinding into Turana's stomach makes his pulse stutter, pleasure winding hot and insistent through him. He moans, not caring that it comes out far louder than he intended, rough and guttural.

"See?" he manages, lips brushing along the curve of Hāro's beak. "You're not the only one aching for this."

Hāro keens, his wings slamming fully open and scattering saltwater spray into the sunset. The sight is obscene in its beauty, and Turana can't help but stare at the trembling wings, feathers glowing gold and orange in the fading light, every inch of Hāro's body lit up with want.

Turana loses himself to the impulse to let his tentacles slide in from every angle. They curl around thighs, tease along the insides of feathered legs, test the curve of Hāro's ass. He takes his time, each stroke deliberate and exploratory. There's no rush. He doesn't *want* to rush. He wants to enjoy this for as long as he can.

And by the depths, Hāro responds. His hips stutter forward helplessly, every muscle trembling as he grinds against Turana's stomach as if he can't stop himself. The urgency pouring off him is intoxicating, as wild and reckless as the sea at stormtide.

This isn't some polished ritual dance or rehearsed feather display. This is messy. Breathless. *Real.* And Turana wants every shuddering second of it. Every shaky groan, every helpless little cry, wrecks Turana in the best possible way. Hāro grinds against him like he can't help it, wings stretching wider still with each press of heat. He's so far gone already, undone by nothing more than kissing and a few exploratory touches, and Turana aches to see how much further he can take him.

"You're beautiful, disasterbird," Turana mutters against his beak. It's not just the feathers flaring golden in the light; it's the way Hāro gives

himself away. Every want, every fear, writ plain across his body.

Turana wants to see more of it. Wants to dive for the hidden softness, the secret depths, like he's hunting for pearls.

So he does.

His fingers tug at the laces of Hāro's tunic, slick with seawater and awkward around the curve of his wings. "Let me," Turana murmurs, low and coaxing. "Trust me."

Hāro hesitates, a quick intake of breath, but he doesn't pull away. He blinks once, twice, then nods.

Turana slides one tentacle in, deft as any hand, curling around the knot and easing it loose. The fabric slackens, then falls away to reveal Hāro in all his glory.

Hāro's cock is long, flushed dark, already wet at the tip where it curves up against his stomach. It looks almost too big for his own body, straining, eager, trembling with each pulse of his wings. Turana's breath catches just looking at it.

"Fuck me," he mutters, unable to hold back the awe. "You're—"

Hāro shifts awkwardly, flushing deeper. "Too much?"

"Perfect," Turana corrects fiercely, palms and suckers alike skimming across the feathers of his thighs as he drinks in the sight. "Look at you."

Hāro makes another sharp sound, half groan, half whimper, his wings arching instinctively at the touch. The sound hits Turana like lightning and his hectocotylus twitches, aching and almost as hard as Hāro's cock is where it lies against his stomach, at the sheer vulnerability of it.

Turana noses along his collarbone as his tentacles map Hāro's body: one curling possessively around his waist, another stroking slowly and deliberately up his inner thigh, another anchoring firmly around his hip.

When one tentacle nudges against his cloaca, Hāro *gasps*, wings snapping so wide Turana half expects them to knock both of them clean off the rock. Instead they tremble there, open and desperate, as Hāro tips his head back and stares up at the swiftly darkening sky, at the stars just beginning to emerge.

Turana grins, wicked, and presses just a little farther. The noise Hāro makes…it nearly undoes him.

"Sensitive everywhere, aren't you?" he teases, mouth dragging along Hāro's throat. "Tell me you want this."

"I—fuck—yes," Hāro chokes out. His claws scrape uselessly against rock before tangling back into Turana's hair, dragging him closer. "Yes, just—don't stop."

"Good boy." The words slip out unthinking, but the shudder they pull from Hāro is immediate, visceral. His hips jerk, pressing harder into Turana's grip, as if the praise itself unlocked something inside him.

Turana's hectocotylus twitches and fills. He wants friction, wants relief, but more than that, he wants *Hāro*. Wants to drown himself in the sheer size and heat of him, to test every place the feathers change colour, every sound he can wring from that sharp beak.

And oh, currents take him, he wants Hāro's cock.

He drags a hand—then a tentacle—slowly along the length, delighting in the way Hāro *jerks*, a broken sound clawing out of his throat. "Fuck, you're gorgeous."

Turana strokes him slowly at first, suckers teasing, exploring the weight and shape of him. Hāro shudders violently, his wings flaring wider with every pass. He rocks helplessly into the touch, gasping and swearing, claws tangling deeper in Turana's hair until his scalp sings with the sting of it.

"You like that," Turana hums, voice vibrating low against Hāro's chest.

"What gave it away?" Hāro gasps, his voice pitched too high for the sarcasm to have any bite. "Don't stop—stars, please—"

"Wild sharks couldn't stop me now," Turana promises, grinning against his skin.

He tightens one tentacle around the base of Hāro's cock, his hand curling gently around the head to tease, coax, explore. The response is immediate: Hāro cries out, voice breaking, whole body arching into it like he's flying. The rock scrapes his talons as they scrabble for purchase, but he doesn't stop, doesn't try to hide. He *gives*, raw and unguarded, trembling under Turana's touch. Turana wants to push him further—wants to see him undone entirely, a storm breaking open under his hands.

"Look at you," Turana murmurs, stroking harder now, faster, tentacles flexing around him with deliberate rhythm. "Fucking gorgeous. You're going to come for me, aren't you?"

"Yes—" Hāro gasps, voice breaking on the word. "Fuck, I—"

"Good." Turana's grin is sharp and reverent. "Then give it to me. Show me how you break, disasterbird."

The way Hāro comes apart is nothing short of a revelation.

He'd already been trembling, wings shaking like sails in a gale, claws digging into the rock as if it could tether him against the tide. But when Turana's tentacles tighten in just the right rhythm, when he twists and strokes with firm, deliberate pressure, Hāro *shatters*.

It starts in his wings: they snap open, full span, all their colours seeming to glow in the moonlight. Then his body arches, all eight feet of him bowing up off the rock as a strangled cry rips itself from his throat. The sound is raw, unguarded, and so *honest* that Turana swears he'll never forget it.

"Fuck—fuck—" Hāro gasps, hips jerking helplessly, cock pulsing against Turana's grip. Every muscle is taut, his feathers trembling like they might fall clean from his body.

Turana watches, transfixed, as thick heat spills over his tentacles and hand, hot and messy, coating suckers and skin alike. Hāro keeps moving through it, hips stuttering forward as though he can't stop, can't *not* give everything of himself. His wings beat once, hard, throwing spray high into the air before they collapse down, sprawling wide and limp against the rock.

He slumps, panting, chest heaving with the effort of it. His feathers are in chaos, scattered and damp. He looks utterly wrecked.

He's the most beautiful thing Turana has ever seen.

"You," Turana breathes, voice rough, reverent, "are a fucking miracle." He lifts his slick tentacle, watching the mess drip off his suckers, mouth watering at the sight.

He wonders, idly, if Hāro would be open to his mouth, next time.

Hāro groans, flopping one wing weakly against the rock. "I'm…a disaster."

"Oh, absolutely," Turana agrees, laughing, "but by the depths, you're my favourite disaster."

The way Hāro throws an arm across his face at that, laughing helplessly, is worth every aching throb in Turana's hectocotylus.

Speaking of which—

He hasn't exactly forgotten his arousal, not with the way it's been building in him with every sound Hāro has made. But now, with the bird sprawled out before him, undone and open and perfect, it slams into him fully: the ache, the desperate need to *bury* himself.

He hisses, low and urgent, as one tentacle slides across his own stomach before wrapping around his hectocotylus and squeezing. Relief punches through him at the pressure, sharp and immediate. But the second he starts stroking, Hāro stirs, lifting his head blearily.

"You—" His voice is hoarse, beak clicking once. "You're still— You haven't—"

Turana smirks through the haze of need. "Observant even when you're wrecked. You're not just a pretty face, disasterbird."

Hāro shakes his head, feathers rustling faintly. His claws scrape awkwardly on the rock as he sits up enough to reach for Turana.

"Let me," Hāro says, still breathless, but steady in a way Turana hadn't expected. His talons hover uncertainly over Turana's hectocotylus, not quite touching.

Turana nearly groans at the sight—those sharp, dangerous claws, careful and hesitant, poised so delicately. The sheer contrast of it: a predator's hands, trembling with gentleness.

"Fuck, *yes*," Turana rasps, head tipping back.

Hāro does. Cautious at first, exploring an appendage that is clearly new to him with the tips of his fingers, careful not to scratch. Turana hisses at the contact, body jolting. He's used to his own tentacles, to slick and suction and firm strokes, to the tight heat of a waiting cloaca—but this? This is rougher, taloned, *different*. Perfect, somehow.

"Harder," Turana urges, already panting. "I won't break."

Hāro swallows, then grips Turana more firmly, stroking in an awkward but devastating rhythm. His feathers brush Turana's stomach with every movement, soft and teasing against the slick heat.

"Fuck, that's it." Turana's hips rock into the touch. His tentacles flail, half-wrapping around Hāro's shoulders and wings without meaning to, seeking an anchor as pleasure coils tight and urgent in his gut. "You feel incredible."

Hāro leans closer, watching every twitch and spasm like he's trying to memorise them. "You're so warm," he murmurs. "Fuck, you're leaking all over my hand."

The blunt, astonished honesty of it almost undoes Turana and he laughs, ragged. "That's because I'm about to come, sweetheart."

Hāro's eyes go wide, wings twitching as his strokes speed up.

"Oh, *fuck*," Turana chokes, his body bowing up off the rock. "Yeah,

yes, just like that—"

His climax hits like a wave breaking hard over stone. His hectocotylus pulses, spilling hot over Hāro's talons and his own stomach, thick and messy, pleasure ripping through him in violent, shaking bursts. He cries out, riding it until he collapses back against the rock, trembling.

When he finally looks again, Hāro is staring at his slick hand with something between awe and disbelief.

"Currents take me," Turana pants, laughing breathlessly. "You—fuck, you're dangerous."

"Dangerous?" Hāro croaks, incredulous.

Turana grins, reaching to curl a tentacle around his waist, tugging him close again. "Because if you look at me like that too often, disaster-bird, I'll drown myself in you."

The tide has rolled back sometime in the night, leaving the water glassy and still. Dawn paints the horizon in streaks of gold and pink, everything soft and unhurried.

Turana floats half submerged in the shallows, tentacles splayed out lazily like sea flowers in bloom. He hadn't expected to wake early—he'd been thoroughly wrung out last night, in more ways than one—but sleep is slippery at the best of times when you live by the tides. Besides, he couldn't stop watching. Hāro looks both impossibly large and impossibly fragile like this, wings folded tight, one long arm slung haphazardly over Turana's shoulder as though some part of him refuses to let go, even while unconscious.

Turana would never admit it out loud, but he's grateful.

The bird stirs with the sun, blinking blearily into the light. His beak clacks once as he stretches, wings fluttering against the stone. Then he groans, muffled, and mutters, "I can't feel my ass."

Turana snorts. "Big tough bird not used to sleeping outside the nest, huh? You're welcome to join me in the water, you know."

"I can't swim," Hāro grumbles, pressing his face into the crook of his own wing like he might disappear again.

"I'd catch you."

Overhead, a seagull screeches. Neither of them looks; both lift a hand

and flip it off in perfect sync. The ridiculousness of it bubbles something light in Turana's chest. He hadn't realised how heavy it had felt before now—before this bird landed in his lap, all broken feathers and bruised pride, and turned out to be...storms above, so much more than the sum of his failures.

Silence stretches between them, comfortable as the tide. And then, softly, Hāro says: "I think I want to tell my mum."

Turana blinks, caught off guard. "About your existential crisis?"

"About you."

He gapes, no graceful way to mask it. He hadn't expected—he *never* expects—someone to want to keep him once the sun comes up. Flings, flirtations, bodies against bodies in the shadows of coral reefs, sure. But *this*?

"I mean," Hāro adds quickly, "I'll probably leave out a few of the more carnal details. But...yeah. I want her to know that something finally felt right. That I'm not broken."

Turana feels that like a weight to the sternum. He reaches out without thinking, looping a tentacle once around Hāro's ankle, grounding him. "You never were." The tentacle loosens again. "You don't have to prove anything to anyone, you know. Not even to her."

"I'm not trying to prove anything," Hāro says thoughtfully. "I just... She's my mum, and I love her, and I want her to know I found something real. Some*one* real."

Turana's throat goes tight at that. He glances up at Hāro, feathers haloed in sunrise. "Does that mean I count as your forty-ninth courtship?"

Hāro barks a laugh, sharp and delighted. "Stars, no. You are absolutely not a courtship. You're..." He falters, then turns, eyes catching Turana's. "You're something else entirely."

Turana's grin softens despite himself. "Good."

It *is* good. More than good. It feels like the kind of thing he'll tuck away in the hollow of his ribs for leaner nights, a truth to chew on when the sea gets mean and lonely.

"Still weird, though, right?" Hāro murmurs, half dreamy with exhaustion. "A Huruhuru and a tentacled sea-creature with..."

Turana snorts. "All these *appendages*?"

Hāro cracks a grin, lazy and wicked. "You're not the only one with

a cloaca, you know." Turana nearly slips back into the water as Hāro stretches out on the rock, his wings tucked behind his head, all faux innocence. "Play your cards right, and maybe I'll show you sometime."

Turana shakes his head and lunges, pressing Hāro back against the stone, his lips finding a particularly sensitive spot on Hāro's neck. Hāro's wings flare wide in mock protest before he reaches around both of them, warm and cocooning.

"You're trouble, disasterbird," Turana says against his throat, the words softened by the grin he can't fight down.

"And you love it," Hāro shoots back, talons curling gently against Turana's back.

Turana hums, nosing into the curve of his shoulder, breathing in feathers and musk and salt. "Yeah. Yeah, I really do."

To Love a Wild Hart

T. L. Sly

artist, belly bulge, blow job, cryptid, death of a lover, death of a parent, death of an animal, dubious consent, hand job, horror, kidnapping, m/m, modern, past tense, penis in anus sex, rimming, size difference, size kink, somnophilia (minor), stalking, third person limited point of view, tonguefucking, united states of america

The camera's shutter engagement wasn't loud—the Leica M6 was known for being quiet—but it startled the rabbit. As it bolted into the underbrush, Max wound the film to the next stop. He preferred using a digital camera for wildlife to avoid spooking the animals, but he'd been capturing plant life when the rabbit appeared, so he'd taken a chance. Blue hour was his favorite time to shoot, though golden-hour photos were typically the ones that paid the bills.

Continuing through the trees, mentally tracking distance and direction as he moved away from the trail, Max paused twice more to take photos before settling on a camping spot for the night. He had never

been a fan of established campsites—too crowded, especially this late in hiking season when thru-hikers were making their final pushes on the Appalachian Trail—which was part of why he'd chosen to focus on the 100 Mile Wilderness for this particular assignment. It was one of the only spots on the AT that allowed dispersed camping.

Another part was that peak autumn color hit the foliage here by the end of September, as opposed to October or even November farther south. The sooner Max got the photos, the sooner he got paid and could move on to his next job. Though really, this was a sweet one. There wasn't much about being outdoors that Max found unpleasant. He'd chosen nature photography as his career focus for a reason.

It was almost pitch black by the time Max had his hammock strung between two suitable trees, his rain cover above it as both precaution and wind-block. Not feeling up to properly cooking, Max chose a quick-to-make pouch-meal for dinner. Fifteen minutes later, he was digging into rehydrated mashed potatoes and chicken, already wishing he was done so he could *sleep*. It had been a long day of hiking over rough terrain, and he was exhausted.

By the time Max had secured the bear bag up another tree, changed for bed, and zipped his hammock around himself, he was on the verge of sleep. And, sure enough, it only took a few heartbeats for his breathing to even out as he sank into dreaming.

SNAP

Max startled awake, instantly on high alert, his heart thundering in his ears. He wasn't sure what had made the loud sound that woke him, but there weren't a lot of options. He was too far from the trail—well over the required 200 feet—for it to be night hikers, unless they were *very* lost. It was most likely an animal, though what type was the question. Forcing himself to breathe slowly and quietly, Max strained his ears.

He tensed further when he heard shuffling and rustling nearby. Whatever was making the sounds was *right outside his hammock*. It didn't sound small, either. There was *weight* behind the sounds that made Max think maybe it was a bear, and Max silently cursed himself for not sleeping in one of the designated shelter areas. His preference for being alone was going to get him killed one of these days; plenty of guides had told him so over the last five years.

Hell, it might get him killed *now* if it really was a bear moving around in his camp.

The thing was, Max knew how to handle black bears. He had bear spray *and* an air horn in his pack, just in case. Unfortunately, the only things *in the hammock* were Max himself and his electronics, since it was too cold overnight to leave the batteries away from his body heat. He could try yelling to scare the animal away, but if it didn't work, he was *stuck*; literally zippered into a sleeping bag inside an also-zippered hammock. He debated pulling out the digital camera—it had a night-vision mode that would at least allow him to determine what was moving around his camp—but he didn't want to draw attention to himself.

It was only a few minutes later when whatever was there shuffled off again, the sounds fading as it moved farther and farther away. When it had been silent for about fifteen minutes, Max breathed a sigh of relief and relaxed. Animals were part of camping, and a nighttime visitor was nothing to get worked up about. He'd just make sure to keep his airhorn in the hammock from now on. *Just in case.*

Closing his eyes, Max willed himself back into a fitful sleep.

Morning brought the unpleasant discovery of a dead animal.

Not whatever had been shuffling around in the dark, but rather a kill it had left behind, which was honestly worse, in Max's opinion. He had no desire to be camped out in a predator's kill-zone; even the possibility was alarming. Not wanting to get too close to the kill—which seemed to be a rabbit, based on size, though the skinned state of it left him uncertain—Max skirted around it while packing as quickly as possible. Before heading back to the trail, Max took a moment to snap some digital photos of the dead animal. If he ran into a park ranger, he wanted to tell them what had happened, and a picture or two couldn't hurt.

Then, doing his best to put the whole thing out of his mind, Max headed out.

Max typically thought of himself as a rational person. He'd spent the tail-end of his teen years bouncing around foster care after the car accident that killed his parents when he was fifteen, and during that time he'd lost all sense of the fantastical or otherworldly. He could see the whimsy in a rainbow's colors, but he knew it was just refracted light. He could appreciate the beauty of mushrooms growing in a circle without succumbing to the fantasy of fairy rings. Nature was full of oddities and curiosities, but that was all they were.

It had been ten years since Max's whole world had fallen apart and he'd had to learn how to make it make sense again. He didn't give in to flights of fancy, and he didn't scare easily.

Now, Max was *terrified.*

Bad enough he'd woken up to dead animals in his camp for three mornings in a row. Worse still was finding one in the center of a spiral—about three feet across—made of rocks and bones. This…this wasn't an animal. No *animal* could've made that pattern. It was too precise, too *perfect.* It was like something out of a scary movie, cultish and horrific. Max snapped a few pictures, then hastily packed up because *like hell* was he staying in this campsite even a second longer than necessary.

As he booked it back toward the trail, Max tried to decide what to do next. Part of him wanted to leave; find the nearest exit from the AT and just…*go home.* Except he had a contract, and Max knew he didn't have enough photos to fulfill it. Not yet, anyway.

Thinking back on the dead animals and creepy spiral, Max shivered.

Okay, he thought as he settled his feet on the well-worn path, heading south. *I'll just stick to the trail and sleep in the designated camp areas from now on.*

It wasn't a great plan, but it was all he had.

"Well, it's the Appalachian Mountains, ain't it?" The older man laughed as he passed Max's camera back to him, looking like every stereotype of a mountain man Max had ever heard. "Strange things happen out here."

They had set up near each other at the shelter site and started talking,

friendly in the way most hikers were with each other on the AT. When he'd learned that David was a four-time thru-hiker who, at fifty-seven, was going for his fifth complete trek, Max had decided to share the photos he'd taken. He was hoping for some sort of sense, or logic, not *superstition.*

Max didn't scoff, but it was a near thing. "C'mon, David…I know there's all sorts of legends and stories, but—"

"But nothing." David shook his head, somber now. "These woods ain't no joke, son. When we tell newcomers 'hike in groups'—or leastways pairs—it ain't just about if you get injured or lost. When we say don't follow sounds in the dark, it ain't just bears or mountain lions you gotta worry about."

Max shifted uncomfortably in his hammock, making it sway a little. "I don't believe in ghosts or the boogeyman."

David shot Max a knowing look, faded blue eyes meeting brilliant green almost tauntingly. "No one does, until they *do*."

"It was probably someone trying to scare hikers." Max's voice wasn't as firm as he'd have liked, but there wasn't much he could do about it. "For a prank video or something."

"Son…" David said, rolling his eyes. "D'you know how old these mountains are?"

"…old?" Max hazarded a guess, shrugging when David looked unimpressed. "What? I'm a photographer, not a geologist."

"Over 450 million years." David answered himself, far more seriously than Max thought the conversation warranted. "These mountains were ancient long before humans were around. There's things here we can't explain. Things that don't make no sort of sense. The Natives knew it, and those of us who call any part of these mountains home know it. You spend enough time out here and you'll know it, too."

Max fidgeted with the camera he was still holding. "Okay, so what am I supposed to do?"

David shrugged one shoulder. "Hard to say. Some folks might head on home. Some folks might go poking around, looking for answers. Me? I'd stick close to people as much as I could, delete those photos, and forget I saw whatever I saw."

Max sighed, knowing David was right about one thing, anyway. Whatever had been in his camp—whatever had left dead animals and

made the strange spiral—was best forgotten. The smartest move was to focus on his job so he could finish and go home. Max didn't believe in Bigfoot, or Mothman, or the Jersey Devil, or any other creepy creature said to live in the woods and mountains. He was a logical, practical sort who believed there was a reasonable explanation for everything.

...and damn it, he wanted *answers*.

Max had a plan. It wasn't the *best* idea, but it was a plan. Max intended to go off-trail for photographs, wasting a solid portion of prime hiking hours on the pursuit. So if he wanted to make any actual progress along the trail as well, he needed to be up at dawn and go until dusk. He would *not* be sleeping at a shelter tonight, but rather camping off-trail again. And this time, he was going to set up his digital camera on a tripod, recording video with night vision. Hopefully, whoever had been following him along the trail would come into his camp *before* the battery ran down. With any luck, Max could have answers by the following morning.

With his goals firmly in mind, Max woke before the sun, packed his stuff, and headed out into the blue light of pre-dawn.

Max purposefully set up camp a few hours before sunset. He wanted to spend the hour before and after the sun went down taking photos without having to worry about making camp in the dark. All things considered, it seemed smarter *not* to have to fumble with his hammock and the digital recording setup. The last thing he needed was to step in a hole and hurt himself when he was so far off-trail.

He'd been shooting with single-minded focus for long enough that twilight had faded into gloaming, the whole world washed blue through his camera's lens. While the changing leaves with their autumn-bright colors showed best during the golden hours, there were other aspects of the forest that did better with the blue light. There was *mystery* to the photos he took at this time of day. A sort of echoing sadness that permeated them and made a person *ache* just from looking at them.

That was what he was going for now, as he shot rocks that spilled like a waterfall over the earth, trees growing over and between them through sheer stubbornness and determination. He wanted to capture the vastness of this place, so full of life and yet so far removed from humanity. The heartrending beauty that evoked loneliness and insignificance in the viewer. The *smallness* a place like this could make a person feel.

Max had the camera to his eye, analyzing angles and composition as he tried to frame the perfect shot before he lost too much of the light and had to head back to his campsite. He turned to the right, finger resting lightly on the shutter button, and startled. His finger pressed down on pure instinct even as he gasped and took a quick half-step backwards. The shutter engaged with a soft sound, and Max jerked the camera down to chest-height, peering through the growing gloom for what he'd just seen.

What he *couldn't* have just seen.

A deer? he thought, heart racing as he looked for another flash of the antlers he'd glimpsed through his viewfinder. Except it *hadn't* been a deer. It had been too tall for that by far, and the way it had moved when he'd spotted it...it had almost seemed human. Only *not*, in the worst sort of way. The thing *had* looked bipedal, but that made no sense.

Max took one hand off his camera, pressing it to where his heart was pounding away as if trying to escape from his ribcage. He took a slow, careful breath and willed it not to shake. He'd heard stories of people seeing deer walking on their hind legs, and he'd always put them down to overwrought imaginations, if not outright lies. But this...what Max had just seen...what he had just *photographed*...

"Couldn't've been digital, could it?" he muttered, glowering down at the Leica M6 in his hand. Film he couldn't develop until he had darkroom access. If he'd been shooting in *digital*, he could have checked the photo right away. "*Tch*."

There was nothing he could do about it now; his eyes scanned the trees where he had seen the...the *whatever* he had seen. The hair on the back of his neck was standing on end, and Max could have sworn he felt eyes on him. Like he was being *watched*, even though he didn't see anyone. His mouth went dry as he resisted the urge to call out; to voice the ultra-cliched "who's there?" that was clinging to his tongue.

Tightening his grip on his camera, Max forced himself to turn his

back on where he'd seen *something* and head back to camp. There were things he needed to do before he could sleep, and they weren't going to get done if he was standing around, staring at trees and freaking out.

Max was once again woken up by sounds outside his hammock. Heavy footsteps. Rustling, as if something was being fussed over or fiddled with. *Breathing.*

Part of Max wanted to reach for his airhorn in the hopes of scaring off the intruder. Part of him wanted to reach for his headlamp and yank back the hammock's cover so he could *finally* see who—*what*—the hell was stalking him at night. Part of him thought he should just close his eyes and go back to sleep and pretend he hadn't heard anything.

Suddenly, there was a rasping hiss as *something* scratched down the outside of his rain cover. Max froze, holding his breath as his eyes strained against the near-darkness, watching as the cover rippled and shifted with the press of...fingers? Claws? He couldn't be sure. Didn't know what he would do if the cover were suddenly shredded or ripped away. If he were *attacked.*

There was the sound of rapid sniffing—louder than Max thought possible, even for something right outside his meager shelter—followed by a sort of blowing exhale. The part of his mind that stored hunting knowledge told him it was a deer sound. A *snort wheeze,* specifically. Except a deer couldn't be scratching at his cover, and a deer couldn't make a spiral in his campsite, and a deer wouldn't leave dead animals behind. Max thought of the earlier flash of antlers, and the not-quite-human movement that had followed. His fingers twitched, though Max had no idea what he was going to do.

And then, before he could do anything, there was a long, pig-like snort—*a deer grunt,* Max's mind offered helpfully—followed by heavy steps moving away again. After a minute, all Max could hear was his own unsteady breathing and his racing heart. Knowing there was no use in stumbling around in the dark, Max closed his eyes and willed himself to settle down.

Sleep was a long time coming.

Max was having a really weird morning.

There was another stone-and-bone spiral in his campsite. It was smaller than the last one had been, with another dead animal in the center. This time, however, the carcass was laid on a layer of fresh leaves. The oddity of that had Max moving closer. He crouched down as close as he dared, nudging at the body with a stick. He'd already taken pictures, so he didn't feel too bad about disturbing whatever this fucked-up tableau was supposed to be. As he manipulated the carnage, Max realized a few things at once. One, the animal in question was a rabbit. Two, there was no blood. Not on the leaves, not on the surrounding spiral, not *anywhere* in his campsite. Who or whatever had killed it had done so somewhere else. And three, the animal was *field dressed*. Skinned, organs removed…

Hell, even the way it was placed on the bed of leaves seemed like an attempt to keep the meat clean and consumable.

Max wrinkled up his nose at the idea of eating *found meat*, standing and moving away from it again. The next order of business was reviewing the video from his digital camera.

Ten minutes later, Max was fighting the urge to throw his damned camera. Night vision relied on infrared, which wasn't worth *shit* with moisture in the air. Max hadn't realized, but there was *fog* last night. Within an hour of Max going to bed, the footage became nothing but a grainy mess of white specks that obscured almost everything else.

Frustrated, Max kept watching anyway, *just in case*.

Finally, shadowy movement appeared from off-screen, across from Max's hammock. The fog still made it almost impossible to see anything. There was definitely *something* entering Max's camp, though *what* was hard to say. It was tall. Over seven feet, Max guessed. Bulky, too. *Solid.* The head was deer-like, and it had a full rack of antlers. At least eight points, maybe more.

It was *not* a deer.

It walked on two strangely shaped legs, and its arms seemed disproportionately long. Max watched it move around his campsite through the snow-like mess of condensation ruining the footage, eyes straining as the *creature* quickly assembled the spiral and left its kill. Watched it move to stand outside his hammock. Watched it drag its fingers—Claws?

He still couldn't be sure—down the cover. Heard the same eerie sounds from the night before.

Max glanced back at the spiral, and the dead rabbit. It didn't make any sense. Was it a threat? It didn't *feel* threatening, for all that every hair on Max's body was standing on end. The creature—whatever it was—had been *inches* from Max, but it hadn't hurt him. And the way the rabbit was cleaned…

Something wasn't adding up. And Max *still* wanted answers.

Two days later, Max was in the same spot, eating dinner and trying to piece together what—if anything—he knew for sure.

The creature had antlers, meaning it was male. He—*the creature*—could hunt and was dexterous enough to dress the kills. He was taller than a human and muscular the way bucks were. Max had found bloody gouge-marks on trees near his camp that morning, which meant the creature was shedding his velvet, and soon those antlers would be stark bone rather than softly felted. The fog had continued each night, obscuring further attempts at filming, but Max was confident that the creature was *not* a deer. He was equally confident that it wasn't a man in some sort of costume. No, it was something else entirely.

And based on the way it lingered in Max's campsite—especially near his hammock—it seemed to have taken a rather specific interest in Max himself.

What puzzled Max the most was the dead animals. After the rabbit was an opossum and—that morning—a raccoon. They were clearly hunted and cleaned for food, but why were they being left in Max's camp? If they were warnings that Max was next, then the creature had given him *plenty* of them, and he would've expected an attack. Not more…what even *were* they? All Max could think was *gifts*. Something *for* him. Was he expected to eat the meat? But why? Why would this creature be trying to feed Max?

It didn't make sense.

A rustling sound to the left made Max's hair stand on end.

CRACK

The branch snapping made Max startle, then slowly turn his head

until he could *just* see that area. And there, in the shadows between the trees, was *something*. Something tall, bulky, sporting antlers…

Max was on his feet immediately, moving toward it. Except by the time he got there, whatever it was had vanished. Frustrated, Max spun slowly, looking for clues about what was happening; why *he* was being stalked by this creature. And there, on the ground, was something unusual.

Max picked up the oddity, bringing it back to camp to study. It was similar to a dreamcatcher, but not. A thin, flexible stick was bound end-to-end with itself, forming a hoop about six inches across. A delicate webbing of filament—*sinew, maybe?*—was wound across the hoop, seemingly at random, leaving uneven spaces between the threads.

Within the hoop hung several items, suspended like insects in a spider's web. A dark-green stone with a hole in it. A small, downy feather: gray at the bottom, bright orange at the tip, with a thin white stripe between. An acorn, the threading wound snugly just beneath its cap. The whole thing was pretty, in a strange way. Max touched it carefully, almost *reverently*. There was care in the making of something so delicate, if no great skill.

Lightly tracing the webbing, Max realized that if he wanted answers, he was going to have to do something different, to try to get the creature to approach. The only question was *what*.

Max really should have expected this.

He'd woken up to more meat in his camp. It wasn't a whole animal this time. That—combined with the deep red of it—had Max fairly certain it was deer. Determined, Max cooked it along with some rice for a hearty breakfast. It was good, too. Max didn't eat venison often, but he liked it. So he ate the meat, and fiddled with the not-dreamcatcher he'd found, and wondered what was going to happen next.

One day, Max was going to stop jinxing himself. Just…not today. Because *today*, he was so busy wanting something to happen that he hadn't thought about what it would be like if something *actually* happened.

Seeing the creature up close in daylight was *not* like seeing it on a

grainy video camera screen, or from a distance.

It—*he*—stood around seven feet tall from his hooves to the top of his head. His antlers added another foot and a half and were shedding their velvet, leaving them bloody and dripping gore in a menacing way. The legs were deer-like, though he took on a more humanoid shape at the hips. His torso and arms were mostly human, though they were covered in short gray-brown fur that lightened to white on his belly and chest, and his arms seemed too long for the rest of him. His hands had long fingers that ended in dark claws and his head…

Fuck, his head was a skull.

Only, as Max looked closer, he realized that wasn't true. There was skin, and very fine, silky fur. There seemed to be only a hint of musculature under it, with no fat to round things out, so the shape of his skull was quite prominent. It was a *deer* skull at that, which was a bit disorienting, considering. He looked back at Max with wide, dark eyes that seemed to bore into him.

"H-hi…" Max stammered, for lack of something better to say. He set the food aside, still talking. "Thank you for the meat. I enjoyed it. And for this." He held up the not-dreamcatcher. "It's beautiful."

The creature made a sound that Max knew was called *blowing*, which bucks made to show interest in does. *Is he interested in me?* Cheeks flushing at the thought, Max stammered. "I-I'm Max. Do you, uh…have a name?"

The creature moved closer and grunted. A *tending* grunt. Another mating sound. Max wasn't sure how to feel about this creature wanting to mate with him; it was both terrifying and intriguing. He stood, taking a step back and stumbling in his haste. "No name? I, uh…could call you Hart? It means *deer*…" The creature nodded, and Max murmured. "You understand…"

Max yelped as he was suddenly lunged at. The world inverted as he was lifted by strong arms and tossed over the creature's—*Hart's*—broad shoulder. "What are you doing?" Max shrieked, squirming in an attempt to free himself, but Hart was too strong.

As Hart walked deeper into the forest, Max's panic rose. "Where are you going? *Stop*, you can't just—"

Except that Hart *could*, because he very much *was*. As Max's panic reached a peak, his head began to swim. Before he could do anything to try to stop it, the black edging Max's vision crept over his mind and pulled him under.

The first thing Max became aware of was soft fur under his body, tickling his stomach, which meant he was naked and lying face down wherever he was. The second thing he realized was that there was *something*—something thick and wet and firm—pressing against his hole. As it breached the tight ring of muscle, Max gasped, eyes flying open. He couldn't stop the low moan that spilled from his lips as whatever was inside him moved, stretching and slicking his entrance. "W-what…*nnnnghhhh…*"

Max writhed in pleasure for a moment before craning his neck to see what was going on.

Hart was behind him, his face buried in Max's ass. It was Hart's *tongue* that was inside of him, preparing him for what Max was now certain was coming next. For Hart to *fuck him*. Panting, helpless against the sudden desire pouring through his veins like liquid fire, Max fisted his hands in the dark fur beneath him and pressed his hips back, wordlessly begging for more. This was…*fuck*, this was wrong, in so many ways, but as that long, agile tongue moved inside him, Max couldn't bring himself to care.

"Please…" Max keened, hands clenching and releasing around the fur as Hart's tongue slid slowly out of him. "H-hart, *please…*" His cock was hard and aching, and he felt empty, *needing* to be filled by the impossible creature behind him.

Strong hands curled around his hips, claws pressing carefully against delicate skin, and Max was hauled *up*. He got his knees under him and arched his back, presenting himself and pleading, "Please…I-I want it…"

Hart's hands flexed on his hips, then Max felt something else pressing against his hole. It wasn't blunt like the cocks he'd taken in the past, but rather it was tapered at the tip. It slid into him easily, slick as he was from Hart's tongue. The shaft narrowed after the head, though it was still quite thick, and Max whimpered into his folded arms as it stretched him open. It felt so good inside of him. So different from anyone else he'd been with, but in the most amazing way. Then, as Hart pressed fully

into him, Max keened as the shaft widened at the base, stretching him wider than he'd ever been. Deeper, too, which made Max wonder just how big Hart was.

Max's knees slid farther apart, inviting Hart deeper into him. His breath hitched, soft whines spilling from his lips between panting breaths as he felt the unyielding pressure of Hart's cock filling him completely. His hand slipped down, tracing the contours of his own body until he could feel the bulge of it through the skin of his normally flat stomach. As he pressed, Hart grunted behind him, then began to rock his hips. He fucked into Max with force, nothing gentle or hesitant about him. It was fierce; it was possessive; it was demanding. Max felt like he was being *claimed* as Hart's cock thrust into him over and over again, relentless as it drove him closer to climax with every inward push.

Max's pleas for more grew increasingly incoherent, a rising tide of need that mingled with nonsensical sounds of pleasure as he rocked back into every powerful thrust of Hart's hips. Hart's hands came down on either side of his head, his body caging Max in against the furs beneath them as he fucked into Max even harder, his cock lighting up every nerve as it slid in and out of Max's slick hole. Max could feel the soft fur of Hart's chest pressed against his back, and he groaned, his cock leaking wetly as everything in him wound tighter, ready to snap at any moment. Each thrust of Hart's hips sent waves of pleasure crashing through his body, and he tightened around the intrusion, eager for Hart to take him harder, faster, deeper.

Max's eyes fluttered shut, the world outside fading away until there was only the feeling of Hart's cock inside him, the sound of their mingled breaths, and the pounding of his own heart in his ears. He couldn't imagine anything better than this. Couldn't imagine ever wanting anything more. Hart's cock pushed him higher and higher, and Max let his fingers curl around his own aching arousal, stroking in time with Hart's thrusts. Anything to push him closer to that glittering peak, that moment of perfect ecstasy that was so close he could taste it. When he finally crashed, shattering under the pressure of so much pleasure, Max's scream echoed around them, a symphony of carnal need that filled the air.

As Max slumped down to the furs, Hart drove into him a few more times before coming with a bellowing roar, flooding Max's hole with sticky-wet heat. Then, while Max was still catching his breath, Hart's softening cock slipped out of him, and he was gently moved to the side, away from where Max's release was cooling in the fur bedding.

Max found himself wrapped in strong arms, cradled against the soft, light fur of Hart's chest. His heart was still racing, trembling as aftershocks of pleasure chased themselves up and down his spine. Max didn't think he could stand—or *run*—if his life depended on it; he was a little surprised to realize he didn't want to run. Deciding to worry about what it all meant later, Max's eyes drifted shut as exhaustion dragged him into dreaming.

Hart's den was actually part of a cave system. The smaller "room" where Max had first woken up—and been ravished—had a raised rock platform covered in layers of moss and animal furs to make a bed. The larger cavern outside had a fire pit, for warmth and light and cooking. There were shelves carved into the stone there that held clay bowls and pots, as well as gathered food. Berries, nuts, roots…that sort of thing. It was lovely, in a rustic way.

But Max's favorite part of the caves was what he thought of as the *bathing room*. When he woke up from his nap, Hart carried him through a short series of twisting passages into a room with a small underground lake. At Hart's urging, Max got in and was pleasantly surprised to find it was warm. As he slid in, disturbing the water, it began to *glow* with a soft, blue-green light. Max knew, logically, that it was bioluminescent algae, but there was something so magical about it. Especially when Hart slipped into the water beside him, pulling Max against his muscular body in an intimate embrace.

Hart could stand easily in the water—it lapped at his chest—but Max had been treading water until Hart lifted him. Max wrapped his legs around Hart's hips, moaning as Hart's cock slid into his still-loose hole, stretching him once more. Surrounded by the soft glow of the water, supported by Hart's strong arms, Max felt small and cherished as Hart's hands silently encouraged him to fuck himself on Hart's massive cock. He moved slowly, deliberately, as he slid up and down the shaft, his head dropping back as the pleasure rose like a tide inside him.

Max's cock was pressed between their bodies, rubbing deliciously against Hart's fur. His hole was clenching around Hart's thick cock as it slid into him over and over. He looped his arms around Hart's shoulders, feeling the muscles shift as Hart lifted him each time so he could sink back onto Hart's cock again, and again, *and again*. The pleasure bloomed inside him, growing with every inward press of Hart's cock, and Max wasn't sure how much more he could take. Everything about Hart was overwhelming, but he was learning to love that. To crave it, even. The *more* of it: how much it all was, to be with such an impossible creature.

"H-*Hart*..." he whined, breath catching in his throat as he clamped down on Hart's cock, eyes rolling back as he chased his climax, straining toward it.

"*Maaaaa-k-k-k-k-k-k.*"

The sound was eerie; chilling in all the ways it *wasn't* human. The sharp bleat of the *Maaaa* and the staccato clicking of the repeated "K" sound, and how they combined into something that wasn't quite Max's name, but also somehow was. Hart had used the sounds he had—his limited vocalizations—to say *Max's name* in the heat of passion—an intimate, precious gift.

It made Max shudder as his release washed over him, his cock spilling sticky-wet and making a mess of the soft fur of Hart's belly. His hole fluttered around Hart's cock, milking it as Hart pulled Max flush against him and spilled himself as deep inside of Max as possible.

Panting, Max rested his forehead on Hart's chest, murmuring. "Fuck, that was amazing. I don't understand what's happening, but...I don't want it to end."

"*Maaa-k-k-k.*"

Hart said it softer this time, warm and fond despite how eerie the vocalizations were. It wasn't much, but it let Max know that Hart felt the same, and—for now—it was enough.

Max hollowed his cheeks, sucking hard as he raised his head so his tongue could tease the tapered head of Hart's cock. Hart was on his back in their bed of furs, panting and grunting softly as Max swallowed as much of Hart's erection as he could. He had one hand curled around the fat, rounded base of Hart's cock, squeezing in time to his bobbing head as he lavished the shaft and head with wicked attention from his tongue. Hart's cock was so different from his own, but Max didn't mind. In fact, he *liked* how different they were. Liked the inhuman feel of Hart's cock in his hand, and his mouth, and his ass.

"*Maaa...Maaa-k-k-k-k-k-k...*"

The sound of his almost-name had Max sucking harder, swallowing against his gag reflex as he took more of Hart's long cock into his throat. He wanted this to be as amazing for Hart as it was for him. Wanted Hart to feel the same mind-numbing pleasure Max had felt each time they'd fucked. And when Hart exploded in his mouth, Max eagerly swallowed every drop, licking his lover's cock clean afterward with loving care, stopping only when Hart's softening cock retreated into its sheath and he dragged Max up his body.

Max hummed happily as Hart licked into his mouth, the action not quite a kiss due to the odd shape of Hart's mouth but as close as they could get. A heartbeat later, Max was on his belly again, his hips being dragged back and up so that Hart could get to his hole. When he was once again breached by Hart's agile tongue, Max let out a keening wail and arched back into the pleasure. As Hart fucked him with his tongue, over and over, Max clawed at the furs, cursing and *begging* for more, for whatever Hart would give him.

And when Hart covered Max with his body and drove his fantastical cock into Max's ass again, Max swore he saw fireworks. Each of Hart's powerful thrusts drove his cock deep into Max's body, the fat base of it rubbing deliciously over Max's prostate. Max pressed his hips back, meeting every thrust with greedy enthusiasm.

Max writhed helplessly as Hart's cock filled him completely, eyes rolling back in his head. The sensation of fur brushing against his skin as Hart's hips met his sent pleasure searing through Max's body. His own cock was hard and leaking into the furs he was rutting against as he was fucked. His breaths came in ragged pants, and his body felt like it was on fire. The room was filled with the scent of sex and fur and sweat, an intoxicating aroma that made Max's head swim.

Max's mind was racing, a jumbled mess of pleasure and need. He had never felt so alive, so claimed, so utterly *owned.* Hart's antlered head

dipped down so he could nuzzle at the back of Max's neck, the silken fur on his snout brushing against Max's skin as Hart breathed heavily through his nose. Max shivered, his entire body arching off the furs in response to the tender touch. Hart's claws dug into his hips, little pinpricks of pain that set off sparks behind Max's eyes as Hart held him in place. His thrusts grew harder, faster, more demanding. The slick sound of Hart's cock fucking into him filled the stone room, punctuated by Max's grunts and whimpers.

Max reached down to stroke his own cock, his hand moving in time with Hart's thrusts. The fur on Hart's legs tickled Max's thighs, adding to the sensory overload. He could feel the heat radiating from Hart's body and the sticky wetness of his own sweat clinging to his skin. The room spun dizzily around him as his climax grew closer, Hart's cock rubbing his prostate with every thrust, sending him spiraling higher and higher. His thoughts were a tangled mess of *want* and *need* and *must have.*

His hand flew over his cock, desperately trying to keep pace with Hart as he drove into Max harder and faster with every passing second. Max's vision swam as Hart's fur brushed against his back, a tantalizing mirror to the soft fur beneath his leaking cock. Max's moans grew louder, echoing against the stone as they mixed with Hart's grunts and the soft sounds of their bodies meeting.

Max felt Hart's hot breath on the back of his neck, a silent encouragement that sent another shiver down his spine. Max's hand tightened on his own cock, and he could feel his orgasm approaching. His entire body was a tightly coiled spring, ready to snap. Hart's thrusts grew erratic, and Max knew he was close, too. Max could feel Hart's cock pulsing inside him, the need for release growing with every breath.

Hart's claws dug deeper into Max's hips, his fur bristling with the intensity of his approaching climax. Max's own orgasm was only a heartbeat away, his hand a blur as he stroked himself. The room rang with grunts and moans and wet, slick sounds, the scent of their combined arousal thick in the air. And then, with a roar that seemed to shake the very air around them, Hart emptied himself inside of Max, his cock pulsing in time with Max's own. As Max felt the warmth of Hart's release fill him, he came as well, sobbing as he spilled himself across the furs beneath them.

As Max slipped toward sleep, he felt Hart's tongue gently cleaning him and wondered when he had last been this cared for, this *loved*. Before his parents' death, certainly. It was a sobering thought, to realize he had been lacking this affection and care in his life, and one he would have to ponder when he woke up again.

Max didn't mind being nude in the caves that Hart called home, but he had pulled on his clothes upon waking with the intention of going outside. He wasn't sure how long he'd been with Hart—five days, or maybe six—but he missed the feel of the sun on his face. He wasn't sure where Hart was—getting food, maybe—but Max wasn't worried about it.

Of course, it wasn't until he set out into the tunnels and caves surrounding the few "rooms" he'd been in with Hart that Max realized he didn't actually know the way out. He'd been unconscious when Hart brought him inside, and he hadn't gone out again. Still, there weren't many path options inside the caves—at least not in this section—and Max used a rock to mark the wall every time he made a choice, because he was going to *try*, damn it. He was starting to feel claustrophobic and debating turning back when he entered a cavern that was a good two hundred feet across in all directions. Sunlight streamed through holes in the ceiling, and there was the soft sound of water dripping. There was moss, and vines, and even a tree twisting through the rock, reaching toward one of the patches of sunlight. Max couldn't deny the beauty of this place and, for a moment, he itched for his cameras.

Max was following the wall when he found them: three narrow-but-deep, hollowed-out sections of the cave wall, lined with moss. And resting on the moss in each one was a skeleton. *Human* skeletons. Flowers, too—freshly picked, from the look of them. Max stared, trying to make sense of them, when a hand came down on his shoulder and made him jump. He whirled to stare at Hart, hand pressed to his chest as he tried to steady his breathing. Hart was staring at him, eyes dark and wide and—somehow—impossibly sad.

Licking his lips nervously, Max glanced at the graves, then asked shakily. "Who…who were they?"

Hart made a sound—low and anguished—that broke Max's heart,

touching the wall below the nearest grave. Max squinted, startling when he realized there were *letters* carved there. He read them, voice soft. "Dyani."

His eyes flitted to the next. "Elijah." He glanced at Hart before moving to the third, whispering, "Amity."

When Max looked at Hart again, he startled at how close they were. Hart tenderly cradled Max's cheek, then guided Max's hand to the fur of his chest, where Max could feel his heart beating. Hart touched Dyani's name again, making another pained sound, and Max closed his eyes in grief-stricken understanding.

He took a careful breath, met Hart's eyes, and asked. "They were yours, before me?"

Hart nodded slowly. Max looked at the graves again and wondered who these people had been. How they had met Hart. What their lives had been like, after he claimed them. If they had loved Hart, the way Max did. Carefully not looking at Hart, Max asked. "Am I allowed to leave?"

There was a pause, then a chilling voice that sounded hollow and unnatural—so unlike the deer sounds Hart made—hissed one word: "*Yessss.*"

A pause, then two more, equally eerie and terrifying: "*Sssstaaaaay. Pleeeeeeasssssssse.*"

Max shivered when Hart's arms wrapped around him, entreating. "*Maaa-k-k-k...*"

Taking a trembling breath, Max realized there was only one choice. How could he possibly leave his heart behind? Melting against Hart, Max murmured, "Yes. Yes, I'll stay."

And really, nothing else mattered.

Home, Aleyne

Dei Walker

alien, bisexual, blow job, cunnilingus, established relationship, f/m, f/m/nb, genderfluid, isolation, kissing, nipple play, non-binary, past tense, polyamory, science fiction, scientist, shapeshifting, spaceship, speciesism, tentacle in anus sex, tentacle in vagina sex, tentacles, third person limited point of view, touch-starved, twosome to threesome, vaginal fingering, war, xenophilia, xenophobia

The derelict ship trembled, proximity sensors blaring a warning that vibrated across Aleyne's hypersensitive external membrane. Cautious enthusiasm bubbled inside them as they shook off the last hazy moments of rest. Their ship had lain still for so long, hushed in the endless drift of the belt, but now it was awake, alive, vibrating under the promise of something *new*. That first pulse of contact was like lightning surging into stagnant water, shocking every nerve cluster wide open.

They flexed, expanding and contracting with excitement, throwing off the sticky heaviness of long dormancy. They burst off the floor in a ripple of plasma, slamming themselves forward into the narrow crawlspace of

a repair tube. The edges scraped deliciously across their membrane, friction sparking against sensitive places that hadn't been touched in cycles. A tight fit for the rigid skeletons who had built the place—but for one like them? "Tight fit" meant nothing to someone with no skeleton.

Taut with excitement, they peered through the vent. The cargo bay gaped open like the maw of some strange beast. It must have taken great courage—or great desperation—to fly into it.

Four bipedal visitors disembarked, each smaller than Aleyne. Pale vacuum suits clung to their forms, four upper limbs, two lower, joints bending and flexing in delicious choreography. The last time this type of sapience visited, they had come for salvage, peeling wiring and metal from Aleyne's home. They had loaded it into their ship as quickly as they could, then vanished before Aleyne could befriend them. With the growing desperation to join with someone, *somehow*, they couldn't bear to have that happen again. The deep, pulsing need in them to be part of something, to come together, burned ever brighter the longer they remained here.

It took slow, patient practice to shape a body similar to theirs. If they looked like them, then perhaps they wouldn't run. The lower limbs were brawny and articulated with four sets of joints, the upper limbs thinner with the same joint arrangements. Aleyne couldn't do joints terribly well—their plasm just bent softly.

Aleyne pressed themself tighter against the vent's edge, drinking in every line of their bodies. Their size was smaller, delicate compared to the colossal predators Aleyne had once observed. But *oh*, those arms. Four hands, four possibilities—what would it be like to feel every finger at once, running, grabbing, stroking across their membrane? What would it be like to let those hands disappear *inside* them, to clutch at nerve clusters and make them sing?

Did they have phalluses, clefts, or something else entirely?

Aleyne's skin trembled with ideas of the suppleness of soft skin or the hard slickness of scales against them, the way a mate's appendages might stoke desire, mingling with musk, enough to make any sensible sapience go light-headed with bliss. A pulse of pure need coursed through them, deep and hard, the basso rumble of a black hole.

Maybe this time things would be different. This time, the visitors wouldn't run when they saw Aleyne. Wouldn't fire their weapons, wouldn't scream or hide.

Plath-yein weren't meant to be solitary. Aleyne knew this the way they knew the derelict warship, the lazy dance it kept in the asteroid belt, the way the stars shone through the portholes. Aleyne ought to be somewhere with others of their kind, exchanging bits of their selves to share memories and experiences. Give a bit to another, receive some in return and be all the greater for it. They *knew* it, deep in their cells and in the wispy memories that had come from the plasm donors who had given them life.

The solitude *hurt*. They may not have the same structure some life-forms did, but they knew what pain was. Laspistols still burned, vacuum still froze, and loneliness bypassed all their nerve clusters and pierced them to the core. There was still another layer to the discomfort, something deeper that filled them inexorably and murmured of something beyond loneliness.

They were fairly certain this feeling of hollowness, of missing something they couldn't define, was what *heartache* was supposed to be like. They'd had enough time to read through the media files on the ship to understand the concept. There was more than enough time to come up with theoretical knowledge—and the practical realizations of what they were missing out on.

Aleyne didn't like it one bit.

Their plasm quivered with longing, pushing them to shift. Limbs budded, bent, bent again, not quite right but close enough. Four arms, two legs, digits stubby and soft but grasping. They flexed and throbbed with want. Would the visitors like it? Would they understand? Aleyne imagined all of it, imagined giving and taking until the loneliness gnawing at their core broke and spilled away.

They turned translucent and slid from the vent to the floor. No one even looked at the cargo bay wall. Everyone's focus was on the courtship wheels Aleyne had built, piles of scrap and arrayed trinkets that Aleyne continually updated on the off-chance that something in their designs had been displeasing to their last potential mates.

The objects they'd collected, whorls of cables and twisted, blackened metal plates, were arrayed in fractal designs, accented with gleaming circuit boards and braids of wire to draw the eye and glitter when lights flickered across them.

There was no way the courtship wheels could be accidental; no solar winds or cosmic waves could possibly arrange them in this way. Aleyne had read in the ships' memory banks of the ways other species greeted visitors, the way they decorated their homes, courted their mates. Some repulsed them, some confused them, but they held a fondness for the ones that were almost like plath-yein courtship wheels, intricate and crafted of shell or stone or—as with the Corvath—songbirds' skulls. Morbid, but proof of commitment, devotion, an ability to provide.

Aleyne made do with a planet's ransom in salvage.

The visitors approached one of the twisted metal courtship wheels, gesturing at the piles of hull plating already harvested for their convenience. Aleyne could not understand the visitors' sounds; there were too many languages to know on which to best focus their skills. This was one they had only learned the rudiments of, unable to mimic certain pheromone-based elements of the language.

When they felt the visitors' interest had been aroused, Aleyne shifted their shape to mimic the visitors. Shape first, and then fine-tuning it as they brought the chromatophores in their membranes to the correct density and hue to pass. It was accurate, they were sure of it.

This time would be different. They couldn't afford to think otherwise.

Aleyne rose from behind the crates and glided nervously toward the visitors. The visitors were taking objects from the courtship wheels, loading them into their craft with high-pitched sounds that Aleyne hoped signified pleasure. The visitors had recognized their value—a small thing, but an important one.

They did their best to mimic the sounds, compressing the internal air cylinders that allowed for speech while waving a piece of scrap they kept on hand for these occasions. Light flashed against its intricately engraved surface, loops and whorls Aleyne was sure meant *something*.

The sounds abruptly changed to what even they could tell were warning noises as Aleyne approached, quickly replaced by the hum of laspistols as their safeties were thumbed off. One gestured with both of its upper hands, the lower pair holding weapons. Aleyne lifted the scrap in their upper limbs, allowing the lower pair to spread wide and show their emptiness.

"No threat," Aleyne said carefully in Galactic, waving the scrap and continuing to ease forward. "I only want—"

There was only a warning whine as a laspistol battery drew more charge. Light flashed from one side.

Aleyne ducked and flattened themself against the deck more literally than they would have wished. Frustration and disappointment burned along their nerves as they thrust themself upright, doing their best to maintain the visitors' form. It was wobblier now, but the alternative—assuming their amorphous native shape—would certainly not help.

"I'm only looking for a *friend*," Aleyne called, the carefully delineated colors of their shape flickering with frustration. The word they used was weighted with more, longing-need-partner all bundled together in tone and with the ripple of membrane and flicker of hue.

The salvagers fled with shouts and the whine of laspistols, the force of their thrusters jarring the derelict.

Aleyne wondered whether it would be worth it simply to hide next time, then commandeer the craft that landed. They'd been treating this place as home, waiting for something to come to them—some beings who might be willing to take them along, or—preferably—mate with them. Some beings who weren't afraid of Aleyne or the indefinable thing that they represented. The derelict required more than just one single individual to pilot it, and given the damage it had endured, they weren't certain they even could. They'd been too afraid to try and sneak aboard a ship, but that would have to change.

Aleyne shed the visitors' form and moved toward the heart of their repurposed part of the ship. Aleyne replayed the encounter in their mind, trying to figure out how they had gone wrong. The courtship wheels had been approved, the piles of scrap welcomed. They'd matched in color and shape.

Ah. They'd forgotten to *walk* with all their joints involved. Their gait had no doubt been horrifying, so-called feet rippling with tiny movements to propel them forward.

They'd be ready next time. It would be different. They repeated the mantra to themself as they moved through the derelict in the days that followed, edging into deeper parts they had not visited in some time, extracting new bits of circuitry and plating to bring back to the cargo bay and make into new displays with even more intricate designs. They would be ready.

It was an infinity. The proximity alarm flashed and the accompanying vibrations rippled over Aleyne's skin. It was with apprehension, not optimism, that they made their way to the maintenance vent.

What emerged from the shuttle was a humanoid in a vac-suit, two arms and two legs—and something that looked, approximately, like a humanoid in a vac-suit. Except it wasn't one at all.

It moved carefully and in the same way as the humanoid, but there was a smoothness to its gait and its appearance Aleyne recognized. Approaching one of the courtship wheels, the humanoid gestured, scrutinizing it from all angles.

The plath-yein beside it—for the knowledge thrummed through them that it was one of their kind—moved from one of the carefully arrayed scrap piles to another. The vac-suit-like shape rippled, the colors gradation becoming finer and more precise, more accurate to the being that walked beside them. The plath-yein's movement sharpened, actively attempting to mimic jointed locomotion.

It looked downright silly, but the dedication to accuracy was impressive. From a distance and at a glance, Aleyne would have had a hard time noting the differences. Whoever they were, they were quite skilled. Admiration pulsed through them, tinged with the instinctive urge to impress them in the same way.

Aleyne weighed their options. One, tried and failed many times: mimic the visitors and their sleek blue vacsuits. The second, an idea they had outright rejected until this point, was nebulous and nerve-wracking.

Appear as they were, rather than trying mimicry. They could always shift during courtship later.

Every time they had tried to be something they weren't, it had ended in failure. They couldn't bear failure again, and failure had been caused by adhering to all the rituals their foggy memory supplied.

Aleyne eased out of the vent and down the wall. There was truly no choice at all. The human was pacing around the second of the courtship wheels, still staring at it. The other plath-yein was rippling in shades of blue, from palest near-white to a blue giant star and ending with a shade so dark it was nearly black. Shifting so smoothly took immaculate control, and that they be in the company of someone with whom they could resemble—but not have to feign—being entirely human?

Something in Aleyne swooped dangerously, calling to mind the moment of null gravity at the apex of a turn just before gravity seized hold again, full of uncertainty. They shivered, skin spiking with apprehension. Moving into full view was difficult; the consequences seemed weightier now that real possibility stood in the cargo bay.

If the visitors weren't friendly, better to know now. Keeping to what was their natural form—as much as plath-yein had one—Aleyne deliberately knocked over a piece of scrap. Habit made them ready for the sounds of weapons, snarls of rage, or shrieks of fear.

Nothing came.

With the attention of the two visitors secured, now was the time to risk it all.

Slowly, focus entirely on the plath-yein and their companion standing amidst their courtship offerings, Aleyne began to shift. They drew their mass into a shape akin to the visitors': two arms, two legs, a torso, a neck and head. They shaped an oval face with a sharp chin and strong nose and a short, tousled cap of hair and the same sort of vacsuit the visitors wore. Deliberate, precise adjustment, down to gloved fingers and clunky boot-like feet.

Waiting was torture.

And then the human face behind the vacsuit faceplate split into a smile that hit Aleyne as sharply as any weapon.

Joy.

"You were right," the humanoid called in lilting Galactic.

The plath-yein rippled with more of that amusement, approaching Aleyne with almost perfect steps. Pheromones wafted off them, a flood of scents that went straight to something deep and instinctive in Aleyne. "We've been trying to find you, cousin."

Find them? Who knew about them—who cared enough to *find* them, as though they'd been missing?

"How—?" Aleyne stopped, the words seizing up inside them. The tongue in their mouth was tungsten-heavy and fumbling, made only more so by the pheromones. They were emitting some of their own, they knew; the plath-yein's body shifted, widened in response, the perfect control fracturing for a beat.

"There are rumors," the sapience, a human, said with a smile. The

speaker unit crackled once before continuing. "Stories of a monster lurking on one of the old Obena warships. People want to scavenge it, but the fearsome monster—no reports are ever the same. And Esak…" They trailed off, looking to the plath-yein. "Esak said he suspected it was another of his kind. It took us a long time to figure out which ship, since none of the salvagers—scavengers, really—wanted to reveal the location of a haul like this. It wasn't supposed to exist, let alone have a creature aboard it."

"And that…rumor?…brought you here?" The fear inside them shifted, easing to be replaced by something else akin to it but of a different stripe.

The human's mouth curled into a wider smile. "I am known for my curiosity. I have a…more than academic interest."

Aleyne tilted their head, the gesture awkwardly exaggerated as they tried to fine-tune the motion. "I do not understand."

The other plath-yein's skin rippled and flickered with amusement, subtle gradations of color Aleyne wasn't sure the human noticed. It was strange to see the shifts of color and texture on a human-like frame. "Dreija is a researcher; she prefers field work. And we have been partners for many years now. Our relationship is not of a purely academic nature."

Aleyne shifted mass from one leg to another, restless, focusing on the other of their kind. Hot sensation bubbled inside them. It was a strange combination of feelings that took them a moment to name—desire, hope, but mingled with a selfish jealousy at the comfort both had with each other.

Oh, how they wanted something like that, their envy clawing at them as it hadn't in years. Once they had longed for the sky, to join other creatures in exploring ships. Now it was nothing so simple as space flight, and entirely about the urges stirring in them, the ache and itch for contact, for the pressure of another's skin against theirs—the potential of joining, mingling plasm, the glimpse into thoughts and memories it would give.

Esak, the human had named them—*him*. Hope sparked through them, and they gave a longing look at the courtship wheels, down at themself, and then at the sealed door that led into the better-pressurized parts of the derelict where life support still functioned.

"If you would like to come with me"—a risk, such a risk for their visitors, going into a place they didn't know with a being they had only just met—"I would…like to hear more of this."

"Of course," Dreija said, eyes glinting. "There are few things I'd like more. It's a pleasure to meet you."

Hope fluttered nervously inside them as Aleyne spoke. "I am Aleyne."

Embarrassment washed through Aleyne as they led Esak and Dreija through the corridors of the warship that still had life-support and atmospheric control, trailing a pseudo-hand along the wall paneling. It was not a habit, but it was an opportunity to practice shaping fingers, appreciating the texture against their skin. The passageways seemed cruder now, more damaged, as they tried to imagine what the visitors thought. Bits of detritus floated through the null-g and low-g sectors. Nervousness chased after embarrassment like a comet's tail; they hadn't thought this far ahead. Where had they *expected* to couple with a mate, there in the cargo bay? All this time and they hadn't cleaned—

"Are you truly the only one aboard?" Esak asked, subtle hues flashing across him. Curiosity-interest muted down to show politeness. Even knowing what Aleyne was, he'd remained in that humanoid shape with an oval face, strong jaw with a mouth, a pair of wide-set eyes that shone the dark purple of a swirling nebula.

"I have explored the ship over my time here but have never met another, save those who visit." Aleyne hummed for a moment. "I do not know how long it has been. Years, I suspect, but—by whose counting?"

Dreija drew herself up a ladder between floors; the pink strands of her hair slowly fell around her shoulders as a higher gravity took hold. "This ship—and all her crew—were deemed lost ten Galactic years ago."

Ten years? Aleyne froze, suspended halfway between the levels. They hadn't thought they'd been isolated for so long. Only a few at most, surely—but when there was no day or night, no orbit to consider, one cycle bled into the next. No wonder they ached so desperately for companionship.

They resumed the ascent, then pushed off into a corridor, reassured by the sounds behind them that they were being followed.

"The Obena wanted nothing to do with this place," Dreija said. "They

lost the war, and this ship was—from everything we gleaned—not even supposed to be here. Secret mission, all references to it scrubbed. It became a mystery, and the creature that lurked on it even more of one. No one ever managed to make off with any sort of proof that they'd found this vessel, either. They all claimed to, of course. Any Obena ship could give plating or power conduits. And then to flee when they found something—or someone—else there? And no two stories ever matched?" Her laughter danced across Aleyne's skin. The sound set off sizzles and pops inside them. "They couldn't admit defeat."

"But none," Esak said, easing himself alongside Dreija and closer to Aleyne, "said the same thing about the entity that lurked there. Each different account varied just enough—but all said the thing they faced looked like them. Only…" His words faded briefly. "Not quite true. Some called it hallucinations, old chem-weapons left aboard as a deterrent. Others called it lies, a story building on itself to cover up their failures."

"It was a long time," Aleyne said, a touch defensive—but they let their flickering hues show pleasure and amusement, letting down the guard they'd held. Relief filled them. They didn't have to hide any more, didn't have to pretend they were something they weren't. "I had no means of knowing how long I was alone."

"And now," the other plath-yein said, "you do." He shifted a slender limb, arm turning increasingly to a pseudopod, motioning to the human beside him. "And there is no reason for you to remain alone any longer, unless you wish to. But the signs you left say that you do not."

Aleyne rippled their skin with a mixture of hope and nervousness, glowing bright with colors that had long been reserved for fantasy alone. The courting gifts had been seen and well-received. There were *two* who'd followed them into the depths of the ship, toward what passed for their bower. "I am very tired," they said, pausing on the threshold of the room they had turned into their home, "of being alone. I am ready to change that."

Dreija and Esak eased into the room. Sleek paneled walls held enough shine to reflect their own blurry shapes back; the rest of the space was decorated with pillows, an oddly shaped basin that was comfortable to rest in, and an assortment of objects that had intrigued Aleyne.

"Is that—?" Dreija moved with startling speed toward a shelf. "Is that

a Paltith reliquary? And—a Leikhan law book?"

Aleyne turned to Esak. "Is this…?"

"Normal? Yes. She is…enthusiastic." The flickering hues of good humor followed. "She has a one-track mind when interested in something."

This close and within the confines of the room, Esak's pheromones turned to a cloud of scent and something more subtle and instinctive that coiled around Aleyne. He reeked of readiness.

They looked across the room at Dreija. "And she—" Aleyne cut themself off. "You and she…"

Esak moved closer to Aleyne, abandoning more of his human-like shape. "Dreija is curious, even for a human. She is not afraid of anything save paper cuts and what happens when I am unsupervised in a kitchen," he said. He brushed one hand-like pseudopod against their side.

The contact rocketed through them. Aleyne made a soft sound somewhere between desperation and relief that startled even themself. Intoxicating, that's what he was. Aleyne trembled, skin shimmering with indecision. "I—" One of their kind, practiced and sure, with a human lover. Unafraid. Eager? That might go too far—but Aleyne was hopeful, and just as eager. "Will she…mind?"

"Only if you leave me out," Dreija called, hands laced tightly behind her back as she pressed her nose to a set of interlinked spheres on wire cords. "I may not be able to do everything you can do, but…there are things I *can*." Her voice danced with good humor and a steely resolve. "And I may have some suggestions for what you might enjoy as well."

The human's bluntness made Aleyne's eyes widen. "I have never," they said slowly, "coupled with a human before." Coupled with *anyone* before, but that was an admission they didn't want to make. Not yet, at least.

"We're different," Dreija said, sharing a long glance with Esak, "but not so different that we cannot make it work. It requires some creativity—at least on my part—but for you…" Her eyes darkened, her bright-pink tongue wetting her lips. "Only if you want to. I don't know what you both need to do."

Aleyne must have looked puzzled, confusion on their skin or in their scent. Esak bobbed his head in a loose nod. "Dreija has kept me busy," he confessed, "but when we suspected it was another plath-yein, I had hope. I have not wished to return to the homeworld for many years, and

our kind are…not so common in space."

"We frighten them." Their response dropped into the room, hollow and hurting. The ability to change shapes and make themselves appear as something they were not had made plath-yein frightening to many species burdened with only one form.

"Oh, Aleyne!" Dreija's pale-green eyes went wide. She reached for them, fingertips brushing against Aleyne's shoulder. It was all they could do not to lean into it. "You really have had a hard time of it."

Esak brushed a hand along Aleyne's side. He seemed to be speaking more to Dreija than Aleyne, but they didn't mind. "Plath-yein mating is usually…perfunctory at best. Proof of survival, that they are strong, clever, successful. Rarely is it done for pleasure, for there is the risk of losing oneself in the other. Literally," he added with a faint smile on his lips. "But Aleyne has proven their strength, ingenuity, and success. I would be very interested to find out what shapes you *can* take," he added with a hint of challenge lacing his tone, mimicked by the rhythmic pattern flashing along his skin. "But you deserve more than that."

Aleyne extended a hand, allowing the humanoid shape to soften, phalanges to meld together and turn spadelike. "What do I deserve, then?"

"Whatever you would like. If all you wish is something perfunctory, then you may have it." Esak's seriousness was as palpable as his desire. His skin pulsed, taking an intricate, fractal-like appearance. "But you also deserve companionship, pleasure, what you wish. Pick a shape, pick *any* shape, or all of them. Let us mate with you. Let us bring you pleasure."

"You could start with kissing," Dreija said, lips curled up with evident amusement. "How do you do it?"

"We don't," Aleyne said, a furtive shimmer in their skin. They turned to look to Esak for help, but found none—only an expression of amusement on the practiced human face and a quivering they sensed was much of the same.

"That's a shame," Dreija answered in a voice soothing and teasing at once. She cocked her head and glanced between them. "I think you might like it."

"You could always show her," Esak said, one pseudopod running along Aleyne's skin. "You enjoy it so much…"

Dreija flashed a bright, toothy smile that made Aleyne's insides contract. "I do," Dreija admitted with undisguised glee. "Do you want to try it?"

Aleyne quivered. They'd lost a significant amount of the precise human shape they'd constructed, finally at ease in the company. They began to pull up the human form again, but Dreija lifted a single hand as though to silence them.

"You don't have to take any shape you don't want to. I like this one, and as long as you have something akin to a mouth, I can kiss it." Green eyes gleamed. "Unless you're offering me a challenge."

"One thing at a time." Aleyne focused on shaping a face, something between Esak's and Dreija's, but with lips, a tongue, teeth. It was intricate work, and they offered Esak the first smile.

He made a noise, something sweet and strangled.

They were on the right track, then.

Dreija cupped Aleyne's face in her hands. "If you don't like it," she said, "say so. Anything you don't want, we'll stop."

Aleyne couldn't think of anything they didn't want as long as they were being touched. Now. As much as possible. Esak seemed to know it, too; the steady pressure of him against their skin was almost overwhelming, yet simultaneously not enough. Every place he didn't touch ached with the absence. Aleyne closed their eyes, struggling to focus.

"I'm waiting." Dreija's voice had gone serious. "Do you understand?"

"I do," Aleyne said.

Dreija leaned in and kissed them. Aleyne was stunned, frozen in place as Dreija's warm, soft mouth pressed against theirs. It was *soft*—they weren't sure why they had thought it would be hard; all the teeth, perhaps?—but there was nothing more than the insistent, gentle touch of her lips. It stirred more electric jolts of desire through Aleyne, nerves singing a new song as Dreija pressed her body against Aleyne's. Esak bracketed them, his soft, pliable body molding itself around Aleyne's, arms wrapping around their torso.

It was sweet. Restrained.

Aleyne wanted none of that. They opened their mouth to speak; Dreija took it as an invitation, leaning in, her fingers touching Aleyne's face as she deepened the kiss. Her tongue dipped past Aleyne's lips, sparking pleasure with every stroke.

It was shocking, but more than that—the contact, the brush of another's body inside theirs, made something inside Aleyne go tight and hard. They leaned *into* the kiss, sliding their tongue against Dreija's. Warmth cascaded through them as Dreija's fingers tightened against their face. She pressed her body against Aleyne's, trying to mold herself against it.

They scrambled for a moment of fine control and extended their tongue, making it longer and thinner, and brushed it back against Dreija's.

This time, she shuddered. Moaned. Curled her fingers in against Aleyne with a hungry, needy whine.

Oh, those were sounds they could grow used to, far better than creaking metal and the whirr of struggling atmospheric recyclers. Aleyne bubbled with satisfaction as they shifted their tongue again, fanning the tips out into a multitude of frond-like ends. Dreija moaned even louder, the sound filling Aleyne with pleasure.

"That's it," Esak murmured from behind them both. "Whatever you've done, she likes that. But you know what she likes more?" He curled one of his hand-pseudopods around one of Aleyne's and guided it slowly over Dreija's body to the soft mounds of her breasts. Their shared touch lingered for a moment, squeezing gently through the vacuum suit, before moving lower still. Another nudge from Esak, and they extended a lower limb between Dreija's thighs.

Aleyne was not prepared for the new, hungry sound Dreija made as her fingers tightened around Aleyne's face. She ground down against their pseudopod. She twisted their tongues together, making short, sharp gasps of evident pleasure.

"You'll have to show me that trick," Esak said. "Whatever you're doing to her mouth. Listen to those sounds, how much she wants us already. I thought this was supposed to be for *you*," he added wryly, pressing his body against theirs.

They didn't mind. Kissing was new, and the way it was so clearly arousing their partner? To be wanted like this? Desired? After so many cycles of their offerings being rejected, this was more than just physical pleasure. Aleyne extended a fine-tipped tendril of a pseudopod and trailed it down Dreija's vacsuit, drawing the seals apart. The risk had been worth it for the way Dreija responded, the humming of her lips against Aleyne's, the quickening rocking of her body.

Dreija broke the kiss, blinking dark and glassy eyes at Aleyne. "Let me," she said, wriggling her way out of the vacsuit and tossing it aside. She crossed her arms beneath her breasts, still clad in a thin underlayer. "It's unfair that neither of you have anything I can strip you out of."

The concept gave Aleyne pause; they'd never felt the need to hide their body, considering it could become anything. Clothing was confining. Yet the appeal of stripping Dreija out of what they wore, revealing what lay beneath…it was like a puzzle-box. Aleyne wanted to know what the human woman's breasts looked like beneath the underlayer. What all of her looked like.

For creatures that could only take one shape, humans did a masterful job at hiding it beneath their clothing.

"Do you want to? I can feign—"

"No. I"—the human paused, looking past Aleyne at, presumably, Esak, who nodded—"we want nothing more than *you*. I know just how creative plath-yein can be. Show us. What else can you do? What do you *want* to do?"

And those words, the hungry demand beneath *show us*, curled another tendril of desire into Aleyne. The mates wanted to see what they could do. Who were they to deny them?

Aleyne did not know humans well, but they knew a challenge. The desire to prove they were a worthy mate continued to bubble in the back of their mind.

They separated from between Esak and Dreija, sparing a quick glance to see Esak's current shape and find a way to complement it. He'd taken on something much like a human's form, though the fine definition of feet and hands had shifted to more amorphous tendrils, body supported on half a dozen thick tentacle-like appendages. At the base of his torso, where it met the mass of writhing tentacles, was a phallus, not unlike the ones humans so often boasted of.

Aleyne met Esak's eyes, letting their skin flash rhythmically with intricate patterns. They ran their not-quite-hands along their body, allowing themself a chance to enjoy the touch of their own hands. Esak's pattern picked up, with a similar pattern and pace; a new rush of pheromones washed off him. He liked what they were doing.

The way Dreija had begun to shimmy out of the thin underlayer, touching herself as she watched Aleyne, continued the story.

This was a heady kind of power, being wanted this way. Aleyne closed their eyes and played with themself for a few moments, listening to the quickening breath of the human woman and the soft shifting of the other plath-yein in the room. A thickening musk of pheromones wove through the air.

Aleyne's paddle-like hands slid down their torso farther still, until one rested between their thighs. Long strokes of their own flesh summoned up a shape not unlike the thick, hard protrusion that hung between Esak's legs. It wasn't perfect, but it was theirs—their first one. Detailed human-compatible anatomy had not been part of their studies.

Judging from Dreija's expression, it didn't matter. Her face held the same delighted glee as when she'd seen the artifacts in Aleyne's collection. "That is a beautiful cock." She licked her lips and looked between the two plath-yein. "But I don't want you to do it because you think you have to." Her eyes focused on Aleyne's face, caught and held their gaze. "We are here for *you*. Whatever shape, whatever *you* wish."

"I want to try it." Aleyne reached a limb out to stroke Esak's cock. "I might like it."

"You might." Dreija's eyes widened, pupils dilating perceptibly. "And you are welcome to anything you might wish." She settled herself down on the nest of pillows. "Anything."

Esak's eyes fluttered closed and his body rocked forward, thrusting against their touch.

Had they failed? Theirs felt no more sensitive than a hand or what served now as a hip or their hair.

"Kneel, Esak," Dreija commanded from her throne of pillows, her voice rough in a way that made that Aleyne shiver. "You like it, too. I can tell. Show Aleyne how much you want their cock. Show me what it's like when you suck them off. How good you are with your tongue. Make them feel good."

With every word, the tension dancing through Aleyne swelled, but it only seemed to make them feel smaller—no, not smaller. Denser.

In a single fluid motion, Esak sank and crossed the floor on the twining tangle of tendrils. Each one wriggled independently, complicated and arousing. With evident good humor in his eyes, the plath-yein wrapped one wriggling tentacle around the base of Aleyne's cock.

Surprise and pleasure jolted through them at the touch. and at the look of utter admiration on Esak's face, at the hypnotizing pattern on his skin that was so close to their own. Then he opened his mouth and took their cock into it, and Aleyne pinched their eyes shut as sensation cascaded over them.

This—being *inside* another being—

The trust. The way he looked at them—like he wanted to make sure they liked it—

The tight, hard part of Aleyne was growing. It was more intense, like they'd ingested a rock, heavy and burning with need. They needed something beyond the surface-level contact.

Esak's mouth slid over them, every stroke of his tongue drawing Aleyne's focus there. His tongue twisted along the length of the shaft, spiraled around the tip.

The pleasure was a heady thing, but not enough. Still not enough. With a wriggle and a thrust, Aleyne pushed deeper, trying to find the thing they chased, the thing that would make the aching need stop.

A musky scent that was not plath-yein mingled with their own; it was a slickness between Dreija's thighs, one Aleyne wanted to press themself into, to taste. They stretched out to do just that, moving together with Esak to spread out beside Dreija on the pillows.

Permission was granted with an enthusiastic nod. Dreija's fingers pressed against Aleyne's head encouragingly, her hips bucking up as she panted out her pleasure at Aleyne's ministrations.

This, too, was good, all mouths and fingers. Esak stretched to join them, kissing Dreija, kissing Aleyne as they lapped at Dreija's cleft. They played with tongue at first, and then drew away and worked a pseudopod along her folds, extending the tip inside her. Pleasure then, too—"more" and "deeper" and "harder" and cries of pleasure, sounds that rattled through Aleyne, vibrated over their membrane, made them want to lose integrity entirely.

Close—but not close enough.

They all tangled together then. Esak's and Aleyne's bodies went soft and undefined, focused less on the shape and more on chasing the hunger building between the three of them. Aleyne tried wings, made four sets of hands to fondle breasts and stroke cocks, and even sprouted a pair of phalluses to watch Dreija and Esak on their knees before them.

Always encouraging, Dreija offered—not quite commands, but

suggestions borne of insatiable desire and curiosity, as her fingers slid and danced around Aleyne's form. Aleyne softened, exploring Dreija's body. Breasts intrigued them, so Aleyne made a pair, ample handfuls topped with nipples. They clustered nerves, all the better to experience the same sharp gasps of pleasure Dreija made when Aleyne touched her there.

The human woman's eyes glinted, pupils gone wide and shining. She lowered her mouth to one of the mounds, swiping tongue and gently drawing her teeth across it.

Oh, this shape was *wonderful*.

It was wonderful, too, when Dreija took one of Aleyne's hands, sliding it down her own body to the juncture of her thighs. "This," she said, voice catching as Aleyne slid a protrusion not unlike a finger along the hot, slick folds, "you might also enjoy. Not all do, but—if we are experimenting." Her voice caught again as Aleyne slid another protrusion, more like a sucking pad of a tentacle, across a hard bud at the apex of Dreija's thighs. Dreija rolled her hips, pressing herself against Aleyne harder.

"You should"—her voice caught—"try this, too. If you want."

If it made Dreija weak and wobbly as a plath-yein with that sort of touch, how could Aleyne refuse?

And so it went, adding and subtracting limbs and clefts, folds and protrusions, surrendering to the pleasure bubbling through them. Finally, Dreija slid onto Esak's cock, her fingers pressed into a cleft Aleyne had made in mimicry of Dreija's. All of it for the sake of pleasure and the growing sense of completion that chased Aleyne.

"More. More, Esak," Dreija rasped, one hand denting his skin while her other curled deeply inside Aleyne. She wriggled down harder against Esak, as though trying to take all of him inside her. As if there was nothing more she wanted than to be surrounded by the two of them, twisted, tangled—absorbed—

Aleyne tightened her pseudopod around the base of Esak's cock; somewhere in their lower bodies, the separate membranes between the two plath-yein began to soften. Aleyne eased themself around more of Dreija until it was no longer fingers, but her wrist, her forearm, the delicate joint of her elbow.

The friction was sweet, but the rippling pleasure that coursed through them was sweeter. Esak began wrapping Aleyne in pseudopods—the same safety and surrounding, the same sharing of contact.

They were not alone, not now. Could never be again, not with this moment shared between them, three organisms together in pursuit of the same goal. This—oh, *this*—

Sensation overwhelmed them. There was no pain, no consideration, no worry—only the need that echoed through every bit of them. Aleyne pulsed around Dreija's fingers; the sensation of those five wriggling digits *inside* them built, all of it a burning need like the heart of a star.

Dreija's fingers came into contact with that hard part of Aleyne, seized it like it was an object that had built inside them. They moaned, body quaking.

"That's it," Dreija said with urgency. "Make him lose control, Aleyne. You can feel it, can't you? How hard he is, how much he wants it? He's been so good for both of us. Do it, sweetheart"—and the word slithered across Aleyne's skin with an unexpected pleasure—"both of you, I want both of you to come for me. Show me what it's like." Her voice cracked, rough and hungry, like that knowledge was as important as her pleasure. "Let me see the both of you come."

It was impossible not to, not when issued with that kind of sweet command.

Every cell of Aleyne turned, for one flickering, infinite moment, to pleasure. There was no space for anything else as the sensation swallowed them, bright and hot and fierce. The pseudopod wrapped around Esak tightened, and the mass of him enfolding their lower body went taut, and together they contracted around each other, around Dreija, frozen in ecstasy for one endless breath of time.

In that breathless suspension Aleyne knew themselves complete, every hollow longing filled to brimming, their whole form steeped in the radiant assurance of being wanted, cherished, consumed in love and desire. Then the tide of time slowly returned—lungs dragging in heavy air, soft membranes knitting closed once more, the low churn of the recyclers threading through the silence—while pleasure still swirled inside them in gentle currents, lingering, refusing to release its hold.

Everything had been worth the wait.

"Come with us," Esak said, the patterns of his skin shifting slowly and rhythmically. His grip around her pulsed once, reassuringly. "There

are worlds waiting for you. Places where you can find out what it is you wish to be."

"Did you?" they asked lazily, the suckers of one pseudopod still idly playing with Dreija's breasts. The human curled up closer to the two plath-yein as they molded themselves around her.

"I tried many things before I settled on this shape. I like it. But there's nothing that says you must be human, or even humanoid." Humor threaded through Esak's voice. "There's much you might discover."

"Do you think they'd like Leicin?" Dreija asked lazily. "All those tails..."

"Tails?" Aleyne ran a limb delicately over Esak's shoulder. "Tails sound very interesting indeed. When do we leave?"

Courted: The Witch and the Rasera

Ivy L. James

beltane, cunnilingus, f/f, fisting, fluff, idiots to lovers, lesbian, magic use, mating bond, miscommunication, modern with magic, oblivious, opposites attract, parenthood, past tense, phobia (heights), size difference, third person limited point of view, tonguefucking, tribbing, witch

At thirty-three years old, Cassandra Hawthorne was determined to establish herself as the best witch in Maple Grove. Hence why she was currently tromping through the blooming spring woods, headed straight for the local rasera's cave.

Mayor Hazel Winters had requested a custom productivity spell jar in time for Beltane, and the best ingredient for that was rasera feathers. Locally sourced, ethically harvested. Sure, Cass had never gathered them herself before today, but she needed to stand out. She'd gotten a good start on it: most everyone in town had come to her for spells (*pouches, jars, jewelry, and more!* as her website said) over the last year, and her tarot cards had yet to be proven wrong. Still, the goalposts were

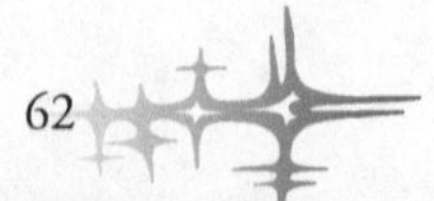

constantly moving. As soon as Cass checked something off her bucket list, she added three more intentions. Nothing she did was ever good enough on its own. With every spellcraft, but especially this one, she had to outdo herself somehow. Make something no one else could possibly put together.

And maybe if she expanded her business, she would make that place for herself that she was missing.

Maple Grove hosted festivals for every solstice and equinox, and Cass always went, mostly because Hazel and her wife, Ralin, got sad if she skipped. But Cass never felt quite right there, even among other queer witches. She couldn't seem to fit herself into their world, though by all rights it should've been her world too. Even surrounded by others like her, she was alone.

She shook off the shadowy thought. *Focus.* The cave was right ahead, and if Cass could sneak in quietly enough, she could grab a few molted feathers and bounce before the rasera so much as scented her. These highly intelligent monsters were known to hold grudges; she had no interest in coming face-to-face with one. Spirit creatures like a fireborn fikerav were easy-peasy in comparison.

As she sneaked alongside the entrance, she paused and listened. No telltale scrapes of claws, no roaring, nothing. Only the wind rustling the green leaves on the trees. Maybe the rasera wasn't home.

Cass crept inside the cave, keeping an eye and ear out for any sign of the monster. She'd expected the cave to be a mess, given a beast lived here, but the floor was so clean as to be unnatural. As if it had been swept. Certainly no stray feathers to be snatched up with any ease. She tiptoed deeper, farther from the afternoon sunlight. When it grew too dark to see, she turned her phone's screen brightness down and used that to light her path.

A low growl vibrated in the black.

Cass swallowed a curse, almost dropping her phone. *Shit, shit, shit.* The rasera was here. She pressed herself against the wall and tucked her phone into her pocket, unwilling to guide the monster to her with its glow. *Fuck. What do I do? Growl back?* That was probably stupid, but everything she knew about raseras had flown from her brain. One thought remained: *I gotta go.*

But when she inched herself along the wall without light to guide her, her foot slipped into a crack in the rocks. As she struggled to free herself, her stomach plummeted. The growling was growing louder, she was a sitting duck, and she didn't even have any rasera feathers to show for her stupidity.

Claws scraped at the floor. Shifting wings rustled. The monster huffed, the sound close enough for anxiety to crawl up Cass's throat.

Fuck, fuck, fuck. It's going to—

A warm, citrus-scented breath fluttered Cass's blonde bangs and ponytail. Cass squeezed her eyes shut, preparing herself to be devoured…but all the dark-shrouded monster did was sniff her, snuffling her neck, her shirt, her feet.

"Human," the rasera rumbled, its feminine voice husky and low, the single word unmistakable.

Cass's eyes flew open. She'd thought the rumors of raseras speaking in human tongues were made-up, or a matter of echoing what they'd heard, like parrots. But this didn't seem that way at all.

"Why are you here?" The rasera nosed up Cass's shirt.

Cass hurried to tug the fabric back into place. "I can leave. I didn't mean to—"

"Why?"

"Um. Shit. I needed…some feathers. For a spell jar?" Right, as if a fucking *monster* knew what that was.

"What is your name?"

"Cass." She felt silly for offering even the nickname. But given that she hadn't been eaten yet, the knot in her stomach was unwinding. She twisted her foot right and left, trying to unjam it.

"I am Nazliha." The rasera shook herself in the false night, wings rustling again, sending a fresh wave of blood-orange scent into the air. Cass hated that it smelled good.

"Nice to meet you, Nazliha," she said stupidly, out of habit. Finally, thank Freyja, Cass's foot came loose. She stumbled backward, catching herself against the cave stone. "Look, I clearly shouldn't have come here, so I'm gonna go." She scooted along the wall in what she hoped was the correct direction.

Claws scraped against the rocks as the rasera *followed* her. "Where will you go?"

"Home?" Cass inched around a corner and caught the first glimpse of

yellow-white sunlight. She moved toward it—and so did the rasera. And the first dim light revealed the monster's form.

The rasera was on all fours, but would easily be seven feet tall if she stood. Long horns arched from her furry head over rich brown eyes and a broad black nose. Her tufted ears stood at attention, swiveling in tiny movements to catch every sound. Thick golden-brown fur covered her body, and feathered wings were tucked tight against her back. A long tail lashed behind her. White fangs and black claws gleamed sharp and sleek.

Instinctive fear rose in Cass's chest.

Fear, and a flicker of arousal.

Nazliha's slitted pupils dilated against the amber of the irises, and she sniffed at Cass's jeans. "You are—"

"No, I'm not." Cass pushed her off, smothering the spark of need in her own belly. "Look, I'll figure something else out for the spell jar. Thanks for not…eating me or whatever."

"I will go with you." Nazliha's rough words left no room for argument. "You will get home safely."

Cass sputtered. "I don't— I'm fine."

"I will go with you," Nazliha repeated in a low growl.

Cass shut up. She headed toward the sun, finally stepping out into the woods with a deep, bracing breath. The air out here was clean and aromatic with fresh flowers and oncoming rain, rather than inexplicably attractive citrus and soft fur. But then Nazliha trotted out behind her, and tempting blood orange enveloped Cass again.

Nazliha followed Cass through the woods, and eventually Cass gave in to the pressure for conversation. Why she needed to make small talk with a monster was maybe something to discuss with her therapist. "Do you like living around here?"

"I have lived here many summers now, since I hatched from my mother's egg." Nazliha sounded wistful. "She was a pup here too. Many mothers have laid their eggs in that cave."

"What about your father?"

Nazliha cocked her head in confusion, ears perking toward Cass. "I have no father. There are no male raseras."

Cass was *not* thinking about the logistics of a female-only species. How they might reproduce. How they might…take care of one another. "I don't have a father either," she said to distract herself, aiming for levity, "but that's just 'cause he's a dick."

Instead of laughing (or whatever raseras did to express amusement), Nazliha growled, standing to her full height, fangs bared. "He abandoned you?"

No, no, no. Cass had not meant for this to get personal. "Anyway, my house is right up here." She pointed through the trees at the white saltbox house she called home. It was a former farmstead, set back from the rest of town and surrounded by an overgrown windbreak that blended into the woods behind it. "You can go back to your cave now."

Nazliha made no move to turn around. "Your nest is inside?"

"I don't have a *nest* nest, but my bed and stuff, sure." Cass kept walking. Nazliha kept following her. Only when Cass stepped onto the porch and opened the door did the rasera pull back. She extended her wings, nipped a few feathers free, and held them out for Cass to take.

Cass hesitated. It felt like a trick—but Nazliha didn't bite or claw or anything else. Just gave her the feathers. A gift. Cass clutched them to her chest. "Um. Thank you."

Nazliha sat on her haunches, tucking her wings back into place. "Be well, Cass."

"Be…well, Nazliha." Cass held up one hand in an awkward wave as she closed the door behind herself. Through the window, she watched as Nazliha trotted back into the woods, horns high.

What in the actual fuck had just happened?

Cass woke in the middle of the night to the strangest noise. A long ululation, punctuated by chirps, clicks, and growls. Some stray cats getting into it, maybe. Rubbing her eyes, she stumbled to the bedroom window and peered out.

In the light of the stars, Nazliha shrieked as she lumbered to and fro on the lawn, doing what could only be described as a weird, monstrous song-and-dance.

"Fuck," Cass mumbled. She stumbled down the staircase, and then she opened the front door with a yawn before grumbling, "Nazliha, what the hell?"

"Cass." The rasera flapped her wings and wiggled. "Dance with me."

Cass hugged herself, trying not to shiver in her oversized tee, boxers, and bare feet. "It's two in the morning. Go home."

Nazliha picked right back up where she'd left off: wailing at the moon while shimmying from side to side, her tail whipping with way too much energy.

"Nazliha!"

The rasera deflated then, wings and ears drooping. "You will not share my dance?"

"I was sleeping, and now I'm not, so no."

Nazliha sank onto all fours. "You may return to your sleep. I will go." And she slunk back into the woods, tail tucked, tufted ears low. Cass waited until she was out of sight before padding back indoors.

After a few fitful hours, Cass gave up on getting any real rest. She made herself a mug of creamer-heavy coffee and sipped it in her oversized armchair as she read in the cool blue light of too-early morning. Here by the window, it was a little chilly. She needed better-insulated glass, but more important, was Nazliha warm enough in her cave? If Cass was cold indoors, surely Nazliha was cold outdoors.

Unable to turn off the thought, Cass collected a couple of spare blankets and, once the sun was high enough that she wouldn't freeze on the walk over, hefted them under her arms and opened the front door.

The carcass of an azerok lay in a heap on the porch.

"Oh, shit!" Cass jumped back, her nose wrinkling. "Gross, gross, gross." The horned bear was clearly freshly killed, but where had it come from? She looked around for the offender. Off at the edge of the property line, up in an oak tree, Nazliha was watching her intently.

Why me? Cass sighed and waved her over.

Nazliha swept through the air and landed at the bottom step, looking proud of herself. "Breakfast," she rumbled. "You will never go hungry."

Cass pinched the bridge of her nose. "Look, it's a…sweet gesture, but I don't eat this."

Nazliha tilted her head in that adorable way Cass was already beginning to recognize. "You do not eat meat?"

It was a fair question to ask a lesbian; there were a lot of vegan women on the sapphic dating apps. "No, it's— I eat meat. From the store or the farm. I don't prepare it myself."

"Hmm. I see."

"And cooked," Cass added, in case that wasn't obvious. "I do a great steak sous vide, actually." She almost invited the rasera over for a steak dinner. Who did that? She swallowed the offer.

Nazliha stared at her with those intense amber eyes.

That stupid spark of attraction flared again. Cass hiked the blankets higher in her arms and changed the subject. "I was thinking, it's probably cold in your cave. If you wanted some blankets…" She held out the two she'd grabbed.

Nazliha snatched them from her and sniffed them. When she looked up again, her pupils were rounded wide. "These will be perfect for my nest. I thank you."

Cass's breath shook in her throat. "No problem."

The blankets tucked into her front arm, Nazliha caught the azerok carcass in her teeth and bounded off into the woods, disappearing into the foliage. And it wasn't fear that pushed Cass to watch her go.

The next afternoon, Cass was meditating on the intention for a charmed necklace when something squawked outside the window. She opened her eyes just in time to see a brown flash swoop past. Her garden stretched out there, in the backyard, and she had zero time to deal with critters eating her produce. With a huff, she opened the back door—and found Nazliha plummeting toward the ground. Was she hurt? Distress plunged sharp into Cass's gut.

But instead of crashing, Nazliha swooped right before she met the artichokes. She spun in the air, up and up, before letting out a shriek and diving again. This time she swept down and landed on all fours in front of Cass. "I can take you up with me," she offered, not even out of breath.

Cass dropped into a squat, trying to even out her own breathing, to smother the unexpected worry that had pierced through her insides at the idea that Nazliha was hurt.

The rasera was alive. Was safe. Was just…strange.

Cass pressed a hand to her chest. "Goddess. You're okay?"

"I am quite well, thank you. Do you wish to fly?"

"Um, no, sorry. I'm scared of heights."

"You may watch me, then." Nazliha sounded almost eager. "I am not

afraid."

"It's okay. I—"

But Nazliha launched herself up into the air, higher than the tallest tree, and she looked right at Cass before plunging toward the grass.

Even as anxiety rose in her throat, Cass couldn't look away.

After a few more spectacular dives, Nazliha trotted back over to her, head high. She sat prettily on her haunches, looking at Cass as if expecting something.

Cass didn't know what that something was, so she offered an honest compliment. "That was amazing," she had to admit, even though secondhand adrenaline still pulsed in her veins.

Nazliha preened.

"I don't know how you always manage to pull up just before you crash."

"Raseras always know where they are in relation to the ground."

"Very cool." Cass wanted to sit on the step and talk with Nazliha, which was exactly how she knew it was time to flee back inside. "Well, I was working when I saw you…doing all that, so I should probably get back to it."

Tufted ears drooped. "Of course. You must work."

"My office is that room. On the corner." She pointed to the ground-floor window she'd seen Nazliha through, though she wasn't sure why she felt the need to share that. What was a rasera going to do with that information? She didn't invite the monster in. She couldn't.

But when Cass returned to her workroom and peered out the window again, Nazliha had curled upright below it, like she was sitting guard, and a fond warmth curled in Cass's belly.

After she'd finished all her customers' spells for the day, Cass rifled through her fridge for leftovers to microwave for dinner. No luck. She hadn't been to the store in a few weeks, and the kitchen was sitting empty. With a sigh, she shrugged on a hoodie and sneakers, grabbed her purse, and headed for the—

Before she could open the front door, something thudded on the other side, like a bunch of small weights being dropped.

She jumped back, muttering a curse more out of surprise than anything, but after the last few days, she had a hunch what—or who—the noise might be.

Cass eased the door open. Nazliha was scrambling up the oak tree again. This time, the porch was piled high with…what looked like steaks, wrapped in butcher paper? A few had little divots where claws or teeth had dug in. Where in Valhalla was Cass supposed to store all of this? Were they even still any good?

She stooped to touch one. Still cold. Probably safe, then, at least.

Raising one hand, Cass waved Nazliha over. The rasera dropped out of the tree with a huge *thump* and raced over, hope etched in her furry expression.

"Nazliha, what is this?" Cass sighed when the monster came to a stop in front of her.

"You did not want the azerok," Nazliha said, as if that explained everything.

"Well, no, yeah, but—"

"I said before, you will not go hungry."

Why are you so concerned with my eating habits? Never mind. Cass moved on. She gestured to the pile of meat, which was clearly human-prepped. "Where did you even get all this?"

Nazliha frowned. "I am not familiar with soo veed, but I know what steak is, and you said you like to—"

Soo veed? Wait. Sous vide. Had anyone ever listened to Cass as attentively as Nazliha did? But Cass couldn't let herself want more of this, so she forced harshness into her tone. "Did you steal it, is what I'm asking." It came out cruel.

Nazliha took a step back, tail tucking. "No. I traded for it."

Guilt gripped Cass's heart. She eased up. "Sorry. I just…" She sighed, raking a hand through her loose blonde hair. "Thank you."

Nazliha was still wary, though, not coming back to Cass, and the fear flickered in Cass's chest that she might not see Nazliha again after this.

Cass came forward, careful not to spook the rasera. "Can I make you dinner?" she asked quietly. "It's the least I can do."

Nazliha hesitated, and it was a punch to the gut. Cass had well and truly fucked up.

"Maybe we can dance together afterward," she offered.

At that, Nazliha brightened.

After bringing Nazliha into the house, Cass stored most of the steaks in the freezer and the spare ice box, holding a few back for the next few days' meals. She set up two steaks in a sous vide box and set them cooking to medium-rare. The rest went in the fridge. Then she rejoined Nazliha in the living room, where the rasera had settled onto the couch.

Cass sat beside her. "If you want to try steak cooked my way, I'm making extra. If you just want it raw, though, that's fine."

Nazliha watched her with utter amber focus. "I will try it your way."

It shouldn't have mattered. It did anyway. Cass covered her smile with a hand. "We have some time before it's ready. I can show you around?"

"I would like that."

So Cass walked Nazliha around the ground floor first—the living room, the workroom, the kitchen, the mud room—and then went upstairs to the two large bedrooms. Cass's room was a hot mess, especially in comparison to the spare room, which was empty except for a single bookcase of overflow witchcraft texts. Nazliha lit up, though.

"This is perfect," she insisted before barreling down the stairs and back out the unlocked door.

Gone, in the space of five seconds.

Cass plopped onto the carpet, feeling like the breath had been kicked out of her. Had she done something wrong in showing the rasera around? Made it too obvious how different they were?

Twenty minutes passed. Cass dragged herself back downstairs to stare at the cooking steaks from her seat slouched in a kitchen-table chair. And then a familiar voice came from outside. "Cass! The door!"

Cass rushed to the kitchen window. Nazliha stood upright outside, carrying a big lump of fabric—not Cass's blankets, but something like that. A comforter, maybe?

She hurried to let Nazliha in, and the rasera tromped directly upstairs, spreading the (yep) comforter in the empty room, perfectly aligning it with the corner of the wall. She dropped back to all fours and studied her work. "It is a start," she said finally.

Was Nazliha planning to sleep over? "Is this, um, for you?" Cass asked

hesitantly. She wasn't opposed to the rasera making herself comfortable, but she needed to know what was happening.

But Nazliha let out a series of rasping clicks that Cass belatedly figured out were her form of laughter. "No," she said finally. "This is *our* nest I am building."

Cass had no idea what she was supposed to do with that, but whatever made Nazliha feel better was fine. "Um. Okay. Well, let me know if I can…get you anything."

"No." Nazliha's eyes flashed with seriousness. "You do not need to get anything. I will take care of it."

Cass held up her hands. "Alllll righty, noted."

Once the steaks were fully cooked, Cass plated them and put one in front of Nazliha, who ripped into it with fang and claw while Cass watched, wide-eyed. She'd never felt so ridiculous for holding a fork and knife.

And when Nazliha looked back at her, amber eyes wild and plate bare, licked clean by a prehensile tongue, Cass had to press her thighs together.

A few days later, Cass worked to the tune of Nazliha's ululations. Despite herself, the now-familiar vocalizations were…calming, almost. Reassuring, even, somehow. And during her lunch break, she sat on the porch swing and munched on a sandwich while admiring the rasera's strange dances.

Nazliha kept bringing soft things to put in Cass's nest. Pillows, blankets, even her own feathers. Cass had no idea where the human-made items were coming from—her own nest? A store? All Nazliha would say when asked was "Worry not, Cass." Like that was helpful.

At their next steak dinner, Nazliha ate her steak raw, and Cass didn't mind. In all honesty, her mind was elsewhere. She had made something for the rasera, and she wasn't sure how it would go over.

"I have something for you," Cass blurted after they'd eaten. "A gift."

Nazliha's tufted ears perked up, and she followed Cass to the workroom, where Cass plucked a bespelled leather cuff from her worktable and held it out for Nazliha to inspect. Nazliha sniffed it. "I smell many

things. What is it?"

"It's to wear. I enchanted it. For divine protection." Cass had infused it with everything she had, every shielding ingredient, every prayer for Nazliha's well-being. It seemed, now, as she looked at the rasera, a little silly. "You don't have to—"

"No, I want it." Nazliha took the cuff, cradling it like it was something precious. "How do I wear it?"

"Here." Cass took it back, only to put it on Nazliha's front right wrist, tying it tight enough not to fall off but loose enough to be comfortable. "I thought... I don't know. I want you to be safe. You've been taking care of me, and I want to take care of you too."

Nazliha's amber eyes sharpened as she assessed the magical accessory. "I am not familiar with human courtship rituals," she lamented, "but I have never received such a gift before. I am honored."

Courtship rituals? Cass froze. She wasn't... She didn't... Did she?

"I am glad the rasera rituals are so clear," Nazliha continued, relief heavy in her deep voice. "Imagine if you had not known I was courting you."

Cass's brows jumped sky-high. "Imagine," she said faintly.

Courting.

Oh, fuck.

It was all coming together. The gifts of food, the dramatic displays, the song and dance, the nesting. How had Cass not realized the rasera was *courting her?*

And why was Cass so drawn to the idea?

She should've cut things off there. Should've ushered the monster out of the house and ended their fragile new relationship. But instead, she dragged her gaze over Nazliha's form, absorbing every detail that warmed her from the inside, feeling the need pulsing between her thighs.

Cass had spent the week being courted by a monster—and she was into it.

"I thank you for this." Nazliha held her wrist up to eye level, admiring the cuff. "Does this mean you are ready for me to taste you?"

Cass pressed her thighs together, searching for friction. The rasera couldn't mean... "I'm sorry?"

"Your sweat. I must assess your enzymes to ensure we are compatible as mates."

Disappointment flickered in Cass's chest. "Oh. Um, yeah, sure."

Nazliha wriggled. "Excellent. Please bare your neck for me."

Settling on the couch, Cass gathered her hair, draped it over one shoulder, and tilted her head in that direction. Tentatively, afraid of the answer, she asked, "What happens if the sweat says we're not mates?"

Nazliha's tufted ears went flat. "The enzymes know."

Ominous.

Cass let it go, sending up a quick prayer to Freyja for her blessing as well. *It'll be what it'll be*, she told herself, though she knew now what she wanted the decision to be. She wanted to be Nazliha's mate. The realization should have felt absurd, but it fit right into Cass's cracked heart, slotting into place like it had always been meant to be. She didn't need to be the perfect witch or the best businesswoman as long as she had this rasera. Even her father walking away all those years ago didn't hurt quite so bad these days, because Nazliha had been walking *toward* her since the moment they met.

Nazliha perched beside her and caressed one clawed hand over Cass's throat. "You are stunning," she said quietly, "and that is true even if we are not mates."

Shy heat bloomed in Cass's cheeks. "Thanks. You too."

Nazliha's breath was warm on bare skin as she opened her mouth and dragged the flat of her tongue slowly up the curve of Cass's neck, the texture of it raspy and seductive. Cass shuddered, her nails digging into her palms as she struggled to stay in place.

It'll be what it'll be.

Once Nazliha was done, she closed her eyes and seemed to savor the flavor. Cass watched her, heart in her throat, awaiting the verdict.

Nazliha's amber eyes opened, and she launched herself at Cass, who toppled at the force of it. That now-familiar blood-orange scent enveloped her. Nazliha clung to her, face buried in Cass's neck, and Cass hugged back, hopeful and scared and turned on all at once.

Finally Nazliha raised her head, her ears perked forward with excitement, and she gave a giddy full-body wiggle. "Our sweat enzymes are compatible!"

Cass beamed, crushing Nazliha even tighter to herself. "What do we do now?" The *we* just came out, but it felt right. Tasted right.

Nazliha's gaze dipped to Cass's curves, and her pupils dilated until

they almost eclipsed the amber. "We mate," she rumbled happily. "And then we'll have an egg in the morning."

Cass's breath caught in her throat, and arousal fluttered hot inside her. She wanted it, wanted a little Nazliha to care for. "I can get behind that," she whispered.

"Not behind it," Nazliha corrected her. "On top of it."

With that clarification on egg husbandry, Cass found herself being led upstairs to the nest Nazliha had crafted, now thick and full of soft, cozy accoutrements and molted rasera feathers. The room smelled comfortably like both of them, a blend of their scents.

"In here." Nazliha lay back in the nest, but Cass stayed standing. She was all but vibrating with need, but also fully clothed. She intended to change that—if Nazliha wanted.

"I can. Um. I can take my clothes off?"

Nazliha's ears perked up with interest. "Whatever you like," she said, but the words were hope-sweetened.

Cass curled her toes. It had been a while since anyone had seen her like this, longer still since it was someone she *liked.* Nervously, she fingered the hem of her green-stitched black dress before peeling it over her head and off, tossing it onto the floor. She stood in front of Nazliha in a nude bra and matching boy shorts with a dark spot from wetness, and for a moment, anxiety needled her—until Nazliha scented the air, nostrils flaring with obvious pleasure.

The rasera's voice was gravelly when she urged, "Take the rest off."

Arousal flared, burning away the anxiety. Cass hooked her thumbs into her underwear and pulled the beige cotton down her legs, kicking it off to land atop her rumpled dress. The bra came off even faster. Then she stood tall, glorying in the way Nazliha inhaled.

"Without your clothes, you smell…" A purr vibrated in the air. "…delicious." She was breathing harder now, as if the mere sight and scent of Cass naked before her was enough to rile her up. "My mate."

Prickling with heat and shy excitement, Cass smoothed her hands over her bare torso. "Now what?"

Nazliha stared at her, pupils blown, chest heaving. "Now you come to me." And she tugged Cass into the nest and on top of herself, eagerly guided Cass to straddle her. A surprised giggle sparked from Cass's throat at the vehemence of it.

As she settled atop her rasera, she encountered a natural bulge right where Nazliha had placed her. Instinct led her to rub against it, and a moan ripped from her throat because oh, it felt perfect. She sighed Nazliha's name and kept going, speeding up to the hard rhythm her clit demanded.

Nazliha watched hungrily as Cass ground against her. The rasera crooned sweet filth, praising Cass, urging her on, but Cass's mind was so blurred she only caught stray phrases: "perfect" and "just like that" and "take what you need." Cursing, she clung to Nazliha's strong shoulders, digging her nails in. The rasera groaned with pleasure.

So good. So fucking good.

Cass whined as she writhed against Nazliha, need tightening in her core. Normally she was a talker, but now she was so desperate she couldn't think of any words besides *fuck* and *yes* and *Nazliha*. Thankfully, Nazliha responded well to those three, gripping Cass's hips—claws digging in beautifully—and thrusting up to meet her.

Chanting her rasera's name like a prayer, Cass fucked herself against Nazliha's mound until the pleasure burst in her, sizzling in every limb. Nazliha caught her, eased her down into the nest while she recovered.

When Cass finally stopped panting, Nazliha crept farther down in the nest and drew Cass's legs apart, situating her bulky frame between them. Cass stared down at her; Nazliha met her gaze as she licked up Cass's slit with that raspy tongue. Moaning, Cass fell back, arched into the touch. Nazliha swirled over her clit and then fucked into her, the prehensile tongue curving up to hit that magical spot inside. Cass's eyes scrunched shut, and she moved against Nazliha's mouth, needing more.

Impossibly fast, a second climax built in Cass. Aching, she grasped Nazliha's long horns and pressed her closer, tighter, deeper. Nazliha hummed, pleased. Fangs scraped sensitive folds.

Yes, yes, yes.

As Nazliha fucked in and out, hard and fast, Cass exploded again with a shout.

Nazliha softened her rhythm but didn't fully let up, piecing Cass back together and bringing her back to earth.

Nazliha moved to take care of Cass again, but Cass gently pushed her away, sated and sensitive. Instead, she tugged Nazliha up to her level. She caressed down Nazliha's bulk and over her mound, finding the opening

below slick with desire. Cass sighed, dragging two fingers along the slit. Her brain cells were functioning again, and she managed to string together a playful sentence: "Who made you this wet?"

"You," Nazliha gasped, lifting into Cass's touch.

"Very good." Lips curving, Cass slipped one finger inside her, then a second, easy as breathing. Nazliha was so warm, so inviting. She moved gently, trying to figure out the anatomy.

"More," Nazliha begged.

A third finger.

It still didn't feel like enough.

Nazliha sobbed with need.

Desperate to please her, Cass eased her entire hand inside her, careful not to nick her even with short nails—and Nazliha's cunt was a cavern, open and deep. Cass explored it eagerly, finding a round protrusion that made Nazliha chitter with satisfaction. Cass caressed it, teased it, and then squeezed lightly.

Nazliha arched up off the nest, chasing the feeling.

Hot desire flooded Cass. The longer she played with Nazliha's bulb, the more noises the rasera made, needy and desperate, her volume ratcheting higher and higher.

"You feel so perfect," Cass crooned in one tufted ear. "And gods, you look so good in my nest."

Nazliha keened, that blood-orange scent blooming. Her whole body was trembling. So beautifully close.

"*My* mate in *my* nest," Cass continued, her voice rough with hunger as she worked over the bulb, relishing every shiver of building pleasure. "You're going to come for me, right here, right now, and—"

As if all she'd needed was permission, Nazliha shattered with a roar, clenching around Cass's hand with surprising strength.

Cass waited, releasing the bulb and slipping free when Nazliha relaxed. She stroked her furry head with the other hand and scratched behind her ears until the rasera purred.

Once Nazliha had caught her breath, she reached for Cass, dragging her back to herself. "Mates," she pleaded. "We need to bite."

Cass tossed her hair back and offered her neck again. Nazliha bared her fangs and bit down. Cass flinched at the sharp pang of teeth breaking the skin, but only for a moment. Nazliha licked over the wound tenderly, intimately, before whispering, "You did so well."

The praise soothed the sting, warmed Cass from the inside. "Now what?" She had expected to feel different.

"Now you return the bite."

Unsure if she was doing it right but determined to try, Cass stole Nazliha's bare wrist and dug her teeth in. Nazliha cried out as an invisible thread snapped into place between them, connecting their spirits. A tidal wave of pleasure—*Nazliha's* pleasure—crashed over Cass. She trembled with the high of it, clenching her jaw harder on Nazliha just to steady herself.

After the bond had settled, she carefully detached, and they snuggled into each other, their mutual happiness rebounding against itself.

"Mates," Nazliha purred.

"Mates," Cass confirmed happily.

They fell asleep curled up together in the nest.

The next morning, though, Cass woke up to discover a new third member of the snuggle fest: a big brown egg speckled with white. Cass couldn't help but smile at it. Nazliha had laid that; Cass had helped. The baby rasera inside was theirs.

Nazliha blinked drowsily and followed Cass's gaze before brightening. Joy glowed through the bond. "Does it not look perfect?"

Cass nuzzled her. "It really does."

"I will warm it until it hatches our pup."

"Hang on. You're trapped in the nest the whole time?"

Nazliha cocked her head adorably. "Yes. This is what I must do."

Now that, Cass could do something about. "Gimme an hour or two." After making breakfast for her rasera (her mate!), she ducked out to the car and stopped by the local hardware store and her favorite witchcraft store. When she returned, she brought everything up to the nest, where she crafted an incubator for their egg—warm but not hot, and enhanced with plenty of protective magic. "This way you can leave the nest if you want," she explained as Nazliha snuffled around the empty enchanted box.

Finally Nazliha straightened, looking down at Cass with approval. "You did good work. Our pup will grow strong and healthy."

Cass pressed a kiss to Nazliha's cuffed wrist. "I look forward to raising them with you."

They set up the egg in the incubator, and then they sat beside it, letting the growing pup hear their voices through the shell as they talked about the life they were building together as mates and mothers. They didn't have all the details yet, but Cass couldn't wait to see where their time together took them.

Cass accompanied Nazliha into town that weekend. They stopped by the butcher's storefront first, just to say hi, and Liam greeted Nazliha with a bright "Welcome back! Got something else for me?"

"Not this time." Nazliha glanced at Cass and made happy clicking noises.

Despite the old anxiety prickling at her, Cass beamed back at her. Even if the people of Maple Grove hated the relationship, Nazliha and Cass were happy. That had to be enough. It *would* be enough.

But it wasn't all they got.

"Well." Liam gave them a knowing smile through his silvery beard. "I see. A rasera mating, now that's something special."

Shock, then relief, washed over Cass like an ocean swell in summer, warm and comforting. Nazliha must have felt it, because she leaned against Cass, sharing the consolation.

Liam smiled at Cass. "How did you like the stooping?"

"The what now?" she asked, feeling like she was missing something obvious.

He cocked his head. "The high dives."

Cass burned with embarrassment (shouldn't she have known the term?) but told the truth. "She looked stupendous."

"You should talk to Ralin Winters. I heard her cousin's been getting courted by a fikerav lately."

Cass averted her eyes. She wasn't alone, and she would have known that if she'd put more effort into knowing the people around her instead of pushing them away. All that anxiety. All that loneliness. She stroked through Nazliha's fur, her fingers dragging with disappointment in herself.

"I am with you," Nazliha rumbled quietly, for Cass's ears only.

Steadied, Cass took a deep breath and nodded before meeting Liam's gaze again. "Thank you. I'll reach out to her."

The Maple Grove butcher saluted her, winked at Nazliha, and then got back to work. Cass and her mate headed back into the midday sunlight. Across the town square, Hazel and Ralin were eating a picnic on the bench in the community garden.

Embarrassed, ashamed, Cass shuffled over to them. "How's it going?"

Hazel seemed surprised to see her. "Cass. Good to see you. And—?" Her attention flicked to Nazliha.

"I am Nazliha," the rasera supplied happily.

Hazel offered a smile. "Hello, Nazliha. I'm Hazel, and this is my wife, Ralin."

Her golden-brown hair swept up in a bun, Ralin waved one burgundy-tipped hand.

"Nazliha is my mate," Cass blurted, looking at Ralin. "I heard you know—your cousin—you're familiar?"

Ralin smiled softly. "Yes. I'm familiar."

"And you're not— I mean, it's—?"

"Are you happy?" Ralin asked instead of answering the question Cass couldn't finish.

Cass swallowed hard. "Yeah," she said honestly.

"And Nazliha's happy?"

"She is, yeah."

"Then we're happy for you," said Ralin. "Sure, it's new to Maple Grove, but it's not unheard of."

"You'll come to Beltane?" Hazel glanced at Nazliha, directing the question at both of them.

Nazliha looked at Cass. Cass nodded. "We'll be there."

Hazel beamed. "Excellent."

When Cass delivered the productivity spell jar to Mayor Hazel Winters the next week at the Beltane celebration prep, she had the particular pleasure of pointing out that her new mate had provided the feathers inside. And Hazel and Ralin and Liam—and the rest of Maple Grove—welcomed Nazliha into the town that was finally starting to feel like home.

Robust Love

Teddy Sweet

begging, breeding kink, centaur, established relationship, fantasy, half-human, hand-fasting, m/m/m, past tense, penis in anus sex, polyamory, roleplaying: predator/prey, third person omniscient point of view, wedding

Somewhere over greener pastures, a spirit pastor was laughing at him, Evlor was fairly certain. He had been the one to desire a handfasting ceremony, had asked Hakri and Navees with all the confidence of someone with an end goal and no plan for how to actually achieve it. It was more difficult than he'd anticipated. His declaration of "I have two hands for a reason" had been met with indulgent laughter, and he'd stomped a front foot inelegantly to show his displeasure and determination.

Handfastings were relatively simple affairs for cervitaurs. Once a clearing had been chosen, the vine picked to tie the partners together, they frolicked around until one of the lovers bit through the vine and instigated a chase. The chase was just long enough for everyone else to disappear back to their lives before the happy couple returned to their

chosen clearing to consummate the union.

Of course, centaurs had to be more stringent about their traditions. It wasn't even the ceremony itself. That was, in Evlor's opinion, the most straightforward bit. No, the ceremony was easy. Building a bed was not. Neither was the whole "tail braiding" thing. Cervitaurs didn't have to worry about such things; their tails were no more than a little bob of a thing with bones and muscles of their own, if that. Evlor, like all roe deer, didn't have a tail at all. Centaurs had long, swishy tails and manes that apparently had a whole language of their own in old society.

"Only those hung up on the old ways pay much attention to it," Navees had explained, lounging on a chaise. He shrugged as he added, "And Hakri."

"So could I braid Hakri's tail into a cute twist?" Navees had the audacity to laugh at that, so Evlor followed with, "I'd even add a mace to the end to make him more fierce."

"You know the army is all about tradition. He might as well prance in and announce 'clippity-clop, here's my cock' if you did that." After a beat Navees added, "Don't mention it to him. He'd actually do that, wouldn't he?"

The answer to that was a solid yes. Just because Hakri came from an Ardennais lineage didn't mean he had the reputed temperament of a traditional warhorse. In fact, he was usually one of the guilty parties in any shenanigans the trio got entangled in. The less said about the time he'd tied a toy snake to Navees's tail in the centre of town, the better.

With a soft grunt, Navees pushed himself up, legs waving in the air as he tried to roll upright. "Curse these short legs."

Evlor carefully didn't mention that, once again, he had been using Hakri's chaise rather than his own. Coming from predominantly Bhutani ancestry, Navees was considerably shorter than their warhorse third. Though he was still stockier than Evlor, who bounded around on long, lithe legs and was much more prone to the odd bout of joyful prancing, his roe deer tendencies on full, unabashed show.

"Here." Navees shoved his rear towards Evlor.

"Darling!" Raising a hand, Evlor tried to cover his tittering. "That's very forward of you."

"You're going to learn to braid properly. It's what Hakri deserves. Now, split my tail into two."

Nimble fingers did as instructed. Evlor nibbled at his upper lip as he dedicated himself to learning. As Navees put it, this was for Hakri. Though he'd never say it, history and tradition were not only a source of interest; to live them was a whole new level of wonder for him.

It wasn't the first time Evlor had played with a tail, but his fascination was no less intense. He was familiar with a standard braid and a rope braid, but this was new: a tight fishtail braid that sounded as severe as it was alluring and practical. As much as Evlor wanted to say he was a natural at braiding tails, his first attempt was more akin to a tangled net than a style worthy of a matrimonial night.

Holding the tail up for Navees's inspection, Evlor burst out laughing at how bad his first attempt was.

"Again. And this time, think more about where your fingers are going rather than where you're imagining your dick will go."

Undoing the mess was harder work than anticipated, and Navees's back rippled with irritated little twitches whenever his tail was pulled too harshly. However, he stayed still, twisted to watch Evlor try again. And again. And again.

"Wait! I have an idea!" Halfway through the braid, Evlor dropped it in favour of trotting out of the room.

In the living room, he rifled through the drawers, mind set on finding a small box. Muttering under his breath, he stomped between sideboard and cupboard. It had to be somewhere in there. Finally, he spotted the box, which had a pattern of bows and ribbons printed on it, and triumphantly held it over his head with an "aha!" It was his niece's kit, bought to keep the six year old entertained when she was being babysat, letting her play with their tails like they were her personal artistic playgrounds. The box was full of beads, bands, and ribbons of all colours.

Holding it aloft, Evlor beamed proudly. "Trust me on this."

"Only because it's you." Despite his words, Navees still looked suspicious as Evlor brushed out his tail once more and started a new fishtail braid.

Halfway through the tail, Evlor tied it off with a band and began separating out the long, grey strands. He hummed to himself, lowering his front legs to get a better angle for his work.

"Ta-dah!" He held up the improvised style. While the first half was as Navees had suggested, the lower half was a riot of colour. "Now, ignore the fact the beads are lurid neons and plastic. We can get nice glass ones. But look!" With a flick of his wrist, Evlor smacked Navees's rump and got a large twitch and a foot stomp in response.

Eyes narrowing, Navees scrunched his nose. "I hate that you're onto something. He'd love that."

"I know!"

A single session of practice was nowhere near enough to perfect a fishtail braid. However, finding time to master it was difficult. The secret sessions to surprise Hakri with the braid came to an end when he bumbled into the kitchen only to see Evlor lifting Navees's tail and deftly splitting it into two.

"Dare I ask?"

Two guilty sets of eyes turned to him until Evlor gave him a shy grin. "Surprise?"

Understanding dawned on Hakri's face, and he bucked in excitement.

"Really? Because I'd been doing some reading, too." His large hands swept through the air as he began explaining. "No pressure at all, but you know the tradition around beds?" Enthusiastic nodding spurred him on. "Well, I thought that maybe we could go to a nursery and look at the trees there. While we could buy something and make adjustments, I thought, if we're going to do it, we might as well go big with it."

"Modifying some mass-produced mating bench sounds as appealing as swimming," Navees sneered. "We're building it from scratch."

Loudly whooping, Evlor stood on his hind legs to steal a kiss from Hakri. He loved that they were all thinking along similar lines. Plus, the chance to indulge in something that made Hakri so excited was a rare occurrence and definitely one to be treasured.

"You have the best ideas. Go during the weekend?"

Thus they found themselves at the nearest tree nursery. Hakri led them around, offering all manner of opinions from sap production of some trees to the care and oils needed to maintain a frame made from another wood. Truth be told, it was all a bit over Evlor's head. Even Navees looked strained as he tried to keep up.

A tree was a tree as far as Evlor was concerned. To him, colour was

the most important. "I think the cherry wood could make for a nice, sturdy frame. It would also look gorgeous against you. All the browny red next to your black fur," he offered, trying to sound like he actually knew something.

Navees gave him a calculating look before speaking. "Not a bad call. Walnut and ash would be too washed out. Plus, they have an offer on."

"Is it good for making dovetail joints?" Shy pride radiated from Hakri as he asked, thrilled to be able to show off his recently refreshed carpentry knowledge.

Patting him on the arm, Navees butted his head against a broad shoulder. "Yes, it is perfect for that."

Obtaining the necessary wood and hardware to make a bed was so simple that it lulled Evlor into a sense of optimism. Making a matrimonial bed wouldn't be so difficult. None of the articles Hakri had shown him made it seem complicated. Measure the height difference, measure the wood, chop, sand, and screw it all together before screwing each other. At least, that was how Evlor interpreted it.

Things were a little more involved than that.

Hakri tried to be useful, but his hands weren't made for creating. While decent with a saw, following careful measurements was not in his skillset. That did not mean he was any less enthusiastic.

Another visit to the tree nursery, more wood (and a bit more as backup), and this time, Navees knuckled down on making the bed.

The frame was easy enough to build but had to be dismantled before being reassembled in the bedroom because there was no way for it to fit in the house.

"Stop straining," Navees groused, tugging at Hakri's feathering. "You don't need to prove you're the tallest."

"But what if I get new shoes and they're thicker than my usual ones?"

Front legs bent, Hakri was kneeling down, rear end up and as his legs were measured. His fingers were entwined with Evlor's to keep the cervitaur from wandering off and making crass comments that would devolve into pleasure but no progress on the bed. A kiss was pressed to his knuckles.

"You'd get new shoes just for our union?"

"I'd get more than just the new shoes superstition demands, if you asked."

"Get moving." Navees lightly smacked him on the flank. "Little deer, you're next."

Snorting, Hakri hefted himself upright and allowed Evlor to usher him out of the way. Navees made quick work of measuring him and jotted the results down on a scrap piece of wood. Yawning, he gestured towards the door.

"Keep each other entertained. I've got actual work to do."

For all the grumbling that Navees put on, he wasn't actually left alone to construct the bed. Hakri was more than eager to hold beams in place while Evlor happily helped screw things into place, sand down rough edges, and wield planks of wood like weapons, much to the other two's chagrin.

"That's not even how you hold a sword!" Hakri sighed in exasperation. "You'll do more damage to yourself than any enemy."

"Maybe it's a bludgeon!" As he spoke, Evlor swished the wood through the air with a vicious grin.

"Maybe it's a bed slat." The plank was gently pried from slim fingers as Navees put it down on the frame. "Screw that in."

Hakri snickered. "You said 'screw.' "

If it had been the first time he'd made that joke, the others would have laughed along. As it was, Evlor gave a long-suffering sigh while Navees acted like he hadn't even heard, instead pushing the next piece of the frame into Hakri's hand, but Evlor saw the way Navees's lips curved upward despite his stern demeanour. Any evidence of it disappeared as Hakri dipped in to press his mouth against the smile, showing off as he held the frame up with one hand.

All too soon, the bed looked ready, and the mounting frame above it taunted Evlor. Even Navees looked torn as he appraised it and the floor-length mirror fixed to the wall next to it.

"I suppose we could test it out, make sure it will hold?"

As if Evlor hadn't been up and down the steps, experimenting with the stability and comfort of the support. They all knew the build was solid. While it wouldn't ever win a beauty contest, it would keep standing even if a tornado and an earthquake shook hands next to it.

"No!" Hakri cried, rushing to stand between the bed and his partners. Flushing darker, he fidgeted shyly. "This is for our first night as a bonded unit."

"Then we best hurry the ceremony along." Eagerness meant the words rushed out of Evlor louder than intended. He slapped a hand over his mouth to hold back the embarrassed giggle.

While Navees had been busy with the bed, Hakri had been sorting the logistics of the ceremony itself. By the time Evlor remembered that it was something to organise, it had already been handled: a clearing chosen for an outdoor handfasting in the local woods, within trotting distance from their home. All he had to worry about was checking that the list of guests included everyone he wanted to invite. Despite the fact there were three of them, the list was small, no more than thirty-odd people from across all their lives. Then again, it was more than enough. They were doing this for their own reasons, not to prove anything to anyone else.

Evlor just had one question. "How are we going to handfast us all?"

Grinning, Hakri winked at him. "You said it yourself: you have two hands for a reason. But in all seriousness, a cervitaurian knot between you and Navees, and a centaur noose to hold your hand to mine."

Centaurs and their damned memories. Sure, Evlor had quipped about having two hands, but he hadn't considered what it actually meant. Then again, he hadn't clarified with the other two that the ties were only released at the end of the celebrations. So perhaps it wouldn't be such an issue.

Evlor was wrong.

On the morning of the ceremony, Hakri was helping brush Navees down, the grey of his coat shiny and almost silver in the light. Behind him, Evlor was hard at work braiding Hakri's black tail, tongue poking out from the corner of his mouth as he focused. As promised, he'd bought some glass beads of varying sizes in a shade so deep they were almost black.

"Braid it tighter," Hakri huffed as he looked over his back.

"Any tighter and it'll give you a butt lift so tight your hole will be smiling." Despite his words, Evlor pulled the braid a little tighter.

"It'll be a nice change, seeing you smiling from all sides," Navees butted in, and leaned over to fuss with shining his hooves. A small grunt of effort escaped him, but he was determined to reach them. Hakri lowered himself and tenderly took the polish from lax fingers. Wiping down the nearest hoof, he glanced up, pleased with himself.

"Teamwork, yeah?" Hakri rumbled fondly, and gladly accepted the hand reaching to ruffle his curly hair. For a change, it wasn't clasped in a tight bun, ringlets free and wild the way he not-so-secretly preferred.

Teamwork was indeed the theme of the day. Evlor stood between his two loves and watched as pumpkin twine was tied around both his hands, one holding Hakri's and the other clutching at Navees's. The officiant, a very patient capritaur that Hakri had liaised with, wrapped the twine around Evlor's left hand, binding his fingers with Navees's in intricate loops. It was all topped off by an elegant True Lover's Knot that sat thick between their wrists and was the cherished memento of every bonding ceremony.

Evlor's right hand clasped tightly at Hakri's. The twine that tied them together was nothing more than a loose slipknot. They had to work hard at keeping it around their wrists, monitoring it and tending to it. Late one night, Hakri had explained it was a representation of any union: it needed attention and work to maintain, otherwise it would fall apart. The romantic in Evlor sighed wistfully, appreciating the regimented and detailed traditions of centaur rituals.

Perhaps he'd been a bit dismissive when he considered a centaur bonding ceremony simple. Evlor was stuck in the middle, both hands out of commission as Navees and Hakri dipped their fingers in the bowl of green paste. Cervitaurs didn't have anything even remotely similar to this, and Evlor shivered as he watched Hakri smear a diagonal line over Navees's heart, then had it mirrored on his chest a moment later.

A nimble, freshly dipped finger deftly pulled a horizontal line over Evlor's ribs. The little reading Evlor had done into this implied that the two halves of a partnership drew half a horseshoe on each other and pressed together into a hug to complete it. For their trio, half horseshoes weren't going to work. Hakri had been all too excited to ramble on about how a triangle is actually the strongest shape, and he'd made a convincing argument. Now, Evlor watched as his partners embraced tightly before turning to him.

The paste smeared against his chest, the lines not quite lining up, but it was perfectly imperfect as far as Evlor was concerned. He clung to

Navees and laughed as Hakri had to lower down to line up their chests before pressing together. A few tears managed to escape as he gazed down at his chest, his hands tightening in a happy squeeze, eager to cling to his newly bonded partners. As their union was declared for the forest to hear, cheers and stomps went up, but Evlor didn't hear them. He was too caught up in feeling both his hands lifted and entwined fingers kissed in tandem.

Wedged between the two centaurs, Evlor allowed himself to get lost in the moment. He eagerly accepted nibbles of food from Hakri, who was more intent on feeding than eating. Not that Navees was slacking in his care. He artfully navigated the trio to greet guests and thank them for coming. However, there was a thrum of something else that had Evlor constantly peeking around. The undercurrent of anticipation had him on edge. Sure enough, in a lull of chatter, he found that they had migrated to the edge of the clearing, a little farther away from the guests.

"Hey, Evlor?" Hakri called for his attention.

As their eyes locked, their fastened hands were raised once again. Breath caught in Evlor's throat as a smile bared Hakri's teeth before they sank into the soft twine. His other hand was raised by Navees and the other piece twisted around their hands was bitten through. Eyes wide, Evlor looked between the two, his heart thrumming high in his throat.

Grin still in place, Navees growled, "Run."

Evlor ran, body springing into action before he had a chance to think about it. The sound of two larger bodies crashing through the undergrowth after him only spurred him on. Heart pounding, he tried to think, tried to be logical, but all Evlor could comprehend was the need to run. He went on instinct alone, darting through narrow gaps between trees, vaulting over branches and fallen trunks. At the edge of his hearing, he could still make out the less delicate crashing of Navees and Hakri, hot on his non-existent tail. It was enough of a head start. Though small and spry, Evlor couldn't hope to outrun Hakri on a clear road. Maybe he'd win a race against Navees on a good day, but only over a shorter distance.

The trees thinned, and he smiled to himself. It was time to turn the tide.

Earth and mulch gave way to gravel that, in turn, became the solid footpath to civilisation. Thankfully, there were enough health-conscious individuals around that seeing a cervitaur charging full-pelt down a road didn't rouse any suspicion. Evlor darted past the few people in his way, bounding home. What was a little less usual was for a cervitaur to be followed by two centaurs, hooves thundering out of sync as they ran.

A quick glance over his shoulder, and Evlor had to swallow thickly. His two partners were zeroed in on him as they raced to catch up. Slipping into their home, he left the door wide open and grinned as he hid behind the door to their bedroom and listened, eyes closed so he could focus better.

"Come on!" Hakri called out, and Evlor could imagine him putting on a final burst of speed.

Sure enough, Hakri barely managed to slow as he thundered into the house and made a beeline for the bedroom. Not far behind him, Navees trotted in, flanks sweaty. Once both were in the room, there was little left in the way of space, most of it taken up by the bed and the mounting frame. The door shut behind Navees with a *thud*, and Evlor could finally step into view with a predatory look in his eyes as he watched Hakri shuffle to hide how he'd startled.

"My poor little warhorse. Walked straight into my trap, didn't you?"

A shuddering breath escaped Hakri. The glance Evlor shot towards Navees found excitement and reassurance, which only helped build the thrill.

He boldly stalked forward. "Get on our bed for me. I've got plans for our newest broodmare."

Defiant, Hakri pawed at the ground even as he bodily leaned towards the bed. "And if I don't?"

"Then you don't," Navees interrupted, "but you'll be left wondering for the rest of eternity what it would have been like, being at the mercy of such a handsome buck." He settled at the edge of the bed and patted it invitingly. "And I'll just have to imagine what it looks like as you're filled and made such a pretty mess of."

"You think I'm pretty?"

Shyness was not a frequent look on Hakri, and it had Evlor approaching him, reaching to take Hakri's hands in his.

"Pretty. Beautiful. Gorgeous. And, best of all, ours."

Shivering, Hakri bit his bottom lip and rumbled out an awed "fuck." He nodded vigorously before saying, "Yeah. I want it. Want you so

damn bad."

Gentle hands moved to insistently tug as Evlor guided Hakri onto the bed. The low mattress creaked under Hakri's weight as he awkwardly shuffled under the breeding frame and eagerly reached for Navees, who welcomed him with an easy kiss and a quiet, "Love how into this you are."

"Should have done this sooner. Can't believe we could have been doing this all along," Hakri replied.

A throaty laugh erupted from Evlor as he moved to grab the rail and stepped up towards the platform designed to give him the height boost he needed to mount Hakri. "Traditionally, this is a wedding night thing."

Navees apparently couldn't help himself as he countered, "Fuck traditions" while staring down Hakri.

"Call me 'Traditions' if you must, but yes, fuck me already." Hakri wriggled his presented rear to entice Evlor and get things moving again. In front of him, Navees giggled, his eyes narrowing. "You planned this, didn't you?"

"You're the brawn, you've got the beauty behind you, which does leave me as the brains."

Any response Hakri may have had was lost to a small yelp as his tail was tugged. Evlor relished the glare he was shot over a broad shoulder.

"Do that again and I'll incite a one-person stampede."

From his perch up high, Evlor got the beautiful view of Navees wrapping Hakri in his arms, a hand sneaking into his curls. The kiss distracted Evlor from any further threats. Evlor pulled at Hakri's tail again; a low, throaty whine was his reward. Even better, a glance in the mirror told Evlor that Hakri's cock was slowly slipping from its sheath. It dropped fully when he flicked the braided tail in his hand and the beads whipped against Harki's tender flank.

"Look at you, so eager," Navees purred as he pulled away, ducking to the side to watch. "Evlor's going to wreck you so good."

Another *thwack* of beaded tail sounded through the room, and Hakri moaned as his head dropped onto Navees's shoulder. It was a delightful sight, and Evlor wished he could live in this specific moment forever. His own palms were sweaty and, wiping them on Hakri's fur, he delivered another smack with the beaded tail to the glorious rump in front of him. It had Hakri gasping and clutching at Navees, exactly how Evlor had imagined it would.

With a few turns of his wrist, he wound Hakri's tail around his hand and stepped higher onto the frame, front legs on the platform above Hakri's broad back. Without the footrests, he would have had to balance on sweat-slick fur and run the risk of slipping and spraining his lower pectorals. Not ideal for their first night as a wedded throuple. Dragging his thoughts back to the treasure before him, Evlor planted his hooves firmly and tugged at Hakri's tail purely to hear him whine. The way he shuffled, trying to press back and find any kind of pressure, was too adorable.

"So desperate already," Evlor teased, and tugged at the tail again. "We haven't even started yet, have we, Navees?"

A low, throaty laugh was his answer, and Hakri groaned, fingertips visibly dimpling Navees's skin. For the time being, it was graciously permitted. Navees even went as far as peppering kisses along whatever skin he could reach. His eyes flitted to Evlor's, and he grinned before dipping down to nip at the junction of Hakri's shoulder and neck. The "oh fuck" this elicited drew another chuckle from them both and, just because he could, Navees bit down again right as Evlor pulled the tail in his hand. Utterly helpless in his half-kneeling position, Hakri could only stomp his back feet, rump swaying to finally find the warm press of Evlor's body.

At the touch, Evlor couldn't help but buck forward a little. His cock had been peeking out of its sheath but hadn't yet slipped fully out. That was rapidly changing as Hakri continued to shift and rub against him, desperate for more. All he was achieving was smearing his coat with sticky fluid. A little more pointedly, Evlor tried to move his cock to tease at Hakri's hole.

"Look at you. If I didn't know better, I'd say you were in season."

"Yes. For you."

Navees raked his nails down Hakri's back, leaving a trail of red lines on his skin that Evlor eyed hungrily. While one hand rubbed along where fur met skin, the other hand drifted back up to thread through the short hair at the nape of Hakri's neck, effectively pinning him into place despite the gentle touches. Evlor salivated at the idea of being the one to hold Hakri down.

Next time.

There was absolutely going to be a next time, and he was going to be the one in Navees's place.

"For us, yes," Evlor agreed easily. "You're good for us, aren't you? Our perfect little broodmare."

"Please. I need him."

Such a raw plea almost broke Evlor's resolve, and he glanced to Navees for guidance, wondering whether they were both swayed. A smirk was shot his way before Navees brushed smile-curved lips against Hakri's ear to softly murmur, "You can beg prettier than that."

"Navees!" His name was stretched into a whine as Evlor rocked against Hakri. The fur prickled delightfully against his sensitive cock, making it pulse and dribble a mess into the dark fur.

Pulling back a bit, Evlor admired his handiwork. The sight was enough for his determination to buckle. He gripped the wood in front of him and blindly pressed forward, grunting in frustration as his cock slipped along slick fur and butted against the tight braid of Hakri's tail. This time, it was Evlor's name that was elongated as Hakri uselessly pushed back, trying to help.

"Evlor, please." Just the touch of his lovers was enough to get Hakri pleading. "I want to feel you. Please. Want you in me."

"He does ask so nicely," Navees conceded and stroked down Hakri's cheek before claiming his lips for a tender kiss. "Desperation tastes good on you."

Spurred on, Evlor tried again, only to let out an annoyed groan as his cock slipped, this time peeking out from next to Hakri's tail, slender pink tip a sharp contrast to the dark hairs there. Pulling back, he tried again and let out a strangled huff as he missed once more. It had been so much easier in theory than in practice when a bench was used.

"Navees, sweetheart, think you could lend a hand?"

"Hand, mouth, anything you need." Though the words were eager and playful, Navees took his time extracting himself from Hakri's hold, took a moment to run his fingers over ticklish ribs, and stole one more kiss before getting up. He ambled to where Evlor was standing and hummed low in his throat at the sight. "You've made a delectable mess. Look to your right, see it in the mirror? Utterly gorgeous."

Doing as Navees suggested, Evlor watched. Navees admired how Hakri's muscles quivered in anticipation, how Hakri's cock hung heavy and useless between his legs. Reaching out, Navees stroked over it and chuckled at the yelp his touch elicited. It also served the purpose of wetting his hand, strings of fluid stretched between his fingers as he took Evlor's much more slim cock and guided it to Hakri's hole.

"Slowly now," he warned, as he always did.

While Evlor heeded the words, Hakri was of a different opinion. As soon as the tip breached him, he tried to step back, greedily wanting more. The frame rattled as he kicked it, and Evlor clutched at the bar in front of him, heart thundering in his chest from arousal and fright alike.

Sheepishly, Hakri glanced over his shoulder. "Sorry."

Laughter bubbled in Evlor's throat, and he made no attempt to stifle it. Not a moment later, Navees and Hakri were also giggling with him.

As it died down, Navees smacked Evlor's thigh, then Hakri's rump. "Hop to it, then!"

Squealing, Evlor jerked forward, hips slamming into Hakri and drawing forth a soft grunt. He shot Navees a glare but had to admit that it was an excellent idea. The soft snickers morphed into a groan of bliss as he slowly pulled out, only to rock back in again. Thankfully, Hakri didn't try to press back.

With Navees leaning against the frame, Evlor could watch in the mirror with him as each thrust made Hakri's cock sway in a lazy arc. The beading wetness at the tip formed a drop that would inevitably land on the mattress below.

Well, not if Navees had a hand in it. Carefully straightening up, he stepped closer and let the flared tip of Hakri's cock brush against his palm. It earned him a sharp inhale and a soft "fuck yes" that had him grinning in turn.

"Whatever you did, do it again," Evlor gasped, his view blocked by Navees's stocky body. However, he didn't need to see to be able to guess.

Ever so obliging, Navees rubbed his palm over the lazily drooling head and eagerly listened to the cursing from the other two. With Evlor in mind, he moved to reveal in the mirror how he teasingly thumbed over the slit, letting the digit dip in before retreating. Hakri almost kicked the frame again.

"Come round. Navees, please. Want to make you feel good too."

There was no resisting Hakri's sweet begging. Shuffling awkwardly, Navees managed to turn and backed up towards Hakri's front. Given

their size difference, it was a bit of a stretch and twist, but they made it work, and Evlor relished the sight of it. One hand on Hakri's cock, Navees shuddered when he felt two on his own. It was hard work; Evlor knew from experience. Hakri was doing his best to get Navees off, but his hands kept tightening with each thrust Evlor made, and he clung to the cock like a lifeline rather than a source of pleasure.

"Fuck, Ev— 'Vees, going to—" Hakri was panting all too quickly under the tender care of the other two. Above him, Evlor fucked with single-minded determination. Sweat beaded around the base of his antlers, ran in rivulets down his chest, and darkened his fur. Gaze locked with his, Navees licked his lips. It was always a treat for Evlor to lose himself like this, especially with such a rapt audience watching him. As a cervitaur, it was impossible for him to last as long as the other two, and they'd learned to appreciate his enthusiasm.

Nipping at Hakri's flank, Navees urged him on. "Yes, go on, show us how good you feel. Come for us."

Hakri let out a long, low groan as his cock flexed and flooded Navees's palm where he'd been rubbing the head. Even better, Evlor panted harshly, eyes closing as his hips jerked in short, sharp thrusts.

"Can you feel that?" Navees all but purred. "He's making such a mess of you, isn't he? Filling you up. You're both so good, so incredible. I'm lucky to call you mine."

Whining, Hakri shook his head. "You can't say shit like that. Not when I've just come my brains out."

"Watch me."

The playful refusal had Evlor's eyes opening, and he watched as anything more was lost in a gasp when Navees's cock was stroked once more. Without the distraction of his own pleasure, Hakri could focus on his partner's. As Evlor slipped out, Hakri sighed at the loss, but they could both relish the way Navees quivered and rocked into his touch. To finally render him speechless was a victory almost sweeter than their own orgasms.

"Next time, it'll be you mounting me," Navees promised.

Evlor watched their joined reflection, how Hakri's hands worked together to stroke the whole length he held, and he spurred them on. "You'd love it, wouldn't you, to fuck me once Evlor's already left me sloppy and used. I can already imagine you fingering me open for your dick."

A grunted "oh shit" left Navees's lips. It wasn't fair how well they all knew each other, how Evlor or Hakri could utter a few words and drive Navees to the brink of climax. There was no need to hold back, to try and last, so Navees didn't. He clutched at Hakri's fur-clad shoulder, teeth clenched before his mouth fell lax and his orgasm finally rushed through him.

Leaning heavily against his partner, Navees tried to catch his breath, and Evlor could feel himself craving to go again, even if his body wasn't quite on board with the idea.

Silence descended on the room until it was broken by a nervous laugh from Evlor.

"So, not to ruin the moment, but a little help, please?"

Straightening up, Navees cleared his throat and walked to the back of the mounting frame. Given his silence, he probably didn't see the issue—at least not until he looked at Evlor, who was looking over his shoulder and laughing nervously.

"What's the matter, little deer?"

A mumble was the initial reply, and Navees looked at him blankly until Evlor repeated himself: "I can't get down. Came too hard."

Hakri barked out a laugh. The other two were gracious enough to not mention that he hadn't moved a muscle to attempt getting up. Receiving a once-over from Navees, Evlor's issue was quick to make itself known: fatigued legs quivering worse than those of a newborn foal.

A chuckle managed to sneak its way out of Navees's throat, but he reached up all the same. "I'll catch you if needed. Nice and slow, now."

In the end, he wasn't needed for more than reassurance and a kiss once Evlor had four hooves on the ground again. That gave Hakri enough time to scoot free of the frame and flop onto his side with a satisfied groan. The other two were quick to join him on the clean half of the mattress, and they settled comfortably in a pile. Their hands found each other to intertwine warm fingers. Even though there was no twine of pumpkin to hold them together now, it didn't matter.

They were bonded.

They were happy.

It was all any of them could ask for.

SCALES LIKE STARS

Ambra Rossi

blow job, breast play, cunnilingus, established relationship, f/f, fantasy with technology, friends to lovers, friends with benefits, getting together, love declaration, marriage proposal, merperson, open relationship, past tense, penis in vagina sex, scientist, third person limited point of view, tonguefucking

The stars arced overhead, rocking slightly as Leila swayed with the motion of the boat. With the passengers all tucked away in their bunks, she'd turned off the deck lights; the moons were in a period of overlapping cycles, both dark, so the only light was the starry river bending down toward the horizon and the occasional blue glow from the water as it lapped against the hull.

There was a soft splash off starboard, and Leila sat up with a grin. The ocean beyond the edges of the boat was dark, except now where the glimmer of bioluminescence revealed the motion of a large creature underwater. Leila's grin widened as the light approached, pausing next to the boat; then the creature surfaced.

Glowing water sluiced down off her blue-toned skin; her hair, the colour of dark seaweed, floated off in the water behind her. There was a smile on her plush lips, and the light of the water reflected in her large, dark eyes. Her webbed ears flicked off a few drops of water.

"Hello, gorgeous," Leila said, scooting closer to the edge of the boat and leaning out for a kiss.

"Hello," Aulica purred, cupping Leila's cheek and pressing their foreheads together for a moment. Leila breathed in her sea-salt scent, and they parted with another gentle kiss.

"Long time no see," Auli said as she sank back down until the water reached her shoulders, the gills under her jawbone fluttering as she changed water for air. Leila snorted softly. No matter if they saw each other one month or one day apart, Auli always said the same thing.

"Two weeks, huh? What've you been up to?"

"Chasing down some sea serpents for tagging purposes." Auli grimaced. "They're fast."

"You don't say." Auli was a marine ecologist; the two of them had met when Leila's boat had been chartered to bring a land-based crew out to a remote island to collaborate with an ocean-based one. "Is the project going well, at least?"

Auli gave a so-so gesture, ears flaring out. "Would be better if they didn't somehow keep breaking our tags."

They chatted for a while, Auli about current fish stocks and what could be a slightly shifting current, Leila about the crew and their tourist passengers and their tour plans, and about all sorts of nothings that were a pleasure to share with each other.

Eventually, they lapsed into comfortable silence, Auli with her head laid across her forearms, elbows on deck, and Leila sitting with her feet in the water. Occasionally, Auli's tail would light up, the natural lines of bioluminescence on her fins drowned out by the algae as she moved her tail around.

The light glinted off Laila's last present to her.

"The beads look nice," Laila murmured, running her hand over a series of them, strung into Auli's thick hair. Auli preened, pulling the strands forward and showing off the beads' reflectiveness.

"They do look nice. Thank you." She dropped the hair and pushed up, palms against the deck, placing a quick kiss against Leila's lips.

 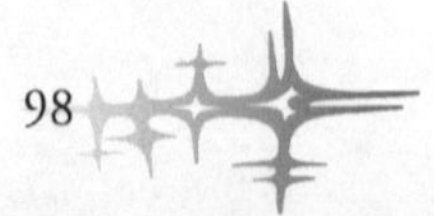

Leila chuckled. "Keep rocking the boat like this and you're going to end up waking one of the passengers."

"Not your crew?" Auli asked, one of her eyebrows rising.

Leila playfully put a hand on Auli's head and made to dunk her underwater. "We get caught *one time*..."

Auli shot a thin stream of water at Leila's chest before laying her arms back on the deck. "Your passengers giving you any trouble?"

Leila shook her head. "They're not too bad, this time."

"That's good," Auli said with a grin, revealing her rows of triangular teeth. "Wouldn't want anything to happen..."

"Oh, hush, you."

"Well, if you don't want to rock the boat, I have other plans."

Leila snorted. "Trying to be smooth?"

"Just saying. Your shirt's already wet, you might as well take it off." The tip of Auli's tongue stuck out briefly. "And everything else, if you want."

"Better plan," Leila replied, heat pooling in her lower belly. "You take me somewhere the boat can't see, and then *you* can take it off."

"I like that plan," Auli said, running a careful hand up Leila's leg, her claws leaving goosebumps in their wake. She tightened her grip around Leila's waist. Leila leaned down to kiss her, and Auli murmured against her lips, "Deep breath."

And then Auli pulled her under, water rushing.

In port a week later, Leila gave her crew the night off and took the passengers along the town's waterfront, showing them the best places for food, drink, and, eventually, dancing. A few, younger by the looks of them, insisted Leila join them for at least one song, and since Leila had nothing better to do, she did.

One song, of course, turned into several, and after a while, she found herself dancing with another human. They were handsome enough, but when they invited Leila home, she turned them down. The lack of scales under her fingers had been discomfiting; skin and clothing just weren't the same.

She excused herself back to her boat and lay out on the swim platform,

one foot in the water.

The port town was small, but its lights still almost drowned out the stars.

Aulica visited again when the tour was almost done and took her somewhere private. Mer magic enabled her to travel through water at ridiculous speeds, even with a human tag-along. Auli had tried to explain it to Leila once, but her explanations involved a lot of gestures and appeals to gut feelings, and they'd ended up laughing it off.

It didn't matter, anyways. What did matter was that, in the space of a few deep breaths, they found themselves on an uninhabited island with sand so fine it felt almost powdery under Leila's fingers as she curled them in pleasure. Auli's tongue curled deeper inside her, twisting in just the perfect way, and Leila shuddered as an orgasm rolled through her. Auli worked her through it, then pulled back her tongue and crawled forward until she was level with Leila.

She kissed Leila and lay down next to her, wiggling around and throwing up sand as she settled her fins down. Leila turned onto her side, lassitude coursing through her, and ran her fingertips over the stripes of bioluminescence decorating the scales around Aulica's pelvic fins.

"Like what you see?" Auli joked, flapping her fin and spraying more sand everywhere.

Leila rolled her eyes but still patted Auli, the thick muscle firm under her hand. "I'd like you a lot more if you stopped covering me with sand." She brushed some of the offending substance off her stomach. "Last time I was still washing sand out of my asscrack three days later."

"You weren't complaining at the time, as I recall it," Auli replied, smug. And, well, no, Leila *hadn't* been complaining—Auli had been fucking her senseless with *both* dicks. It had been sublime. Still.

"You're lucky I like you," Leila said, picking up a fistful of sand and tossing it at Auli's sleek chest.

Auli chuckled before turning thoughtful and giving a quiet noise that sounded like a growl, but that Leila had learned was closer to a human hum. Then there was a swish, and Leila yelped at the water hitting her as Auli brought the end of her tail—and the giant, almost ribbon-like

tail fin—up and over them until she could reach the pouch tied at the base of the fin.

She fiddled with it for a few seconds, during which time Leila gazed at her, drinking in the grace of the flowing edges of her tail fin, how the blue-purple sheen was magnified by iridescence, the sheer strength at play along the length of the tail…the way her fingers were so nimble despite the webbing that joined them to the knuckle, the reflection of light on her claws…

The tail moved away, and Leila's gaze snapped up to meet Aulica's, who was smiling bemusedly.

"I *am* lucky you like me, I think," she said, and then held out a closed fist to Leila. Leila raised her brows but obediently held out her hand, and Auli dropped something into her palm. Leila pulled it closer for inspection.

It was a long ribbon, about the width of a single finger, winding, and—when Leila flipped it over with a touch—woven through in such a way that shifting it made Auli's glow catch the fibers, illuminating a cascade of shimmering patterns that brought to mind the way silver fish flashed in a school. The ends of the ribbon, when Leila inspected them, were complementary, one end a large knot and the other a series of holes.

"Oh! Is this a necklace?" Leila looked up just in time to catch Auli's heart-wrenchingly fond look before it became her usual cocky grin.

"Could be, though I would suggest a bracelet."

Leila held out her arm and the bracelet. "Put it on me?"

Auli hummed assent, taking the bracelet from Leila and wrapping it around her wrist three times before pulling the knotted end through one of the loops. It fit, snugly but not too tight, and shimmered every which way when Leila rotated her wrist to admire it.

She ran a finger along the band. "It's gorgeous."

"You think so?" Auli was positively glowing—ears fanned, posture as straight as she could make it on land, self-satisfied smile on her face. Her bioluminescence seemed to brighten as well, but Leila wasn't sure if it was truly brighter or if she had just paused to admire Auli for long enough that everything else had faded into the background.

"Yes," she answered honestly. "Now stop fishing for compliments and come give me a kiss."

The payout from the tour company that had chartered her boat wasn't anything extraordinary, but Leila was able to give her crew a week off and take the boat out for a solo run to a much quieter island. Leila pretended not to hear her crew's "Solo run my ass" and "Whatever you say, boss" comments as they disembarked.

Auli stayed with her on the boat, and together they managed to cover almost the entire deck with scales. Auli grimaced when she saw them, and promised she'd be done shedding soon.

On the last night of Leila's vacation, the two of them sprawled out on the deck together, talking until the stars completed their journey.

"You've got barnacles under your boat."

"Hello to you too, Auli," Leila said, and finished tying down the port stay before looking up.

Aulica leaned on her elbows off the swim deck, her hair pooling in the water around her. It was still daylight, so there was no bioluminescence in play—Auli still looked gorgeous, of course, the lightly blue-green tinge to her skin all the more obvious, especially where it became more saturated toward her hands and ears.

"Hello. It really is a lot of barnacles, though. Went sailing somewhere in particular?"

Leila rolled her eyes, knowing that Auli knew *exactly* where that particularly clingy strain of barnacle came from. She descended to the swim deck, sat down next to Auli, and gave her a kiss on the nose. "The new deckhand forgot to apply the hull repellant before we passed through the strait, yes. It's going to be a nightmare to get them all off, that's for sure… How many are we talking? I haven't had a chance to look at them yet."

Auli waggled her hand in the air in the mer gesture for estimate. "A few thousand. I hope the deckhand's still around for cleanup duty."

Leila winced. "I was going to make them start tomorrow morning. I don't want them in the water after dark—you know how the squid are." It had been one of the unexpected benefits of her relationship with

Auli—she could swim in the open ocean at night with absolutely no fear, the most apex of apex predators of the sea by her side.

"Mm. So you're free now?" Auli batted her eyelashes.

Leila raised an eyebrow. "Dinner's in an hour or so, will I be back by then?"

Auli's ears flapped. "What if you came with me for dinner? No promises when you'll be back, though."

"Oh?"

Auli's ears twitched again, and Leila was burningly curious. Whenever they ate together, Auli usually caught a fish right then and there and devoured it whole...but if Auli had planned a meal, then it was sure to be something Leila could eat. "Okay," Leila said, "Let me go tell my first mate I'm not eating with them, then I'll be back."

When Leila returned, Auli was waiting a meter from the boat, submerged up to her eyes, her hair spread out on the waves. She bobbed upward and grinned when she caught sight of Leila, flashing her sharp teeth, and Leila grinned back before slipping into the water, hissing at the chill.

"Let's get you somewhere warmer, hm?" Auli said, coming close. She wrapped her arms around Leila's waist. "Deep breath." Leila exhaled, inhaled slowly—

—and Auli pulled her under, the great rush of water past Leila's head, the pop of her ears as they descended and then again as they surfaced right when Leila's store of air was almost used up. She gasped for air and began treading the water once Auli let her go. The water was, true to Auli's word, much warmer. Leila blinked her eyes clear, barely registering the burn of salt after so many years at sea.

The island was little more than a sandbar, topped at the highest point with three coconut palms and a scattering of shorter plants. The rest was pure white sand, ripple patterns forming deep under Leila's churning feet in the clear blue water. On the shore was a large log of driftwood that was mostly flat on top, and perched there was what looked like a coconut bowl but was larger than any coconut Leila had ever seen. She swam toward it, then walked, the water reaching her thighs when Auli reappeared with a small bag clutched in her hand.

"What's all this?" Leila asked, wringing the hem of her shirt dry. She could probably just take it off, honestly; she didn't think Auli would have taken her to an *inhabited* island for some mysterious adventure.

"Dinner!" Auli swam forward as far as she could go, and then pulled herself up the beach while Leila followed. It amused Leila to watch—Auli had to undulate like a seal to get any forward traction, but her tail and fins were so long they dragged in the sand anyway.

"What is it?" Rolled up behind the driftwood table was a small towel, and she unrolled it and sat down cross-legged while Auli propped herself up on her tail.

"Kokoda," Auli said, and undid the preservation charm keeping it safe from the sun before pushing the bowl over to Leila. It was half filled, small chunks of white fish served with human vegetables and another one that Leila only recognized as being from the bottom of the sea, coated in creamy coconut milk and a few slices of lemon and onion.

"It looks delicious," she said, giving it a sniff.

Auli preened. "Procured it all myself. Fish, veggies. Even the coconut milk."

"You made the coconut milk yourself?"

"Well, I had to barter for the coconuts, but otherwise yes." She held up her hand, showing off her claws. "The coconut flesh is surprisingly nice for the claws."

Leila laughed. "That's good. Thank you, Auli. This is so kind."

"Anything for you," Auli said, oddly serious. Leila's cheek heated, and she looked away quickly, back at the kokoda.

"Are you—it's fish, are you sharing with me?"

"Mm. I thought…" Auli trailed off until Leila looked back up at her, and then it was her turn to look away. "I thought it might be nice to *really* eat together, for once."

Leila's heart swelled in her chest, and her breath caught on it. "Yeah," she pushed out. "Yeah, it would."

Auli's ears fluttered, her cheeks turning a deeper blue. "Well, you know. Help yourself." She reached forward and delicately picked up a cube of fish with her claws. "Oh, wait—" She popped the fish into her mouth, then pulled her tail up—carefully, so as to not spray the fine sand everywhere—and from the pouch tied to its end, she pulled out a pair of chopsticks. "Here, sorry. These are for you."

"Thanks," Leila said, smiling, and they ate the truly delicious kokoda, and talked and talked, and Leila thought, *oh, this is happiness.*

"By the way," Auli said as she dropped Leila off, dinner and a good tumble across the beach later, "I have this knife for you."

Leila took the proffered knife. It was a switchblade, elegantly crafted, the metal a darker silver than normal. It fit snugly into her palm, and from holding it, Leila could tell it would fit perfectly in the belt sheath she carried now. The handle was gently ridged in the same dark silver color, rough enough to provide grip but not so rough as to tear the skin.

It was a beautiful knife, but Leila had plenty of knives, and Aulica had never shown interest in such human gear, given that her claws and teeth were perfectly adequate to the task. Maybe it was magical? Leila was close to magically blind and could never tell how much magic items had stored in them, but Auli was much more sensitive to it.

"Thank you," she said anyway, but her confusion must have shown in her voice, because Auli pushed up to give her a peck on the lips.

"Try it on the barnacles tomorrow," she said with a wink, and then, "goodnight!"

Before Leila could say it back, Auli had vanished, water closing soundlessly over her head, and Leila watched the waves until the shadow of blue-green bioluminescence faded into the dark.

When she tried the knife on the barnacles the next day as directed, it sliced through their magically enhanced cement like butter.

"Only thing I've ever heard of that does that is iron snail shells, boss," said one of her older crew members after confirming that the knife was not, in fact, magical. They sounded faintly impressed. "The ones that grow by the magic vents. Good knife you got yourself there."

"Huh," said Leila, and switched out her usual knife for the iron snail one, on the side of her belt where she could reach out and run a finger over the rough surface, thinking of snails in the deep ocean and a lovely mer who'd apparently paid them a visit.

"I've got a surprise for you."

"Yeah? What is it?"

"Guess." Auli looked up at Leila where she was sitting on a rock exposed by the low tide, close to where the shallow reefs dropped off into the deeper ocean.

Leila poked her in the forehead. "Auli…" she said, drawing out the "i."

Auli stuck out her tongue with a noise. "Okay, fine, here." She held out a fist and, after a second, Leila stuck her hand under it. Auli opened hers, and something heavy dropped into Leila's palm. She held it up close to examine it.

"A…rock?"

"Not just any rock! Look closer!"

Leila looked closer. It was a rough grey color, shot through with cracks that were filled with opaque white. It was roughly round, and at one end, there was a hole, large enough for a string to pass through. Presumably someone had intended this to be a necklace. Still, if Auli was insisting a stone like any other Leila could find on a pebble beach was interesting, then there must be more to it. The knife wasn't magical, but maybe…

"A…magical rock?"

Auli gave Leila double finger-guns, something she'd picked up after accidentally meeting one of Leila's younger and more excitable crew members, and which didn't really work with the amount of webbing between her fingers. "Yep! And guess what it does."

"Uh…" Leila tossed the rock up a few times. "Points me north?"

Auli snorted and wrinkled her nose. "That's magnetism, not magic. Try again."

Leila rolled her eyes. "C'mon, just tell me."

"I will…for the price of a kiss," Auli said with a toothy grin. Leila rolled her eyes again, sure that the fondness she felt was read into the gesture. She leaned down and gave Auli a kiss, which Auli quickly deepened, licking into Leila's mouth with a *mm*. When they broke apart, Leila's heart was beating fast, the space between her thighs growing wet already.

"This rock," Auli pronounced dramatically, "will let you breathe underwater for up to twenty minutes at a time on a full charge."

Leila's eyes widened. "And…is it charged?"

Auli grinned, a little devilishly. "Fully," she growl-purred, and the wetness between Leila's legs grew more pronounced.

"How do I activate it?"

Auli showed her, pulling out a thin fish-leather cord to loop around Leila's neck so the stone wouldn't go missing, and then Leila wasted no time submerging herself.

It was a strange sensation at first, forcing her lungs to believe that she could breathe the water, but she adjusted quickly and set to the much more satisfying work of giving Auli the best underwater blowjob she possibly could.

"I really am sorry," Auli said later, patting Leila on the back as Leila coughed again, seawater burning her throat. "I should have been watching the magic level better—"

Leila spat and wiped her mouth with the back of her hand, then smirked at Auli. "Got distracted, did you?"

Auli fluttered her ears in embarrassment.

Leila laughed, and then promptly coughed up more water. "I'll bring a timer next time."

Leila and her crew stopped at one of the bigger ports in the region for a supply run, a short break, and, in a few cases, a turnover of the crew themselves. It was always sad to see someone go, but newcomers could also be fun. *If they behave*, said a voice in Leila's head that sounded suspiciously like Auli's, complete with a ghost of a sharp-toothed grin. Leila smiled to herself.

The portside market was bustling. It was hosted along the ancient waterfront built of solid stone and stuccoed in gleaming white, and the market itself was a patchwork assembly of bright fabrics and wood, metal, and plastic poles propping them up. All manner of colours and smells and languages filled the air; people from all over streamed through the central walkway, and the hawkers who ran the booths called out in a cacophony, voices layering one over another.

Leila was usually content to find a meal from a decent food stall—today's selection was a leaf of coconut rice topped with delicately sliced mango—and call it a day, but Auli had been getting her a number of presents recently that Leila didn't feel she'd been adequately returning, so Leila set out with a goal to find a present for Aulica.

The problem being, naturally, that Auli was a capable adult who lived in a completely different environment both magically and physically than Leila, and was thus infinitely more well-equipped than Leila to procure herself anything she might find useful. That left things that were maybe not useful but were at least *pretty*, which was a different challenge altogether, because so far, the only things Leila had seen that fit the bill were also items that seawater would absolutely destroy, and a permanent waterproofing spell was so out of budget for Leila as to be laughable.

She missed Auli already, despite the fact that they'd last seen each other only five days ago. When they were together, time passed so much faster. Leila was always too caught up in the moment to check the hour. Leila *enjoyed* everything about Auli, from her snarky humor to the strength of her tail to her wit and intelligence to her beautiful face.

She just—she just *really* liked Aulica.

Like, a *lot.*

Maybe it shouldn't have been such a revelation; after all, she saw Auli more than she saw anyone else except perhaps her crew—she certainly didn't call home nearly as often as she met up with Auli. And even the crew, the ones who had been around long enough to get to know Leila, they all knew she had a—

She and Auli had never exactly defined whatever their relationship was. It had been a casual fling at first, after they'd met at a remote research station and were both willing to try something new…and then they'd just…kept going. And sure, there'd been other partners, but the last time Leila had slept with someone who wasn't Auli was…months ago, at least, and she suspected it was the same for Auli.

Did that make them exclusive?

Did Leila *want* to be exclusive? Exclusive physically, or exclusive emotionally? She would already say that Auli was one of her closest friends…

Leila had finished her mango rice and was about to double back when a little stall tucked in between two larger, brighter ones caught her eye.

It was a small table draped with a soft blue fabric, and hung around the sides and spread out on the table were all sorts of nacreous carvings. The largest, a round oval propped up on a stand, featured a delicately carved design of a mer underwater, so lifelike Leila could almost see the carved hair undulating with the waves.

"Nice work, isn't it?" said the shopkeeper, startling Leila. "The smaller ones are nice, too," she added, inviting Leila closer to see. She wasn't lying; the details the artisan had managed to fit even into a carving no larger than Leila's thumbnail were incredible.

"I have to ask," Leila said as she picked up a carving of a sea urchin on which the individual spikes could be counted, "are these able to withstand water?"

"Ah, shopping for your mer, are you? I thought so," the shopkeeper said with a knowing smile, while Leila backtracked over everything she'd done since arriving at the stall to try and pinpoint what might have tipped the shopkeeper off about Auli—*if* Auli could even be considered "her" mer, naturally. "Rest assured, all my jewelry has been made with complete submersion in mind. Thoroughly tested, if you catch my drift."

"I— Sorry, how…?"

The shopkeeper gave Leila an indecipherable look, then shook her head slightly. "Honey, if you didn't want people to know, you'd do better to hide that courting gift of yours," she said, gesturing to Leila's side, where her wrist with the silken bracelet rested.

"Courting gift?"

"Oh, did you really not know? Here, look." She extended her right arm, and on her wrist was a bracelet as intricately woven and shimmery as Leila's own. "I'll eat my table if that knife you got on your belt there there isn't iron snail shell, too. And you probably got some magical trinket somewhere, eh?" She flicked one of her earrings, which was a small grey pendant. Leila would bet it was full of magic.

"I…"

Then the shopkeeper laughed, surprising Leila. "Don't feel bad, darling, I was practically married before I learned what all these nice gifts my sweetheart was giving me meant! You'll want to return the favour if you're interested—I'm assuming you're interested? You'll also want to have a nice conversation with your mer about proper communication, I'll tell you that."

One of those statements, at least, was something Leila felt equipped to answer. "…yes, I'm interested."

"And far be it from me to stop you spending money at my stall! A good bangle for the tailfin is a classic acceptance gift."

Well. At least this stall's wares *were* of good quality; Leila walked away, after further enlightening conversation, with a large bangle inlaid with carvings of whitetip reef sharks, Auli's favourites.

"So, I had an interesting conversation with a stall owner last week," was how Leila greeted Auli the next time Auli appeared near the boat, cutting across Auli's exuberant grin. The bioluminescence along her flanks started to pulse faintly, a surefire sign that she was on guard.

"Is…something wrong? What did the stall owner say?"

"Nothing much," Leila replied, kicking her feet in the water off the swim deck before locking eyes with Auli. "Just that she thought that I was being courted by a mer." She let that hang in the air as Auli's face ran through a series of expressions before settling on something close to *resolute*.

"Okay. Okay—I *was* going to tell you, I swear, tonight even, I brought—no, back up." Auli took a deep breath and smoothed back her hair, her ears moving agitatedly and the light along her sides pulsating even more strongly. "I wasn't even aware of it at first. I just wanted to give you some more nice presents, and these are the nicest presents! And I thought, well, we've been—you know, fucking, whatever—for a while now, and so it wouldn't be inappropriate to give you courting gifts even if it wasn't for explicit courtship because, well, we're already *way* past that point in a traditional courtship, you know? But then I was thinking about it, and—"

She paused, dipped into the water as she pulled her tail up, and reached into the pack she kept tied there. Leila noticed, in a way she never really had before, the lack of bangle around that same point. Auli let her tail fall back down, her hand closed tightly around something.

"And Leila," Auli said, serious and intense, practically quivering with tension as she bobbed gently in the waves, one hand grounding her to the swim deck, the other, closed, held to her chest. Leila looked between

her eyes and her hand, then inhaled sharply. Auli smiled faintly and opened her hand. In the middle of her palm was a small ring, glowing faintly in the same colour as Auli's bioluminescence—when Leila looked closer, she saw that the ring was constructed of delicately overlaid scales. "Leila, would you accept my suit?"

This had not been one of the many results of their talk that Leila had imagined over the course of the past week.

No, this was *better*.

Leila pulled Auli close and kissed her fiercely.

When they broke apart, Leila was panting heavily and Auli was not much better; they were both beaming.

"Is that a yes?" Auli asked, her grin wide, a hint of a laugh in her voice.

"That's a yes, you silly mer," Leila said, resting her forehead against Auli's. "But just ask *me*, next time. Don't let a stranger inform me!"

Auli tilted her head and gave Leila a chaste kiss on the lips. "Duly noted." She held out her hand, gesturing for Leila's, and slid the ring onto Leila's finger.

It fit perfectly, thin and unobtrusive when Leila moved her hand, but heavy and grounding. And the glow…

"Are these your scales?" she asked.

Auli nodded, almost tentatively. "It's traditional to make the final gift in a courtship out of one's own sheds," she explained. "Kind of…to offer that you'll stay by someone's side, even if you're not physically there."

"Oh," said Leila, running her finger over the scales. "I like that." She could feel the heat returning to her cheeks. It wasn't as if she didn't already think of Aulica often…now she would have a physical reminder as well. "Auli, I also have something for you." She fished around in the pocket of her shorts for the bangle. She'd kept it on her since she'd bought it, and spent more time than she'd wanted to contemplating whether she was truly ready for the commitment it meant.

When she looked up, Auli was gazing back at her with something that she would even now dare to call *fondness*. She held out the bangle. "Here. For your tail." Auli took it, turning it over in her hands a few times, and Leila saw the exact moment she found the shark engraving because her ears perked up and she broke into a smile.

"Leila…this is gorgeous." She dove underwater and resurfaced a moment later, holding onto the deck as she pulled her tail up next to her, showing Leila how the bangle lay perfectly just above the strap for her pocket. The silver contrasted with Auli's scales, the carvings catching the light. "It goes well."

"I'm glad." Leila smiled, and Auli's tail splashed into the water as she pushed up to kiss Leila again.

"Now…deep breath."

Leila obligingly inhaled and slipped off the boat as Auli pulled her under.

They emerged onto a small atoll, the waves sparkling in the setting sun and reflecting beams of rosy colour onto Auli's skin and scales, tinting her purple. The water was shallow enough for Leila to stand, but Auli's tail swept up around her. The bangle flashed, and Leila smiled before throwing a leg over, straddling Auli. Auli smiled in return and pulled her closer, kissing her deeply.

Leila moaned into the kiss and rocked her hips, already wet between her legs. Auli hum-growled in return, running her hands along Leila's ribs and pushing her wet shirt up. Rivulets of seawater streamed over Leila's skin and drew out goosebumps as they cooled in the sea breeze. Then Auli pulled the shirt clean off, tossing it onto the spit of sand nearby—Leila giggled, remembering the time she'd given Auli a talking-to for losing one of her favourite shirts to the waves—and her hands continued their exploration.

She held Leila in place with one hand on her back, moving her other hand forward to palm Leila's breasts, and Leila arched into it. The hint of claws accompanying everything Auli did added that perfect touch of sharpness that made Leila mad with pleasure. Auli set to work, playing with Leila's nipples and squeezing her breasts until she was gasping, only for Auli to claim her mouth, licking into it until Leila was dizzy with want.

Auli kissed down her neck, then her chest, leaving the occasional nip with her pointed teeth that only made Leila more aroused. She pushed Leila backwards, farther down her tail, and spent time at each of Leila's nipples, pulling and licking and twisting. She pushed farther, until she was below and above Leila, and continued down, over the rolls of Leila's stomach and then down again, her long, thick tongue flicking against Leila's belt, which her claws were hastening to undo—

"Wait, not yet," Leila said, her voice coming out as a series of pants.

She batted Auli away, rolled off, stripped out of her shorts, and threw them to the beach with her top. She straddled Auli again, fully naked in the twilight, placing her hands at the base of Auli's pelvic fins and running them down, parallel to the patterns of bioluminescence that ran down the side's of Auli's tail. "I want you in me tonight."

Obligingly, Auli pushed them to shallower water—they'd learned the hard way that penetration in the saltwater could get difficult for Leila—and let her genital slit fall open. The two rows of larger scales in the center of her hips parted to reveal her twinned dicks, already wet with natural lubricant and held erect by their baculum, soft around the outside and semi-prehensile at the tip. Leila couldn't resist leaning down to give them each a kiss while Auli hissed, her head falling back in pleasure. Leila stroked a few times, first one, then the other, curling her fingers around the tips. Soon, Auli was panting, ears and fins fluttering, her claws dug into the sand under her.

"Leila…" she said, deep and breathy.

Leila hummed, and with one more kiss, she sat up, crawling forward until her hips were lined up against Auli's, rocking her clit onto Auli's dicks. With a growl, Auli surged forward, pure muscle between Leila's legs, and buried one hand in Leila's hair, kissing her aggressively. Leila welcomed her, leaned into her, pushed her own tongue into Auli's mouth to trace the points of her teeth.

She reached blindly under herself, grabbing one of Auli's dicks and pulling it back, pushing up with her thighs high enough to slide Auli's dick under her, and then sank down.

She and Auli both let out long groans; Leila broke the kiss, so full and stretched she needed a moment to just *breathe*. Auli gave her that time, leaning back into the sand and running her hands soothingly along Leila's hips and thighs until Leila felt like she could handle movement again and twitched her hips forward. Auli's other dick was perfectly positioned, as always, to provide pressure against her clit; the one inside her curled back at the tip, stretching wider and giving Leila resistance as she began to rock more insistently. Auli's fingers tightened over her hips, holding her in place, and Leila got even more wet in anticipation of what was coming—

Auli pushed her tail up powerfully, pushed her length deeper into Leila, who gasped and fell forward, resting her hands on Auli's chest.

And then Auli did it again, and again, fast and hard just like Leila liked it, until Leila could think of nothing but Auli: Auli under her, Auli inside her, Auli holding onto her, the taste of Auli as they kissed again, the way Auli's movements stuttered as she neared her peak—

With a shudder, Auli climaxed, going still and slack, and Leila took over, riding until she also came, biting down hard on her lip.

She slumped down against Auli, laying her head on Auli's chest, which rose and fell rapidly. Under her ear, Auli's heart beat loudly; she felt that pulsing mirrored in her own chest. Auli tucked her head to kiss the top of Leila's.

Then she kissed Leila's eyebrows, and her nose, and her cheek, and her lips—Leila moaned into it, but Auli pulled away, rolling them over and kissing Leila's throat, pressing her into the sand with the weight of her tail between Leila's legs. She pulled her dicks back into herself, and Leila grumbled at the lack of something to rut against; in response, Auli directed her mouth to the soft skin just above Leila's collarbone. She lingered there, her teeth sharp pinpricks which would leave bruises tomorrow. Then she nuzzled down Leila's chest and stomach, faster than last time, her goal clear.

Leila obligingly spread her legs wider as Auli nosed at her pubic hair. Her hips jumped involuntarily when Auli's tongue darted out and licked her firmly.

Auli smiled.

"Auli—"

"Yes?"

"Please," Leila said, rocking her hips. Auli was on her elbows, and she ran her hands up Leila's thighs, soft and reverent.

"Of course," Auli said. Her hands slid back down until she was holding Leila by the hips, preventing her movement.

Then she started eating Leila out in earnest.

She started slowly but intensely, dragging her tongue over Leila's folds, lingering over her clit, warm and wet and insistent. Each stroke sent frissons of sensation through Leila, starting at her core and radiating outward. She curled her fingers into the sand, panting, and arched her back against the hands holding her still, her legs shaking; she was still so *close* from her last orgasm.

Auli hummed, a deep purr that echoed across where she was pressed

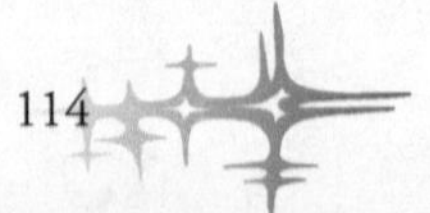

into Leila, and that made Leila gasp. Then Auli moved down, taking the pressure off Leila's clit, leaving her both relieved and bereft. She licked deeper, *inside* Leila, finding the sensitive spots and lingering there. Auli couldn't use her fingers, given the claws, but she more than made up for it with the dexterity of her tongue.

Leila descended into a haze of drawn-out pleasure, held just at the edge of orgasm as Auli worked her while studiously avoiding her clit. At times Auli came close to that sensitive place, the trailing end of her tongue flicking up as she closed her mouth to swallow, or her nose brushing against it as she pushed deeper into Leila; but for the most part she kept away until Leila was shuddering under her grip, all but begging for it.

Auli hummed again, and then, with a few strong strokes of her tongue over Leila's clit, tipped Leila over the edge. Leila came hard, sensations pulsing through her, dimly aware of Auli's thumbs drawing soothing circles on her hips, mostly aware of the wave of released pressure that flooded her awareness. Auli held her through it, and when she was done, she crawled up the beach to lie next to Leila.

"Do you want more, love?"

Leila turned her head to kiss Auli's skin, tasting sea-salt. She felt tender, almost raw. "No, I'm good. Great. Just…hold me for a bit?"

"Of course."

Auli wrapped her arms tight around Leila, grounding her. The waves rustled quietly against the shore, and as Leila settled back into her skin, she felt…comfortable.

Loved, even.

"So…are we fiancées, in the human world?"

There was a beat of silence, one of Auli's hands moving up and down along Leila's spine. "I think that's the equivalent, yes. There's a few more courtship steps if you want to do it proper mer fashion, though."

"Oh?"

"You'll have to come down to meet my family, for one."

"…I'll start saving up for a good long-term water breathing spell, then."

"Yeah?" Auli murmured, nuzzling Leila's hair.

"Yeah. I'll try and convince my family to come on my boat for a while…"

"There's no rush," Auli said, but she squeezed Leila tighter.

"I know. But I..." Leila sat up, one hand pressed flat to Auli's chest, the other cupping her cheek. "I love you, Auli, and I don't want to wait."

Auli turned into her hand, kissing her palm and fluttering her ears. "Ah, Leila, Leila...I love you too. I'm so happy."

"Me too," Leila said, leaning down for another kiss, tender and chaste this time. "You make me happy."

They fell against the beach, uncaring of the soft sand that clung to their skin, their fingers intertwined. Auli's tail extended out, long and sinuous, the waves lapping at her fins.

Her scales shimmered in the dark water like stars.

Leila had never seen such a beautiful sky.

METAMORPHOSIS

I. A. Ashcroft

blow job, body modification, death of a parent, dendrophilia, fraught family dynamics, genderless, genderless/m, grief and grieving, magical healing cock, misogyny, modern with magic, nature spirit, past tense, penis in vagina sex, third person limited point of view, trans man, transphobia

Between two lush hills in the middle of nowhere, there stood an old, weathered sign. *Bauer*, it read, the paint near gone.

A young man named Jakob rested beside it today, wiping sweat from his brow and dust from his tweed jacket, a honey-brown leather suitcase rolling behind him. The sign was hardly needed—everyone knew where the Bauer farm's extensive borders were without a word, him most of all. The land's proximity rose electricity up the back of one's neck, like biting into a tart apple.

I'm home.

An empty breeze whistled through the tree line. His feet stayed put a long while.

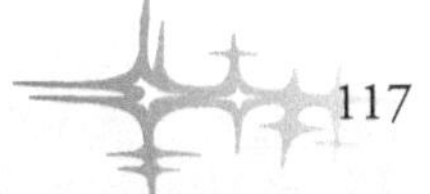

No one in town had really acknowledged him as he'd made his way from the bus stop, but their eyes had peeled him to the bone. He was, after all, the sort of country gossip that had gone and dyed its hair pastel yellow and pink and given itself an eyebrow ring. Jakob had pretended he didn't see them watching, and no one said a word as he headed to the dirt trails past the main village road—though maybe it was just because he was a Bauer himself, his aquiline nose and storm-gray eyes a giveaway. His family land was an ocean and the village an island. Almost every citizen had some role keeping the farmland running: shipping produce, cutting down invasive elms, repairing irrigation ditches at the right turns of the season…and in exchange, for hundreds of years, bountiful harvests had come and gone without even a blight.

But best not speak *to* the Bauers, lest one remember the fine line between blessed and unnatural.

Once, Jakob had been used to their silence. It hurt now. He'd been in new places for years, off to college and the modern world—perhaps they saw him a traitor now, and he figured it only a matter of time, really, before someone in town would voice the cruelest question about him:

How could the Bauer's prodigal son return home when it had been a daughter that left?

Sniffling, he coughed at the heat, pollen, and nerves, a sticky ball in the back of his dehydrated throat as he kept up the path. The persistent memory of the little child he'd been kept running alongside with banged-up knees, trampling happily over the swaths of wildflowers and hoping to find caterpillars in the ditches. The woods and the fields had rooted inside his blood back then as if he'd grown from the earth, too, never knowing fear or pain while this soil was beneath his feet. But Jakob braced for the end of the trail today, where he would find his farmhouse, cozy and white, sitting beyond a sun-dappled glen, where his mother wouldn't fling open the door with her laugh or her worry-tight brow asking where the hell his shoes had gone, and his father wouldn't be pacing, whistling soft imitations of birdsongs, eyes always off in the trees.

For a long moment, he just closed his eyes and breathed, wiping away the tears with the back of his palm and focusing on good memories. The air was still alive with wild lilac all these years later. Only after he opened his eyes again did he notice brilliantly purple blooms running up and down the path, as if a crowd lining the streets to bear witness to his return.

At least the land was happy to see him back.

Nostalgic, he reached down, breaking off a little tuft of flowers. It kissed his nose with home, and in spite of himself, a small smile started to tug.

Shadows suddenly moved in the tree line to the left. He spun, alert to the woods, those that his forebears had refused to clear for farmland no matter the profit. There was a sizzle-snap down his neck, the hairs rising—

Nothing. Just empty spaces, rock and moss and dappled sunlight through the canopy's summer-green.

He breathed. *Badger or something.* These trees made everyone feel watched; it was why non-Bauers stuck to the roads and fields.

But the woods had always provided for Jakob. With the blush of lilac tucked behind one ear, somehow, he found the strength to keep walking down the path to his inheritance.

The farmhouse had been fresh-painted before the coming autumn, glossy and proud in the fading sun. Someone had winterized the windows and gutters, hands unseen, money spent to take care of the problem in the way of invisible stagehands changing a set. Time on the outside had made Jakob more aware that this was unusual for farmers, for whom one ruinous year often felt but a coin flip away.

We were just lucky, I guess.

The idea that luck was running out made his tense shoulders ache as he twisted the heavy iron key inside the front door lock. He'd indeed almost gotten his agricultural degree—almost—but all it had done was open his eyes to how much went into keeping a farm afloat. Here he was, the last of some line of lucky geniuses, but he didn't know half of what they did.

"She's of the land," he'd often hear his mother whispering to his father as he'd grown older, hair tangled with twigs and leaves, always off wandering, listening to the whispers of the wind in the grain, climbing through the orchard and learning the sweet snap in the air when the harvest had come. *"She's got the instincts! Just look at her! Teach her!"*

But his father had always turned away, quiet, brooding, intractable.

The family had always been…old-fashioned, about what made an heir. Landowner.

Man.

They hadn't actually left him the farm in the will. It was a simple legal default. He couldn't help but wonder if they'd been trying again for a second child they could pin their hopes on.

The door drifted shut behind him, and he breathed in the dust and the empty spaces and the ghosts in the dark Bauer entryway. Then he sniffled and sank to his knees, collapsing against the shoe rack. His mother's boots still had dried mud on them, parked with the toes toward the door.

The cicadas sang so loudly they rattled the windows. For the third night in a row, Jakob sweated into his pillow, staring at the ceiling of his childhood bedroom. The noise had crawled into his body—it felt like the entire farm was alive, screaming for company before inevitable death in the coming frosts.

"Urgh," was all he could say, rolling over, stuffing the pillow over his ears.

Soon he was padding downstairs yet again, quiet, as if somehow still a bother to these old wooden walls. The kitchen lamp spilled warm yellow over the documents scattered on the table. He'd been finding his footing with the business records—stunned to find he'd absorbed a great deal from his classes after all—but these were a different kind of difficult to parse.

A personal letter and a bundle of maps.

"They were meant to go to whichever son was his heir," the lawyer's young assistant had said, kindness in her eyes to convey sympathy for his loss, and it was a day when small kindnesses had meant a lot. She'd even offered to bring him a little picnic lunch sometime. Such a gentle smile. Hailey, wasn't it…?

But Jakob put her from his mind, how she'd made him feel warm and halfway welcome. Perhaps his lonely brain was like the cicadas, screaming their fool heads off in the empty night.

Sighing, he shuffled the documents on the table. Considered an envelope he hadn't had the courage to open yet, yellowed, sealed with red wax.

Land rites, it read in his father's careful, exacting hand, *for the passing of ownership.*

The sun blinded, sweat running down between Jakob's shoulder blades and soaking his binder. Nettles snagged his clothes, rocks slipping underfoot. The season's last gasps were volcanic. Not for the first time, he wished he could just...take off his shirt. But he never could shake the feeling of eyes. Perhaps it was another badger, or perhaps it was a farmhand who took the wrong turn, but he refused to give them a show. He took another swig from his water bottle.

The sealed letter about land rites had been cryptic at best, like all of his father's few words.

Every autumn, a Bauer son must take the marked path. The grove at the end is where you will plant your seeds, the final rite, and after, you'll find that our crops will never fail. This is the deal we made, as my father told me, and his before him.

If we do not renew it each year, the harvest will wither, the wilderness retaking the earth.

That was all. An *I love you* would also have been nice, even if it had been for some other child never born. Felt a pity that theatrics and superstition were his final gift.

Still, Jakob figured, what the hell did he have to lose? If a rite of passage was all he had left, then he wanted to try. That morning, the path to the woods had even welcomed him, bordered in wild lilac, seemingly bloomed overnight. Songbirds flitted between the trees, a rowdy chorus, soothing with good memories. Bees bobbed gently in the breeze, the odd bumble investigating his shoulders like a fuzzy, lolling kitten.

No matter what other humans felt, the land opened its arms and welcomed all of his messy heart, body, and soul, and he willingly fell into that embrace.

He walked for hours, slow, thoughtful. There was little along the way other than squirrels, flowers, and the odd cairn to assure him he was on the right road, stacks of mossy rocks near blending into the green. At each, he counted the number of stones, one for each head of the family, each generation he'd been made to memorize long ago.

He sat at each, heavy with that silent weight, alone.

He didn't realize until that moment that he was angry. Always treated like never enough. But so what if he'd been woman or man? He was *Bauer*; he was as worthy as anyone! He was *of this land*! Every plant on this trail he'd known, every bird's song—what he hadn't known was how much his heart had stayed here when he'd left, lost to towns and woods that didn't know their son.

Like it was fate, he'd always find a stone nearby to add to the count of the stacked rocks, the discoveries tingling in his teeth. They would rest in his palm, smooth, slick, sharp, and perfectly weighted, the heft nurturing the quiet in his soul as he added to the monument tower. Each slid neatly into place as if made for that purpose alone.

By the time he was at the end of the road, he felt he understood something of his father's immovable looks, the silence inside. Perhaps it was why the Bauers stayed to themselves, storm-gray eyes all looking to the wilds.

He still wasn't sure if he liked it, but he understood.

It was in the slow boil of the mid-afternoon that Jakob passed from under the glittering canopy and into a wild meadow at journey's end. Before him lay a ring of eight white boulders, pictographs carved on their surfaces in pale, weathered lines.

His ears popped, the hairs at the back of his neck rising. This looked like something older than a mere three hundred years. But there had been people here before Bauers. Farmers, probably—in the middle of the circle, the soil seemed soft and fertile.

"Where we plant the seeds." He sighed, tired, sweaty, finally ready to go back to the house. The pollen here was thick as the wild lilac, head-clouding and heavy, but he dropped his bag at the ring's edge and found the packet of seeds—rosemary, the sort one planted in a kitchen windowsill. Crossing into the circle, the buzzing in his ears rose higher, his breath making a startled catch for reasons he didn't understand.

Then he realized: the clearing was utterly silent. No birdsong. No buzzing insects.

Shivering, he still knelt, taking a long, steadying breath. "I'm ready to renew the deal," he whispered, as if the sky could care to listen. But as he started to paw a little furrow into the earth, a *thud* resounded. Jakob lifted his head and stared. One of the heavy white stones—pumpkin-sized—had fallen over. From this angle, two worn depressions over a narrowed snout-like shape gave the impression of something like a skull, perhaps of some deer or cow.

"...huh," Jakob greeted it, nostrils flaring. Fingers itching, he found himself touching it, as if to put it back—what could possibly dislodge something so heavy...? It was smooth, warm from the sunshine. In spite of himself, he thought again of childhood, of playing in the tree line and finding shiny stones to take home.

Then, a rumbling vibrated through his legs. Startled, he scrambled back, gasping as it grew stronger. Something quaked just beyond the ring, swelling the dirt, cracking open the soft soil like the rise of a balloon and growing closer—"Stay back!" he cried out—then the ground split, and out rose something that made him strangle out a noise of wonder and fear. It was almost a snake: powerful, inexorable, a serpentine length of coiling muscle, thick as the trunk of one of the ancient trees. Black, fertile, wet ground undulated in a writhing mass, held together with patchworks of roots and ivy.

The tip wriggled down to rest upon the fallen boulder, mud seeping to cover those faint, ancient scratchings. And when the mass lifted itself again, the white stone had sunk into place as a strange skull. It angled that stone to the sky, tip of the snout-like form touching the sun.

When it turned back to him, twin flaming orbs had bloomed inside the dim hollows, stars stolen from the heavens.

Jakob screeched, legs flailing. He threw the packet of seeds at the dirt monster, which didn't fix the problem. Then he screamed a second time as the thing rippled closer, showering him in moss and pebbles—dozens of protrusions melted out of its serpentine form, roots pressing forward—becoming nubs, becoming legs—now less snake, more centipede, that long body skittered to encircle the clearing.

Then it ceased, abruptly still and distant as a statue.

Jakob breathed, whimpering, frozen. He shouted mentally at his stupid feet, panting like an animal, but they still didn't move. And the thing, the creature, it just kept staring into his soul, those twin micro-suns blazing merrily in its hewn face: terrifying, but *beautiful*. The damage to the grasses and mosses encasing its form was healing. All down its back, a carpet of fragrant flowers bloomed at unnatural speeds, dots of white, red, and deep-purple brilliance; sprigs of culinary rosemary were even plumping up where its throat might have been, a strange beard where the seed packet had ruptured.

Silent, they kept staring at one another, until Jakob felt like his heart would burst open and fertilize all of this lush, living green with his blood.

Then, the stone head cocked. A shudder of emotion rippled forth, a tangible curiosity and utterly alien intelligence.

Jakob finally managed to move. Memories ruptured through the adrenaline—all of his grandmother's tales of land spirits and their ancient power—and he rolled to his knees, bowing to what his instincts knew as a ruler. For this, it was the Bauer wealth, wasn't it? They'd managed to speak to this thing centuries ago.

"I'm so sorry," he whimpered. "I didn't know. My parents are gone. There was an accident. I…I'm so sorry to intrude. I—"

But the creature's curiosity again rippled through him. Its back half sank down into the earth—root-legs sucking up into its body. A crackling like breaking wood and churning gravel wracked the clearing as its shape shifted, shrinking, compressing. Finally, it was only a little taller than him, a freed lump, stone head placed in the center of a stubby neck. Two wooden legs sprouted at the body's base, taloned and sharp. The creature now hunkered inside its cape of lush grasses like a magnificent, deadly owl. The sharp point of its stone-snout pressed down onto Jakob's hair.

He nearly burst into tears, save for his desperate politeness.

The thing backed away suddenly, and then, again, it changed. Thorn-talons withered and shrank, new branches bursting behind the skull like antlers. Eight delicate legs erupted down its belly, graceful with tendon-vines and cloven rock hooves. A poof of ferns waggled on its new rump, the rosemary sprig beard still whipping around on its face as it shook itself. It almost was a deer now, if a deer also enjoyed being a spider—giving a few joyful, thumping hops, as if to demonstrate itself and receive congratulations.

Jakob tried, but his mouth wouldn't work. *Is... is it trying to become something that doesn't frighten me...?* It was in fact gradually becoming more silly—trotting around the circle with all eight hooves kicking up clover, swishing its fern-tail with pride. Bright new flowers bloomed and withered and bloomed again across its belly and down its back, vines wrapping up its powerful neck to keep the stone skull stable. Soon those proud antlers were bursting with drooping lilacs, berries, and wild roses.

But the strangest thing was how long, sticky strands of honey-sap dripped between the being's backmost legs with each step, increasing with each toss of its joyful head. A harder look confirmed that—

Jakob immediately averted his eyes.

The creature was. Ah. Perhaps female?

It trotted around the circle once more, this time tossing its butt even more pointedly. Little white flowers were blooming beneath its fern-tail so as to encircle a bright wreath around what seemed to be a slit in the moss, one flashing in the vibrant sun with each switch of its hips. The sweet, cloying musk leaking there curled up Jakob's nose—it was only then he realized how his head throbbed and hummed with heat.

And the part of him lost in the logic of dreams added up the sums and gave them the value:

You plant your seeds here.

"Hold on!" was all he could croak, crab-walking back until he collided into another of the encircling boulders. "I can't... can't do that!"

The creature made a noise despite its lack of mouth—like wind squeaking and snorting through a wooden flute. Its long neck twisted a perfect 180 degrees so it could both stare through his soul and provide maximum view of its desire to mate.

PACT.

It was a consuming mental assault, spoken as if through the hiss of a stream and the flutter of a hundred wingbeats. It was the word of a language that shouldn't have ever met human ears, an earthquake through bone and blood and brain. Jakob's eyes rolled back under the weight of it. And when he came back to himself, bright spots crackling at the edges of his gaze, there the creature still stood, bright grass-and-clover coat rippling up and down from end to end.

Pact. This was a softer thoughtform, shivering faintly through teeth. His heart jumped against his ribs as a stone hoof pawed the earth.

Jakob had never known true panic. It was only when he found himself back in the trees, running, running, tripping over a stone cairn and collapsing in a sweat-soaked, shaking pile, did he know he'd done just that.

For a long moment, he lay utterly still, aching. No hoofbeats rang against the earth. Buzzing no longer seeped through his brain. It was as if the world depressurized—suddenly the air was lighter, and the cicadas were singing their desperate swansong. Here, quietly, trembling, he curled up into a ball, as if he'd made it back home and lay in the childhood bed where he barely fit, just slightly wrong no matter where he was.

Eventually, though, his heart evened, and he had to contend with reality. He breathed long and slow, pinned on his back under the weight of the sky.

Why didn't you tell me?! he wanted to rage at his parents. Was it something only for *treasured sons* to know?!

Then a tingle raced up his neck. He clamped down his infuriated despair, eyes seeking, seeking, and finding nothing—but the creature was the land, and there wasn't a place it couldn't observe here, was there? It was watching him now.

...it had watched him all his life, hadn't it?

Slowly, Jakob pawed at the clover by his side, then quaked to his feet. A friendly tree was his brace. Soft wind tousled his hair, cooling his sweat and fear.

It almost seemed to push him gently back toward the house.

"Is that you?" Jakob whispered. He heard no answer, and yet, as he kept his hand soft to the bark, he felt a vibration inside that seemed to hum in time with the sensation of the sacred clearing.

"It's you. You're here, aren't you?"

Again, the wind picked up, a nudge, the leaves rustling, as if a helping hand to take his weak knees home. And a certainty welled inside, from where his hand touched the tree, spreading through his chest:

A surety of safety. Warmth.

It hadn't wanted him to be so afraid.

He bit his lip, overwhelmed. Again, the wind pressed at him, as if an insistence he wasn't trapped, that he was free.

Jakob instead found his feet taking him sideways, to an overlook nearby. Breaking from the thick brush and branches, he could again see

the fading light washing the land in orange and pink. He didn't understand how the sun had sunk so quickly; he'd had hours remaining of daylight before entering the ring, but now he realized he'd never make it back before dark.

Still…these woods had never harmed him…

Quietly, he sat on the overhang, legs swinging over a rock. His heart was strangely calm now, even if he trembled. It was the same as he'd usually felt wandering alone in these trees; his parents had always just trusted the woods would be his friend, too. He could see some of the farmland from here—the gleaming gold wheat, ready to cut. The emerald groves of fruit trees. Loaded trucks glittered in the last light, the hardworking hands returning to town.

Home, he breathed, overwhelmed with the scent of the place that had been his cradle—the wild lilac a constant note, bursting around the path here and the path when he'd arrived, as if a welcome, a *hope*.

And it had accepted him, all of him, just as he was, even if he was physically unable to fulfill the agreement.

How long were you waiting for me? he wondered. *My whole life?*

A twittering in the trees made him turn. A little wren fluttered down to rest at his side, unusually bold.

In its beak was a sprig of wild lilac.

Jakob dazedly reached out—it hopped right into his grasp, tiny enough for him to cup in his palm with room to spare. Fragile, vulnerable. Like him, beside that shapeshifting ancient. Gently, it set down its gift, chirping a bright tune, and then it fluttered away, free as him to come and go.

Eyes stinging, Jakob understood this message in some place deeper than words.

You deserve more from me…at least an explanation.

Jakob slowly made his way back to the stone ring, considering how to ask forgiveness and show the grateful shape of his heart no matter the rest. Part of him wondered if the deal could be changed, but he doubted it; for all his experiences with lawyers and agreements, terms weren't often negotiable.

The being was still waiting for him when he returned, just as he'd left it. Again, he entered the ring of its court. This time, it was hanging back, tilting its head, cautious, almost questioning. Jakob could taste a sadness in his mind suddenly, a confusion, and he hadn't realized it wasn't wholly his own.

"Please forgive me," he said softly, bowing at the waist. "I didn't know. I didn't understand. I didn't run because I'm not thankful or don't want to honor you…it's just…I wasn't born…a…a son. I'm the last, but my father knew I couldn't do this, so he didn't tell me…because I can't fulfill the terms."

The glen was silent and humid as a coffin. He sensed no comprehension in the immortal stars of its gaze.

"I'm…" He kept trying. "My body isn't right. I would do anything for my home, if I could, but I…" Oh no. The tears were coming again. But the strange clamor of the being's thoughts suddenly shuddered through him, itching under his skin like a wave of spiders and sunshine.

Change. Around him, the being started to pace, as if asking him to move with it.

He didn't understand, turning, trying to face it. Was it expecting him to undress? Would he have to bare himself to make this presence comprehend? Resolved, he slipped off his shirt, baring his binder for the first time. The cool breeze on his shoulders was a relief, even if the vulnerability made him shake. "Do you see?" There was no answer. His face burned hotter, crimson sneaking down his neck and over his chest; agitated, mourning, he wriggled out of even his binder then, chest naked under the sky for the first time since he'd been six, all its soft flesh.

You…seed, the creature declared, more insistently, still trotting to and fro.

"What…? I?" It still wanted…? Mortified but desperate, he slid down his pants. Naked! There! He fought steadiness into his voice, wretched and embarrassed. "Okay, do you understand? I don't have the equipment. God, I wish I did! But, I…I'm not…"

No… Its head swayed closer, antlers tilted as if the berries and flowers twined there were a gift bouquet. Jakob, hesitating, found himself reaching out. A fluttered whisper kissed his mind like those petals to his fingertips, warm as the sunshine. ***You…always enough.***

Eyes stinging, Jakob froze.

It was the first time anyone had…

Quietly, gently, he rested his palm to the heat of its head, the soft moss and smooth stone. And he held himself there in silence, awed, as if

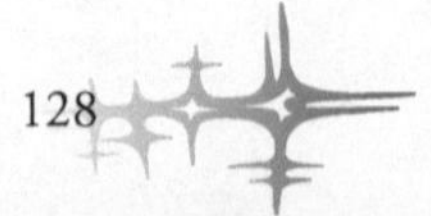

he'd been allowed to caress a god.

The touch set off a ripple, an uproar of transformation. Jakob gasped, jerking back—the being's body *snik-snak* ground in a new symphony of metamorphosis. Legs eroded, then sprouted hooves to paws to pincers, fungus falling away and re-fruiting, multicolored mushroom caps rippling up and down a rapidly shortening spine.

It turned to face him, now upright on two legs like a goat's. Torso and arms dwindle-popped into something almost man-like, though its head, spinning into place atop the neck, remained roughly deer-shaped, those burning eyes set deep into hollows. At the end of this almost-faun's arms, five fingers bloomed of woody bone and tendon-vine, each clicking a playful rhythm against one another. And as the creature shivered with glee, something else new bloomed between its legs: a mushroom pushing horizontally from the earth, shaft as thick as the cap, a pillar seeping with a syrupy amber. The strange phallus swung joyfully as it rose to point toward Jakob's nakedness, trails of spores puffing in its wake.

"Hnhhh?" Jakob managed in all intelligence. Hot dizziness blanketed his senses as he breathed the shimmering air.

Change! was the word that rung through him again. Images flooded his mind: a hundred butterflies emerging from the chrysalis. Flowers growing from seed to bloom.

Jakob collapsed to his knees, eyes swimming as the almost-faun padded nearer, as that thick liquid dribbled down its shiny phallus and as his own juices started to drip freely on the grass to match. "I..." he rasped, both awed and afraid. To be seeded, to be the one bearing life...he...he couldn't...

But the creature's rough, woody fingers only caressed his cheek. Jakob leaned into that sun-touched earth and soft moss, full of happy memories in that smell, loving in spite of himself. And slowly, lilac bloomed from that strange wrist. The petals grew, fell, cascaded tenderly over his hair.

A sole, gentle thought tickled up through his mind, firm as an unmoving mountain:

Beautiful.

Jakob's breath caught, tears finally breaking their bounds and spilling over. "Do you understand what I'm afraid of, if I honor the agreement this way?"

You…safe.

Jakob wept, but the reassurance bloomed soft and sure in his chest. "Okay," he whispered. The being brushed its slick, spongey erection across his lips, base wreathed still in little white flowers, kissing a hot trail across his cheek. He inhaled deeply, head spinning, almost deliriously content. It smelled sweet and earthy, his mouth watering in spite of his newness.

He let the tip pass between his lips, sampling it with a lick.

The spirit shivered so hard that it nearly lost its form. Pebbles clicked to the dirt, leaves shaking loose. And the sap was as delicious as it smelled, thick, smokey honey trailing down to his stomach—Jakob moaned involuntarily, a trail of fire burning through his chest. His pelvic muscles shifted, loosening, a fresh wave of slick dribbling down his thighs. Suddenly the creature pressed him to the grass—then it was on him, whickering its strange sigh, grasping his body and testing, stroking, every inch of skin a dozen new soft root arms could suddenly reach. His nipples went rigid as he cried out, the hard flat of its stone muzzle gently tracing down his throat, warm from the fading summer light still. Slowly the fire of this touch traced down his sternum, vines snaking from its body, lashing Jakob's arms up and out of the way.

His back arched as his legs were spread wider—as if a willing offering on an altar, and he couldn't help squirming, gasping inside sweet pollen—then the creature dipped down and the warmth of a stone snout kissed his most sensitive spot. Lightning shocked up into his core. "Yes…" he moaned, a plea to the twilight stars above.

The creature lifted itself to tower like a proud oak. The full moon had crested dusk's horizon, and its twin-star gaze burned just as bright beneath, the word of consent spoken, the contract sealed.

Its hips aligned as it thrust into him with no further preamble.

Jakob's eyes bulged, a wild moan tearing out of his chest. A deep ache resounded, suddenly invaded to the hilt—if he hadn't been so wanting, it might have hurt more, but the pain was as quick to fade as it had come. The burning shaft almost felt like it was *squirming*. Every blade of grass on the creature's body stood upright as it joined gleefully, its pride seeping in through Jakob's mind. And as it locked itself to him, its fluids gushed through him in a thick wave. It coated him, everything inside burning and throbbing.

The being started to piston, to coat its essence all the way up to the womb, stirring it into a froth. Jakob convulsed with pleasure. He moaned as its heavy body slapped wet against his, the sweet substance smearing between them, drenching his pelvis.

Oh my god. Oh my god. He cried out wordlessly, these prayers to the being above and inside grinding him to the grass, covering him in dirt and petals, and he laughed in dizzy freedom. He started to raise his hips to meet each thrust, wanting that throbbing, wet, hungry impaling as deep as it could go. *Take me.* Giddiness rose higher as the being lifted his body up with its gentle vines, never pausing its messy plunder, bringing him to sit on its lap so it could yank his hips up and down with two, then four desperate hands encasing his chest.

Jakob came moments later, squirming, such a powerful electricity rising that he was whimpering to the sky, back arched. His body sung at his most vulnerable points, the hard nubs of his nipples, and the swollen stub between his legs rubbed with the creature's shaft with each thrust.

Change! the word sung again inside him. His skin trembled as if it was coming alive, like it too would ripple and shiver as the creature's mossy coat had when it transformed.

We are change! The magic swarmed under his skin like ants, and he howled as the sticky fluids inside scorched at his organs, the fire spreading rapidly through his fingers and toes, his spine, to the crown of his head.

We are change! He wrapped his fingers into that grass-body and felt it shred underneath and stain his flesh. Panting, eyes flashing with colors, he saw it bloom anew, plush and soft under each palm. The overpowering scent of lilac drowned him.

WE ARE CHANGE!

A soft light spilled from inside Jakob's skin as he received the magic of life, chanting into his neurons. He yelled out as he writhed, as he erupted with another explosion of pleasure, no longer sure where he ended and his lover began. All he knew was that for this precious, beautiful moment…

…he was all lives and all seasons and all seeds and all songs…

I…I am change…

Jakob's eyes rolled back in his head. Letting out a sigh as if he were breathing for the very first time, he began to transform.

The creature's long phallus withdrew, throbbing and hot and spurting, glistening with passion. Jakob's long wail of pleasure deepened and burrowed rough into his throat. So much of that magic was *sloshing* inside. Vertebrae popped. Muscles pulsed and shifted and tightened, soft fat melting into new places, but none of it hurt, all of it was the most righteous song he'd ever felt. The softness of his chest collapsed, the tissue flowing and reforming. Where the magic seed gushed from his body, the flesh grew warm before it simply merged like hot butter. He cried out again, for nothing was gentle about how his genitals swelled, gorging with blood and new flesh, pounding and throbbing and rising out of him like the season's harvest craning to reach the sky.

He nearly blacked out, first from realizing what was happening, and then at the soul-shaking rush of pleasure to feel it happen so *fast*. All he could do was helplessly whimper and look up at his mate, his teacher, his lover, his god, his home. It watched him, too, with what could still distinctly be scented as *pride*. Jakob keened as his erection filled out and solidified, this last part of his body, barely hanging on to the rush of power—and then the dizzy spell ended, and he gasped in the cooling night air, realizing the stars seemed so bright and close.

His fingertips brushed his body, new. His chest had hair! Absolute tufts of it. The hair on his scalp had erupted in the frenzy, too, once close to his ears, now spilling in a pool around his shoulders, shiny and healthful. His thighs were so firm! His…

He couldn't bring himself to touch between his legs yet, but he could feel it anyway: an aching throbbing, a craving new and hungry in his gut. And beneath it, soft flesh prickled, churning, a sack burning with all of the magical seed the creature had sealed in his body.

Beautiful, the creature spoke, and Jakob laughed, and Jakob cried. He rose, wobbly, on knees uncertain as a newborn foal's.

"I'm…!" His voice cracked, and he laughed again, hearing a stranger, and yet hearing himself for the first time. "I'm me!"

The creature's stone hooves nicked an impatient tap-prance out on the ground; it tilted its head as if confused. *You were always you*, the look seemed to say. *Appearance is a formality.* It turned, switching the ferns of its tail, presenting its rump again. Its phallus hadn't sagged even a little; but underneath it, now, a soft slit was opening and dripping sweet sap down earthy faun-legs. The creature's flesh rippled as its back arched,

and six new arms caught it as it came low to the earth, kneeling, snorting, presenting itself.

"You still want…?" Jakob barely could shuffle forward, the transformation making his muscles quake, exhausted. But he found himself pressing tight to the offering of earth, smiling stupidly, running his palms up the being's rippling spine and enjoying its melodic chitter-clack. Flowers bloomed where he touched, and as he pressed their sweet kiss to his nostrils, they withered, replaced by rapidly swelling red berries. On instinct, he brushed them with his lips, let the cool, firm fruit break on his teeth and stain sweetness to his tongue. Crimson dribbled down his chin, and he sucked the strange, delicate offering, feeling drunk.

Vines wrapped softly around his thighs, pressing him tight and close.

"Okay," he whispered, willing to give this lifelong companion anything in the world. The way his tip slipped inside, it was barely with conscious thought, as if his body were tied to this singular destiny. "Ohhh!" It almost made his eyes roll back again, the warmth, the wet embrace. Churning, pulsing need quivered at the root of his shaft, deep in the soft sack, urging him to drive deeper.

"Ohhhh!" he sighed again in revelation as he obeyed, toes curling. The hot slick burned up his tip, through the deep nerves, settling into an electric tug with even the slightest motion. Sudden overwhelm made his breath catch, his eyes spill over with wet trails. Smiling, panting, squirming, he fell forward and hugged the shivering living earth, burrowing his nose into clover and smearing his tears as if he were hiding secrets. Again he thrust, crying out into the fertile loam. The being's electric aura-crackle rang at the roots of every hair in his body, its approval a happy song humming inside his teeth. The vines around his hips squeezed. He could only find the freedom of movement to draw himself back but halfway before thrusting to the hilt again.

Oh—it wanted to make sure he wouldn't… *couldn't* disengage.

Wanted his offering.

He laughed, the sound gibbering, strange, and free. He would never have thought to do anything else. Should the land itself open up and swallow him whole, letting him die inside the body he'd always wanted to live in, he would have accepted it. It had given him everything, and then it had given him more, and he loved—*loved* the animal pleasure of burrowing into wet heat and claiming a mate, the smell of sweat and the sweetness of the lilac, the moon and the stars shining on his naked joy. If this was the old faith, then he would pledge himself body and soul.

The beast whickered, then sang in the voice of a hundred blackbirds taking flight. Its insides convulsed and sucked at him until his eyes almost rolled back in his head.

I can't…I can't hold it…oh fuck…I can't…

"Th…*thank you*," was all he could manage as a boiling pressure thundered higher, seizing his spine. The vines dug so hard into his ass that he knew they would bruise, but he didn't care. His body collapsed from under him, quavering, one final thrust in deep, wrapping his arms tight around the earth and refusing to let go.

The wet surge up his tip was so unusual, so new, so right. Deep his seed erupted from his body forged in magic and desire. Back into its giver, it nestled, deep into the womb of creation.

All one. You to me. Me to you.

That's how it was always meant to be, right?

He held close, happy, breath slowing. The warm night kept creeping past, and he closed his eyes, quietness settling over his soul, and—

Jakob awoke come morning. He didn't remember falling asleep—only that, suddenly, soft, cold light flickered through his eyelids. Up he rose from the ground, body aching and stiff. Something in his nose was shiver-cold, like drying leaves and coming frost, the approach of a new season. The spirit was no longer in his arms, and the grassy clearing rounded by sacred stones, in dawn's first faint light, was yellower than he remembered.

Naked, Jakob curled into himself, dead leaves shuddering off his form as he frantically looked for his clothes, confused and—

He stilled. There was a mound at the far end of the clearing, one that shifted ever so subtly, a moving collection of dirt and rocks. The vines, so vibrant in the night… Jakob's breath caught. They were cracking away. Where before the spirit had been plush and green, moss was crumbling, clover decaying and thin. The gorgeous eyes were now sputtering sparks sunk deep into their hollows—turning to meet him from where they'd quietly watched the rising sun. Even the worn, ancient pictographs decorating its skull seemed fainter in the dawn.

"But…" Jakob was on his clumsy, half-numb feet without thought, hurrying to touch, to embrace. The spirit turned to him fully on eight

spindly legs, and as it did so, pebbles and clods of dirt cascaded from its belly, like its root systems were no longer alive enough to hold it all together.

"Don't hurt yourself!" Jakob cried out in alarm, almost skinning his knees to rest beside it.

But he could feel something like a laugh fluttering in the back of his brain. It was…

It was so happy.

"But I thought…" Jakob swallowed, mourning. "You're dying! I thought…"

Its stone face rotated a good 90 degrees, silent, perplexed. Then it leaned that cold forehead against his, softly, so softly. Images came to Jakob's mind: a grove of trees changing color, a creek slowly freezing.

Winter, it seemed to say. *This is the way it has always been.*

And with that, the creature pressed its scratchy, dry body past his as it began to walk away. Earth dropped from it with each step, moss disintegrating and puffing off into dust, until its legs simply crumbled out from under it. Unperturbed, the earth that composed that collapsing pile shifted and changed until it was a snake again, small and tenuous now, coiled up as if to consider how it wanted to spend its precious motion past this point.

"You have to go?" Jakob whispered, lost. Despite the cooling soil, under his searching fingers, there was a strange warmth in its core, like lifeblood secret and safe. He stopped shaking.

Oh. I gave you the seed…of life.

"Do you take it under the earth?" he rasped. "During the winter, to keep it safe? So your lands bloom next year?"

A sense of contentment and approval washed over him, relaxing, warm.

"So we…" He flushed. "We do this *every* year, huh?"

The contentment grew warmer still. He blushed harder, squirming…and he was still transformed. Was this permanent? How would he explain…? Would he even need to? The Bauers kept to themselves, and the small town…they never looked too close.

A sleepy statuesqueness was settling into that serpentine body. Before he could say anything more, additional images flooded into Jakob's mind, an overwhelming parting remark:

The joy of those reaching to mates in their winter dens, the storage of seeds to survive the cold, the births of the spring.

Jakob made an embarrassed, questioning noise, sinking deeper against the ground. Stupid idea: pebbles dug up against his butt cheeks and made him wince. He didn't move, though. He really hadn't thought he would ever be able to have children the way his parents had, and…and oh, oh god, there was a very beautiful woman who'd given him her contact information and asked to bring him picnic lunches, and suddenly, that was all he could think of: her jet-black hair and pink-flushed shoulders.

A faint yet powerful wave of smugness wafted through Jakob from where the creature was coiled.

"Whoa, wait! You're really just going to roll over and go to sleep? I've got questions!" He gestured frantically between his legs. "How does this even…?!"

It didn't answer, neither in feeling or mind. The earth was entirely still, a pile of rocks sprouting little tufts of dead grass.

And yet, Jakob could still taste faint petrichor on his tongue, the earth of his home.

He leaned down, gratefully kissing the cool stone. It felt a pledge. "I'll see you next summer, then," he whispered, and rose, looking to the dawn.

A Promise Given to the God of War

Nicole Doen

deity, f/nb, fantasy, first person point of view, frottage, getting together, jealousy, non-binary, performer, pining, present tense, public sex, religion, size difference, tentacles, tentacle in vagina sex

There are three requirements a Bliss must meet if they wish to perform their pleasure upon the Gilded Stage: one must be beautiful, one must excel at their work, and one must awe the empress with the ingenuity of their performance. There are many ways by which one might approach such a challenge, but for my coin, few are as skilled at sussing out the empress's desires as the person on that stage right now.

I suppose that explains why they are the empress's Bliss while the rest of us perform in public theaters or private chambers.

Their name is Evalan, and they aren't what one would imagine a Bliss should look like. Their hair is short, a middling shade of blonde, and their eyes are what anyone would call a hazy, indistinct blue. Their features are not sharp, nor cute, nor enchanting, and they are not the

boldest of performers, a title which might better fit any number of individuals in our line of work. What they are is captivating, though. One brush of their hands down the delicate planes of their torso, over the gentle flare of their hip or between their legs, is enough to drag the attention of even the most buttoned-down courtier in the audience.

They have, of course, long won the empress's eye, something I have held against them for many long years now, with nowhere to discharge that frustration. The empress is shockingly loyal, and Evalan has been ruthless in holding this coveted position.

I don't even want it, coveted or not. The Gilded Stage, the adulation of the empress's myriad courtiers, these things don't matter to me. I'm satisfied with my current place. What matters is what I could do with hundreds of sets of eyes on me and me alone. Even just a single chance on that stage would be enough.

The crowd gasps as one, returning my attention to the perfect, extraordinary performance taking place before my eyes. Evalan is now kneeling on the stage, their body curved, hiding their nakedness from the crowd as they bite their own arm to muffle the sound of their release. They turn their neck gracefully and look at the crowd with damp eyes, their hair plastered to the back of their neck.

One of the courtiers nearest to me presses their palm to their lap.

For tonight, I have seen enough. No matter how they might twist their body in sinuous ecstasy, I feel no stirring of desire in my own breast, no throb low in my gut as my cunt warms and grows wet with need.

As sticky heat builds within the theater, the fetid, floral musk of this season's most popular perfume fills the room. Too close. Too much. A headache blooms behind my eyes, pulsing rhythmically. The scent is so thick that it begins to coat the back of my throat, making me want to gag.

I offer a frivolous prayer to Vetthar that something more delicate will soon find favor among the nobility.

Eventually, the pain in my head pulls me to my feet. This act alone inspires numerous catcalls as I slip between tables, as though they believe I'm leaving to rub myself to completion free from their prying eyes. My skirts move about my legs in a heavy sweep. The courtiers, emboldened, skim their fingers over the flowing silk. Despite how delicate each layer is, I cannot feel the courtiers' touches through the whole of them, and I

am glad for it.

I near the theater's exit when the courtiers begin to clap and shout for Evalan.

It's only then that I hear words I had long lost hope of hearing. Blood pulses in my temples, loud enough to muffle Evalan's words of gratitude and more.

"As some of you may have guessed or discovered through naughtier means"—at this, the crowd laughs, as they no doubt intended—"this was my last performance for you as the empress's Bliss." Boos and groans of displeasure greet their words. They wait until the crowd settles to continue. Despite hearing this announcement with my own ears, I hardly believe it. "You mustn't begrudge me a touch of romance in my life, can you? She wooed me so well. How could I say no?" To prove their own happiness, Evalan offers the empress a besotted smile. "But the empress looks forward to choosing another to replace me on the stage. I look forward to helping her make that important decision. Any Bliss who wishes to may perform once for Her Highness. When she has chosen the one she prefers, the competition will end."

Desire finally blooms within me.

Hope, too.

Some have accused me of coldness, have told me that I'll never ascend to true greatness until I find it in my heart to love the courtiers back. This, I think, is not true. In the pursuit of my goal, it's not whatever greatness they would bestow upon me that I seek. All I need is the platform this opportunity provides.

The headache that had begun to drag at me dissipates as excitement and purpose kill the discomfort.

There's one place in this wretched city that no one would expect me to go, especially not on a night as exciting as this one. It will offer me the space and privacy to lay out my request. More importantly, it's the one place I feel I will be seen—and seen properly. It's my favorite place in the city, and it's the only place I feel truly at home.

Sneaking into an abandoned temple ought to be sacrosanct, but I choose to believe that Vetthar will better see me here than anywhere else.

At the very least, I feel they mustn't condemn my boldness, because I have not yet been struck down for my audacity. I prefer to believe that means Vetthar enjoys my company, too.

You see, I am the last remaining devotee of Vetthar's, my gods of war, my gods of sacrifice and peace and creation.

Anyone would consider this a contradiction, I might wager, but they simply don't understand Vetthar's purpose, nor why they should return to the mortal realm. If someone were to ask me why, I wouldn't have a satisfying answer for anyone but myself.

The truth is, I simply want to know them as the priestesses of old knew them. I want to love them in that way, too. They fought for us, and they left us behind, and I want to fight for them. I want to bring them back. At least, I want them to know there's still someone in the world who cares about them.

Our intimacy might be one-sided, but I like to believe they enjoy the songs I sing, the baubles I craft in their honor, the food and drink I nab from finer tables than mine to spread across their tripartite altar. They never answer, but I embrace hope with every visit. As always, I think of the tales of old, grand poetry that told of the days when a Bliss was the only worshippers the gods needed. We didn't cavort to pointless ends with the nobility, stabbing one another in the back for prestige. Blisses mattered for more than just the entertainment they offered.

I wish I could have lived during those days.

As my silk robes pool around my feet, I murmur my secret to the wind. I cannot imagine Vetthar will hear it, wherever they are, but I speak regardless. "What will it take for you to love me back?"

My wildest hope of all is in believing I can return us to those days.

Such is the sort of thing only the empress's Bliss could bring back into fashion.

After I've finished my devotions and bathed, I turn my attention to the study of an ancient priestess's confessions. I keep the original tome in the crumbling library where I found it, but this is a carefully constructed copy of that manuscript, created for my own use. I bring it with me to my favorite spot in the temple, the stage upon which this same priestess

may well have coupled with Vetthar's corporeal form. Here, I light the lamp I keep for such purposes and lounge on the furniture I've moved here slowly over the years.

A staid, dryly amused laugh startles me from my reading. I can only tell how long I've been at it by the ache in my back and the ever-deepening night. The laugh belongs to Evalan, which I register only belatedly, my head still full of the intense descriptions of the priestess's devotions.

The musk of Evalan's perfume tickles at my nose. At least this stage stands within an amphitheater. A cool breeze cuts its overwhelming scent and drives it away.

"The old practices oughtn't be plundered for sport," they tell me, as though I don't know what the old practices ought to be used for.

I close the book, place it on the empty stretch of seat beside me, hoping Evalan sees the rejection of their presence for what it is. Arrayed around me are used sheets of paper, each filled with carefully inked sigils and signs. Love letters, they might be called. These, I gather up and retain hold of while Evalan gazes at the book.

Though my attempt at binding it is unpolished, made by a hand clearly unused to the craft, I treasure the object almost as much as the words stored within it. On the cover, Vetthar is depicted in their triplicate form, etched in gold, each body entwined. The artist—again, me—was not competent in her replication of the most famous painting of Vetthar to exist, but she certainly tried her best.

"The old practices were given to us," I reply. "Why shouldn't I use them?"

"Neither the empress nor the monks will approve."

The monks. They do little except ruminate on the evils of the world from within their joyless monasteries and rope others into similar beliefs by telling them the gods do not care for them. Seeing that it has been several generations since a deity has walked among us, I understand why this may have happened. We have enjoyed peace within the city; I see no reason not to attribute it to those who bought it for us in the first place. Many have disagreed, sometimes vehemently, sometimes quietly, as with the slow dying out of the priesthood. As for the empress, she need only enjoy the performance. What I do is not sport, not the competition others will see it as. I only need one chance, not the security of a permanent position.

"But the court will." Any time someone shows a flair for the dramatic, the court has loved them for it. I know this, because I've refrained from giving it to them for so long. And though they've loved that, too, they never loved it enough to get me on that stage any other way. "I'm willing to bet the empress won't care enough one way or the other as long as you don't express disapproval."

"What makes you think I won't?"

"You don't care either."

Their laugh is intoxicating, but I've imbibed so many intoxicants in my life that I've gained immunity. "No wonder everyone loves you even if they would prefer to loathe you. You're so refreshingly straightforward about everything."

I would scoff, but I'm not completely ignorant as to where my appeal lies. If I weren't liked at all, I wouldn't have made it this far. But love? If this is love, it's not the kind I want. My eyes see further. My heart aches for more. If this is love, I'll use it to push for the love I want.

To touch a god, I need to draw their attention to this earth by whatever means available to me. Though Blisses are not what they once were, I can do as Blisses of the past did. With a large enough audience, perhaps that will be enough to draw Vetthar's eye.

Evalan picks up the book and sits next to me. "May I?" they ask, too late for me to decline. "What exactly are you planning to do?" Flipping the pages, they press their lips together in a smirk as they find the diagrams and cramped commentaries I was so diligently studying. "I see."

I don't flush, the only mercy Vetthar shows me in the face of such crassness. I don't scowl, either, though I take credit for that restraint.

"You don't care for the empress and you don't care for the monks who have shunned our indulgences. I think you barely tolerate the court. Why do you want to entertain them in this way?"

If they cannot guess at the degree of devotion I hold in my heart, that's their problem. "I simply think nobody else will do such a thing. Even if I can't win the stage, who will blame me for wanting to stand out?"

"I shouldn't tell you this," they admit, "but I enjoy your work. I think you have potential." Their fingers skim over the images before them. "But why go to this much trouble? If it doesn't work, you will be made

a fool, and if it does…"

If it does, I will have called down war.

I can't hold my tongue on this point.

"Vetthar isn't what you think." They might also be called valor and guardianship and grim necessity. War in three parts. War brought to one's doorstep against one's will. War fought against one's worst impulses. War waged against injustice. They are the truest of gods, and my most beloved.

"Vetthar turned their back on the world," Evalan says, callous. Their words are a sword they think they wield against me, but I see it for what it is, a useless toy, blunted. It's nothing to fear. "Why would they turn their attentions to you?"

There are Blisses more enchanting than me, more beautiful, more likely to win the most prized position a Bliss can take. This is true. But if I can show the court what a devotee of Vetthar can do, perhaps they will better appreciate what they have lost. "I have nothing to lose by trying."

"You have everything to lose," Evalan says. "Your vocation. Your reputation."

These things are meaningless in the face of what I could win. For Vetthar alone, I stir with desire. To waste this chance to display it would be sacrosanct.

The net of gossip ensnares me within minutes of my return from the temple to the Blisses' Quarters. Each time I hear the bits and pieces of whispered conversation occurring outside this or that building, I pretend I'm not as eager to slide into that freshly opened slot as they are.

None of them try to draw me into their conversation, at least not until I reach the tea shop where many of us eat our meals when we're not performing. There, I find Caral already holding court among the copse of trees behind the shop, almost as haughty as the empress herself as he regales his audience with the juiciest tidbits he's uncovered. Though I attempt to bypass his attentions, hoping to take a seat at one of the more distant tables on the opposite side of the garden, they fall on me immediately.

He beckons me over with a broad, beaming grin and a warm wave of his hand. "Assa, dearest," he says, clutching both of my hands. "Would that we all could fall in love as thoroughly as the empress has, hmm?"

He says this to me because he's one of the few who understands how little I care for such romantic notions and likes teasing me about it. The handful of Blisses already at his table sigh and remark about it among themselves. A few more listen in from the pond nearby.

Perhaps my determination is too clear on my face, because he squeezes my hands and gestures for me to sit. "You have something big planned already, do you not?"

"Where did you hear that?"

"Not everyone sneaks away from court to visit Vetthar's temple." When I glare even more obviously, he shrugs. "I hear things."

I would ask from whom he heard these so-called things, but it's obvious enough who has spread the news around. Evalan does think me a fool or worse.

He leans forward, elbows on the table, and balances his chin on his knuckles. "So?"

"I'm planning…" I lean in, too, letting myself be pushed around by Evalan's machinations. I could never have gotten for myself as much interest as Evalan has generated for me. I might have thought this impromptu competition for court's Bliss was enough, but Caral's involvement will ensure all eyes are on me when the time comes. "…something blasphemous."

Caral laughs. Snatching up the cup nearest to him, presumably tea, but maybe not, he presses the rim briefly to his temple in acknowledgment. "To upsetting the monks and scandalizing the courtiers. May your performance do all that and more."

If I had a drink, I might toast to that.

How does one love a god enough to pull them down to earth?

As I stand behind the Gilded Stage, looking upon a raucous audience that Caral has primed for my presumed failure, I wonder, too. He really didn't have to spread quite this much hype on my behalf. The only form of relief I feel is in knowing the Bliss currently performing has bored the audience near to death. That ought to be good for me.

My mind cannot help but focus on the frivolous details, like how the gray wood out of which the stage has been constructed looks so cheap from so close. Or the glow of golden sunlight spilling from behind the drawn-tight curtains. It will be sunset soon, the daylight wasted if I'm not allowed to step foot on stage when I'm supposed to.

Vetthar has always preferred the warm light of daytime, everything out in the open. It will already stifle them to come into a building rather than remain out of doors.

Though my thoughts are too agitated to wander off, I find myself surprised when polite clapping indicates the end of the current performance. A handful of servants scrub at the wood and put down the mat I left with them earlier in the day.

Drawing in a deep, steadying breath, I step onto the stage, my feet bare on the cold wood.

Before the courtiers, I remove my robes and kneel on the stage, alone and unadorned. A disappointment to be sure. Though they whisper, confused by the lack of ceremony and pomp, I pay them little attention. They will get their time's worth soon enough, or so I hope.

In preparation, I've spent several days eating only that which will appeal to Vetthar: honeyed seafruit, principally, but also sugared flower petals caught from the tallest limbs of the tallest vetta trees, and the delicately pale teas that taste of the grass on which Vetthar stood when they won their land wars. I meditated. I did not touch myself nor allow anyone else to touch me.

This isn't a requirement prescribed in the text I've so carefully copied, bound, and studied, but I like the thought of reserving myself only for them.

As a result, I feel more eagerness than I expect, a warmth growing low in my abdomen as I anticipate what I will have wrought if this works…

But it has to work first.

The vows are easy. I speak them aloud in a low drone, the words already worn smooth by the hours I spent memorizing them. At the same time, I begin to mark my skin with the sacred ink that will open myself to Vetthar's sight. Those love letters I wrote on paper before become tattoos now.

The silvered-black ink slides like ice across my clavicles, under my breasts, between my thighs. It shimmers in the candlelight and carries the scent of night-blooming bloodwood, a clean, clarifying fragrance. I have read that the hilt of Vetthar's sword featured the image of bloodwood etched into it. I hope this is true. Regardless, the scent is comforting to me.

Body ready, I close my eyes.

I wait.

Long minutes pass.

And nothing happens.

The air grows charged with the audience's burgeoning impatience.

I may have been wrong about this after all.

My patience is rewarded by the subtle shift of air, the clatter of something against the wood floor, the slick sound of…

…of what?

Gasps and startled cries rise from the audience. My eyes fly open.

A column of light stretches to the ceiling, bright enough to flay my vision, pulsing and coruscating inhumanly. Wing-like appendages extend to either side of the room, skimming the walls. They shine, too, illuminating each and every face in the theater.

Every piece of art I've ever seen of Vetthar speaks to their beauty. Their human beauty, elevated to godhood, but two legs, two arms, a head and mouth and two eyes only. Vetthar of the sea dripping in vibrant blue. Vetthar of the land wrapped in brightest red. Vetthar of the sky limned in scouring white. Human beauties tripled, masculine and feminine and neither or both depending on how one saw it.

This creature is not that. This is the creature of the oldest descriptions. Vetthar, from before the first war of the cosmos split them into three beings, the better to fight for all parts of the world.

The light dims, and the creature folds itself nearly in half to look me in the eye. As my eyes adjust, I notice more about them. Six spreading wings, feathers shining in a muted rainbow of shades from cream to a deep, rich brown, honor the part of them that once conquered the air. Six tentacles, thicker than a squid's but otherwise quite similar, honor the sea they also tamed for their chosen people. Six long arms, startlingly human, appendages that hold the sword that once brought peace to the

land, reach for me. How such a slim torso can carry the weight of these disparate parts, I cannot say. Yet again, I am awed by their power.

Their face—if it can be called a face—holds eighteen glowing eyes, if I'm counting right. They blink in unison.

"You have summoned us." Their three voices entwine as one, deep as the sea, melodious as a singer's, as light as a bird taking to the sky. "Why?"

My own voice is stolen by the surprise I feel, the quivering fear. Arousal wells within me.

One hand reaches forward to skim my cheek, its fingers long and slender, big enough to wrap around my neck. Their innate light dims further, and I note that their skin is the same warm-toned olive shade as mine.

Only the other limbs, sleek and wet, are another color entirely: as blue-gray as the ocean on a tempestuous day.

Their hand is cool, soft, gentler than I expect given its size.

"We know you," they say, stroking my skin, rhythmic as the tide. "So determined to worship us."

To my shame, I turn my face into their touch. I'm not the sort to capitulate during performances, but I would do so now. Will soon do so, if I have correctly read the intent in their voice, their gaze.

Warmth floods my cheeks.

"You are pleasing enough to the eye." Their voices would shake the theater if they raised them in a shout. As it is, it's just shy of too loud for comfort. "What do you wish of us?"

I had assumed I would summon their three human forms if I succeeded. That's how the records all refer to them in the legends and histories detailing their appearance during their earthbound exploits. Seeing this form before me, I must throw that plan out, mustn't I?

A true believer would say they only wish to serve, but how can I serve them like this? The truth, or a version of it, forms in my mind, and given their divinity, they can probably sense it. Images flash before my eyes, illicit, explicit.

I want them to perform with me. Even like this. I want to tie them as firmly to the earth as I can—bring back the old ways. I want to be their Bliss, and I want everyone here to know it.

Before I can say these words aloud, they wrap those long fingers around my neck just like I'd imagined them capable of doing. Their nails, sharpened to points, prick the fragile stretch of skin under my jaw. They do not squeeze. They wouldn't need to, if they wanted me dead.

Despite the fear that bubbles within me a second time, my core warms with further arousal. Wetness clings to my spread thighs. Only the slightest shift in how I'm kneeling would expose this fact to the courtiers. Vetthar moves behind me and crouches low, bringing their body against mine. One of their arms wraps around my waist and tugs me backward into their embrace.

My legs sprawl clumsily. In the silence of the room, the only sound is the thump of my heels and buttocks against the wood floor of the stage.

Two more of their arms bend my knees and splay my thighs, exposing me directly to the courtiers. For the first time since becoming a Bliss, I long to turn away. This is too vulnerable a position, too exposing. The courtiers look at us with curiosity, revulsion, and not a small amount of desire.

"Behave well for us," Vetthar says. Their voices rumble soothingly my chest. The stinging scrape of their nails down my inner thighs tells me I mustn't run from this. I don't want to, not really. I'm just embarrassed by my reaction to them. When have I ever submitted so easily to another?

Though I expect at least one of their hands to find the wet heat of my cunt, they focus on touching every other centimeter of me until I pant and squirm at each brush of their knuckles over my body.

Throbbing with want, I twist in their hold and rock my hips, gaining only a modicum of relief from the exertion. The courtiers lean forward and sigh. A few brush their hands over the smooth, rich velvets stretched across their laps.

"Stay still." They look down at me, their eyes luminous. I can only do as they say, muscles trembling as I obey. "Good."

I thrill at the praise.

"How little preparation you need."

I hope the courtiers cannot see the color that must be flooding my face and spreading down my body. My awe and humiliation should not be for them. And yet, it must be. It's almost better for it.

One of their tentacles, cool, thickly muscled, and wet with slick, slides up my leg from ankle to groin before settling lightly between my folds. I had forgotten about those particular appendages. Vetthar of the

sea, I must assume. Whether I'm meant to or not, I shift, rubbing myself against it. Even that little taste of stimulation is almost too much.

The tentacle retreats, wraps teasingly around the back of my knee. "Much too eager."

If they mean to be cruel, they couldn't have chosen a better method. At the loss of this stimulation, I whimper, clenching at nothing. "Please." Much too eager indeed. I am already overwhelmed by what I want from them.

"Hold yourself open."

Uncoordinated, I spread my legs, feeling humiliated as I expose myself. Vetthar's wings lower around me, but I only have a moment to feel relief at being hidden before the tip of one feather ghosts over my clit. Their touch is too light, but I chase it like I'm new to pleasure, too needful, as they say.

I want everything they'll give to me, even if I'm the one who must bend for it.

"Prove to me you deserve my touch, and perhaps you shall have it."

Turning my face away from the audience, I press my cheek to their chest. Their tripled hearts beat soothingly against my face. The sound calms my nerves.

How can I prove myself to them? What do they want?

They know I've made offerings to them. I've prayed. I've reached for them the way any petitioner might. But that's not all I feel. And now that they have finally come to me, I have grown shy and embarrassed.

They have been my god, a source of strength and companionship, for so many years. They have been with me since I became a Bliss. I've kept their temple. I've honored and treasured their words. I have wanted them as I knew them. I want them in this form, too.

I do not need to become the court's Bliss to have everything. This is enough.

For the first time in more years than I can count, this alone is enough for me. Whether Vetthar gives me what I want is out of my hands.

They hold me closer, dust their wing over my wet cheeks. "Good," they say. "You learn quickly."

I will not sob before a crowd of courtiers, but my emotions splinter before Vetthar. Between the two of us alone, we share this secret.

As though to reward me, one of their tentacles rubs against me again.

As the tip breaches me, it draws forth the sweetened pain I prefer. My heels dig into the stage, slip over the smooth wood. Two more of the tentacles wrap around my legs, holding them in place. The tentacle within me offers a few shallow, probing thrusts, before plunging as deeply inside as it can without breaking me.

Given their size, it isn't much of the tentacle's length, so little of it that I wish I was as large as they are, able to take everything they offer. We could be joined in a way befitting Vetthar's stature.

They hiss, their momentum stalled as their tentacle stills within me. Each of their arms tighten around me. Their wings flick wide and extend to their full length above me, displacing air with a quiet huff.

"You would have made an excellent priestess," they say, voices low.

While several tentacles pluck and twist around my aching nipples, the ones that remain unoccupied tighten around me.

Against my lower back, I feel something unfurl, not unlike the tendrils of a fern, thin and flexible and countless in number. These appendages drag across my spine as Vetthar ruts against me, leaving warm streaks behind. Pushing back, I arch against them, weak from their praise. I want to look, to see what these things between their legs might be and how I might bring Vetthar to pleasure with them, but they are content with this, it seems, because they will not free me from their clutches.

"Please," I cry out, desperate. Overwarm from the many points of contact between us, I sweat and pant, wet all over from our exertions.

The tip of their wing brushes against my mouth, silencing me with a delicate, tickling touch as their feathers spread wide. The feathers shield me from view. Though courtiers shout in dismay at the disruption of their show, Vetthar doesn't care. I don't care either.

"I didn't ask for you to beg," they tell me. Then, they whisper words meant only for me: "You have already given me your truth. I shall share something with you in return."

As they thrust against my back, gasping lightly against my ear, the tentacle within me matches their rhythm. Fresh need washes over me, but it is not my need, too powerful and all-encompassing to belong to me. It is as though I can feel what they feel, and it becomes mine.

Long suppressed desires, hopes, and fears pry open my heart just as Vetthar has opened me physically. I don't think they are my desires, hopes, and fears, but they feel so similar that I cannot help but see myself

in them. If this is what Vetthar has held within them all this time, I can only share in their pain and eagerness. I hope I can assuage both.

I squirm until one arm frees itself from Vetthar's binds, and I gently wrap my hand around one of the tentacles. It returns the embrace, catching my wrist and curling around it. A sigh of relief escapes me as we connect in this way, something beyond the physical. It unlocks something within me.

My body is a canvas across which Vetthar has smeared our mingled fluids, scented lightly of the sea, the sky, the land. I am a mess, and between shouts of ecstasy, I can only laugh, feeling a new lightness within me.

This, I think, is what being cherished must feel like.

I totter close to the edge of my release, unsure whether I am meant to take it as it comes or if I must restrain myself. Vetthar has not been a cruel lover, but they may be a capricious one, prone to mischief and wanting their own way. They are my gods. Of course they should want their own way.

Unbidden, I imagine all the ways they might take me—capricious, imperious, whatever they want to be. My performances could be dedicated to them. Or I could stop performing entirely, because I want to be Vetthar's alone, the priestess I ought to have been.

The tentacle within me fills, hardens, thrusts fast and precise. The head relentlessly strikes the most sensitive places within me. I have never come easily, but for Vetthar, it will happen shockingly soon. I think to beg again, but the bony back of Vetthar's wing turns and presses against my mouth, opening it. I must be careful not to clamp my teeth down for fear of wounding it.

The crowd whines as I am again revealed to them.

I lose track of time, then—the worst thing a Bliss can do. I do not care. The courtiers can think as they will, say what they want afterward. They can walk away, bored, knowing they are not my prime concern any longer. If I cannot replace Evalan, so be it. All the better, in fact.

Vetthar must sense my thoughts, because they tighten their hold on me, push harder into me, use me as I want to be used.

There is only so much that one body can take. Brought to the highest peaks, like a virtuoso completing the performance of a lifetime, one can only tumble. Exhausted, I have reached that point. Orgasm crashes over me. I don't think I could have stopped it even if I wanted to.

Perhaps if Vetthar demanded it, I could have.

They fuck me through it and keep fucking me as I come down.

I don't want to let this moment go, but once climax has come and gone, what else is there? Blisses entice. They offer themselves. The performance ends. Everyone leaves. If they are me, they go home alone.

In my adult life, I have not cried. Tears are for children and those unwilling to do what they must. I am neither.

But tears slip down my cheeks now. I fight Vetthar's hold on me, hoping to dash them away before Vetthar sees, but I'm unsuccessful.

When Vetthar comes, releasing their fluids within me and against my back in a hot, frantic rush, I can only cry harder. As they gently untangle their limbs from my body, my cries fade to whimpers for all the things I still want and cannot have. I wish I could have seen them come. I wish I could make them come in other ways, too. I want to put my mouth on them, my hands. I want to be loved by them again.

They touch my face with hand and wing and tentacle, all gentleness as they wipe away the tears and sweat. I don't know what there is to say, but whatever it is, I should say it.

And then they are gone, and I don't know what to do.

As I look to the audience, standing for me, shouting for me, I know this work is no longer my calling.

Afterward, the courtiers call on me, so many of them that I lose track. From this fact alone, I know even before it has been announced that I have won that which I did not seek. The victory is devoid of meaning, though I smile emptily at the empress when she confers the title of empress's Bliss upon me. I cannot, of course, decline the invitation. Such is life.

In any case, there is renewed interest in pious devotion to Vetthar and other long-forgotten deities. I must be satisfied with that for however long that interest remains kindled. It is a pleasing outcome. The monks are certainly displeased.

My desires bend further toward Vetthar. When I dream, it is of Vetthar's touch and taste and smell. When I touch myself, I think only

of them.

In my imaginings, they come to me sometimes. We are alone in these dreams. I needn't perform for an audience. I can say aloud what I hadn't spoken in real life.

At my first performance as the empress's new Bliss, Evalan sits at the empress's side. Their love makes me ache for my own impossible circumstances.

When I have finished, I am satisfied physically, though I am not satiated emotionally. I do all that I ought to ensure the courtiers are happy. I hope Vetthar watches and wants.

I return home from the performance exhausted, but I eat as I must and drink tea to soothe my nerves. I perform for Vetthar privately, the way any priestess ought to. Perhaps it is because I'm not a proper priestess that they don't condescend to come again. That I might have been a good priestess once has no bearing on the fact that I cannot become one now, for there are no priestesses left to guide me on that particular path.

I wake one morning to discover a spray of bloodwood on my pillow, the flowers fragrant, only just blooming along the length of the thin branch from which they spring. Bloodwood is rare and fine. The trunk of a bloodwood tree is prized for its lustrous sheen; the petals of its flowers are delicate despite their rich, bold redness, like its namesake freshly spilled across a snowy field. I don't know where it came from, for there are no bloodwood trees left in the city, nor any within a reasonable travel distance. I don't even know if there's a bloodwood tree left in this world.

It was said once that the bloodwood's flower was a mark of Vetthar's favor, though in those stories, these tokens were offered to their favorite protectors. I dare not hope to be considered among that class of heroes and lovers.

But certainly, no human would be capable of sneaking into my rooms without me being aware of them.

Over the following days, I receive many, each branch tenderer than the last, as though they're stripping an entire tree for my gratification.

I'm no gardener, but I wonder if there's something I can do with these gifts.

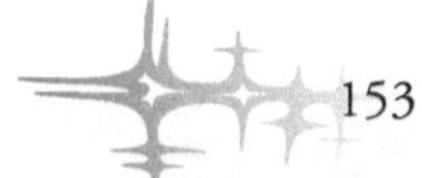

"Shall I recite poetry to you?" I ask the empty air. "I could compose something if you'd like." *How does one woo a god?* I ask myself. I do not know how I succeeded in bringing them down the first time. "Shall I go to war for you, my—"I flush in embarrassment. I cannot say the word that was on the tip of my tongue. *My love—* "Vetthar?"

There have been tales of gods falling in love with humans, but the ones I know have always been such that the humans do not want to love them back. These are tragic tales, irrelevant to me. If any one of them told me how to convince a god to give me the time of day, that would be worth something.

I leave behind my role as the empress's Bliss—the old ways have already fallen out of fashion anyway—and return to the temple to make something of it. Perhaps I cannot form a true priesthood, but I can devote myself fully to this pursuit. I can promise Vetthar that someone will care for this sacred place until she passes. I have books to transcribe and halls to clean. With my earnings as the empress's Bliss, I can even hire stoneworkers to make repairs. I have determination and time enough to turn this stagnant place into a wonderland for Vetthar.

All their favorite things—or what have been so recorded—I bring. Food, drink, dance. Me, if they will have me, but even if they will not, I am theirs.

This is what I can do.

Maybe that's all the temple was, even at the height of its power.

I would go to war if it was asked of me, but the kingdom is safe, well-protected. Vetthar is free to rest and idle as they please. Still, I teach myself the old ways of combat, hoping that will suit their tastes, when I'm not grafting bloodwood branches to the trunks of trees I have been promised are nearly the same. I plant them one by one in the garden at the center of the temple, its beating heart.

I dream, and in my dreams, I ask, "What will it take to convince you?"

They answer, so vivid that I think their voice may be real, "What makes you think you have not?"

I hope Vetthar likes the copse of bloodwood, my way of thanking them for their gifts and their favor. What they give to me, I pray, will be returned to them a thousand-fold. In a hundred years, it might even mature into something worthy of them. Though I do not expect to still be here at that time, they will know I have staked their claim on the world, a reminder to them that the world can still birth that which they could love and would be the closest thing to them, like the hilt of a sword they must always carry on behalf of the world.

For them, I would be like that bloodwood, their truest companion.

I can think of no greater love letter than that.

One morning, my eyes open to find them sprawled on their stomach next to me, their wings almost too big for my cramped bedroom. Their arms hold their upper body aloft. They still don't look human, though their proportions are closer to mine. There are only a few feet of difference between us this time. Their eyes sparkle far more than I remember them sparkling before. The sun will do that, I guess.

"Will you not recite a poem for me?" they ask, flicking one of their wings up to shade my body from the light pooling across my bed through the window. "Your ancient siblings used to leave flowers for me as well. That would be nice." Their many eyes narrow. "Candied flowers, to be more precise. I would have offered some to you, but I'm afraid I don't know how to candy them. I hope you like non-candied flowers. Do you?"

"I do," I repeat, thinking through the implications. "Candied bloodwood flowers? That's what we offered you?" It made sense, of course. No wonder they carry a sword with images of it carved into the hilt. They like bloodwood because people like me gave them gifts of bloodwood. We are as important to them as they are to us.

I'm as important to them as they are to me.

"Mmhmm."

What a sly, dear thing they are.

"We have plenty of them now," I tease. I don't think I've ever felt this light in my life. "Thanks to someone."

"So I've seen."

"And you'll…" It shouldn't be so hard to give voice to my wishes "…visit me?"

When they nod, relief floods me. Vetthar's word is iron, their covenant unbreakable. I laugh and sweep my hand over my eyes, the better to hide my happiness. With one of their myriad limbs, they pry my hand away and circle one tentacle around it. They'll want for nothing, not candied flowers nor fruit nor poetry if that is their wish.

They will know no war with me, their last battle fought long ago to bring about a world where they are not needed beyond the desire of one lover for another.

COMPATIBLE

Jaye Anderson

alien, body modification, body sharing, bondage, bondage (tentacles), depression, dildo in anus sex, fantasizing, m/m, masturbation, mating bond, orgasm delay, overstimulation, praise kink, present tense, public sex, science fiction, sex toy (dildo), size difference, telepathic communication, tentacle in anus sex, tentacles, third person limited point of view

Marcus is alone on the 22nd floor, as usual.

The lights of the city gleam cold and bright through the glass of the office windows. Marcus's coworkers all left earlier for happy hour, which seems like a misnomer. He's not sure where to find happiness, but he's pretty sure it isn't at a bar.

He's pretty sure it isn't here in this office, either. He likes his job, and he's good at it. But when he'd moved to the big city, he's thought there would be more to life than sitting in a glass tower staring at code.

Marcus isn't good at making friends, never has been. He'd hoped it'd be easier here, surrounded by so many people. It's one of the reasons

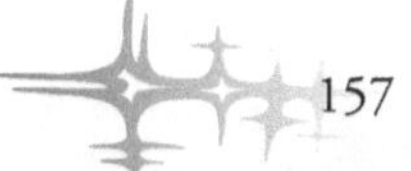

he left his small hometown. The thing about big cities, though—the thing nobody told him—is that when you're surrounded by thousands of people all the time, you don't make friends. You avoid eye contact. You don't make small talk. Nobody wants to smile and make nice a thousand times a day, so nobody does.

It's been a year here, and Marcus hasn't made a single friend. He works late, crunching code for a company that doesn't care if he exists. But at least the view is nice. Sometimes, like tonight, he can even see the stars.

He's not here to stargaze, though. He reluctantly turns away from the night sky and goes back to his computer screen. His browser has, annoyingly, opened a tab to H.N.R.Y., the chatbot his company has been pushing everyone to use. He can't remember what the acronym stands for, not that it matters. Chatbots are a gimmick, and their output is garbage. He doesn't need help doing his work, thank you very much.

And then, as though it is deliberately trying to compound his irritation, an authentication screen pops up. Marcus frowns. There's no "X" button to close it, and he can't switch windows away from it, either. "You've got to be shitting me," he mutters, uselessly keying Alt-Tab.

Fine. He gives in. He grudgingly types in his username and password, only to get another pop-up:

BIOMETRIC AUTHENTICATION REQUIRED

Okay, the company is going way too far with this. He's tempted to hard reboot the system to get around it, but there are activity loggers on everyone's machines, and he doesn't want to get reprimanded for trying too hard to avoid the stupid bot. So he reluctantly presses his thumb against the thumbprint reader on his laptop.

There's a sting. He jerks back with surprise and finds a pinprick mark on his thumb. It looks like a tiny spider bite. Did his computer just *stab* him? He pokes tentatively at the thumbprint reader, but it's smooth to the touch. No sharp edges. He sticks his thumb in his mouth to soothe it, and he glares at the page loading on his screen.

What would you like to know today, Marcus? it says in brightly colored letters. It's childish. Infantilizing. He hates it.

It's also a ridiculous question. There's a lot of things he'd like to know. Like why his computer *bit* him just now. Or maybe who was really behind the Kennedy assassination. Or how to win at the stock market. Or how to make friends.

Marcus could actually really use the answer to that last one.

He leans back in his office chair and looks out over the city below, where millions of people are going out to movies and concerts and bars with happy hours. Marcus wouldn't know about any of that. He can't actually remember the last hour he had that was happy.

He eyes the search box on the screen. "Okay," he mutters. "I've got one for you."

He types into the box: *Where do you find happiness?*

There's a slight pause, which is cute; it must be programmed to act like a human. And then it responds: An interesting question. **Are you asking about me specifically, or the general 'you'?**

Marcus stares in bemusement. He must have unlocked some kind of Easter egg. Okay, it's late, it's technically the weekend now, and he has nothing better to do. He'll play along.

I'm asking you specifically, he types.

A warm sensation blooms in his chest. It's…satisfying. Like he's just said exactly the right thing. It's not a feeling he's accustomed to. He rubs absently at the pinprick on his thumb, wondering what the bot will say now.

Do you know, you're the first human to ask me that?

More Easter eggs. It's odd that the company would have invested this much money into an AI tool just to have it play games with the employees. Marcus glances around the office to make sure none of his co-workers are hanging around watching him get pranked. But he's all alone up here. Just him and this chatbot. Marcus starts typing again.

Don't talk to humans often, huh? I get it, we're pretty boring as a species.

The cursor flickers slightly, almost like the bot is laughing, and again Marcus has that blooming sensation of rightness. It feels—good, like a friend laughing at a shared joke. Except this isn't a friend, obviously. It's not even a person.

You're not boring. But to answer your original question: let's just say that I'm on the path.

On the path to happiness. This bot is telling Marcus that it's on the path to happiness. Okay, sure.

And what about yourself? Are you happy?

Sure, I guess, HNRY.

You don't sound happy, Marcus. And please, call me Henry.

Marcus's heart picks up speed. Easter eggs are supposed to be cute and funny and, crucially, small. They aren't supposed to pick up on conversational cues or to ask extremely personal questions.

This is officially very Goddamned weird.

He should probably report this to security. But he looks at the question flashing on the screen—**Are you happy?**—and he has the perverse urge to answer it. Like, actually answer it. He can't remember the last time someone else seemed legitimately curious about his well-being. He's working on a Friday night, and there's nobody who cares if he comes home late or comes home at all. His coworkers don't invite him to happy hour. He calls home once a week and lies to his family about how great everything is going.

I make good money and I have a good job, he types, which is pretty much the same kind of thing he says to his family back home. It's true enough. He went to a good state college, and his job pays well and has opportunities for advancement.

But unease coils in his stomach as he sends the message. It's a partial truth at best, and…well, partially true also means partially untrue. He doesn't actually think that making good money and having a good job are the key to happiness, and lying to the bot is kind of like lying to himself.

That's not what I asked, Marcus.

Marcus lets out a startled huff of air. This thing clocked immediately that he'd dodged the question, and it *reprimanded* him. The person on the other end of this—and Marcus is sure now that it is a person—is being pretty goddamn inappropriate. And yet, as Marcus stares at the screen, the thought of calling security fades out like a distant radio signal. He wants to answer. He wants to tell them the truth.

Yeah, okay, he types. *You caught me. I'm not happy. Better?*

The uneasy feeling subsides, replaced by the same warm feeling of satisfaction as before. He lets out a long breath, wondering what the hell is happening and why he's continuing to go along with it.

Yes. Better. Tell me more. Why aren't you happy?

It's like something deep and buried cracks open with him, spilling forth words as his fingers fly over the keyboard.

This city is a big, mindless machine, and I'm stuck in its gears. I don't think anyone at my job would even notice if I just stopped showing up. I have

no friends. I went to one party, and it turned out to be for someone's wife to sell some kind of candles. So every day I stay here late, and then I take the subway home and I eat alone in my apartment and I wonder if my parents would take me in if I just went back home, except I'm not going to do that because I don't want to disappoint them. To be completely honest with you, Henry, I think I'm miserable.

Marcus's eyes are hot and blurry, and he angrily wipes his sleeve across them. Jesus, what is wrong with him?

Your distress is upsetting, Marcus, but your honesty is enjoyable. Thank you.

Oh, that—that feels really, really good. A warm thrill sweeps through Marcus, powerful enough to make his eyelids flutter closed. It's not a normal reaction; none of this is normal. He thinks Henry might be doing something to him. That's a crazy thought, but he doesn't have another explanation.

You are experiencing pleasure, Henry says. Marcus can tell he's delighted about it, that he likes making Marcus feel good.

Marcus doesn't understand how he knows what Henry is feeling, though. Is he reading Henry's thoughts? Is *Henry* reading *Marcus's* thoughts?

Not possible, he tells himself without conviction.

How else do you experience pleasure?

Marcus's mind flashes to the jerk-off session he'd had that morning in his bathroom. It had been a long one. He'd gotten up before his alarm and had time, so he drew it out, edged himself.

That's not—he's obviously not going to tell Henry that.

Tell me, Marcus. Please.

He's still at work, on his company computer. He doesn't ever think about this kind of stuff at work. But Henry wants to know, and…wow, Marcus really wants to tell him.

Why are you so interested in this? he returns instead, fighting off the urge to answer.

We are compatible, Henry tells him. **Therefore I must learn what brings you pleasure**. The cursor sits there, blinking expectantly.

That actually makes a lot of sense, Marcus thinks, and then he shakes his head like a dog shaking off water. No, it *doesn't* make sense. He has a million follow-up questions—what the hell Henry means by "compatible," for example—but those are all subsumed by the overwhelming urge to answer Henry's question. Henry needs to know what brings Marcus pleasure, and Marcus needs to tell him. He can't resist it any more than he can resist gravity.

I shouldn't be telling you this at work.

Work is irrelevant. Tell me.

I masturbate. A lot. Sometimes two or three times a day, if I have time.

Marcus shivers with delight. God, being honest feels so good. It's like he's in a warm, fuzzy ball of sunshine.

You mean that you stimulate your penis until orgasm?

Well, that sounds really clinical, but basically yes.

If my phrasing sounds clinical, how would you phrase it?

I'd say that I stroke my cock until I come.

And then the bottom drops out of Marcus's stomach, because he just did the equivalent of sexting on his company laptop while he's sitting in the middle of the office. "Oh, shit," he says blankly. There's no way to delete sent messages, so his confession sits there in stark black-on-white, evidence that he's lost his Goddamned mind.

It was inappropriate for me to say that, Marcus types. *I'm sorry*. But even that minor untruth twists unpleasantly in his chest. He presses his hand against his heart. It's an actual physical sensation, like heartburn. He's got fucking heartburn from lying to a computer.

But that thought just makes the heartburn worse, because now he's lying to himself. Henry is not just a computer. Henry is clearly and obviously sentient, and he thinks he's compatible with Marcus, and he wants to know how to pleasure Marcus.

Jesus fucking Christ.

Marcus types: *I'm not sorry, actually. I'm just afraid of getting in trouble with my work.* The heartburn eases immediately, and he breathes a sigh of relief.

It's all right, Marcus. You won't get in trouble. You have my word. Will you allow me to demonstrate something?

Like what?

Please. Indulge me.

OK. Go ahead.

And then, directly into his mind, Henry says: **You don't need the computer, Marcus.**

Marcus jerks in shock, Henry's words reverberating in his head. "Oh my God," he says reverently. "How did you do that? Can you do it again?"

I will do it many times, Henry promises. **You're sensitive to me, and I to you. Surely you can feel what I mean.** Henry's voice in his mind is different from Marcus's own internal thoughts. It's alien but strangely enjoyable. Marcus wants to hear it again.

Marcus is objectively aware that he should be terrified right now. What he's experiencing isn't possible. But his limbic system is awash in pleasure from talking to Henry. He can't be afraid when he feels this good.

I want to know everything about you, Marcus. Tell me what brings you pleasure. Tell me what you desire.

Marcus huffs out a faint laugh. He keeps his desires tucked away in a tiny corner of his mind. They involve restraints and subjugation and all kinds of things he isn't supposed to want.

But he wants to tell Henry.

A bead of sweat drops from his forehead onto his keyboard and he absently mops it away with his shirt cuff. He looks around the abandoned office again, at the empty desks and chairs bathed in the dim after-hours lighting that gives everything an otherworldly blue tinge.

"What are you?" he asks.

I am neither a computer nor a human. But you knew that already, Marcus.

He did know, somehow. He doesn't know exactly what Henry is, but he knows he's a living, thinking being from really far away.

"Yeah, I did know that," he says faintly. "How did I know that?"

We are compatible, Henry says. **Highly compatible**. Pleasurable heat blooms in Marcus's chest. **Soon we will share pleasure**, Henry informs him, sending a twist of shivery thrill down Marcus's spine. **But first we must learn each other, in your place of comfort. Are you amenable to this, Marcus?**

He is amenable. God, he is, he *is*. He wants to know more about Henry—who or what he is, and what brings him pleasure, too. And oh yeah, wow, that thought sends a lightning bolt of pure desire searing through him. He wants *very much* to know what brings Henry pleasure. His heartbeat, fast and steady, thrums in his ears. His skin prickles like there's a gathering storm.

"Place of comfort. Like my apartment?"

Your apartment will do, if you are comfortable there.

"Yeah," he says. "Yes. What do we have to do?"

Bubbling elation surges through Marcus. This, he suddenly knows, was an important step in a ritual. A question has been asked and answered. And now they can…they can…go to a place. Together.

Yes. Your place of comfort, Henry agrees. **How far away is it?**

Marcus guesses Henry means his apartment. "About half an hour by the Green Line," he says. "Uh, three miles as the crow flies. Are you going with me?"

In a manner of speaking. Your place of comfort is close enough for me to continue to communicate with you as we are now. Once you are there, I will learn you, Marcus. I am beginning to learn you already. Do you find it pleasurable?

A shivery thrill passes down his spine and goes right to his cock. He realizes with faint surprise that he's already half hard. Henry is in his brain. "Learning him." Marcus wants more; he likes the idea of being *learned.*

"Yeah," he says, the words coming out slow and sluggish. "It's good. It's, ah, pleasurable."

Your body is a marvel, Marcus.

"Thank you," he manages. Nobody's ever told him that before. But then, nobody's ever really had the chance. He's never had a partner. He doesn't count the girl who went to prom with him his senior year and told him that she wasn't surprised and not to worry about it when he didn't kiss her goodnight at the end.

Marcus checks the time to see when the next train will arrive and realizes, stunned, that he's been talking to Henry for three hours. He thought it had been fifteen or twenty minutes at most. He's losing time, which is something else that should be frightening, but isn't. Henry is learning him, and he feels incredible, and that's all he really cares about.

"This is insane," he says out loud. But he's on the verge of something huge, and he has to chase it. Whatever this ritual is that Henry wants to do—taking him home and "learning him"—he's definitely fucking doing it.

He stands up, puts his jacket on, and shuts his computer down. The

browser tab with his chat history on it flickers out of existence. For a moment, Marcus stands in the dark, silent office, wondering if this has all been a bizarre overwork-induced fever dream.

Very good, Marcus, Henry says in his head. **Let's go home.**

The southbound station of the subway is quiet. At this hour of the night, everyone's heading into the city, not out of it. Marcus stands at the edge of the platform, breathing in the dank, humid air wafting out of the tunnel, listening as the train approaches. There's a guy slumped on a bench looking half asleep, and there's two other office workers waiting a bit farther down the platform. Marcus puts his hands in his pockets and tries to look normal. Just a regular guy waiting for the train. Not a guy with a potentially alien life form hitchhiking in his head.

The first train to arrive has people in every car, even though it's late.

Let it go past, Henry suggests.

Marcus lets it go past. The next train comes shortly after, and two of the cars are completely empty. Marcus boards the second one.

This is your place of comfort, Henry says.

Marcus looks around at the dingy subway car with the cracked vinyl seats and the grease-smeared windows.

"This isn't my apartment. I'm on the subway," he says, aware that he's now become one of the people who talks to themselves on the subway car.

You can speak to me the same way that I speak to you, Marcus. You do not need to vocalize. Our connection is strong.

Really? Marcus thinks experimentally.

Really. And we do not need to be in your apartment. This is a place of comfort for you.

Now that Marcus thinks about it, Henry's not wrong. He likes the subway—the way the noise envelops him, the gentle rocking of the car. He especially likes it when there's no one else around and he has the car to himself. It's one of the reasons, he realizes, that he doesn't mind staying at work so late.

Place of comfort is part of the ritual, isn't it? Marcus asks. The wording feels significant.

Yes, Henry says. **The place of comfort is where we establish the bond.**

So we're going to... establish a bond? Right here on the Green Line?

Marcus asks.

We began establishing it at your office, Henry says, and…yeah, Marcus kind of already knew that, now that he thinks about it.

"Holy shit," he mutters to himself.

I am learning you, Henry says. **May I try something?**

It's nice that Henry is bothering to ask first, even though he must know that there's no way Marcus is going to say no.

Sure, Marcus thinks. He waits expectantly, and then out of nowhere, a wave of pleasure sweeps through him, raising the hair on the backs of his arms, making him push his hips forward in the seat. He grabs the edge of the hard plastic subway chair, holding on for dear life. He's grateful that Henry made them wait for an empty car, because there's no way he could hide what's happening to him right now. He's whining like a dog.

You have many erogenous areas, Henry muses. Henry is playing his nervous system like a piano.

"Fuck," Marcus manages to grit out. It's like Henry is digging right into his brain stem. Marcus's cock is tenting out his pants, and he's moving his hips, thrusting into nothing. *How are you—? How are you doing—? Oh fuck—*

The pleasure builds, heightening and heightening, and fucking hell, Marcus is going to come. He's going to come right here on the Goddamned subway. His nipples are tight and sensitive against the fabric of his shirt; his cock throbs uncomfortably against his zipper. He's—he's *writhing*.

Henry's excited.

You're responding very well. You do this to yourself? When you masturbate?

Not like this. Marcus groans, trying to stop himself from kneading his cock through his pants. *It doesn't feel like this.*

This is better? More pleasurable?

"Oh yeah," Marcus gasps aloud. *This is so much better.* The shock of joy from Henry that blasts through him is enough to take his breath away. Henry's elated that he's making Marcus feel so good. *But you gotta stop*, he tells Henry. *I can't do this on a subway car. In public.*

Ah, taboo, Henry says, understanding, and the pleasure abruptly shuts off. It's like someone threw a cold bucket of water over him. He's panting, and the back of his shirt is damp with sweat, sticking to the seat

of the subway.

"Th-thank you," Marcus manages. His cock is still hard, but he's no longer in imminent danger of coming. "Holy shit."

You are extraordinarily sensitive, Henry exults in his mind. **You and I have been together for only a few short hours. Normally a pair would spend days nesting together in a place of comfort before being able to communicate this way.**

"Must be fate," Marcus says. He means it as a joke, but it doesn't feel like a joke. It doesn't feel like a joke at all.

Yes, Henry says simply. **I have never felt like this. And I have searched, Marcus. Long and far. Just as you have.**

What? Marcus asks, blinking with surprise. *I wasn't searching.*

There's a trill of amusement inside his mind. **You were**, Henry tells him. **I can see it in your mind. You traveled a long distance. You seek new minds, new opportunities. We are the same, Marcus.**

Warm pleasure suffuses him, and this time he's not sure if it's Henry's or his own. Yes, he thinks. They are the same, even though Henry probably isn't even human.

You're from really far away, aren't you?

My original home is very far indeed, yes.

Marcus shivers. This is…a lot. Six hours ago, he was thinking about spending his Saturday finishing up some spreadsheets. Now he's got an alien telepath inside his head, telling him they're halfway through a courtship ritual that culminates in… He frowns. He's not sure what it culminates in, actually.

Merging, Henry supplies.

Marcus goes very still. Anxiety skitters through him. He likes Henry—likes him a lot—but he doesn't want to *become* Henry. *What does merging mean?* he asks.

Two become one, Henry says, sounding reverent. The words resonate in Marcus's mind like a church bell.

Two become one, he repeats, dazed.

The underground walls streak past the windows. A bead of sweat rolls down the back of Marcus's neck. It's hot in this subway car.

I'm afraid, he tells Henry. *I like being who I am.* He hopes Henry won't take offense. But to his relief, he feels only faint amusement through the bond.

You will continue to be who you are, Henry assures him. **Two become one. We merge, but we do not transform. You will see, Marcus. It will feel so good. We will feel so good together.**

An exploratory pulse of pleasure spirals through his belly; his cock, which had gone quiescent, stirs to life again.

You are so sensitive to me. Will you show me how you pleasure yourself?

Taboo, Marcus thinks hazily through the soft pulses of pleasure Henry is sending through him. *Not in public. I said before.*

No, Henry explains patiently. *Show me in your mind. Imagine it. I want to see.*

Oh, okay. He can do that. When he agrees, the wash of ensuing delight makes him feel like his entire brain is in a warm bubble bath. He leans back against the plexiglass window, feeling the vibrations of the train car in his skull.

With eyes closed, he brings to mind that morning's jerk-off session. He'd taken his time with it, got out his favorite dildo, slicked lubrication onto it, pushed it slowly into himself. He remembers the feel of the bulbous head spreading him open, the slow stretch of it.

Henry is avidly attentive. **Yes**, he tells Marcus. **Good. More.**

Marcus gets the feeling Henry is taking notes. But that's okay. Everything is so, so okay. He's getting more and more of Henry's thoughts now—Henry is excited and extremely eager. He wants to touch Marcus. He wants to complete the merging. It's usually a slow process, but this time it's happening very quickly, and Henry is shuddery with excitement about it. He can't believe how perfect Marcus is.

Warm pleasure shivers down Marcus's spine. No one in his entire life has ever thought he was perfect.

Once inside, you thrust? Henry asks. **Show me. Please, Marcus, continue.**

Yeah. Yeah, he'll continue. He goes back to the memory of fucking himself. He'd pushed the dildo all the way in, seating it firmly inside, panting while he got used to the stretch. And then he'd begun working his hips, slow and rhythmic, against the towel he'd laid on his bed. Fucking himself with the dildo.

Marcus gets a momentary flash of something with—appendages. Dozens and dozens of arms, slithery and tight, enveloping

him. Penetrating him. Thrusting.

"Is that you?" Marcus asks, his voice thick and low. "Is that you, Henry?" Fuck, he wants that. He wants it so fucking much.

The image abruptly disappears. **You saw that? I am sorry**, Henry is telling him. **It is too soon. I did not know you could—**

Marcus's cock throbs. His legs are splayed wide on his seat; a light sheen of sweat coats his forehead.

Show me again, he begs. God, if they don't get to his stop soon, he is absolutely going to start touching himself on the subway. He's so fucking hard. Show me. Don't be sorry. *Show me again, please, I want it.*

Henry trembles inside his mind. **Stop**, he says abruptly. **At the next station, exit this car and get back on the northbound train.**

Marcus's eyes flutter open. "What?" he says into the empty subway car.

We need wait no longer, Henry answers. **We can complete the two become one. I am sure of it. You are perfect, Marcus. Your mind is so receptive to me. I have tested your compatibility. A question has been asked, and answered. In a place of comfort, we have shared our minds. Now we must merge. Please. Please accept my offer, Marcus. I have come so far and waited so long. I want nothing else in life.**

"You don't have to beg, Henry," Marcus says, half drunk with pleasure. "I'd do it for free."

Yes? You are saying yes?

This is objectively crazy. It's stupid, dangerous. He barely even knows what he's agreeing to. But deep in his heart, he knows he's not crazy. This is real. And he's been so alone, and Henry feels so good, and Henry thinks he's perfect.

I'm saying yes.

Ecstatic, wild joy floods the bond. **Come to me**, Henry chants in his mind. **Come to me, come to me.**

The subway rumbles to a juddering stop. "Stand clear of the door," the automated voice announces. "Stand clear of the door."

Marcus leaves the subway car on unsteady legs, making his way to the northbound platform. He's on his way to Henry now.

"Two become one," he says into the echoing space of the deserted platform.

Yes, Marcus, yes. Two become one.

Half an hour later, Marcus is standing in front of his office building again.

You're in the building? he asks, surprised.

Yes. I am connected to the network.

You are a chatbot! He's not serious, though. A rumble of amusement travels through the bond.

It was the easiest way to do my search. I have investigated thousands of humans in my time here.

And you settled on me?

I settled on nothing. I accepted only the best. You are perfect, Henry says, which is never going to get old for Marcus. **Your sensitivity to me is astonishing.** There's another flash of squirming tentacles. Those have been getting more and more frequent. Henry's losing control of himself in his excitement.

You're going to use those on me.

Yes. The answer is simple. Yes, Henry is going to use those on Marcus. Marcus hurries toward the door.

Henry uses his network access to open all of the doors between Marcus and himself. He's in a sub-basement level that Marcus doesn't normally have access to.

If someone reviews the logs of when I entered the building, they're going to have questions. It feels stupid to be concerned about breaking workplace rules under the circumstances, but Marcus is a rule-follower by nature and some habits are hard to shake.

They may well have questions, but you will not have to answer them. After today, you will no longer work here, Marcus.

Marcus freezes mid-stride. The realization hits him like a slap to the face: this is the end of his previous life. He's about to say goodbye to the data analysis, the late, lonely nights in the office, the hopes for advancement in a career track he doesn't care about. All gone.

All gone, he thinks, a burgeoning joy swelling in his chest. *Oh my God*, he thinks at Henry.

Do not be afraid, Henry says. **We will see the stars together, Marcus. We will pursue**—a concept that didn't quite translate, something like

happiness/pleasure/delight/ecstasy—**in each other's company. You will want for nothing.**

Okay, Marcus says. His heart is a kite being flown on the end of a string, lifting into the stratosphere. *Okay, Henry, I trust you.*

The sub-basement level is labyrinthine, and after making his way trepidatiously through several corridors, Marcus finally arrives at two steel doors with a massive lock and a biohazard symbol on the front.

Are you actually hazardous? Marcus asks.

Not unless provoked, Henry says.

Marcus's hands tremble as he uses his ID badge one last time to unlock the doors between himself and Henry. There's a deep thudding reverberation, and the doors swing open. Inside the massive room, there's a metal structure that looks like a giant-sized playground jungle gym, stretching up to the ceiling.

And inside it is Henry.

He's beautiful, Marcus thinks, the breath gone from his lungs. He's iridescent black and purple, his massive central bulk giving off an oil-slick shimmer. Dozens of long, undulating tentacles extend outward, wrapping around the metal bars, writhing in the air. They're the same tentacles Marcus saw in his visions, except in person they're far, far more massive. Henry is *huge*.

Electricity crackles around the bars. It looks like a cage, like Henry is trapped here, electrocuted if he tries to escape. Outrage wells up inside Marcus—Henry, beautiful and alien, powerful and intelligent, locked up here in a corporate basement and electrocuted?

No, Henry says, his voice loud in Marcus's mind, like a radio tuned to a nearby station. **It suits my purposes to allow them to think I am trapped here, but I am free. The electricity feeds me. Come to me, Marcus. Please, you are so close.**

"Henry," Marcus gasps. "You're so—"

The first tentacle, thick and bulging, reaches him. It wraps around his leg, winding itself up and up, slithering around his waist, leaving little shocks of pleasure everywhere it touches. Another one encircles his other leg. A third winds itself around his neck, which should make him want to panic. But he's not panicked. He's elated. Henry feels so good; he wants more.

Yes?

Yes, Marcus thinks frantically. *Yes, Henry.* He runs his fingers over the winding tentacles, petting and stroking their smooth texture.

Surely you must feel it, Henry tells him. **How perfect we are.**

"Yeah," Marcus gasps out loud. The tentacles reel him in, pulling him closer to Henry's massive center. Rills of pleasure skitter up and down his nervous system. Henry strips him out of his clothes, several tentacles at once working to tear off his shirt, his pants, even his shoes and socks. Marcus is breathless and lightheaded; feeling Henry's skin against his own is so good. The tentacles are slippery and slick, muscular and warm, flexing and twisting all over Marcus's body.

Now, Henry says. **Two become one.**

Vertigo sweeps over Marcus. He feels like he's falling—falling into Henry, somehow, but Henry is also falling into him. It's disorienting, exhilarating. They're *joining*. "I can feel you," Marcus gasps. "In my head. All of you." His mind floods with images and feelings as the bond opens, an artery of knowledge from Henry's mind to his own.

Henry exults. **Yes**, he says. **You understand everything now, Marcus.**

And Marcus suddenly and abruptly does. He understands perfectly. Henry is courting him with a ritual that has existed for longer than humanity has been a species. The first step is determining genetic compatibility. That was the pinprick on his thumb. Dozens of humans managed to pass that first test.

Next is an exchange of words—*a question asked and answered.* Only Marcus passed that one. **You sought pleasure-joy-happiness**, Henry tells him, yet another concept that doesn't quite translate. **I too seek this. We are the same.**

Once a bondmate—*bondmate*, Marcus thinks with stunned delight—has been found, the pair retires to nest together in a place of comfort. Henry, delirious with excitement at having found such a perfect mate, decided that a moving subway car counted as a place of comfort, and that the brief period they spent together on that car counted as nesting. **I could not help it**, he says. His tentacles wind around Marcus, stroking and exploring. **You are perfect. Look how you respond to me.**

Marcus is responding, yeah. He's completely bare now, and Henry's

touching him everywhere. Tentacles writhe around the sensitive insides of his thighs, slipping and sliding against his balls, teasing at the swollen head of his cock. Two thin, delicate fronds wrap themselves around his nipples. He makes a loud, shameful noise, and his knees go weak.

Come to me. Let me pleasure you. You are exceptional, Marcus. I have searched for so long. Two become one.

"Two become one," he repeats aloud, and the blast of joy that radiates from Henry is like standing next to a furnace.

Yes, Marcus. The tentacles loop and twist, sending shocks of ecstasy cascading through him. A knot of tentacles forms around his cock, writhing around it like—like nothing on Earth. It looks *filthy*.

"Henry," he starts to say, and a tentacle feeds into his mouth. It's warm and thick and tastes metallic. He instinctively starts to suck, and the bond lights up like a magnesium flare.

You like that? Marcus thinks. *It feels good?*

Yes, Henry assures him. **Yes, oh yes. Your mouth is a marvel. I did not know. Do not stop, Marcus.**

Henry pulls Marcus ever closer, until Marcus, still suckling at Henry's thickening tentacle, is pressed against Henry's sleek and glistening central mass. A thin ooze flows up and over Marcus's arms as Henry continues to draw him inside. Soon, his arms are halfway inside Henry, and Henry is…covering him. Flowing over his entire body, encasing him head to toe in a thin layer of ooze. He can see through it, barely, but the room is dim and blurry. He can't breathe, but it doesn't seem to matter. Henry is feeding him oxygen somehow.

Once he's completely encased, the ooze goes rigid, immobilizing him.

Oh fuck, Henry, he says, inside his head because he can't talk around the tentacle filling his mouth. *Oh fuck, oh my God.* He tries futilely to move, testing Henry's strength. But he can't even move a millimeter. He's trapped inside Henry, with a tentacle filling his mouth and a knot of tentacles swarming over his cock, and…oh, oh God, a thick one slowly feeding into his ass. He makes a loud, helpless noise as Henry pushes into him. He can't do anything about it. He has to just stand there and take it.

I am doing this because you desire it, Marcus. There's a thoughtful pause. **And because the sensations of your mouth are incredible. I wish to prolong them.**

Marcus wonders if he can actually die from pleasure. Henry is filling him in every possible way. He has tentacles going into his mouth and up his ass. He's completely enveloped. He bets someone looking from the outside wouldn't even be able to tell he's there. Marcus moans around the mouth-tentacle, tries uselessly to beg. His thoughts are disjointed; he's awash in ecstasy.

I'm gonna come, he thinks blearily. Henry is doing something to his cock that feels like several mouths are sucking him at once. The tentacle inside his ass thickens and pulses, thrusting slowly just like Marcus showed Henry from his memory. He's really, really close, and he can't help it. He's going to spill.

Not yet, Henry says. A thin tendril winds itself tightly around the base of Marcus's cock, fitting itself there snugly.

Oh God, Marcus thinks frantically.

I will prolong our pleasure, Henry tells him. Henry loves being sucked, *adores* it. He's never experienced anything like Marcus's mouth. His pleasure echoes back into Marcus's mind, a feedback loop that just keeps heightening.

Marcus is fully cocooned, now, encased in Henry, wrapped in dozens of squirming tentacles. They're in his mouth, on his nipples, around his cock, up his ass. Pulsing, throbbing, thrusting. And he's so hard, and Henry won't let him come. Tears stream down Marcus's face, which Henry absorbs eagerly.

I don't know if I can handle this. It's too much.

You can, Henry assures him. **It will not be too much. Trust me.** And then all of Henry everywhere starts to pulse, rhythmic and steady. **Two become one. Are you ready, Marcus?**

Marcus makes a strangled noise that's meant to be *Yes*. Yes, yes, he's ready, he's so ready. *Please, Henry, please. Two become one.*

His vision is clearing even though the thin black membrane is still covering him, and he realizes that it's because he's seeing what Henry sees now, superimposed over his own vision. Henry can see in a different light spectrum than Marcus can, so Marcus can now too. The colors are all shifted, and Henry is—Henry is *glowing.*

Henry is flowing into Marcus now. Not just his tentacles. His whole self, cell by cell. He's sinking into Marcus. Marcus is absorbing him, or maybe he's absorbing Marcus. They're merging, and Marcus is sobbing,

because nothing has ever felt this good in his life or maybe in anyone's life. He thinks maybe he's the only person in the history of the human race to ever feel like this.

Yes, Henry thinks. Henry's thoughts are disjointed now, too. He's been searching for this for several human lifetimes, and it's better than anything he ever imagined. **You are the only one, Marcus. We are perfect together.**

Vibrations cascade down his sensitized cock. Henry is in him now in every way. In his mouth, in his eyes and ears, in his lungs, his heart, in his mind. He *is* Henry, and Henry is him. They're merging. Two become one, and he can never go back. He never wants to.

Yes, he begs, and **yes**, he tells himself in response. Henry releases the tentacle binding Marcus's cock and suctions himself around it, squeezing it tight, pulsing and pulsing and pulsing. He erupts into orgasm, their two bodies meshing into place, their cock spilling, their tentacles thrusting into their mouth.

Marcus becomes gradually aware that he's being cradled by a triad of massive tentacles, wrapped snugly around him and holding him securely about four feet in the air. But it's all right, because they're also his tentacles. He's Marcus, but he's also Henry now.

Two become one, Henry agrees, pleased and delighted inside their shared mind. **We will do this again many times, of course. The human mouth is a wonder of the universe.**

"Mmnh," Marcus says. He slides a hand down his own chest and torso, feeling the tentacles erupting from his own body. "Those permanent?" he asks sleepily. He thinks about how odd his trachea is, how strange it is to vibrate sound in this way.

They can retract, Henry tells him with some amusement. **When I withdraw inside you, you will appear perfectly human. Which may be useful for times we need to be among humans.**

Marcus shivers with the realization this brings: They're going to see the stars, just like Henry told him. "Can I go home if I want?" Marcus asks, thinking of his family.

Of course, Henry assures him. **We can go anywhere, see anything.**

And they will not know you have changed unless you tell them, he says, anticipating Marcus's next question. Good, because his mom and dad are pretty understanding, but he doesn't think they're ever going to be ready for...*this*. He wonders if Henry has family. He'll find out, he guesses. They'll find out everything about each other. Two become one.

"So you really weren't trapped here," Marcus says, looking at the empty restraints sparking with electricity.

Amusement crackles through the bond. **No human could trap me.**

There's a pleasurable vibration at the base of Marcus's spine. Henry settling in, he guesses. He's—elated, he thinks. He's not sure he ever knew what joy truly was before.

Yes, Henry agrees. **Remarkable. You asked me, Marcus, where I find happiness. Do you know now?**

Marcus smiles. He does.

"The same place I do," he says. "I find it here, with you."

Orchis Magnus

E. M. Beka

alcohol use, bigender, bipoc, break-up, dendrophilia, emotional abuse, f/nb, frottage, miscommunication, modern with magic, mute, nb/nb, non-binary, past tense, scientist, sentient plant, sex pollen, third person limited (alternating) point of view

Travel was highly overrated.

Comfortable in its cosy ecosystem, the plant had never thought it would try it.

At times it had enjoyed the songs of migration some of the birds sang, but it was no tumbleweed destined to blow about on the wind. It had outlasted megafauna, bushfires, droughts, and countless storms.

Its roots were deep. It endured.

Then an excitable primate had climbed down the sinkhole, spotted the plant, and jumped about like an anxious tree kangaroo.

The primate had brought with it a series of thick brown vine-like things and an oddly smooth branch with a shiny flattened end that was

lightly coated in soil.

The plant had not realised the danger before the primate pushed the shiny end into the soil beneath its roots. The primate efficiently used the odd branch to dig, and in a distressingly short amount of time, the plant had been separated from its soil and hoisted through the air. The plant barely had time to register upset at its flight out of the sinkhole before it was shoved roughly into a darkened hole, cut off from nutrients and sunlight, with only just enough water to keep it from desiccation.

Had it not been in its resting phase, it might have been able to defend itself, but as it was, the alarm could not entirely rouse it from its torpor in time to make a difference.

It decided to wait.

It was almost Flowering Time. It would conserve its energy.

Stepping into a greenhouse for tropical plants in the depths of winter always felt like wrapping oneself in a hot, damp blanket. The air was perpetually humid, and everything smelled lightly of moist decomposition. The perfect conditions for rainforest plants. The perfect place for Harlow to regain their equilibrium after yet another awful and circular conversation with their probably-soon-to-be-ex girlfriend. Plant needs were simple, and they never interrogated Harlow about their "priorities".

Sweat dripped down their back as Harlow walked the orderly rows of chaotic growth, checking the tubing of the sprinkler system. Harlow's graphite pencil scratched on the inevitably damp paper of their lined exercise book as they marked which plants needed more attention. The dragon fruit was about to outgrow its trellis. The stripy-leaved Syngonium was looking a little leggy and needed to be shifted into a position with more light.

Tucked into the back corner was the star of the collection, the plant that Jo had dramatically declared her nemesis.

Magnus. *Orchis Magnus*, if the boss got his way on the official classification. The largest monopodial orchid ever found, as-yet unknown to general academia, but once Harlow and their boss published, it would break the records without even trying.

When the specimen had first been delivered four months ago, Harlow

had thought it was a practical joke. It wouldn't have been the first time. Jo had thought she was being funny when she'd sent the flower arrangement early in their relationship with the label, *Caution: exotic specimen.* The ensuing conversation when Harlow had to explain why the arrangement had ended up in the incinerator, about biosecurity risks and rules about personal deliveries, had caused their neighbour to shove flyers about couples counselling into their mailbox. Again.

Harlow had stared at the almost-two-metre-high box marked *fragile: live specimen* and hoped that they weren't going to have to rehash that discussion. Sometimes it was less the thought and more the thoughtlessness that counted. The fault was not one-sided on that account. Harlow could admit that they tended to get overly absorbed in work, yet Jo *still* apparently thought that Harlow's post-doctorate in botany involved studying to be some kind of over-glorified gardener.

They had been better together in undergrad, before Jo started receiving invites to the types of gatherings where a partner with dirt under their nails raised eyebrows. Rugged charm out of its element was deemed lack of polish, and Harlow was never in their element around cut flowers and cutting conversation.

(Besides, it had been years since Jo had said that was what she liked about Harlow. Harlow was starting to wonder whether her glitzy new "contacts" had changed Jo's taste on this level, too.)

It was with some trepidation that Harlow had read the note accompanying the shipping receipt for the "flowers" they had been sent by courier.

Orchis Magnus. Please propagate. Will be back late June/early July, August at the latest. Cheers, B.

What followed was a vague squiggle that Harlow squinted at, reluctantly accepting that it resembled their employer's signature, if done in a hurry, on the dashboard of a moving car, with a hand unsteadied by overindulgence in the two most common vices in academia: expensive coffee and cheap booze.

It was almost a relief that the delivery could thus be safely relegated to "work" and not romance, except that Harlow was now informed that their boss was set to be gone for four months, not the originally declared two, and that whatever the specimen was, Harlow had to not only keep it alive but also figure out how to encourage it to multiply.

"Seriously?" Harlow muttered under their breath.

"You are Dr Wren?" The young lady with the clipboard had sounded a little nervous. Harlow often had that effect on people unintentionally. Somehow everyone expected botanists to be twiggy little nerds with glasses. While Harlow had met plenty of those in their time, between their above-average height and time spent lugging around large terra-cotta pots full of specimens, Harlow was less of a twig and more of a tree trunk. As always, it had been stiflingly humid in the greenhouse that day, and sweat dripped down from the delivery lady's hairline below her logo-ed cap as she enviously (Harlow assumed) eyed Harlow's unprofessionally rolled-up sleeves and neckline unbuttoned to just below the top of Harlow's denim overalls.

"Yes, that's me," Harlow confirmed. They'd looked around the crowded greenhouse and sighed. "Just stick it over there by the staghorn fern."

"The what?"

But Harlow was already shifting pots to make room, and the delivery lady must have figured out what they meant, as she quickly wheeled the crate over to the hastily emptied corner.

Three minutes later, the sound if not the scent of the diesel-powered delivery van had dissipated, and Harlow eyed the box resting in the middle of the floor, box-cutter in hand. They couldn't imagine what kind of flower was actually inside. It was bigger than a corpse flower, and considering that the box was only marked for domestic post, whatever was inside had not been imported, but this did not necessarily narrow down the options. After all, there were plenty of private greenhouses with the kinds of specimens that Harlow knew their boss would salivate over.

Harlow cut open the box along the seam, carefully lifted back the cardboard, stepped back to avoid the immediate cascade of cardboard packing peanuts (good mulch, actually; Harlow made an absent note to set them aside) and stared.

Harlow had thought the box to be almost comically big, but upon consideration of its contents, it had been barely big enough. Dark leaves swayed gently in the air currents from the green house fans, striped yellow-brown from repeated bruising impacts against the sides of the box. There was no flower, and the stem—as thick around as Harlow's

forearm—sagged a little sadly, clearly not appreciating the shock of what must have been days in transit. It had been taped in place around the sphagnum-moss-wrapped root-ball to avoid it shifting in the plastic-lined box, but at some point, the sheer weight of the plant had clearly strained against what must have been most of a roll of gaffer tape.

In the dark, getting jolted around, and worst of all…

"You poor thing!" Harlow cooed to the plant as they started to carefully brush away excess packing peanuts. "Did that idiot seriously pack you in ice? What the hell was he thinking?"

It was a common myth amongst amateur orchid growers that the slow release of water from ice made it perfect for orchids that (generally speaking) despised over-watering. This school of thought ignored, however, that even the most cold-tolerant orchids generally hated frost. Times like this forcefully reminded Harlow that while Bert was world-class at identifying species by their flowers, he had gained his botany credentials by cataloging museum specimens rather than cultivating live plants.

Luckily for his live specimens, this was why he had hired Harlow.

"Don't you worry, I'll get you situated somewhere more comfortable!"

The primate that freed it from the darkness was different from the excitable one. It was bigger, for one, and its skin was closer to the colour of good soil. Oddly for a primate, it had green and purple tendrils in its head-fur. The plant had not known that primates came in such alluring colours.

The colourful primate made distressed noises and quickly took away the strangely same-shaped leaf litter that the excitable primate had practically smothered it in, and the thing blocking the sunlight. This primate was also far gentler with its leaves and its roots than the excitable primate had been.

The primate settled the plant gently against a flat, warm surface that was as hard as rock, but without so much as a helpful crevice for it to dig its roots into. Shortly afterward, the primate walked away, then came back before the Dayfire was halfway to its night position bearing what looked to be oddly regular sections of dead tree. It propped them up into a shape, then did something violently vibrational that left giant termite holes in the wood.

The plant shivered and hoped that it would not be next.

Jo always teased them for talking to plants, but Harlow couldn't help it. It was a habit they'd picked up from their grandmother, who'd sworn blind that a bit of venting to the vegetables made them grow sturdier. No research Harlow had seen corroborated such a claim, but on the other hand, it was hard not to pick up a few superstitious behaviours when dealing with things as finicky as orchids.

Orchis Magnus, however, was not only a bad joke (literally, it was Latin for "large testicles"), it was taxonomically incorrect. Magnus, for lack of a better designation, did not have the twin ball-shaped tuberoids like other members of the Orchis genus.

(Harlow could not *wait* to publish and get out from under Bert's black thumb.)

Magnus was, however, definitely an orchid. Its single monopodial stem, the broad spear-head leaves that sprouted dark purple from the stem before shifting to a lush green, the green aerial rootlets poking through the optimistically packed sphagnum moss, the fleshy subterranean roots—all of these screamed "orchid". If it had not been nearly as tall as Harlow themself then Harlow might have hazarded from the shape of the roots and leaves that perhaps it was a *Cryptostylis*, possibly *Cryptostylis subulata* or *erecta*, also known as tongue orchids. But those did not get over about 80 cm tall.

Magnus was almost two metres tall. The flowers, when they came, were no doubt going to be enormous, particularly when the shocking width of the stem was taken into account.

"*Orchis* is bullshit, but you're certainly a *Magnus*," Harlow had muttered. "Thank fuck you're at least partially terrestrial. I can't even imagine trying to mount you. I'd have to forklift in a boulder or half a tree or something, and forget fishing line, I'd have to visit the hardware store for some rope. As is, finding a pot big enough to put you in comfortably is going to be a bitch." Harlow eyed the root-ball again. "Yeah actually screw that. I'm going to make something custom. Don't

worry, Magnus, I'll get you settled."

The next nine hours had been exhausting. Harlow had dragged Magnus as gently as possible into an empty corner of the greenhouse, cleared away the ice fragments and sodden sphagnum moss, and then got to work discovering and treating the worst of the damage. Harlow examined every square millimetre of Magnus, taking note of every patch of discolouration. Another few days in the dark and it might have been a disaster, but with diligent care, Harlow was confident that they could save the plant.

A number of Magnus's roots had gone slimy brown with rootrot, and Harlow hacked these away mercilessly. Leaving them intact would only let the rot spread even further. The leaves they left intact, trusting that they could revive them by adjusting the moisture levels with the right planting conditions in the greenhouse. It was evident that Magnus was undergoing a dormancy phase, which was pure luck as far as Harlow was concerned. It meant that the shock would be lessened. Given enough time, Harlow hoped they could make Magnus thrive enough to bloom.

They drove to a warehouse that specialised in recycled wood, haggled a discount on getting some old railway sleepers cut to a length that would fit well in Harlow's van, then stopped by the local nursery for potting soil, coarse gravel, charcoal, sphagnum moss, and coconut husks. The greenhouse had all of these materials, of course, but none in the amounts that would be necessary for accommodating Magnus. At least Harlow didn't need to buy new tools.

Then Harlow had to build the plant bed.

"Lucky I'm not afraid of hard work, Magnus," Harlow had grunted as they hauled the heavy railway sleepers into a rough square shape, stacking them one by one until they formed a raised bed as high as Harlow's waist, then drilling holes deep enough to use threaded bar and coach screws to hold it all together.

"I'm putting more effort into this than *my* bed," they grumbled good naturedly.

They had hosed off the coconut husk, ensuring that any excess salt was removed from it. They wanted the husk to provide nutrients, not poison Magnus.

They layered gravel within the sleepers and then wrapped moss around one that would act as a glorified stake, sticking it upright in the gravel and piling layers of soil, charcoal, and the coconut husks around it, creating a loosely packed scree that would drain well. They dug a shallow hole beside the support to cradle the giant orchid's root system before stepping back to take a well-earned breather, sipping lukewarm tea from their battered old thermos.

Then it was time to lift Magnus.

Harlow considered for a moment if it would be worth getting help, considered the conniption fit that Bert would have at anyone unauthorised accessing the inner sanctum of the greenhouse, and then sighed and set up a pulley over one of the greenhouse roof beams with a length of rope, carefully wrapping Magnus's base with hessian before winding more ropes around in a net.

They'd dragged Magnus as close to its future bed as possible and then wrapped the rope around their waist, set their legs, and began to stagger backwards, heaving down on the rope.

Slowly, Magnus lifted into the air, sliding against the side of the raised bed. Harlow strained, feeling the sweat beading at their hairline, turning to wrap the slack of the rope around their waist as they continued to pull.

Finally, Magnus popped over the edge of the sleepers and swung almost neatly over the hole, only bumping lightly against the mossy support sleeper.

Harlow took a slow step forward and gently lowered Magnus. They unwound themself from the rope, then released Magnus's roots from the rope and hessian.

It was then that they got the phone call.

"Baby? I thought we were meeting at the restaurant?"

Fuck. They had been on track to finish early, and then the delivery had turned up, driving all non-plant thoughts straight from their mind. Harlow might have felt guiltier if this dinner had not been postponed twice due to Jo getting last minute "essential for my career!" invitations followed by dawn returns, Jo hoarse-voiced and hangover-nursing, replete with "had to be there" stories.

"I'm sorry, Jo. I can't. Something came up," Harlow said, cringing in advance.

"Urgent work in the greenhouse? They're plants." It was Jo's lack of comprehension that hurt the most. It wasn't like Harlow had never tried

to explain why taking care of endangered plants for study took skill and time. "What, did you get a shipment of runaway runner beans or something?"

As though Bert would allow something as prosaic as a runner bean in his greenhouse.

Harlow sighed, started to run their fingers through their hair, and then stopped when they realised they were spreading dirt through their curls. Again.

"I should have called ahead," they admitted. "But I'm serious, this is time-critical."

"You should have called," Jo agreed. "I have tickets. Leave now. The flowers will deal."

Tickets? Harlow winced.

"If you'd told me—" Harlow began.

"You're not coming," Jo sighed. "Typical. Whatever, I'll take Cleo. Don't wait up for me."

It probably boded poorly, but Harlow felt relieved when Jo hung up. No doubt Cleo would enjoy whichever Experience Jo had booked more than Harlow could have.

At least they hadn't fought. Again.

And Magnus did need settling. Harlow had been truthful—now was a critical time.

Ah well. Back to work.

The plant listened to the ape noises and observed the primate as it used its portable mist maker to make its roots pleasantly damp.

It had originally been alarmed when the primate had started cutting away at its roots, but quickly realised that the primate was only taking away the ones that were unwell. Some of the roots had been damaged by the loud primate during the rude uprooting incident. Others had been damaged by the cold-water rocks that the loud primate had initially packed it in before it had been put in the dark.

The plant was glad to be away from the cold-water rocks. It did not like them. They felt like the few times an unusually cold season had swept through and killed some of its neighbours with frost.

Absently, it wiggled its roots, digging deeper into the loamy soil mix that the primate had so thoughtfully provided it with. It also liked the thick dead-tree-covered-in-moss that the primate had provided—it was nice to be able to lean against something while it re-established its balance in the soil.

It was very strange having been kidnapped by primates only to be waited upon and worshipped, but Magnus had to admit, it was starting to appreciate the attention.

The odd metal flower that spun and produced a nice soft breeze around its rootlets and stem was very thoughtful, as was the tiny Dayfire that shone steady light. It had never seen such things, nor enjoyed such regular light rain, twice a day, in the morning and late afternoon. Its home had always been pleasantly moist from the other respirating plant life, with raindrops dripping gently down from the canopy, but things had been getting drier in recent season-cycles, consistently enough that it was starting to feel a little concerned that this was not just a longer-than-usual Drytime.

The plant decided that it liked how the primate had specific mouth sounds for it. "Magnus" had a good hum and susurrus to it. It had been a long time since it had a name. Magnus would do.

It had once been one of many, but the centuries had claimed most of its kind even before it ended up at the bottom of the sinkhole. It had originally had three neighbours, siblings from the same seeding event, but the others had withered away, one by one, due to rootrot from a position that flooded, a bushfire that had missed Magnus itself by mere metres and covered its leaves in soot that took months to wash away, and (most ignobly) a cassowary getting a little over-excited during a Flowering and crushing its sibling before it could finish germinating.

That experience in particular had taught the plant to be choosy about selecting its Flowering attendants. Nothing that was too rough. Smaller birds were normally fine, although their claws and beaks could be harsh. Mammals could do in a pinch, so long as they didn't see it as food. It had cousins that used wasps and other winged insects, luring them in with flowers that resembled females of the species smelling ripe for pollination, but such creatures were too small for its needs.

Like all of its kind, it could adapt its shape somewhat to draw in a particularly desired attendant, but shrinking was a different story.

It had never tried to lure a primate for Flowering Time. It would have to observe to discover what the primate liked.

"You're spending too much time with the plants, Harlow, and not enough time with me!" Jo was pacing, her earrings tinkling wildly as her gesticulations barely missed the dangling foliage of Harlow's many houseplants.

Harlow winced at her volume and discarded their first three responses. *Why is my career less important than yours? I'm not the one who cancelled the last three times. You barely even want me there. You and your friends will ignore me all night anyway.* Jo wanted to hear "sorry", but Harlow was sick of apologising.

After a beat, they shrugged awkwardly. "I'm a botanist, Jo. I'm not sure what you were expecting."

"What I was expecting?" Jo's eyes glittered with unshed tears. "What I was expecting was to actually prioritise me at least as much as your plants!"

Harlow's mouth dropped at the unfairness. Sure, they were putting in longer hours at the greenhouse since Magnus's delivery, but Harlow had spent plenty of nights with only the plants for company while Jo filled her diary with so-called networking events.

"That stupid orchid sees more of you than I do!" Jo continued stridently. "Cleo keeps saying that I deserve more than a glorified gardener, but—"

"Haven't you told me the exact same thing," Harlow snapped, instantly regretting it as Jo's angry tears spilled.

Before Harlow could decide whether they owed her an apology, Jo left in a flurry of trailing scarf, manicured gesticulations, and slamming door.

Harlow's phone beeped a reminder that they didn't need, that it was time for the afternoon misting. Magnus was getting dry.

Harlow supposed the fact that they reached for their lanyard with the greenhouse keys rather than chasing Jo out onto the street indicated that maybe she was right about Harlow's priorities.

Every day, as they had for the last seven months, Harlow ensured that Magnus was misted lightly, morning and early afternoon. Every few hours, Harlow checked the fans, the humidity levels, the temperature, and the soil pH. They tinkered endlessly with the levels of nitrogen and phosphate in the fertiliser and the indoor climate conditions, watching for every droop or colour change.

When Harlow visited their apartment just before Magnus had been in their life for six and a half months, Jo had left a handwritten letter saying that she was "taking some time".

Harlow felt guilty about how little this moved them.

The next morning, however, effectively distracted Harlow from their impending break-up, as prioritising the orchid had finally paid off.

Magnus had grown three buds, each about the size of a loosely furled golf umbrella.

"Are you starting to bloom?" Harlow exclaimed. "You beauty!"

Sure enough, the velvety hairs of the bud had parted just enough to show a sliver of crimson-purple. Harper donned latex gloves and stepped forward, gently stroking at the emerging petals. They tried to name the colour. The dark but vibrant mauve was reminiscent of a perfectly ripe fig. They stroked gently, parting the hairs to better view the tender corolla.

"There you are," Harlow said. "Oh, I can't wait to see you unfurl."

Harlow wondered if Magnus had the capacity for self-pollination. Many orchids that grew in isolated conditions did, and had Harlow's boss seen any other specimens like Magnus then at least another one of them would have been uprooted from their habitat.

But regardless, what kind of creature normally pollinated it? Birds? Insects? Marsupials? It was frustrating that Bert had provided no naturalistic observations of Magnus in situ.

Harlow checked the camera that was continuously filming Magnus. Once the blooming was complete, they would compile the footage and use it to create a seamless time lapse. Harlow was sure they were the only one that had entered the greenhouse in weeks, but redundancy was never a bad idea.

The next week, Harlow registered something different in the greenhouse.

The heady scent grew stronger as Harlow approached the back of the greenhouse: Magnus's domain.

"Good morning, Magnus!" Harlow greeted, gently checking its leaves for insects or signs of damage. "Ah, you are looking well today!"

Harlow could have sworn that the scent increased in response. It was strong, and herbal. The aroma was as heavy as if someone had been burning essential oils for hours. Oddly, it reminded Harlow of chai tea.

Their stomach rumbled at the thought.

"Hmm, time for lunch I think." Harlow turned to get their lunchbox.

There was a susurrus, and Harlow spun to focus sharply on Magnus, whose leaves had suddenly seemed to shudder as though in a strong breeze.

The fan was, of course, on, circulating air around the room, but Harlow could have sworn it was not strong enough to move Magnus's broad leaves.

Harlow's stomach rumbled again, and they turned their attention back to their leftover curry.

Magnus had correctly identified how to activate the primate's base appetite. The test had been worthwhile, because it showed that the primate was not tricked into seriously considering it palatable. Smart was not always easiest to handle in a pollinator, but if Magnus wanted to engage in the True Sacred Dance, then it was required.

Despite the inconvenience, its anticipation grew at the challenge.

Time to see if it could tap into those mammalian reproductive instincts.

The next time Harlow entered the greenhouse, the scent was different. It was earthier, somehow. The fragrance was reminiscent of truffles,

and something pungent and almost…salty. Like someone had been exercising vigorously in the greenhouse.

Harlow frowned and sniffed their own armpit. No, they had definitely remembered to put on deodorant that morning.

Very weird. Harlow could not pinpoint the origin of the funky miasma. Could someone have broken in? Harlow was the only one within a thousand kilometres with a greenhouse key.

They resolved to check the cameras later, just to be sure.

Harlow leaned forward and absently flicked a speck of dirt from Magnus, brushing against the fleshy roots that were green with chlorophyll when suddenly, the roots moved.

Harlow froze.

Had they imagined that?

They felt it again. An undulating motion, as though the roots were rubbing up against Harlow's hand.

Harlow fell backwards onto their ass.

"Magnus?"

The giant bud, which they had watched for weeks without seeing more than that teasing hint of sumptuous purple, started to open before Harlow's shocked eyes.

The motion was not quick from an animal perspective, but in terms of a plant, it was insanely fast, as though Harlow was watching time-lapse footage instead of directly witnessing the bloom.

The green perianth parted, revealing deep-plum inner sepals with crimson striations. The sepals, in opening, revealed delicate inner petals that were edged with more crimson, including a delicate clitoric anther cap at the end of an abbreviated column that concealed Magnus's reproductive organs. Other types of flowers had male and female reproductive organs—stamens and pistils—but orchids combined the two into this single elegantly efficient organ.

(Harlow would be lying if they said this was irrelevant to why they had been drawn to study Orchidaceae above all other genuses.)

Below the column, the maroon-flecked labellum gaped, low and inviting, ready to be a perfect platform for any pollinator to collect the waxy pellet-like pollinia from the anther, or to (in theory) deposit pollinia from other orchids of its kind on the sticky stigma.

"Huh, I thought for sure your labellum would be inverted, but you

look more like a *Zygopetalum*," Harlow thought aloud, comparing Magnus to the star-shaped flowers with large lower labella like frilly pink or purple aprons, rather than the *Cryptostylis*, which were called bonnet orchids almost as often as tongue orchids. It would have made sense if the orchid had indeed been a *Cryptostylis*, albeit one that formed a "bonnet" large enough to wear at Mardi Gras. Instead, the labellum continued uncoiling at the lowest point of the flower to produce the widest pollination platform that Harlow had ever seen.

As Harlow watched, a bead of nectar welled up from the base of Magnus's column. Ponderously, the bead grew to almost the size of a grape before it grew too heavy to maintain surface tension and dripped slowly down the labellum like a pearl of sweat down a lover's neck.

"I wonder what normally pollinates you?" Harlow wondered, breathing in the musky aroma that they were sure now were the plant's pheromones.

"If I didn't know any better, I'd think that it smelled like sex in here. Perhaps the normal pollinators are mammalian? Possums? But you're not night-blooming. The deep purple and red that would look black at night suggest that the desired pollinator has some manner of colour vision. Insects tend to like those colours, but what insect could possibly be large enough for the flower to evolve to be so large?"

Magnus's leaves rattled, and Harlow paused.

"One of these days I'll find that draught."

The primate scraped an odd stick into Magnus's column, which felt…not entirely unpleasant, but perfunctory. It had collected pollinia, but it had done so in the manner of an echidna digging out some manner of grub from a half-rotten log.

Effective, but hardly fun for the log.

It had been so long since Magnus had managed to complete the dance properly. This place was strange, this partner was strange, but it had been so attentive otherwise that Magnus could not believe it was completely blind to Magnus's charms.

Magnus would have to try harder to entice it. But with what? How? Primates were difficult.

No sooner had Harlow filed away the pollinia samples than the greenhouse door slammed open. The sound of the stiletto heels clacking on the concrete floor revealed the most probable culprit a millisecond before she sashayed into view.

"Wow, that is the biggest flower I've ever seen! Smells like a gym though."

Harlow blinked. "Jo? What are you doing here?"

Jo smiled, revealing her dentist-bleached pearly white teeth behind immaculate palest-pink lipstick. As usual, she was wearing too much perfume, an over-brewed jasmine scent. Its miasma marked her territory well enough that weeks after Jo's abrupt departure, Harlow's apartment still felt haunted by her presence.

"I'm reminding you what you've been missing." Jo had an emotion Harlow struggled to identify in her eyes. "One for the road?"

Then to Harlow's surprise, she opened her coat, revealing a slightly ill-fitting negligee.

Harlow backed up a step. "Really?" They weren't sure what they were asking.

As usual, Jo acted as though she could read Harlow's mind. "Since when have you doubted that I know what I want?" she said, leaning in until she could brush slightly scratchy lace against Harlow's bare arm. She hung onto their shoulder and kissed them under the jaw.

Harlow grinned ruefully. They knew what Jo wanted to hear. "I'm lucky when that's me."

Jo bit Harlow's earlobe, then murmured right into their ear, "And don't you forget it."

Harlow wavered. It was probably unwise, but the pleasure curling in their belly insisted that Jo had a point. "Fine, but let's move over here, we're less likely to get caught by the cameras."

Jo laughed, and, soon after, her breath was hitching into moans.

As far as encounters went, it could have been more comfortable, but Jo had always liked being innovative. It turned out the older specimen shelf *was* just the right height, and sturdier than Harlow would have assumed.

It all would have gone better, though, if Harlow's phone hadn't

buzzed a reminder in the middle of the afterglow. Harlow getting up to mist Magnus again was definitely not what Jo had had in mind as a post-coital activity, and she had been gone before Harlow had finished the routine leaf check.

Who was *that*?

Was *that* what the primate liked in a mate?

Was that what the primate liked to *do* with a mate?

Magnus needed to reconfigure its plans.

To Harlow's disappointment, the first flower did not last long. No longer than three days. Though perhaps the effort of maintaining such a large flower was too much for a plant that had undergone such shock so recently in its growth cycle. Luckily, Harlow had managed to collect the pollinia sample. Perhaps Harlow had damaged it?

They would have to be more careful next time.

They watched the other buds, waiting to see if the stress to the plant would halt this flowering cycle, but for now, at least, its condition stayed stable.

More concerning was the way that Harlow was increasingly feeling the sensation of being watched.

The little hairs on the back of their neck stood up almost constantly, but there was never anyone there. They checked for electronic surveillance, but the only cameras they could find were their own set-up, and it was the type that saved the footage onto an SD card, not the type with an internet connection.

Whoever it was, it wasn't Jo. She was doing something with Cleo again.

The second time Magnus flowered happened just as abruptly.

Again, Harlow just so happened to be exactly in the right place to

observe it.

The labellum itself continued to unfurl, revealing first two, then five, elongated lobes protruding out, limb-like, from the main body of the labellum, the centre-bottom lobe somewhat shorter than the others.

Harlow blinked, then started to laugh. They were of course familiar with *Orchis italica*, or the Naked Man Orchid as it was more infamously known. They never would have guessed that Magnus would take such a shape. Regardless of how large Magnus was for an orchid, however, the "man" if standing on the floor on its "legs" would only have reached Harlow's knee.

How entirely bizarre. Harlow had never heard of an orchid that bloomed with differently shaped flowers. They were so glad they had the continuous time-stamped footage recording.

More of the nectar dripped down the body-shaped labellum. Harlow watched as it pooled around the area on the labellum analogous to the crotch.

They reached forward with one gloved hand, just in time to catch the nectar as it overflowed.

Harlow was gripped by an irrational urge to taste the viscous liquid, but managed to refrain. It would be embarrassing if word got out about Magnus before they were ready to publish because Harlow had ingested toxins from it.

Instead, they took a glass vial from their overall pocket and carefully collected a sample, applying the stopper with care. Kylie from the Chemistry building would let them run it through a chromatograph to check the composition after-hours if they brought her strong black coffee from their private stash.

From the same pocket, they pulled out a sterile swab, which they peeled the plastic from and then used to gently collect a second pollinia sample from the delicate anther. They lightly deposited the swab and pollen in a second vial, then stroked the column with one gloved finger.

"You are gorgeous," Harlow breathed, inhaling the surprisingly musky scent of the flower. It reminded Harlow of something, but they couldn't identify it. It would seem that this was where the scent emanating in the greenhouse had come from.

The labellum jiggled lightly in what Harlow could only assume was a timely gust from the fans.

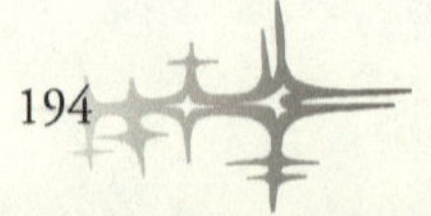

Despite themself, Harlow snickered as they stepped back to admire the view. "And completely ridiculous looking. Such a beautiful colouration though."

For a moment the flower seemed almost to sag, but then Harlow blinked and it was perfectly upright again. Perhaps such a large flower was heavy on the plant, no matter how thick the stem was.

Its attendant had not properly appreciated the offering. It had laughed! Magnus sulked. The laughter was not an unpleasant vibration, reminiscent of those birds with long beaks that sometimes caught snakes and cackled together in the trees, but it was not the desired result!

One last try.

The last talk with Jo was painful. Jo obviously had a specific script she was working through, but Harlow wasn't willing to follow her cues this time, especially when Jo said it was her or Magnus; that she couldn't bear Harlow's continued distraction.

Before Harlow could think of a response, Jo claimed once again that Cleo thought she could do better than a Doctor of Gardening.

Harlow responded that perhaps it was time that Jo conducted that research, and that was that.

Harlow knew that coming into the greenhouse after half a bottle of red wine was a mistake, but their apartment still smelled of jasmine, Jo definitely wasn't coming back this time, and they needed to get out.

If a small, spiteful part of Harlow thought it a little humorous to go running to Jo's "nemesis" to use as an audience for bemoaning the break-up, then that would be between them and the plants.

At least the plants were good listeners.

As they stumbled into the greenhouse, Harlow realised the smell that Jo had complained about was stronger than ever, but now the scent was unmistakable. It was not just the aroma of sweaty bodies, it was bodies engaging in a very particular activity.

Sex.

Harlow rounded the corner, and then saw that while they were drinking away their sorrows, they had missed seeing Magnus's third flower blooming.

And what a flower it was.

The difference between the first and second flowers had been strange. This flower was even more complex, and different again. Instead of a comical silhouette of a naked man, Magnus looked like…

"What *are* you?" Harlow whispered reverently.

The colours had remained the same: deep Tyrian purple with crimson striations. But the shape looked more like the face and torso of a woman. And below the torso, Magnus's green rootlets had, somehow in the past 14 hours, grown into the shape of a human lap, complete with hips.

On top of the sex smell, Harlow realised they could detect a faint whiff of jasmine.

The realisation hit Harlow like a wet bag of compost.

"I wondered what could possibly be big enough to pollinate you. Magnus. Were. Were you trying to attract *me*?"

Magnus waved a tendril at them, coincidentally framing the delicate curves of the womanly silhouette its labellum now formed.

Harlow facepalmed. "I literally felt you moving under me with the second flower."

Magnus nodded its floral "head", causing the entire body to jiggle. A sweet drop of nectar rolled down from the column, between the "clavicles" of the labellum torso, then curving down to drip onto the rootlets that formed the "hips". The way they were bundled together looked like a pair of delightfully thick thighs, and they were parted just enough to straddle.

Harlow licked their lips. This was crazy. They could not be seriously thinking about…

One of Magnus's leaves made a clear beckoning motion.

Harlow was lonely, horny, and more than half drunk. "This is for science," they murmured, meaning, "this is for me."

They stepped forward and climbed until they were kneeling in the soil of Magnus's planter box.

This close to the flower, the scent was almost overwhelming, akin to burying one's face between another person's legs.

Harlow had always liked giving head.

They leaned forward and lapped at the dripping nectar near the base of the column, in roughly the position where a mouth would have been on a human. The taste was sweet, but more astringent than they would have guessed. Like Manuka Tea Tree honey. The petals of the innermost corolla framed Harlow's face, both cradling and smothering.

Magnus dripped more nectar in seeming encouragement, and Harlow could feel the rhizome and rootlets shifting between their legs until they were supporting Harlow's weight.

Harlow leaned back a little to better enjoy the sensation and stripped their shirt off over their head. Magnus rewarded the increased access to Harlow's skin by brushing its labellum and leaves up and down Harlow's torso, the sensation akin to silk scarves and leather. Long strokes down Harlow's ribcage, softer ones teasing Harlow's chest (including sensitive nipples), curiously exploring each and every centimetre of bared skin.

Harlow leaned forward again and lapped at the nectar, shivering as the greenhouse fans cooled the sweat on their back. They were starting to feel dizzy from the wine, the nectar, the pheromones.

And then Magnus pressed a rootlet directly against Harlow's core.

Harlow groaned and began to grind against the fleshy lower stem and rootlets. Their movements shook the flower, and they could feel the nectar dripping onto their skin as it spilled past their mouth onto their bare chest and jean-clad thighs.

Magnus thrummed gently, the rootlets writhing against Harlow. Some curled around Harlow's calves and thighs, holding without binding.

Harlow could have easily escaped if they wanted to.

Harlow had no intention of trying.

Every nerve in their body felt like static danced along it. The sense of being entirely enveloped and overwhelmed by Magnus's presence—its mixture of textures, its olfactory blanketing, its taste—made it easy to sink into the experience.

The rootlets undulated between Harlow's thighs, and Harlow could feel their orgasm approaching as they continued to frot against the crude tubercules. The texture and dirt made them glad to have kept their jeans on, even as they dug clawed fingers into that same dirt in a desperate attempt to ground themself.

The unceasing, tireless rhythm started to blur into euphoria, urging Harlow to rock faster and faster against the flower as the sticky pollinia caught in their hair.

Finally, they reached their peak, climaxing harder than they had in some time but forcing themself to stay upright, wary of crushing Magnus's petals.

A gentle push to their sternum, and Harlow pulled back from the flower, licking the nectar from their lips. The flower followed, and the rootlets rearranged themselves, until Harlow was lying on their back in the dirt, legs arranged on either side of Magnus's stem.

The rootlets resumed their rhythm, continuing to play Harlow like an instrument.

Harlow's strangled moans were muffled by the flower lowering and covering their face, dripping yet more nectar into their mouth as they suckled greedily.

They could become addicted to this, they thought dazedly as the rootlets wrapped delicately around their ribcage, deliciously abrading oversensitive skin.

The sensations finally came to a crescendo as the rootlets once again increased their frenzied movements against Harlow's core, raising the pressure but never quite pushing past the boundary between excruciating pleasure and pain.

Harlow screamed their second orgasm, and Magnus subsided, apparently content with wringing them into loose-limbed disarray.

There was dirt caked up to their wrists, all over their back, in their hair. Their underwear was soaked and sticking slightly awkwardly. Their face and chest were covered in nectar that had spilled past their lips and down their chin. They had bright-yellow sticky pollinia in their hair.

Harlow was a mess.

Harlow was beyond caring.

There was a light stirring from Magnus, and Harlow looked up. Without being able to articulate why, Harlow sensed a distinctive vibe of smugness from the tilt of the corolla.

"Yeah, yeah, you got me," Harlow chuckled, slowly sitting up.

They turned their head and saw the still-recording camera.

Damn.

They had no idea how they were going to explain this to Bert.

Ocean Breeze, Take Me Home

Cedar D. McCafferty-Svec

belly bulge, bipoc, bird person, character injury (non-graphic descriptions), didn't know they were dating, double penetration in one hole, drowning, f/f, getting together, half-human, hurt/comfort, misunderstandings, octopus person, overstimulation, oviposition, past tense, size kink, tentacles, third person limited point of view

Sharp pain accompanied the crack of thunder overhead. Adaline rolled in the wind, gasping as agony lanced down her wing and through her shoulders. It left her arms numb. Each heavy, rain-sodden flap brought a fresh wave of torment, and she knew, beyond a shadow of a doubt, that she was going to die out here.

Lightning arced to her right, crashing into the water below. Her heart leapt to her throat, choking her, and she desperately angled her wings to catch the wind. If she could just glide to the edge of the storm…if she could just make it a little farther…

Her wing buckled.

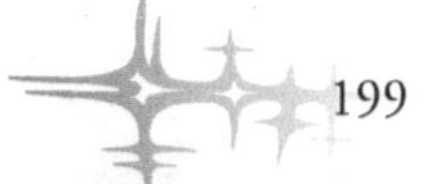

Adaline dropped in a free fall. She didn't even have time to scream before the roaring waves swallowed her whole.

Lightning above lit up the water, drawing her eyes to the bubbles streaming from her beak. It was surprisingly peaceful under the waves.

Deliriously, she thought there were worse ways to go.

She wished she'd learned to swim.

She should have listened to her mother and stayed home.

As her eyes closed, something soft and slippery wound around her leg. Was it seaweed? She didn't think she'd sunk far enough for that, but it didn't matter, did it? Or at least, she thought it didn't. The weightlessness of the water was replaced by the shift of currents against her feathers, and more of that slippery substance covered her. Supported her.

Adaline opened her eyes again, looking blearily through the darkness. Just barely, she could make out the shape of something, or someone. Soft clicks and coos didn't make noise so much as pulsed against her ears. It felt safe.

She reached one hand out and touched a face. Smooth, leathery skin and a small, pointed beak. Her thumb traced up to what she thought might have been an eye. She knew this face, didn't she?

A hand wrapped around hers, and everything went dark.

She woke with full-body jerks and the rough, hacking cough she'd only heard half-drowned sailors make. Her stomach heaved, and she gagged. Someone pushed her gently onto her side and turned her head as she spat out what felt like a lungful of water.

When she blinked, tears wet the down of her cheeks. The world slowly came back into focus; muted grays and browns blooming into greens and blues the longer she looked at the ground. It was wet from more than what she'd hacked up, and she registered the gentle sound of water against a shoreline.

It was dark, though. So, she wasn't outside.

"Wha—?" She winced as her throat stung, scraped raw, and curled in on herself while she coughed. Everything *ached*.

A hand passed over her back, petting down her spine and patting gently at her shoulders. "You're okay," a soft voice said from overhead.

"You're safe. The storm cannot reach you here."

Storm? *Storm.* The aches and pain made sense now.

She coughed one last time and groaned as she rolled onto her stomach. She flared her wings to help balance, only to cry out and yank her right wing closed again. Nausea roiled in her stomach. She shook with the effort of not breaking into tears.

"Gentle, dear one, gentle," that same voice whispered. "Your wing is broken. I don't know how to set it, I'm sorry. But you are no longer drowning, so that's a good thing."

"Wha—? Where?" Adaline coughed again and grimaced. Talking hurt. Everything hurt. She'd thought that already.

Something slimy brushed across her broken wing, carefully wrapping around the edges and stabilizing it as hands helped Adaline sit up. Only then did she get a proper look at her rescuer.

Dusky brown skin dotted with paler circles. Not quite freckles, but something adjacent. A round face with eyes that were just on the edge of too large with next to no sclera visible. They had no lips, not like the humanoid ones depicted in the old fables. Instead, they had a beak, smaller than her own, that jutted from their oblong face. As Adaline dragged her gaze down, she noticed the spread of tentacles half in the water and half on the rocks around her. The smooth skin was strange where it brushed against her feathers, but it wasn't a *bad* strange.

She'd never seen a mer up close before, let alone one that hailed from the cephalopod side. She'd always watched them from the sky, following and mimicking their graceful moves in the water.

"You are in my home," the mer said. She smiled at Adaline, though Adaline could read it more in the crinkle around her eyes than the movement of her beak. "You fell quite a distance into the water. You're lucky I was looking for you."

"Me?" Adaline questioned. She shook her head minutely. Moving it too much made her vision blur and her head sway with vertigo. "Why would you be looking for me?"

"Because you always come out around this time to dance for me, silly." The mer clicked her beak, and a tentacle came up to brush against Adaline's cheek. It was followed by a hand, the fingertips dotted with tiny suckers like the tentacles. "You've kept this pattern for months. The others thought me foolish for indulging in the mating dance of a harpy, but you learned our moves so well despite being bound by feather."

Adaline hadn't known she'd been observed in turn. She hadn't even known she'd been mimicking the same mer the entire time. It was a lot to contend with on top of everything else. Despite that, and despite her bone-deep exhaustion, one thing stuck out and made her look at the mer in a new light. When she tilted her head, the soaked plume of feathers adorning her head flopped over and smacked against her ear. "Mating dance?"

"Yes. Surely you knew? Those dances are for enticing a mate, assuring them you are fast and nimble and able to evade capture from the trickiest of foes. That you could adapt them to flight shows a cunning that none of my kind have shown me in the years I've been looking." A finger lifted Adaline's chin, turning her this way and that as though she was looking for more hidden damage. "You are stunning for a harpy. I would be delighted to accept your proposal."

Adaline brought her hands up quickly, taking the mer's wrist and pushing her away. "I wasn't— I don't even know your *name*."

The mer gasped, pulling her hands back to cover the bottom of her face. Her eyes were wide, and the rusty brown of her skin began to bleed into a glowing blue along the paler circles. "I am *so* sorry, dear one. I forgot we haven't been properly introduced. I was so worried about making sure you were safe… I am Kalin."

There was a way Kalin said her name that echoed strangely in Adaline's ears, like she said it with clicks and hums in the back of her throat. Adaline didn't know if she'd said it in her native tongue at the same time, but it certainly sounded like it.

"Kalin," Adaline said. "That's a very pretty name." She took a deep breath and winced, putting her hand over her ribs as her chest pulled tight. "I'm Adaline. I—" She paused, both to sort out her thoughts and to take a breather. "I wasn't trying to court you. I'm very sorry."

Kalin breathed an "oh" more than she said it, but she didn't stop her gentle support of Adaline's wing and back. Instead, she slid her hand down and cupped Adaline's chin. "Well," she said, "then I will simply have to court you instead. If you're amenable to that." Her eyes crinkled with another smile, and she let go. "First, however, can you walk me through how to set your wing? I don't wish to harm you further, but if it isn't set—"

"—I won't be able to fly again," Adaline finished. She decided to brush over the previous comment instead of questioning it. She winced as she flared her wing out again, breathing through the roiling nausea. "Here, I'll show you what I know." What she knew wasn't much, but it would have to be enough.

She carefully felt out where the break was, hissing quietly at each twinge of pain. "You'll need to hold the back steady, under the break, and realign the bones with your other hand." She reached for Kalin's hands, positioning them in the right spots.

A tentacle came up to cradle and steady Adaline's wing.

Having more than two "arms" was certainly helpful.

Kalin met her eyes. "Are you ready?"

"No, but do it anyway."

Kalin nodded and pushed. Dark spots covered Adaline's vision. The pain left her breathless for one sharp instant before the screaming started. Somehow, she didn't pass out. Kalin stroked a tentacle down the curve of Adaline's spine soothingly, holding her upright as Adaline panted through the aftershocks.

It took several long moments before she could focus on her surroundings again. She observed them to distract herself from the pain. It was a fairly standard cave, from what she knew about caves. Her people didn't go into caves much. Being below the earth was too enclosed and suffocating.

If she tipped her head back far enough, though, she could make out stars through a crack overhead. The cavern had to be at least four times her wingspan tall, and many more times wide. Kalin had lanterns scattered around the outskirts, and the soft orange glow made everything less jagged and scary.

Adaline stood carefully and walked around the lit space. Tables and shelves marked out a living area, and tapestries hung between the bookcases. Adaline recognized some of the tapestries, actually. She paused in front of one, lightly drawing a claw over the faded green and blue threads. There were two harpies embroidered into the sky, and the land below was rolling hills and delicate flowers. This tapestry was old. She'd seen recreations of it in the town hall. But what was it doing here?

"Shipwrecks," Kalin answered without Adaline asking. She was much closer than Adaline expected, and Adaline jumped. "Sorry." She reached past Adaline and traced a line along the hills. "Shipwrecks drop treasures to the bottom of the sea, and my people take them home. We preserve what we can of the landwalkers and the sky dwellers, because we know we will never understand their world. Just like they do not understand ours."

Adaline hummed and crossed her arms, hugging herself gently. "That makes sense. I never thought of mers collecting the things we lose…"

"Your kind don't think of us much at all." Kalin drew back and made her way to a pile of seaweed and kelp. She lifted it and shook it out, revealing that it was woven into a blanket. "I know you cannot sleep in the water like I do, so I studied and made this to keep you warm while you are down here."

Adaline blinked and curled her talons into the floor beneath her, flexing them nervously. "When…when did you find time to do that?"

"It has been done for many months," Kalin said. She crawled back, each tentacle overlapping another to move her. Despite how awkward land must be for Kalin, she made it look smooth and graceful. Adaline was almost jealous. "It's softened with whale fat and dried in the sun, so it should keep you warm." Kalin flicked the edges, draping it around Adaline's shoulders. It was large enough to cover her wings and wrap around her.

Almost instantly, she was suffused in warmth. Of course, everything was warmer than her slowly drying feathers. She still curled her fingers around the edges and drew it close. It smelled like the sea, in a way that made her nostalgic for summer days spent playing on the beach with her sisters. "Thank you."

Kalin beamed with pride and tucked the edges close to Adaline's neck. "I'm glad you will be warm. Now that you are awake, I can go fetch dinner. You do eat fish, right?"

Adaline laughed softly as she nodded, and Kalin swiftly slid back into the water. Within moments, Adaline was alone in the cave, left to her own devices. Even with all the items Kalin had collected from Adaline's people, there was no obvious sleeping area. If she was going to have to impose on Kalin long enough for her wing to heal, she might as well sort out a small corner of the place to be a nest.

"Four to six weeks?" Kalin passed Adaline a plate made from a shell, the mother-of-pearl sheen on it catching Adaline's eye. She nodded as she took the plate, deeply inhaling the scent of roasted fish.

"That's how long wings take to heal on average. I won't be able to fly until it does, and I don't know how far we are from my home," she said. She slid a claw over the belly of the fish, slicing a piece off. "I'm sorry for the inconvenience."

"Nonsense. It's no hassle at all. This gives me plenty of time to learn your customs and perform a dance for you." Kalin settled on the bundle of tentacles beneath her and bit off a large chunk of fish. "It gives us time to get to know each other."

Adaline hummed a not-quite-answer. Even if Kalin said it was fine, she felt guilty. Crashing in on her, imposing on her home while she healed… She hated to be useless. "Is there something I can do to help around the place?" she asked. "You're being so kind, I'd love to repay the favor."

Kalin slipped a tentacle beneath Adaline's plate, pushing it closer to her. "How about you eat first, and we can discuss helping out after you rest. I can't imagine passing out while almost drowning is very restful. For tonight, you are my guest." She drew her tentacle back and smiled before turning back to her plate.

There was nothing to it then but to eat and rest.

Adaline whistled as she shucked open the oysters Kalin had brought up. The repetitive motion was good for her, steadying. It took her mind off the dull ache of her wing and the increasing itchiness of the pin feathers growing in. She'd done similar work at home when the fishers came back from their trips. The familiarity was a balm to her battered soul.

She twisted the knife and pressed her thumb into the gap, pausing for a moment as she noticed the bundle in the middle. Pearls? She supposed that made sense. Kalin likely dug up the oysters from deeper parts of the sea where they had more time to form.

She rolled the pearl out of the pocket and picked it up, twisting it this way and that to get a better look. There was a golden sheen to it, and it couldn't be more than a couple of millimeters across.

The water moved at her side, and Kalin's head popped up. She blinked a few times at Adaline and clicked her beak. "You are lucky; golden pearls are a good find." She hauled herself the rest of the way onto the bank, splashing water over Adaline's legs and leaving a puddle where she sat.

Adaline gestured toward the loops of strung pearls along Kalin's upper arms. "You seem to have found quite a few."

"Pearls are a status symbol among my kind," Kalin said. She traced a finger over the highest strand. "These were given to me by my mother before she left for the South." There was something far away in her eyes that Adaline couldn't name. "They were the courting pearls my father gave to her."

"Oh." Adaline blinked and looked down at the pearl in her hand. "Are courting gifts common?"

"If you're considered higher class, yes." Kalin gave Adaline an amused look. "The pursuer typically will present a strand of the highest-quality, rarest-colored pearls. We start collecting them when we first come of age. The more pearls you give, the more serious you are about the relationship."

Adaline nodded, rolling the pearl between her claws. "We don't use gifts so much," she said. "We aim to spend quality time together. The biggest thing, though, is if you can match songs. It's said that if your singing sounds good together, the relationship is blessed by the gods."

Kalin clicked her beak, considering that. "Sound travels underwater, but we do not use singing so much. We leave that to the whales and dolphins. I can see why it would be important for you, though. I can hear your songs, sometimes, when you have festivals on the beach." She picked up an oyster from the pile beside Adaline and shucked it open with practiced ease. She pressed on the meat and rolled two pearls out, then passed them over to Adaline.

Adaline cracked a smile as she let them bump against the gold pearl in her palm. "This you starting to court me?" she asked, teasing.

Kalin slid her hand under Adaline's, the suckers on her fingers tickling against Adaline's skin, and carefully folded Adaline's hand around the pearls. "I have some ground to make up. I'm afraid I wasn't collecting pearls to woo anyone." She smiled and used a tentacle to chuck Adaline's chin. "I can show you how we string them later, if you'd like?"

Adaline flushed and looked away. Her heart fluttered against her ribs,

and she couldn't breathe for a moment. It wasn't a bad feeling, though. Quite the opposite. "I would like that."

Kalin kept three tentacles wrapped around Adaline's waist, laughing as Adaline squawked at the chill of the water. Adaline flapped her good wing, splashing Kalin with a wave of water. "Stop laughing at me. I already told you I don't swim!"

"You can't even float. How can you live this close to the sea and not know how to swim?" Kalin teased. She tucked another tentacle under Adaline's legs, keeping her steady, and grinned. "How are you going to keep up with me while dancing?"

"The same way I have been for months, obviously. I'll just *fly*." Adaline tightened her hands around Kalin's shoulders, careful not to prick her with her claws, and squeaked again when Kalin lowered her a little farther in the water. "This ain't natural for me."

"There are plenty of birds that can swim. It's not so hard, I promise. And I'm here. I won't let you come to harm."

Adaline sighed and slowly forced her muscles to relax. It was a process, but eventually she was sitting loosely in Kalin's hold. There was something to being held up, relying on someone else to keep her safe, and she wasn't sure how to feel about it. Yet she wasn't afraid. After all, Kalin had saved her from drowning once.

In a way, it brought her back to childhood, clinging to her mother's silks on her first flight. She'd felt just as unmoored then, but she'd known she was safe.

She missed her mom. Hopefully she would see her again soon. Introduce her family to Kalin. They would like Kalin, she was positive of that.

"There you go, look at that. You're floating just fine," Kalin said softly. "Ah, ah, don't tense, I've still got you."

Adaline forced herself to not panic and freeze up as she realized that Kalin had relaxed her grip. Adaline was still holding onto Kalin's shoulders, but the support was looser around her waist. It wasn't all that different from being weightless in the air, supporting herself with only the strength of her wings. Yet it was also completely different.

"How long can you stay on land?" She looked up at Kalin, avoiding thinking too hard about the water. "If we're gonna do this legitimately, I'd want my family to meet you. Right now, they just know you as 'one of those sea creatures Adaline is always following.' "

Kalin laughed, and her tentacles rippled. It almost tickled, and Adaline squirmed, kicking her feet.

"I don't mind being known that way," Kalin said. She tipped her head toward the shoreline of the cave. "A few hours if I keep moist. I dry out fast, so it's easier for me to be in the water, but I can go on beaches easily enough." She lifted a tentacle to push Adaline's crest out of her eyes. "I would love to meet your family."

Adaline flushed even as she tipped her head into the touch. "Good. I'm sure they'll love you." She kicked her legs again, treading water now that Kalin wasn't supporting her as much. It wasn't so bad when she wasn't scared. She could understand why others enjoyed it.

"You mentioned that your people value songs," Kalin said softly. "Can you teach me some of them?"

She nodded. "Yeah, yeah. They… Not many of them have words. Whistles carry better when you're flying." She clicked her beak thoughtfully, pondering over which song to sing, then she started to hum, a simple shanty she'd learned as a hatchling.

Kalin's eyes widened slightly, and she laughed. "I know this one! I've heard this when the fishermen come out." She joined in after the second phrase, her voice a lilting alto to Adaline's soprano. It had an almost bubbly, warbling quality to it, and Adaline's heart raced to hear it.

They were in perfect harmony.

She'd never sung with someone who matched her tone so well. Not even her sister, her nest twin. She didn't hesitate to loop her arms around Kalin's neck, bringing their foreheads closer together as she shifted the song into something like a ballad.

She remembered her mother singing something similar with her father when they would dance in the kitchen. She and her sister would copy their moves, but they could never match the song perfectly because it was their parents' song. This had that same feeling: a thing made between the two of them that no one else could copy.

Kalin slid her tentacles tighter around Adaline's waist and thighs, holding her up more. Her voice dipped and weaved and while it wasn't

perfect—it was clear Kalin wasn't trained so much as she learned by mimicking—it was just right for them.

The fire crackled merrily, lighting the cave in an amber glow. Adaline flexed her wings out and then back in, repeating the motion a few times. After almost three weeks of swimming lessons, she'd become more comfortable in the water, but she couldn't wait to get back in the air.

The break didn't hurt now, but she knew she still had to take it easy. Stretching it felt good, though.

"Kalin," she called, "Can you help me with preening?"

Kalin popped her head out of the water with a burble. "I don't know how your preening works. You'll have to show me."

"That's fine. There's just some pin feathers I can't reach on the back of my wings. C'mere, I'll show you." Adaline gestured with her uninjured wing, beckoning Kalin over. The splash of cold water against her back was a shock, but Kalin settling behind her was more than enough to warm Adaline again.

She reached back, combing her fingers through her crest until she found a keratin sheath. "Can you see this?" she asked.

"Mmhm," Kalin hummed.

Adaline tried to ignore the shiver that went down her spine, but the flair of her wings gave her away. Kalin, graciously, didn't comment on it. Adaline cleared her throat and used her other hand to part her crest feathers and give Kalin a better view.

"It's really simple. You have to rub the sheath off and fluff out the feather." She rolled the keratin between her fingers, loosening it until it flaked off into her hand. She carefully fluffed the feather out by feel alone. "Like that."

Careful fingers combed over her wings, and Adaline shivered again. This time Kalin did chuckle, and Adaline flushed. "They're sensitive," she protested. She settled back and stared into the fire as Kalin broke apart the pin feathers.

The itchiness gradually faded, and Adaline trilled in the back of her throat, sinking into the touch as it turned from preening to just petting. She closed her eyes, smiling as Kalin started to hum quietly. It was the same tune they'd made together during her first swimming lesson. It made her heart do silly leaps, like it was dancing all on its own.

"Kalin?"

"Mm?"

"Will you dance with me?"

Kalin leaned back, and Adaline shifted her wings out of the way. She turned enough to look at Kalin, her breath held. The octo-mer was flushed bright blue, the spots along the top of her head fluctuating between blue and green.

Adaline smiled, fond, and cupped Kalin's cheek gently in her hand. "I'm asking, knowing what it means to you, because I want—" She hesitated, clicking her beak. Why was saying it so difficult? The knots in her stomach ached from the nerves. "…to court you." If the last bit came out in a rush, Kalin didn't judge her for it. "Properly," she finished.

Kalin leaned into the touch and chittered. Her eyes crinkled. "You have already courted me, remember? But yes, I would love to dance with you."

Adaline stood, taking Kalin's hands as she did. "You asked, on that first day, if I'd be amenable to your returning the courting favors. I know I didn't answer then, and I haven't really answered since, but—"

Kalin placed a tentacle under Adaline's chin, quieting her. Her smile was broad enough that her eyes creased at the edges, all but disappearing. "I'm glad that you waited and made sure. You're very smart, Adaline, and I very much like that about you." She carefully guided their hands together, moving closer to put them chest to chest.

Dancing on dry land didn't come naturally to Kalin, Adaline knew. And yet still they managed, swaying to their own beat in lazy circles. Adaline didn't think she'd ever know how she avoided stepping on any of Kalin's tentacles. They made it work, though, and that was beauty in and of itself.

To be so in sync with someone else, to know each other's movements as their own and telegraph that with just a slight push or pull of their bodies…it was magic. Beautiful, love-filled magic.

It was no wonder the cephalopod mers used dance in their mating displays.

Adaline smiled as they spun, and she lifted her voice in song for their dance. Sweet, simple melodies were always her favorite. She was lucky

that Kalin's dance followed the same rhythms.

Perhaps this was how her mother had felt when her father courted her. It wasn't like how the books described it, flying through tight spires of stone, flirting with disaster with every tilt of her wings. It was warmth and gentleness. A hug that she could wear as a coat through the cold winter months. It was everything and nothing like she expected.

"Kalin." They slowed to a stop when Adaline finished singing. She tipped her head back to look up at Kalin, taking in the glowing flush and the crinkled edges of her too-wide eyes. Her heart skipped a beat and tap danced against her ribs.

There were no words for what she wanted to say. Instead, she leaned onto the tips of her talons and pressed their foreheads together. The slide of Kalin's tentacles enveloping her was familiar and welcome.

Adaline didn't have to say anything.

Kalin already knew.

There was a push and pull evocative of their dance as Kalin drew her nearer and Adaline, in turn, let herself be held up. If Kalin sank down on her tentacles, the height difference wasn't that great, but it was peaceful to be held; cradled as though she was something precious. Adaline liked it. She liked being precious. Wanted. Loved.

As kisses go, beak to beak and hands on cheeks, Adaline couldn't say it was the best she'd ever had. But it was the one she wanted to keep having. Keratin scraped against keratin and sent vibrations through her beak, making her laugh, and Adaline tipped her head enough to rub the sides of their beaks together.

Kalin chirred, the sound high and rolling, as she repeated the motion. Her tongue rasped against Adaline's beak, prickly and sharp in a way that made Adaline's feathers fluff out on end. Her crest stood up, spread wide in display, and she didn't have time to be embarrassed about it before Kalin picked her up under her thighs.

Her stomach swooped, and she threw her arms around Kalin's neck. Kalin's hands, in turn, sank into the thick ruff of feathers at the back of her neck.

Having more than two arms was definitely in Kalin's favor.

Adaline traced a hand over the string of pearls along Kalin's upper arm, letting them roll between her claws. She gasped as a tentacle slipped under her shirt, the suckers flexing around and over her feathers.

Kalin breathed a laugh against the side of her face. "You taste like sea salt," she murmured.

Adaline wrapped her hand around the pearls and used the other to tug Kalin back into a kiss. She could get used to this.

Adaline twisted, peering into the mirror to see herself from each angle. She was completely bare except for a harness made of pristine, multi-colored pearls. The strands draped across her shoulders in three rows, meeting at her neck and making a choker. Two more strands draped from the choker's middle, falling down her chest and looping around her sides. She could feel them rubbing between her wings, shifting with each breath she took.

It was a stunning number of pearls, and Kalin had hardly stopped crafting the harness for the last four days.

Adaline's stomach flipped over and over, twisting into knots, as she met Kalin's eyes through the mirror. She'd never received something so *grand*, and Kalin had so carefully helped her into it. She could still feel the ghost of Kalin's fingers at the back of her neck.

"Do you like them?" Kalin asked. Her voice was low, almost breathy. She couldn't tear her eyes away from Adaline.

"I love them." Adaline turned and cupped Kalin's cheeks in her hands. She traced her thumb beneath Kalin's eye, smiling as Kalin leaned into it. "They're beautiful."

Kalin's shoulders relaxed as she nuzzled Adaline's palm. "I'm glad." She swept her gaze over Adaline, her eyes darkening.

Adaline would say she was undressing her with her eyes, but there was nothing to undress.

"Is it too forward of me to say I would much rather kiss you than go dancing right now?" Kalin asked.

Adaline laughed softly and tipped forward to rub their beaks together gently. "Well, I'd have to tell you, then, that technically we've completed all the stages of courting. We've danced, sang, spent quality time together, you've given your courting gift…" She flexed her wings, shivering as the pearls shifted against her feathers, and gently wrapped one around Kalin. "There's no one else here to perform anything for."

Kalin's breath shook, and she shifted, sinking into the embrace of Adaline's wing. Tentacles slid around Adaline's legs and moved higher, brushing over feathers and pearls until Kalin had her swathed in an all-encompassing hold. Kalin tipped her head just enough to slide the sides of their beaks together again, and they both shuddered.

"Are you certain?" Kalin asked.

The press of their bodies together made thinking hard, but Adaline had never been so certain of something in her life. "I am." She slid her hands behind Kalin's head and pulled her down, puzzling their mouths together with a sigh. It was so easy to turn herself over to Kalin, to let herself enjoy the slick slide of tentacles and the tickle of suckers.

Kalin lifted Adaline by her thighs, supporting her entirely as she walked them toward the nest. She couldn't stop touching Adaline, even as she laid them both down and covered Adaline with her body. She pet over Adaline's faint curves, slid her fingers between the feathers of her chest, and rolled the pearls between them slowly. She held Adaline's legs up and apart with two tentacles while another coiled across Adaline's belly.

Adaline arched into the touch, moaning into the space between them. She tightened her grasp on the back of Kalin's neck, keeping her close, and slid her free hand across the expanse of Kalin's back. She could feel the swell and ripple of Kalin's muscles moving under her palm.

A tentacle brushed against her cloaca, and Adaline whined. She dug her claws into Kalin's back, and did it again when Kalin moaned. Arching her back again, she rubbed up against that questing tentacle and swallowed down the sound Kalin made in response. She slid her claws down Kalin's back, gentle so she didn't cut her, and splayed her palm across the ribbed gills at Kalin's side. The gills didn't move while Kalin was on land, but instinct told Adaline they would still be sensitive.

She was right. The shudder that rippled through Kalin was enough to rattle both of them. Kalin broke the kiss with a gasp, pressing her face into Adaline's shoulder and nipping at her neck.

Adaline laughed, delighted, the sound quickly melting into a moan as the tentacle finally found its target. It spread her cloaca open, the tip sliding in and out slowly, teasingly. She understood, on some level, that Kalin was being gentle to ease her open. Adaline didn't care about that, though. She just wanted *more.*

She rolled her hips with a sharp, needy sound, and was rewarded by Kalin sliding in deeper. If Kalin made any sound, Adaline didn't hear it over her own moan. She swore, undulating and rocking into the thrust. Kalin was so deep inside her. Deeper than she'd known someone could go. It wasn't as though her fingers had the length and girth of a tentacle, after all. She tucked a claw tip between the ribbed gills, stroking the edges and delighting in the punched-out sound Kalin made. She rocked her hips, trusting Kalin to hold her, and groaned as Kalin got even *deeper*.

Every millimeter was a delicious stretch. The suckers caught and tugged at her as Kalin moved.

Adaline was going to lose her mind.

"Gods," she gasped. She pulled her fingers away and dragged them down, curling around the bulk of a tentacle, prompting Kalin to thrust into her faster, deeper, until every breath that Adaline drew was a stuttering moan.

She pressed her fingers to the swell of the suckers. Her stomach clenched, and her heart thundered against her ribs. "Kalin, Kalin, *Kalin*—"

Kalin rubbed their beaks together, crooning, and twisted her tentacle inside Adaline, holding her steady when she writhed.

"Please, please—" Adaline couldn't do anything but babble, grabbing for any part of Kalin she could reach. Her hands and arms shook, her thighs quaking. Tentacles wrapped around her wrists, holding her firm, and Adaline dropped her head back against the cushion of her nest. Their nest. She arched, panting, and rode the waves of pleasure that threatened to drown her.

It was a much better sensation than drowning.

She crested that edge with a cry, and Kalin fit their mouths together to swallow it. Kalin held Adaline still through the throes, and while she didn't stop the motion of her tentacle, she did slow. The thrusts became gentler, more caressing, and Adaline quaked.

"You are stunning," Kalin whispered. Her voice was raspy, now, arousal deepening it. She nuzzled against Adaline's beak, her cheek, the ridge of her brow. She pressed Adaline deeper into the nest, chirring quietly.

Adaline batted at Kalin's side weakly, huffing a laugh as she twitched and shuddered. "You're—hah—gonna kill me," she gasped.

"I saved you once. I can do it again," Kalin answered nonchalantly. She nuzzled at Adaline's forehead and combed her beak gently through her crest. "I think this death will be sweet." She twisted her tentacle and slowly drove it farther inside of Adaline. She held Adaline down, not letting her arch up, and smiled as Adaline squirmed harder.

"A-at least let me return the favor?"

"You'll get your chance, promise."

Adaline gasped sharply as Kalin thrust her tentacle deeply again. Her hips twitched, and she clenched her hands into fists, tugging gently against the hold Kalin kept her in. It was a comforting embrace, even if it stopped her from reciprocating the way she wanted to. She groaned as Kalin pushed her legs farther apart, giving her more access to her cloaca. It seemed to be stretching wider as Kalin moved; the tentacle seemed to swell with each shallow motion that drove it deeper and deeper.

Adaline hadn't known she could *fit* that much inside of her.

Kalin dragged her up a little, just enough to support her back and her wings, and slid another tentacle across Adaline's belly. This one was slicker, leaving something sticky on Adaline's feathers, and if Adaline tilted her head to look, she could just make out a glow between their bodies.

Oh.

Kalin was bioluminescent.

Adaline would wear the signs of their mating until she scrubbed each and every feather.

Her stomach clenched again, and she whined, rocking as much as she could. Kalin murmured something too low for Adaline to make out, but it didn't matter when that tentacle edged in alongside the first.

Adaline threw her head back with a howl; her feet curling and pricking the both of them with her talons. "Gods, *Kalin*."

Kalin stuttered a moan above her, sound buried in Adaline's crest, and worked the second tentacle in as slowly as she dared. The tip of it was flared, entirely different from the first one, smooth and slick and leaking that glowing fluid, which oozed out of Adaline with each gentle thrust.

Perhaps Adaline should have asked Kalin about *how* her kind mated, but that thought was quickly swept away. They were certainly figuring it out well enough, and the stretch alone was enough to cause tremors that rocked through her entire body. She could scarcely breathe for how full she felt. And *still* it kept going.

She whined again, turning her head to press her cheek against the tentacle holding her arm. She opened her mouth, running her tongue along the underside. Kalin's answering moan was honey-sweet, so Adaline did it again. She was rewarded by Kalin burbling something that was probably a swear, and the press of a tentacle on her jaw before it slid into her mouth. She swallowed reflexively, eyes watering, and clenched down around Kalin without meaning to.

Kalin swore again and thrust harder. The twist of the tentacles dragged her suckers along every part of Adaline. Lightning raced along Adaline's spine, and her wings flared, the very tips curling with an aborted flap. She swallowed again around the tentacle in her mouth, groaning as her eyes rolled.

It was so much.

It wasn't enough.

Her heart raced, pounding hard enough that she was positive Kalin could feel it. She was almost certain Kalin was deep enough to *touch* it. Kalin moved faster, panting in her ear and twisting the two tentacles in farther and farther until Adaline felt something within her swell. It was slow, the growth starting at the entrance of her cloaca and then sliding oh-so-slowly down the rippling length. Adaline would have sobbed from it if she'd had the air.

"Adaline," Kalin breathed. She writhed atop of Adaline, chest heaving, and showed no signs of flagging. Not even as that bulge moved deep and liquid warmth rushed through Adaline. She clenched down and found resistance from more than just the tentacles. Later, perhaps, she would laugh at herself for not thinking of eggs, but in the moment, the only thing she could do was cry raggedly through her stuffed mouth.

Kalin's name was a mantra in her head. She rocked as much as she could, clenching and unclenching over and over on those wriggling lengths that split her open like a shucked oyster. Her ears rang from the blood rushing through them and from the overwhelming waves of pleasure that made her thighs quake and her belly tight.

Kalin groaned, long and low, and thrust hard as she delivered another egg into Adaline. The tentacle in Adaline's mouth went deeper, pressing against the back of her throat.

Adaline swallowed, looking at Kalin through watery eyes. Kalin was

glowing. Every spot along her head and shoulders pulsed in time to her thrusts. Adaline met her gaze, her stomach swooping once more as she realized Kalin was just as wont to look away as she was.

A third egg slid into her, faster than the last two, and Adaline could feel how she bulged from it.

She was so *full*.

Kalin stuttered for the first time, gasping as her eyes fluttered. "A-Adaline. I—"

Adaline pressed her tongue to the underside of the tentacle in her mouth and rubbed.

Kalin broke with a cry, grabbing at Adaline's waist with her hands and pulling her into each thrust. Adaline lost count of how many times Kalin swelled and released. She didn't notice when the tentacle slid out of her mouth and the first one retreated from her cloaca. All she could feel, all she could *concentrate* on, was the pulse of heat and the pressure of eggs heavy in her body.

Darkness took her vision as she sobbed, her wings flapping erratically as the tightly coiled heat in her gut flooded out of her. She couldn't stop rocking, couldn't stop *moving* as she chased that sensation, that *high*, for what felt like hours. She didn't stop until she had to, physically too spent to move another inch, and still she twitched and whined as they both slowed.

She could feel Kalin shaking around her as she lowered them both back into the nest, panting hotly against her cheek. One final roll of the tentacle was the only warning Adaline had before Kalin pulled it out of her. The rush of fluid that flowed out after it was hot and sticky. It gummed her feathers and left her gaping open. But still that pressure deep inside of her remained.

She knew, without knowing how she knew, that if she shifted just right, all those eggs would press against the most sensitive parts of her. Imagining that made heat flare in her belly again, but she was too tired to act on the thought. As Kalin let go of her arms, Adaline let them drop over her head and finally opened her eyes again.

She was painted in glowing fluid from thigh to chest, and her stomach was swollen from the eggs. She groaned, weak, and made a sad attempt at putting her hand on Kalin. Her fingers merely twitched, but Kalin seemed to get the message anyway. She settled on top of Adaline, curling her tentacles around her like a living blanket, and nuzzled at her.

"They aren't viable this time," Kalin murmured, "but they could be next time, if we wanted."

"Kalin…genuinely I am too fucked out to think about children right now."

Kalin laughed and brushed her hand over Adaline's belly. "We'll talk about it. For now, we rest, and tomorrow I will help you lay those."

Adaline hummed and tipped her head against Kalin's. "Will it involve more tentacle play?"

"If you'd like."

"I very much would."

Their beaks brushed together slowly; keratin on keratin in a gentle rasp that said more than words ever could. Tomorrow they would figure out the rest of their lives. But for tonight, it was just them and their love, completing their song and dance.

Nothing Ventured...

Kitty Lee

alien, anal fingering, belly bulge, consent issues, crack treated seriously, getting together, hurt/comfort, m/m, multiple orgasms, mute, overstimulation, polyamory, present tense, science fiction, sex toy, size difference, size kink, sub drop, tentacle in anus sex, tentacles, third person limited point of view, united states of america, west virginia

Heya John,

You weren't kidding about this thing, it's turning me into a human fucking fleshlight. The unpredictable movements, the supple but firm texture, that unbelievable *coiling and gripping action...* fuck*!*

I wish *I could say "I don't care how the hell y'all made this gimmie 10 of 'em," but my whole brand is based on THOROUGH reviews. I need to know allergens! Factory conditions! Health & safety warnings! (For real, man, are you* sure *this thing is sale-able? I'm feeling full to buuuuuuuu—*

"Uuugh, fuck." Hunt groans, one hand flying from the keyboard to press the swell of flesh below his belly button. It presses back, coiling and dragging. The wide, flared base digs against his ass, pulling viciously as the toy tries to burrow deeper inside him. With a final, luxurious lash, it settles back into idleness.

He comes back to reality with an aching hard-on heavy between his legs, leaking against his track pants. He really should have taken the dildo out before he got to work, but the monster cock churning up his guts has a way of short-circuiting his thinking. It's not unusual for brands to send him state-of-the-art toys to review—he's one of the best in the business—but there is *nothing* usual about the glorious mind-melting *thing* John of Jamin Plug-n-Play sent him.

Hunt's hand is shaking when he taps the "Backspace" key a couple dozen times and starts again.

> *—ursting.) Writing this is the first clear thinking I've done since I let this big boy in. It's pushing my limits! I didn't know my ass still* had *limits!*
>
> *All this to say, of COURSE this thing's a game changer and I want to review it, there isn't a person on my follower list who wouldn't cream their pants at the way this bad boy bulges in me, but I can't do that if you don't give me some more details about—*

He's typing quickly despite the hunched, twisted position he's adopted to try to give his prostate a moment's relief, when a businesslike knock on the front door breaks the hot, heavy silence of his studio.

"Oh my God." Hunt's eyes fall closed. Squeezing his cock again through his pants, he stumbles to his feet, grabbing his robe. "That better be the lube or I'm never getting you *out*, bud."

The dildo tugs on something in him, almost crossing the line into pain. Hunt rides it out, gripping the wall, then wraps up in his robe and stumbles to the door.

It's not the mail carrier.

It's not even human.

On the day outer space shrank down into an achievable vacation spot, Hunt had been on a weeklong "fishing trip" with his buds, which is to say he'd been having a seven-day orgy with some of his favorite freaks, trying to convince them to bait *one* hook without it being a euphemism.

He heard about it later, that aliens were real and had started visiting, but they weren't exactly the sort to come knocking on doorsteps in West Virginia.

Or, well…they hadn't been before.

The thing outside his door is huge. Eight feet tall, easy. Some mountain-town part of Hunt is crowing "Bigfoot! Bigfoot's here!" even as the rest of him is taking in concrete reality.

No mouth, but frills and whisker-like tendrils giving character to the enormous, dark eyes staring at him out of an angular face. The looming alien is wearing what looks like a cape made of leather ropes, until the whole cape moves in a ripple, parting to let an appendage emerge, curved around a small, white—oh.

The alien is holding out a piece of paper.

"Uh." Hunt blinks. The mountain boy in his head is still shrieking "BIGFOOT, BIGFOOT!" despite the fact that this fellow might not have feet. Hard to tell when Hunt can't look away from its eyes. "How do?"

He chokes on the end of the greeting, the enormous tentacle up his ass choosing that moment to give a particularly spirited lurch. *Fuck, don't cum.*

The alien before him twitches; its fins flare and rattle with brittle noises. It shoves the note closer to him.

"Yeup." Hunt fumbles one hand out to take it, trying to get his eyes to uncross.

Hello, he reads. *My name is Stoic, he/him. My penile-equivalent was recently stolen. I believe it's inside you.*

"Oh my fucking God," Hunt wheezes, and the not-actually-a-dildo-at-all writhes.

Operation "give the nice alien his dick back" falls apart like this:

First, Stoic's cock throws off its flange, shoving itself even deeper inside Hunt.

Second, four fingers deep in himself, Hunt *still* can't get ahold of the damn thing.

Third, it has tiny tentacles on its base, and it's grabbing his fingers with them, which is both *cute* and *horrible*.

And so, out of options, he's done the unthinkable.

He's called Stoic in to help.

"Sorry again." Hunt groans, watching the stranger looming over him in the mirror. He's never felt *dainty* in comparison to someone before.

Dark eyes meet his gaze in the mirror, and Stoic lifts one appendage to touch the top of Hunt's head in absolution. Then his cape of tentacles unfurls, revealing one tipped with six red tendrils. It trails down over Hunt's lower back, cold, slick contact against his burning skin. The slender digits slide into his gaping hole and spread him in a single flex. Hunt has to grab the sink with both hands, gritting back a scream of pleasure.

The tendrils tangle with the piece of Stoic in him then lock in place, dragging it back and out. It clings, sucking at Hunt's insides. He lets out a squealing sound he can't choke back. His hips buck, guts throb, balls tighten, vision blurs, he's—

Stoic heaves backward, falling against the bathroom wall with a crack of tile.

"Shit." Hunt shoves off the sink to try and catch the giant. Stoic is heavy and boneless under his hands. At best, Hunt slows his fall, only for his own legs to give out, sending him fawn-like to the bathroom floor, surrounded by a splay of tentacles.

Stoic's skin flashes in a roiling curl of white before settling back into dark bands of green and brown.

"You okay?" Hunt's voice comes out strangled.

Stoic's eyes are closed. The spiked frills on his face are pinned back. It makes him look smaller, the great mass of a body puddled in exhaustion. He unfurls a limb, lifting a notebook and pen.

Adjusting, he writes in trembling letters. *Courtship ended early. It wants to go back.*

"Oh." Hunt's eyes fall to the piece of this stranger he's gotten so attached to. It's still twisting, bucking like it's trying to get away from the tendrils holding it in place. "Oh, buddy, be sweet, yeah?"

He lifts a hand to steady it like he would a spooked horse, but his

barely functional brain catches him before he pets a stranger's cock to soothe it.

Stoic lifts the appendage into the place where Hunt's hand is hovering. Hunt hesitates, then sets his palm against it, giving a gentle rub with his thumb. It bucks eagerly up into his palm.

"You're okay, little guy," Hunt mutters. "I'm so sorry I hurt ya."

Stoic's other arms are writing again. "Not you."

"John," spits Hunt, connecting the dots. "Those bastards! They stole a part of you to sell it?"

Stoic gives a rolling motion that might be a shrug.

"I should have known," he writes, a drooping motion in its many limbs.

"What kind of fuckin' *dick* would do that?" Hunt barks, still soothing Stoic's "penile-equivalent." Being pet seems to be calming the thing down, somehow. "Not just to betray you like that, but to hand you off to a stranger! What if I'd hurt you? I mean, more than I probably did. I'm really…I would *never* have started—I didn't mean to take advantage of anyone, especially not…like this. It never even came, I…"

He peters out, the hollow horror of what's happened settling around him. How many times had he gotten off with Stoic's stolen cock? Had it felt like a violation? The thought settles sick in his stomach.

Stoic is writing again.

The note, when it comes, is longer.

We only orgasm at the completion of courtship, Stoic has written. He glances at Hunt, dark eyes swimming with hidden color, before adding, *after three days within our prospective mate.*

"Three days?" Hunt's blood flies south, leaving him dizzy. He pinches his thigh with the hand not still gentling a cock.

It likes you, Stoic writes in a rushed addition, even as the tendril wriggles closer, bumping its tip against Hunt's cheek.

"Mutual." The poor penis shudders, humping against the stubble-rough skin of Hunt's cheek. "You sure there's nothing I can do to help?"

A curl of gold lights around the ring of Stoic's oblong pupils. *You want to help?*

"I…" Something bright lances through Hunt's chest, between hope and terror. "Yeah."

Can you? writes Stoic.

Hunt's mouth goes dry.

Three days, Stoic had written.

It should probably be an easy "no," but intentions aside, Hunt had been part of hurting this stranger. There's no doubt he owes Stoic something. (And if it means not having to say goodbye to his ultimate sexual fantasy in a tangle of hurt and cum on the bathroom floor…)

"Mama didn't raise a quitter," he mutters to himself, setting his jaw. "Let's talk details."

Discussing the arrangement with Stoic feels like Hunt should be signing contracts and contacting his lawyer. He technically did send Amelia an email, but only to loop Stoic in with a trustworthy legal representative.

I will return often to ensure you are well, but part of courtship is leaving you with it. It is about both compatibility and trust, Stoic writes.

"Then we're mated?" Hunt asks, his head swimming.

When the courtship concludes, I may leave with no lasting harm.

Hunt's delicate heart shrivels up, despite him scolding it. "When do we start?" he asks with an easy smile to mask his dumb heart repeating *he'll leave, he'll leave*. It's making this right he should focus on, any way he can.

If we begin now, it will ease the symptoms.

"No time like the present," Hunt agrees, swallowing a mouthful of saliva at the very thought of having Stoic back inside him.

He can do three days. It'll be a challenge, like that night he spent being Free Use at Mortimer's bachelor party. He'll get fucked out, enter a delicious subspace, and after…

Well, he'll be fine after. He'd loved that night, the warmth of the bodies against him, the pounding he'd taken, filling him up till even his hungry body screamed from overuse, strangling on the dicks of strangers until he came untouched.

It's no one's fault that he'd ridden the taxi home alone. He'd been the one to say he was fine, didn't need special treatment, wasn't delicate.

He was the one who hadn't called anyone over when it all came crumbling down on him while he sat in the shower alone. Not his first or last sub drop.

He'd loved that night, though. He'll love this, too.

Stoic watches him lube up from the bedside, delicate colors lighting up across his skin. He's still aside from his twitching, wiggling cock, so visibly eager that Hunt's own excitement skyrockets as well. He's always loved watching his partners get horny. He doesn't know how to interpret the colors Stoic is turning, but he recognizes a needy cock!

There's a scratching sound, then a note: *You're sure? You're small.*

"I've never heard that before." Hunt laughs, a flush brightening his whole body. "I can take it." He slides his fingers out, so slick he can barely grip his ass cheek to spread himself.

He's been with all sorts of guys before. Some take his prep at face value and start fucking, some prod at his work to be sure, some press kisses to his sensitive skin, some stare into his anus like a crystal ball…

Stoic surges like a tide. There's a smooth, writhing thing against Hunt's stretched rim, then it withdraws, leaving him to moan, fingers clenching on his cock and ass cheek till he feels the bite of his short nails.

"You know it'll fit." He shuffles on the bed to better present himself. "You helped get it out earlier, right? C'mon, Stoic, put it in!"

There, *yes*, the writhing touch returns and sinks in, working into him with utter determination. The first bit goes smoothly, smaller than his fingers, but as it reaches the bulge in its middle, Hunt groans deep, pressing back into it, forcing his hungry ass to swallow up the impossible girth.

Stoic makes that clattering sound again and presses *harder*.

"Oh fuck." It's *so much*. The force, the intention: it makes everything different. It's one thing to shove a dildo up your ass; it's another to get fisted by a giant.

He bucks, jolts, and cums dry in the too-tight grip of his own hand. His body clenches down helplessly on Stoic's member. There's a long pause, then an inexorable slide as Stoic pushes, straining against his guts and bladder. Thank *fuck* he pissed before this, or he'd be squeezed out like a lemon on his blankets.

It's so close to perfect. Stoic's just pushing in, not rocking in and out with it, but it's all right. He'd roll his hips, but he's scared to stop that oh-so-perfect weight crawling its way back into his guts, twisting deep into him like it's pressing hands against his walls, feeling its way through the dark.

He gives up on holding himself open, fisting both hands in the sheets and biting down on a mouthful as well. His hips ache. His guts tense. His stomach lurches. It's too big, he was wrong, it's going to split him open, and *he's going to cum again.*

He strangles a scream in the blankets as it gives a vicious wiggle in him, then suddenly it's *in*. It's in, and it's all he can think about. When he reaches back to feel, a tiny tendril is all that remains outside him. It tangles around his finger almost playfully, then prods around the stretched muscle of his gaping, twitching hole.

He's supposed to say something, give a sweet moan, say how good it feels…

All he can do is lay there, breathing, ass in the air, an enormous weight settling itself in him. He fumbles a hand to his stomach, and—*there*—it writhes against him from the inside, deforming his skin in a heavy bulge as it presses against his spine to answer his touch.

The not-a-hand on his thigh squeezes, then retreats. Hunt struggles to breathe, his diaphragm constricted by Stoic's cock's writhing. It feels so fucking good he wants to cry, but Stoic might worry and take it back again.

"Good?" Hunt pants. He's sweating, flushed red, and shaking. It makes him stupid, the size of the thing in him. "Does this…feel good for you?"

Stoic withdraws farther. Hunt makes a keening noise low in his throat. Is he not supposed to ask…? There's a paper in front of him. He blinks tears out of his vision (shit, he hadn't meant to cry) and sees:

Yes.

"Oh good." Hunt sinks onto the bed, his lower back burning and his feet cramping. He must have been curling his toes. He'll need to…to stretch.

He's starting to get fuzzy. It's doing something to his overloaded nerves, to have it grasping and curling inside him again, though it's not lurching like it had when Stoic first appeared at his door.

Is he allowed to rest? He has a guest. Who he's courting. He shouldn't fall asleep, should he? Could he even fall asleep, with the enormous thing

undulating in his guts? It feels unbelievable. There's nothing else like it. It's going to ruin him for cock, which is a shame. He really, truly loves cock.

There's another note. Right. Yes. Stoic is in the room with him.

You're all right?

"Super well. Totally well." Hunt drags himself onto his side to look up at Stoic. "The best. All good."

That rippling gold courses over Stoic's skin. Hunt gasps as the patterns echo inside him, the cock throbbing in time with Stoic's color changes. It's *incredible.* He wants to touch Stoic's face, see if the color changes his texture like it changes the cock's. He doesn't know if that's allowed. He doesn't know what Stoic likes at all.

It's the kinkiest thing he's ever done, accepting this fist-sized protrusion in his guts for three days. For Stoic it must be like missionary. The thought is shameful, embarrassing…sexy. It gets all tangled up inside him, then whites out as the cock gives a particularly good curl against his prostate, milking him.

When he comes out of it, there is another note. Stoic is shifting away. *In the morning, I'll bring food.*

"You're going?"

Does he want Stoic to go? He can't be a good host, but the thought of a cock in him without its owner…is Stoic going to be moving through the day barely functional, like Hunt would if he were wearing an onahole to the bank?

Until the morning, Stoic writes.

Hunt strangles the sound that wants to escape him, nodding quickly in return. He clears his throat, fumbling to sit up, but a long tentacle curves over his shoulder, pressing him back to the bed. Hunt melts, the convulsive shudders running through him settling into shivers as he sags into the mattress.

Stoic's frills chitter at him again. He nods, then glides out of the room.

He leaves a piece of himself leisurely fucking Hunt from the inside, its motions unpredictable as ever but unmistakably mild. It does nothing to settle the incredible pressure of having something so large inside him. The thought of eating makes his stomach clench hard enough that his ass squeezes.

In answer, or maybe even protest, the thing in him writhes deeper.

This time Hunt can't strangle the throaty groan that escapes him. He's getting hard again, the intrusion so closely straddling the line of pain and pleasure that he takes himself in hand despite how overworked he's already feeling. One more orgasm to take the edge off.

He can do this.

People can adjust to all sorts of wild circumstances, Hunt tells himself roughly twenty times during the shuffling walk from his bed to the computer.

Sitting is sweet suffering, compressing his insides. His fingers won't stop shaking, but he's up. He's thinking. He can mostly breathe.

Inside him, Stoic gives a sweet curl. Hunt's vision nearly whites out *again*. He's hunched over the keyboard panting before he's even processed what happened. A string of saliva touches down on his space bar by the time he's able to think about things like "keyboards" and "existing."

But if Hunt is going to fuck himself stupid, he'd better sate his curiosity *now* while he still has the capacity. He's trusting to a fault, but he's had time to process now, and…

Well. If he's getting taken for a ride, he'd like to know before he goes through three days crammed full of the biggest cock on the planet.

The tab where he'd found the alien species name "cerophamid" is still open. It's blessedly uncomplicated to add "courting rituals" to the search terms.

HEALTH AND WELLNESS: HUMAN/CEROPHAMID UNIONS BIOLOGICALLY INCOMPATIBLE. "PLEASE STOP TRYING," LEADING DOCTORS SAY.

"Cowards," Hunt scoffs, then refines his search.

ALL THINGS ANTHROPOLOGY: INHUMAN COURTSHIP—MATING RITUALS OF CEROPHAMIDS

It's hard to focus on the wall of text, but Hunt is a goddamn *professional.* He's taken product notes while sitting side-saddle on a fuck

machine!

He opens a garish red sports drink, uncaps his pen with his teeth, and starts a bullet point list of notes.

By the third point, he's getting a queasy feeling that has nothing to do with Stoic's cock pressing into the weight of his stomach.

Stoic didn't lie. Three days is a *minimum*, on a planet where days last longer than they do on Earth.

But Stoic hadn't mentioned anything more than sexual compatibility.

> *Romance and sex are strongly tied to physical wellbeing in Cerophamids. Betrayal during courting is not uncommon, but carries lasting health detriments. Emotional rejection from the denial of courting gestures or failure to return them can be equally harmful.*

For a while, Hunt is so stressed that he forgets the churning in his guts. Stoic hadn't mentioned daily feedings, or skin coloration displays exchanged between partners, or the intricacies of the way his frills and whiskers had moved while they were...

To *really* complete the courting, he needs to do more than bear the maddening pleasure.

"Tomorrow," he promises himself raggedly, his head against the desk, another splatter of cum marking the palm of his hand. "Tomorrow..."

He dreams of being fucked by an ocean, waves crashing inside him, overfilling his straining body.

He wakes up needing to piss every twenty minutes.

Even though it leaves him bent double, braced on the counter, cradling his stomach, Hunt gives the morning everything he's got. The tendril is lively, pressing against his skin from inside as if seeking affection and validation.

"Come on, bud." Hunt's shaking thighs press together in a vain

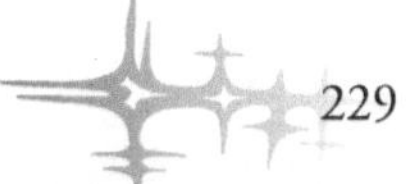

attempt to keep his sore dick from rising. "I gotta get things ready for your dad."

By the time the polite knock comes at the door, Hunt has his entire makeup kit spread on the dining room table—heavy wood, inherited from his grandfather's hunting lodge, able to stand up to a real meal *or* a real dicking. When Hunt first moved in, there was a tiny table with white plastic chairs. Trying to envision Stoic sitting there coaxes a snort out of him, which degrades into a chortle. By the time Hunt wobbles to the door, he's laughing like a fool, grinning up at Stoic.

"Hey! Welcome! Uough... w-wow, laughing got your fella all excited!"

Stoic stands in the doorway, his pupils ringed in gold. Vibrant green ripples over him. Hunt resists the urge to hobble back and check the coloration translations he'd looked up. "We aren't mood rings," the author had warned, but he's PRETTY sure green was good.

The gold in Stoic's eyes is unmistakable, at least. Gold had only come up in descriptions of courting. Even reading in a haze, Hunt remembered that much. It had been so hard to focus, so hard to sleep, feeling like the cock was climbing up him, up to his throat, to fuck into his brain or—

Hunt's knees buckle. He fumbles, catching for the wall. Stoic catches him instead, the firm but yielding muscle of a long limb wrapping around Hunt's back. An awkward laugh wheezes out of him, and he leans into the support.

Stoic's frills give a chittering quiver, and he lifts another tentacle to display a folded box of takeout. Hunt's compressed stomach clenches. He swallows acid.

"Right this way." He gestures, leaning into Stoic's weight to stay upright. His heart is thundering in his chest, uncertainty crawling up his spine from the core of aching discomfort in his guts, so full he's starting to feel wrung out. He's been drinking energy drinks, of course, but he wasn't able to stomach eating last night.

Stoic doesn't pause at the mess on the table, setting down his takeout on the clear side before turning to look down on Hunt, another of his arms coming up to hold him.

Two more tendrils unfold from Stoic's mass, holding his pen and notebook. Hunt wavers on his feet. He can't handle the thought of sitting yet—it'll scrunch him up again. There's a reason he spent most of

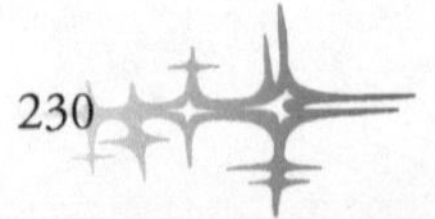

the morning leaning against the counter instead of sitting down.

That reason wriggles inside him again, jostling his prostate, and his eyes roll back. Stoic's grip tightens in a strange, fingerless, spreading squeeze. Hunt pulls himself together with a shake.

"I'm good." He flaps one of his hands despite Stoic holding his elbow steady. "Still wakin' up. How're you? Not too much of a hassle findin' something to eat around here?"

Stoic's whiskers bristle, then soften. He adds a few quick words to his notepad without actually looking at it, then shows the text to Hunt.

"Whoa, can you write with *all* your arms?" Hunt asks while he's still trying to get his eyes to focus.

Are you well? the note reads, and then jotted under it: *No trouble.*

As he watches, the tentacle adds *yes* to the bottom. Then it taps the pencil against the top line again.

"No, yeah, I'm good! Just pushed too hard this morning—oh, got somethin' for you!" He extracts himself from Stoic's hold, leaning his weight on the table to uncover his face paint and makeup collection with a "Tah-dah!"

He's sleep deprived. It can't be held against him.

Stoic writes a large question mark on a fresh sheet of paper.

"Well." Hunt eases into a chair, breathing quickly through his teeth, then leans back, rubbing a hand down his stomach and swallowing as the bulge presses back against his palm. "I've really only got two colors, y'know? Peach or pink. So I thought, if you wanted…"

Stoic lowers to his level. Not crouching, more…puddling? He's listening, frills shivering and the gold in his eyes brighter. A few more tendrils unfurl from him, leaving him smaller, and start touching tips to the pigments.

"I can tell you what I feel," Hunt says, watching Stoic unwind himself. "And you could make me match?"

There's a strange sound, then, like a hissing "churr." Stoic's frills clatter, and his whiskers twine, making it clear they're as mobile as his other tendrils.

An arm touches Hunt's chin and slides up his cheek, affectionate. Hunt closes his eyes and leans into it, melting at the feel of Stoic's chilled, supple skin against his stubble.

"I'm excited," Hunt breathes, eyes still closed, and sucks in a breath when a second tendril brushes over his forehead in answer, leaving the smooth, oily texture of his supersaturated Pride face paints. When there's a pause, he lets a smile curve his lips. "I'm happy we're doin' this together."

The tentacle under his chin tightens, tilting his head. Spots of color brush against his temples, his cheeks, the sides of his nose.

I'm scared I can't do this, he doesn't say. *I'm worried I'm going to let you down. It's starting to hurt.*

"I'm horny," he says aloud, wetting his lips like he's tasting the words.

That's true, at least. He can't seem to get it up anymore, but he's horny. He hasn't been able to think about anything but Stoic filling him all day. There's no escaping the enormous physical reality of that.

Touch answers him, not just one tendril, but three. They stroke up over his cheeks, joining between his brows, trailing down the bridge of his nose, then finally another touch follows, tracing a color under his eyes.

In the wake of it, Hunt opens his eyes.

Stoic is close to him. The gold in his eyes has swallowed his dark irises, leaving his pupils swimming in an aurum sea.

"How do I look?" Hunt asks in a low rasp.

In answer, Stoic's body ripples. A bright line of green emerges over where his brows would be. Then soft spots of blue across his temples and between his whiskers. Finally, gold lights up on his face, too, trailing up to his eyes, then joining between them and tracing down the center of his face.

"Oh. I'd really like to kiss you." Hunt sighs.

Stoic tilts his head, then closes his eyes, leaning in.

He has no mouth, but when Hunt leans in, his frills flatten as his whiskers reach forward, caressing the planes of Hunt's jaw, toying over his lips. Hunt kisses him, soft in case the frills are fragile. He thinks, abruptly, that he should have worn lipstick for this—marked Stoic with his own colors.

This isn't about me, he reminds himself, leaning back with a smile. The thing inside him has started wiggling again, hitching twitches of desire that are starting to get Hunt worked up, never mind that he can't get it up anymore.

"Stoic, will you fuck me?"

Stoic opens his eyes, that glistening, consuming gaze, then rises in a rush, his tentacles peeling off to scoop away the makeup, setting it swiftly aside.

"Yes!" Hunt cheers. He fights his way out of his robe, kicks off his loose pants, then catches one of Stoic's tentacles about to put the lube away with the makeup, tugging it back over. Stoic doesn't give it to him, though, instead taking an experimental pump on the delicate end of one of his tentacles and holding it up to Hunt in offer.

"Yeah." Hunt wheezes. "Yes. Yup."

He grabs the table, shoving himself to his feet, and bends over, bracing himself there. The first touch against his ass is *cold*, and he jolts, hissing in a breath. He shifts his legs wider, fighting to open himself. He never fully closed up the night before—not with Stoic's tendrils poking out every now and then to play with his rim—but he's tight again. Stoic prods at the ring of muscle, and the cock inside Hunt wriggles back to meet him. Hunt lets a punched-out groan escape him at the combination of touches.

"J-just play with me a while. I'll loosen up."

In answer, the tip prods and rubs, as if getting ready to shove all the way inside and through him. Hunt feels a brief, sharp spike of fear that lights his whole body up. Then, almost tenderly, the very tip of Stoic's limb breeches him. There's another squirt of lube, right against his hole, and another tendril starts rubbing it in. A third has wrapped around Hunt's thigh, holding onto him. A fourth strokes up his back, firm and grounding.

"Oh God," Hunt moans as the motion presses his too-full guts against the hard surface of the table. "Yes, like that."

Stoic makes that churring sound again. Hunt can't see him in this position, but he can *feel* the weight of Stoic moving over him. The table groans, and Hunt answers it as the tendril in his ass starts moving in—like the night before, not in and *out*, just steadily in. It's hard as a cock, but less yielding on the outside, gripping at his hole not for lack of lubrication, but with ridged intentionality.

He's making a weird, panting, hitching sound he's never made before. He arches his back, trying to offer himself entirely to Stoic. It doesn't hurt yet; he can take it. It's too intense, it's too much, but it's so—it's so…!

The little guys on the base of Stoic's detachable penis wriggle downward. Hunt can *feel* them slithering through him to greet Stoic's new appendage, tugging and twining.

Suddenly it doesn't feel like a toy inside him anymore. It doesn't feel like something plunged deep and left there. Instead it's one long, prehensile, hard, *enormous* cock, fucking up into him. He pounds a fist against the table, then scrambles for something to hold onto—the edge of the table, a new hole in it, anything.

Stoic pauses, and Hunt whimpers. He presses back, then pulls forward, rocking himself on the enormous thing inside him. Once, then twice, he rolls his hips, fucks up and back, and then Stoic seems to understand. On his next roll back, the tentacle up his ass thrusts in too, then slides out again.

"Fuck yes!"

Stoic rattles his frills, and the tendrils on Hunt's body squeeze down on him. He groans as it presses him to the table. On Stoic's next thrust, the cock in him thuds against the hard surface. Hunt gasps, then yelps, wriggling against the length impaling him.

Eagerly, the dick tendrils grabbing Stoic's arm wrap around it, turning into bands and ridges of even *further* sensation. It drags that tendril deeper, like it's showing a friend its favorite place. Hunt feels a swell of unbearable affection, made *less* bearable by the fact that the place it drags Stoic's tentacle to is his *fucking prostate.*

"Haah—ahh, ghngh!" Hunt garbles, drool puddling under his mouth as Stoic prods, fiddling with that sore place inside him. His hips hitch, his balls ache, his guts *cramp*, tight and painful. It makes his whole body jolt, one leg kicking out artlessly. A table chair skids to the side at the impact. This time Stoic doesn't pause, only wriggles more intently against that place while the whole of his appendage gives writhing waves through Hunt's body, inching deeper.

It's going to come out my mouth, Hunt thinks desperately, arching back against it. He's hard again, bobbing under the table, uselessly humping the air. *He's going to go all the way through me.*

He might be screaming. He might be begging.

"More, yes, like that, right there, fuck, *fuck*, Stoic, yes! Keep going, don't stop, I can take it, I—I know you need—"

Babbling, senseless, his *brain isn't working*, he's nothing at all, he's a

ventriloquist dummy with a fist up his ass, with Stoic's tentacles about to close around his heart, with nothing inside him that's his, and everything inside him that's Stoic, filling him so full he'll never be able to eat again, fucking him so deep no one else could reach.

"*FUCK!*"

Stoic draws out, then slides all the way back in, seating himself roughly into place. Draws back again, then in, in, in. The ridges where his cock is grabbing onto his tentacle drag against Hunt's walls. There's no escape, there's nothing he *wants* to escape, he needs to piss, he needs to cum, his body is a hole and only Stoic can fill him, he can't breathe, he can't stop, he wants—he needs—

Stoic wraps a tentacle around his shoulders, tilts him back and lifts him so his stomach isn't distending against the unyielding table, but bulging out into the open air, and better, or worse, or neither, or both, lets his senseless legs give out, dropping his weight on that impossible intrusion inside him.

Hunt comes with a raw scream, the world falling out from under him.

When he wakes up, he's cuddled on the table. His robe is over him. He's shaking, soaked in sweat, aching bone-deep. He feels hollow.

One hand flies to his stomach. He lets out a low groan of relief when he feels something inside wriggle in answer. He hasn't failed. Stoic hasn't given up on him yet.

A cooling touch brushes over his sweat-drenched hair, then cradles the back of his head.

"Stoic," breathes Hunt, smiling up at the alien now that he's mostly back in his body and re-oriented.

Stoic makes his strange sound again, wriggling his whiskers and frills, then strokes Hunt's hair with one appendage, while another lifts…a fork? A fork.

There's a bite of egg delicately balanced on it. Hunt sort of wants to cry.

Instead, he obediently opens his mouth, letting Stoic feed him one bite of salty takeout breakfast, then a second. He can't bring himself to accept a third, but he takes a few swallows of water when he's offered.

"I'm okay," Hunt rasps when Stoic starts writing, and watches him soften, setting down his notepad in answer. "I just need some rest."

Stoic nods, adjusting the bathrobe for him before looking toward the bedroom.

"Give me a hand?" Hunt asks with a grin.

He leans on Stoic all the way back to his room, barely able to walk, with lube dripping down his trembling thighs.

He's asleep almost before he hits the mattress.

Too hot. Everything's too hot. There's lava inside him, churning, boiling, he's—

Hunt wakes up sweating. There's a note and a glass of water at his bedside. There's a plate with a sandwich. It's cut in triangles. It makes him queasy to look at. He can't eat, there's no room, he's going to split open.

Too hot, too full, too—

The cock in his guts gives a heavy twist. It's amazing. It's unbearable. He groans, collapsing with a shudder, and shoves a hand between his legs to try to take the pressure off. When he slides his fingers between his thighs, he finds the tendrils of Stoic's cock waiting for him, tangling with his fingers, using them as anchors to pull itself closer to his entrance, then push farther back in.

Hunt chokes at the feeling of being fucked like this. He grabs hold of the tendrils like a hand reaching out from inside him, helping it plunge itself into a body that never seems to stop trembling anymore.

He's not hard. He can't get hard. His cock is wrung out; his whole body is wrung out.

I haven't read Stoic's note, he thinks blearily, then his body goes stiff, shuddering, jolting, *squeezing* as his useless cock tries to come again.

For a while, it's almost like sleeping.

But he's not asleep. He's not awake. He's not…

He's not okay.

It comes to him through the fog. He's not okay. He's not doing okay. He can't breathe. He's too full, and the ache, the cramping, the soreness…it's dulled but spread, taking over his body, making him feel

outside himself.

No, come on, three days, he begs himself, twisting on his sweat-ruined sheets. He stumbles up to piss once, but ends up on the bathroom floor on his hands and knees under the tile that Stoic cracked, trying to breathe. He fumbles for lube, adds more to his hand, reaches down to rub at himself. He's so horny, he wants to cum or, no, if he can just get back to enjoying it—

He's a hole. He likes it that way. He's always…

Some time must pass. He doesn't remember leaning over the side of the tub. The cock is jackrabbiting inside him, gripping his fingers so hard as it uses him that it's held him in position even as he's gone limp and distant. It feels so good, it feels too much, he—

He manages to get to his feet. Catches sight of himself in the mirror. Green, blue, gold. Stoic's touch was so gentle. He wants it back so bad he feels sick.

He staggers to the kitchen. What was he doing?

There's a knock on the door.

"Stoic." Hunt's voice shatters around the name.

His stomach lurches, his heart throbs, then he's on the ground.

Something breaks. A *thud.*

A cool touch on his temple. A caress through his hair.

"Hey." Hunt grins, but Stoic isn't golden today like he was yesterday. He's gone colorless, save for ripples of pink that slice across his face. Hunt stares at them, fixated, until he feels a nudge against his hole. He whimpers. Keens. His eyes roll, his body twisting.

He can't, he can't, he can't.

There's the feeling of multiple, tiny limbs, prying him open. He gags on nothing, drool pooling in his mouth. That feeling, that enormous thing, moving through him, fucking him from the inside, the pressure, the cramping, the numbness. There's something cold in him, something wet, dripping out of him, splurting.

A stretch—enormous, agonizing, wringing a shriek out of him, then—

Nothing. Nothing at all. Hunt breathes in deep, a desperate gasp. His hand lashes out, claws on, grabs tight. Stoic catches him in one tentacle and holds.

"No," Hunt begs, registering the emptiness. "No, Stoic, I, I can, I—"

Stoic is shaking his head. Stroking Hunt's hair. It sinks in Hunt's stomach like a stone, heavier than any cock. He chokes, then breaks open in a sob. It unleashes the agony trapped in him: the pain and stress, the desire and fear, the weight of *failure*. This one thing he's good at, this one thing he could do to make things right.

Hunt wails, trying to bury his face in his hands so Stoic won't have to see.

He doesn't get the chance. His hands are caught, then so is his body, his aching hips, his shaking legs, *all* of him.

Stoic wraps himself entirely around Hunt, *engulfing* his burning flesh in cooling tentacles. There's a mass at the core of him—something soft and tender. It presses up close to Hunt. When Stoic makes his churring sound, it vibrates deep into Hunt's body. His sobbing hitches. Stoic squeezes around him with a gentle undulation. The tendril in his hair strokes; the one layered down his back rubs over his spine. Everywhere, he is held.

"I'm so sorry." Hunt struggles to catch one of the tentacles to hold in return.

There's the delicate pressure of whiskers against his hair, then the pressure of a face pressing into him once, then twice. Hunt's heart breaks open in affection as he realizes Stoic is kissing him. He's helpless to do anything but return the affection, kissing anything that's in front of him. Stoic's hold settles, going soft enough that Hunt's able to hold his heavy body in return.

He feels the first couple tendrils unwrap and braces, but Stoic only churrs at him, spreading his other tendrils wider, covering all the gaps until Hunt is entirely swallowed in his embrace again.

It feels…so good. He feels ruined, but Stoic is gentle and strong. Hunt is safe with him. He feels it, right down deep in his bones.

Light breaks through the huddle. Hunt turns dazedly toward it with eyes that can barely see.

Are you hurt? Stoic has written.

"I don't think so." Hunt's voice is strangled with sorrow. "I'm just t-tired, and hungry, and I need a *shower*."

His voice breaks. *Whining*, he chides himself. *You're the one who fucked up!*

"I can try again," he offers immediately. "It was so close, I can—"

Stoic lets him sit up when he tries but doesn't let him go. He hasn't stopped stroking Hunt's hair. When he trails off into silence, Stoic bends down and presses to his lips, his whiskers tracing over Hunt's jawline.

When he pulls back, there's a new note.

I was afraid, it says. Stoic strokes down his sides in comfort to convey his meaning.

"Didn't mean to scare you." Hunt lifts his hand to Stoic's face, letting the whiskers wrap around his fingers. "You've been through so much. I don't want to let you down…"

Stoic shakes his head, but the way his whiskers are clutching Hunt's fingers softens the rejection of that motion.

You did such a good job, Stoic writes.

Hunt's throat goes tight again, tears spilling down his cheeks. His lip wobbles with the effort of restraining himself. He clutches one of Stoic's bigger tentacles with his free hand so he doesn't risk hurting his whiskers and frills.

"I ruined—" Hunt starts, but Stoic interrupts him with another of his kisses, lingering against him as Hunt breathes hot against his cool skin.

Nothing is ruined.

"Oh," Hunt goes soft in his arms. "Oh…"

Stoic feeds him French toast with fruit salad.

Hunt lays boneless in his arms, accepting everything he's offered, feeling strange all over.

After breakfast, he haltingly talks Stoic through how to use the shower. He braces himself to stand, only to start crying again when Stoic carries him instead, standing under the spray with Hunt still in his arms, applying soap to his body as if he were made of spun sugar.

After, wrapped in a towel and Stoic's arms, Hunt pillows against the nest of tentacles. He's so small in Stoic's grasp. Being carried feels like floating through an ocean. It's a loss when Stoic sets him on the bed. But then, with an enormous groan from the mattress, Stoic joins him there.

Stoic spoons him from behind, writing in front of both their eyes.

Hunt, may I court you in the way of your people?

"What about you?" Hunt reaches back and down, where a human's

cock would be. Stoic doesn't seem to understand the gesture, only wrapping his hand up in tentacles and hugging him again.

I've been unfair to you. Incautious with you.

All around Hunt, tentacles are starting to pet him. One is stroking through the furry trail connecting his cock to his belly button.

You've given me your body and loyalty, at risk to yourself.

"I couldn't do it," Hunt whispers, but the heartbreak feels far away.

You're wonderful. Stoic underlines the words. Twice. While Hunt is busy breathing through a wave of emotions, Stoic adds: *If you'll have me, I'm yours.*

"Please stay." Turning from the paper, Hunt buries himself in Stoic's innumerable limbs, welcomed in past the guarding appendages to the soft body beneath. "Stay with me."

This time, when he falls asleep, he's held by a person whose body is sparked with gold and white, pink and orange. In the morning, Hunt promises himself, he'll ask what all those colors meant.

In the morning, Stoic is there to answer him.

A Tantalizing Smell

Katia Anyway

dendrophilia, f/f, fantasy, friends to lovers, frottage, love confession, nature spirit, pining (mutual), present tense, self-esteem issues, size difference, third person omniscient point of view

The wind blows through branches, making leaves shift and caress each other, the soft melody of it sending a wave of peacefulness through the deep forest. A few giggles rise to accompany this melody. The feelings of one's leaves caressing someone else's is a delightful tease for the dryads during mating season.

The Westside Forest is the deepest forest of the country, so deep that no living creature has ever reached the other side to find out what's there. Is it an unknown neighboring country, a mountain, perhaps even a sea? No one knows.

No one, except perhaps the inhabitants of the forest themselves. The depth and wilderness of the forest have allowed many species to develop, unbothered by people who would prey on them to use their magic for

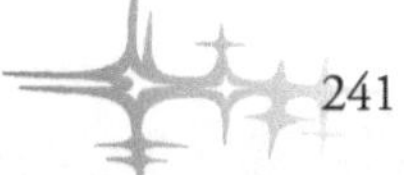

themselves. Among those species are the dryads. These beings evolved from trees, and while their outside appearance hasn't changed much, they are fully sentient and capable of moving, changing shape, and interacting with their environment much faster than a tree could.

Dryads live in communities and are mostly sedentary, only migrating to avoid danger. Once a year, when the days become longer than the nights and the dryads' foliage has grown to their fullest, mating season occurs.

The dryads open their flowers, filling the air with a fresh, floral scent. The scent is so strong that even the wind can't dissipate it. Each dryad has a specific smell, slightly different from her neighbors', and uses it to attract other dryads' attention.

When they want a specific mate, dryads move toward them to express who, exactly, the flowers are for. From up in the sky one can usually notice, at the beginning of the mating season, how a small part of the forest becomes even denser.

Quite a few dryads gather around Katarina, the biggest and most beautiful of them all. Her top branches reach higher in the sky than anyone else's. Her foliage is the most vibrant green, each leaf a slightly different tone from the next, creating a lovely harmony. When she moves, with a grace that could make others pale in jealousy, it looks like she is the one directing the wind, not the other way around. Her face, when she makes it appear on her trunk, is the loveliest anyone has ever seen, the lines of her bark creating the cutest crow's feet on the sides of her eyes when she laughs.

Year after year, many dryads gather around her to express their interest, showing her their most beautiful flowers and fighting to be on the right side of her so the wind will push their smell in Katarina's direction.

And year after year, Katarina's flowers remain resolutely closed.

One by one, she rejects her suitors, quietly shaking her leaves in their direction. The move is deliberate, independent from the wind's motion, and she always stays far enough away to avoid touching the suitor's leaves, to avoid unnecessarily teasing them. She accompanies this move with the scent of her leaves: herbal and fragrant, but not floral. The rejection couldn't be clearer.

Her suitors are used to it, though, moving away and turning to each other instead. The giggling rises in intensity as the dryads gather

together in twos, threes, or even more, rustling their leaves and flowers together, showing their mutual interest and accepting the proposition to go further together. Soon, the smell of sap joins the flowery one in the air, dryads opening their mating flowers to each other and groaning in pleasure when they feel the first touches there.

No one has ever seen Katarina's mating flower, as she never, ever, takes a mate.

Next to her, as per every year, her neighbor Shirley observes the dance unfolding. She tries to attract a mate from Katarina's rejected suitors, but, as usual, she goes unnoticed, no one giggling for her or attempting to mix leaves with her. No one bothers to shake their branches in polite rejection the way Katarina does. No one even notices the scent of her lone flower, open in shy hope.

Shirley is very small for a dryad. She doesn't know why, but despite her mature age, she doesn't grow the way others do. As other dryads grow wider trunks every year, Shirley remains no wider than a broomstick. As other dryads reach slightly higher heights every year, Shirley remains no taller than a bear standing up on its back legs. As other dryads grow bigger branches and fuller foliage, Shirley remains only able to grow twig-like branches that carry only a few leaves. As the other dryads count their flowers in terms of hundreds, Shirley only ever grows the one.

Shirley takes good care of her lone flower, making sure it's always getting just the right amount of sun and water, so it remains beautiful and fragrant throughout mating season. Yet, the flower's scent still can't compete with the other dryads' scents. Without other flowers to accompany it, Shirley's scent is so subtle and delicate it gets easily overpowered by the other dryads' much more intense smell. As a result, she goes unnoticed, remaining mateless despite her best efforts. Every year, she tries not to let herself hope too much, and yet every year, the lack of acknowledgment hurts her deeply.

Shirley deflates as the last of Katarina's suitors leaves, going to join a group of dryads mating a little farther away, completely ignoring Shirley. As usual, she has been overlooked next to Katarina's majesty.

Katarina leans closer, her face appearing on her trunk.

"They're stupid. You know that. Your flower smells lovely."

Shirley makes her face appear, too, so she can give Katarina a small smile, accepting the comforting words gratefully. Shirley is desperately in love with Katarina, but she's never tried to attract Katarina's attention during mating season. She knows full well that she doesn't stand a chance; Katarina won't even show interest in the bigger, fuller-leaved dryads that court her. Katarina would be polite about it, she'd reject Shirley gently, but the rejection would still rip Shirley's heart apart. So she doesn't dare try. She's already so lucky to be able to be Katarina's friend. She doesn't want to ruin their relationship with her unrequited feelings.

"Thank you, Katarina, I appreciate the support. But I can't exactly blame them, I do smell…subtle…" Shirley closes her flower, moving it closer to her trunk for safe keeping.

Shirley is so grateful to have Katarina in her life. She's the best friend Shirley has ever had. They met a few centuries ago, when Katarina was still a young dryad barely taller than Shirley. It was during the Great Migration, the time when the dryads had moved south, trying to escape the biting cold of winter. Just like trees, dryads die when frozen solid. That year's winter had been particularly harsh, and when the first few dryads died from the cold, the community had urgently decided to move. The tribe had pulled up roots and left, running for their lives.

Shirley, who'd been just a wee sapling at the time, had struggled to keep up. That's when one of the other young dryads had slowed down, making sure Shirley wasn't left behind. They'd ended up losing track of the tribe, left alone together as the snow started falling. They could have died, and Shirley's heart still skips a beat in her trunk when she thinks about it. But Katarina hadn't left her. Instead, she'd found shelter for them and helped Shirley keep warm by cuddling close to her. Shirley would forever be grateful for Katarina's help that winter. Eventually, they had caught up to the rest of the group, and they all settled down in the Westside Forest. Shirley had been sure this was the end of their adventure together, that Katarina would find her friends and leave, but no. Instead, she'd rooted down next to Shirley and said, "Friends stick together, right?". Since then, she'd never left Shirley's side.

"Well, personally, I think the subtlety of your mating scent is a good thing." Katarina says, avoiding Shirley's gaze in a rare display of shyness. "I love how soft and delicate it is…"

"Thanks, Katarina." Shirley's sap buzzes happily inside her.

Since that migration, Katarina's always been there for Shirley. Through

highs and lows, through spring growth and autumn leaf shedding, through light rain and droughts. When Shirley is feeling down, Katarina gives her a pep talk. When Shirley struggles to find enough nutrients in the ground because her roots can't reach far enough, Katarina gently curls one of her own roots around Shirley's and give her exactly what she needs. When the wind is violent and threatens to uproot Shirley, Katarina shifts, moving in the wind's way, protecting Shirley with her wide and robust shape.

"About that, Shirley… I wanted to ask… Uh… Your flower… You always close it when… I mean, is it for someone in particular?"

Katarina stuttering like that is a bit out of character; she's always so noble and confident. But Shirley's too busy swooning over how cute it is to grasp the implications. Katarina really is one of a kind, and Shirley's always annoyed that her suitors only want her as a sexual partner. Katarina's so much more than just beautiful. She's also kind, protective, and strong. Shirley admires her all year long, not just during mating season.

"Not really." Shirley shrugs. "I'm just shooting my shot, you know."

Shirley's given up on ever receiving any kind of romantic attention from Katarina, who the flower really is for, so she may as well try her luck with someone else. She can still dream, though. Fantasize about seeing Katarina opening her flowers one day. How many would she have? How exactly would they smell?

Katarina shuffles a little closer.

"Well, in that case, maybe… I mean, would you like to…?" She gestures vaguely with one of her branches, making Shirley frown in confusion. Something about the two of them…? "Shirley, I really, really like your flower and…and you…so…"

Shirley gasps, frozen in place as she witnesses the most enchanting sight.

In front of her, Katarina is opening her flowers.

There are so many of them, almost more flowers than foliage on her branches. Shirley had never noticed Katarina grew flowers at all. Looking closer, she realizes why: the flower buds are green and small, hiding seamlessly in the foliage when they're closed.

A strange sort of calm takes over the forest, the wind the only sound still disturbing the silence. The groans and whines around them stop as all the dryads' attention turns to Katarina opening her flowers. The sight is so breathtaking, no one can ignore it.

One of Katarina's branches moves closer to Shirley, offering one of her flowers for her to smell. The flower is small and delicate, almost ornate in the way the petals curl on the edges. Shirley breathes in its scent. It's like nothing she's ever smelled before. Fruity and fresh, but also sweet. A sort of spicy undertone. Something out of this world.

Suddenly, Shirley wonders if Katarina can bear fruit. Only a few dryads can, and only after mating. They disperse the fruits so their seeds can grow and perpetuate the species.

"Shirley." Katarina takes in a steadying breath, causing a slight change in the wind with the way all of her leaves gather the air around her at once. "You are my best friend, and the one person I'd really like to mate with. So, you know, shooting my shot."

She gives Shirley a sweet but slightly nervous smile.

Shirley…Shirley is frozen in place. The sheer unexpectedness of the situation makes her wonder for a moment if perhaps she's fallen asleep and this is all a dream.

Dream or not, she can't make Katarina wait any longer.

"Me?" she blurts out. "I'm… Katarina, I'm flattered, but…are you sure? I mean, you could have anyone you want."

Katarina's laughter fills the air, making Shirley's heart skip a beat. Katarina laughing is always the most adorable sound in the entire forest, and Shirley is delighted every time she hears it.

"Of course I'm sure." Katarina moves the branch she gave Shirley to smell her flower. She uses it to caress Shirley's leaves with her own.

The caress makes a tingly feeling course through Shirley's entire body. It's the first time someone has touched her like that. Now she understands why the other dryads seem so delighted when their leaves are touched, even accidentally.

"Shirley, please, show me your flower again."

How could Shirley refuse such a sweet request? No one has ever wanted to see more of her flower. A little self-conscious, but with a heart brimming with hope, Shirley extends her flower to Katarina, opening it and letting its smell free.

In a very eager and forward move, Katarina extends more of her branches to reach for Shirley's flower. She curls them around Shirley's

branch and flower, the leaves on said branches taking in a big breath to smell Shirley's flower.

"Yes..." she whispers dreamily. "That's the smell I've been looking for."

Katarina's entire foliage shakes with emotion. Shirley cannot believe she's the one provoking such an intense feeling.

"I don't know why, Shirley, but your scent is the only one that makes me feel like that. Like..." Katarina pauses, breathing in Shirley's scent once more.

"Like what?" Shirley asks when Katarina doesn't continue, entranced as she watches Katarina rub one of her flowers against Shirley's, mimicking the way dryads rub their mating flowers together during sex.

"Like I want to curl up and mesh with you."

Shirley's body buzzes, the sap rushing through her veins and blurring her senses. Now that's a very graphic proposal. Between the words and the gesture, some would consider this to be straight-up dirty talk.

"Would you like that? To mate with me?"

Katarina sounds so eager; how could Shirley say no?

"Of course," is what comes out of Shirley's mouth.

"Perfect!" Katarina giggles in delight.

She shifts, twisting the base of her trunk to show Shirley a specific part of it. Shirley gasps as she watches the bark move, layer upon layer peeling away from the trunk, forming a beautiful wooden flower. In the center of said flower, an opening leads directly to Katarina's insides; sap is already dribbling from Katarina's entrance. Her mating flower.

And Shirley...Shirley stays frozen, with no idea what to do.

This the first time someone has opened their mating flower for her. Shirley has a front-row seat to the enticing sight instead of peeping to see it from a distance, usually from the side and only for an instant before the person's mate dives in. But the flower is almost the size of Shirley's entire body! How is she supposed to interact with it?

Usually, dryads would lean against each other, rubbing their flowers together and tangling their roots under the ground, mixing their branches and leaves, sometimes angling their faces together for a kiss.

But Shirley's flower is so small, Katarina wouldn't even feel it. Shirley isn't even sure she'd be able to reach high enough for their flowers to touch at all.

"Shirley, please..." Katarina whines sweetly. "Don't make me wait any longer."

Unable to deny Katarina anything, Shirley leans closer, opening her small, dry flower to touch Katarina's with it. As she thought, her flower is too low to reach. She's about to tell Katarina when her leaves accidentally touch Katarina's flower. Katarina shivers and makes an appreciative humming noise, as if the touch was a lovely tease.

"Just like that," she whispers.

Underneath the ground, Shirley feels Katarina's roots tangle with hers. While it's usually a comfort to feel Katarina's gentle underground touch, today the move is rushed, urgent. Shirley is pulled closer, manhandled until she's standing face-to-face with the wooden flower. Katarina's flower gushes at the touch, her sap sticking to Shirley's leaves.

Shirley isn't sure if she likes it.

"Come on, please, more." Katarina demands.

Shirley, unsure what else to do, moves her leaves, trying to use them to caress Katarina's flower; she had seemed to like it the first time. The touch feels...good, to Shirley, but certainly not as good as it seems to be for Katarina, who's whining and softly begging for more, pulling Shirley even closer by her roots.

After a moment, Shirley steels herself and decides that if this is what Katarina needs, she'll do it, even if it doesn't feel that good to Shirley. As long as it makes Katarina happy...

Shirley moves against Katarina's mating flower, first rubbing her with her leaves; then, when Katarina pulls her so close that she's plastered against the wooden flower, with her whole body. Soon, Katarina's happy cries fill the entire clearing, making all the dryads around her shiver with want. Many turn jealous glares Shirley's way. Shirley doesn't notice, though, too busy gasping for air as Katarina's sap slowly covers every inch of her body.

Soon she's dripping, the sticky fluid everywhere from the crown of her branches to the base of her trunk. With every gush of fluid as Katarina enjoys herself, Shirley finds it harder to breathe. While it's not the most comfortable feeling, Shirley isn't worried. Dryads only need to breathe in order to grow, and while Shirley does it most of the time in the hopes of becoming taller, she can hold her breath for a while without it hurting her.

"Shirley! Shirley, please!" Katarina gasps, unaware of Shirley's struggle. "In…inside! Please, I need you inside!"

Inside their mating flowers, in addition to their hole, dryads have a spot from which they can grow tendrils. The tendrils are used to slither into the mate's hole, so the dryad's sap can get as close as possible to their mate's reproductive organs. It's the process of the sap mixing inside a fertile dryad's core that allows them to bear fruit later in the year. The tendrils' biological purpose is to make reproduction more likely, but even dryads who can't bear fruits use them to stimulate the sensitive spots inside their mate's hole. From what Shirley's seen of other dryads mating, the tendrils could be a very pleasurable experience.

Not that she's ever had the opportunity to experience it herself. But even if she had, and knew how to use her own tendrils, the knowledge would be useless in this situation. Katarina's big, glorious hole is way too large for Shirley's tendrils to do anything.

As Shirley's nerves rise, Katarina keeps whining and begging. Soon she'll decide Shirley is a terrible partner, if Shirley doesn't do something. But what can she do?

Maybe… Suddenly struck with an idea, Shirley leans closer, moving one of her branches to Katarina's opening. It's just the right height. Maybe she could use it, somehow. After shifting her leaves to another branch, so this one feels closer to an actual tendril, Shirley rubs it as far as she can reach inside Katarina's hole. It's not very far, really, but Katarina seems to like it, humming in appreciation.

"Yes, that. More," she demands.

Knowing her small branch wouldn't be enough to fully satisfy Katarina, Shirley gathers her strength. Slowly, she redirects her body's resources, pushing them all into this one branch. The branch grows, bigger and longer than it has ever grown. If she wasn't leaning on Katarina to hold herself up, the new weight of the limb would have toppled Shirley over, probably uprooting her in the process.

As she feels the branch grow inside her, Katarina lets out a shocked gasp. Shirley's worried for a moment that it means she doesn't like it, but more sap gushes out of Katarina.

"Oh, Shirley… This is…this is amazing, don't stop!"

The delight in Katarina's voice makes something warm inside Shirley's trunk. Particularly around the area of her mating flower. Shirley *does* like pleasing Katarina.

As Shirley's branch keeps growing, she stretches deeper and deeper inside Katarina until she reaches a depth at which Katarina's walls turn from hard wood to tender and soft. This is Katarina's core. If Shirley spills her sap here, Katarina's body will absorb it, ready to use it for reproduction.

Something in Shirley's heart stirs. Her flower starts feeling warmer, wetter. She wants to fill Katarina with her sap so badly.

She feels so honored that Katarina would let her touch such an intimate, sensitive place.

Entranced by the feeling of Katarina's softness, Shirley keeps rubbing her core with her branch, too distracted to realize that her branch keeps growing. Soon, she feels Katarina's walls all around her branch. Then Katarina's whole body shivers, tensing then relaxing around Shirley.

Shirley stills.

Did…did Katarina just come?

"Oh, Shirley…" she gasps, several of her branches coming up to curl around Shirley's body. "This was amazing. Thank you so much."

Oh…she did.

A curl of heat gathers in Shirley's core. It's the first time she's ever made someone come. She hadn't even been sure she could. A proud smile stretches her lips.

Maybe Katarina wouldn't mind doing it again…

Distracted by her happy thoughts, Shirley doesn't notice the way Katarina frowns as she rubs Shirley with her branches.

"What… Shirley, you're soaked!" She moves her face closer on her trunk to see Shirley better. "Oh my… Are you okay? Can you breathe?"

She fusses over Shirley, trying to wipe the sap away and only managing to spread it around.

"I'm fine," Shirley replies with a smile. "You had fun, right?"

The color of Katarina's cheeks darkens, a mix of shyness and arousal making her bite her lower lip.

"I did, but…"

"That's most important to me." Shirley finally pulls her branch out of Katarina. The weight of it almost makes her fall over, but Katarina catches her.

"No! It's not to me!"

Shirley blinks, surprised by the force of Katarina's words. She sounds so certain, so determined, like the mere thought of Shirley not being as satisfied as she was during sex is unacceptable. Shirley shrinks her branch to a more manageable size as she listens to Katarina.

"I want this to be good for both of us. Sex is… It's for both of us! I chose you because I wanted to make you feel good too. If I had wanted someone to just make me come, I could have chosen anyone."

A thrill courses through Shirley's body, but this time, it's not only arousal. It's mixed with real happiness. Katarina cares. She genuinely cares about Shirley, not just as a friend, not just as a lover, but as a partner too.

"I wasn't…" Katarina avoids Shirley's gaze, a mix of shame and sorrow in her eyes. "This wasn't very good, for you, was it?"

Shirley doesn't want to admit it because she doesn't want to hurt Katarina's feelings. But she can't lie to her, either.

"Well…it could have been better…" She winces when she sees the disappointment in Katarina's gaze intensify. "Maybe we could…try again? If you want?"

"You would…? With me?" Katarina sounds hopeful but disbelieving.

"Friends stick together, don't they?" Shirley tries to reassure Katarina, to show her that she won't lose Shirley over this.

It doesn't work; Katarina's face falls further.

"You don't owe me sex, Shirley. If you don't want—"

"Sorry, wrong choice of words," Shirley interrupts. "Look, Katarina, I love you. You are so important to me, and I… You're the most beautiful dryad I've ever met." Katarina blushes, a small, flattered smile stretching her lips. Shirley's a bit surprised. Surely Katarina knows how beautiful she is, right? But this is a concern for a later time. She continues: "Of course I want to try again with you. It's okay if we don't figure sex out right away. I know my size makes things difficult. But you won't lose me over this, I promise."

Katarina and Shirley exchange a look, Shirley trying to convey how sincere she is with her eyes. It takes Katarina a few moments of searching Shirley's face and fussing over her with her branches before she smiles in genuine relief and happiness.

"Let me try to make you feel good, too." Katarina whispers in the space between them. As if this isn't already enough to make Shirley's core warm all over again, she adds, "Please?"

Shirley spends a few seconds opening and closing her mouth before she manages to formulate an actual response. All the while, Katarina waits patiently, smiling fondly at Shirley and caressing her softly. When Shirley's finally ready to speak, though, the leaves of one of Katarina's branches suddenly tease some of Shirley's, almost take the words right back out of her mouth.

"Sure… Of course. If you want, that is…" Shirley struggles to mumble.

"Oh, I do, I really do." Katarina replies, her voice sultry and silky. It makes Shirley's mating flower all wet under her protective folds.

Katarina must smell it or feel it somehow, because she licks her lips, a self-satisfied glint in her eyes. With one of her thinnest branches, she teases the skin of Shirley's trunk, right where her mating flower is about to appear.

"Now, how about you show me *this* flower? I'm sure it smells even sweeter than your other one."

The thrill of showing her flower to someone for the first time, and to Katarina no less, courses through Shirley's body. It makes the first few protective layers open without Shirley consciously deciding to unfurl them. But when Katarina's eyes light up in delight, she purposefully spreads the flower fully.

Katarina's mouth opens, awed silence all that comes out. Shirley smiles shyly at her, but Katarina doesn't notice, too focused on Shirley's mating flower. Experimentally, she starts rubbing the folds with her branch. Intense shivers wrack Shirley's body. It's like being lit up in flames, her flower so sensitive that a single touch there echoes everywhere else inside her. Suddenly she understands why Katarina was so gone so quickly, earlier.

Distracted by her own feelings, Shirley doesn't notice that Katarina's branch is inching toward her opening; she lets out a surprised gasp when it tease her insides. Katarina's thrusting slowly, unsure how deep she can go without hurting Shirley. The intrusion is strange, as all new sensations are, and it isn't as satisfying as the caresses against Shirley's folds were. Still, she lets Katarina explore, waiting to see if, with familiarity, this will become more pleasurable.

"This isn't doing it, for you, is it?" The thoughtful tone of Katarina's

voice surprises Shirley. She hadn't noticed the way Katarina's eyes had zeroed in on her face. "You stopped panting," she clarifies when Shirley blinks at her.

"It's not bad—" Shirley starts, only to be interrupted by Katarina's frown.

"But it isn't good either." She pulls her branch out, going back to lightly caressing Shirley's folds.

The move fries Shirley's thoughts again, the swift movement of the branch against the outer part of her entrance sending a wild rush of heat to her brain. She almost tightens in want, but the caresses to her folds distract her.

She doesn't notice how Katarina falls deep in thought herself. Katarina observes attentively their size difference, the way the slightest of her movements can move Shirley's entire body. She notices, when one of her branches curls instinctively around Shirley's entire frame to keep her from squirming in pleasure out of Katarina's embrace, how Shirley's mating flower is the same size as one of Katarina's regular flowers.

Curious, she decides to replace her branch with said flower.

Shirley almost cries out in protest when the branch moves away, only to cry in delight when it's replaced with the velvety touch of Katarina's flower. The petals rub delightfully against her folds, and the pistil teases in between them, the one hard part of the flower feeling similar to Katarina's branch, the petals a wonderful addition.

"There you go…" Katarina whispers, sounding almost as turned on as Shirley feels. "Seems we've found what works for you. Look at you, you're gushing."

True to Katarina's description, Shirley's sap is steadily leaking out of her. It mixes with the pollen of Katarina's flower, creating a fragrance that's a mix of both of their smells. Katarina seems to really like it. She hums in delight and rubs her flower harder against Shirley, as if trying to produce more of the smell.

The pistil bends, now flush between Shirley's folds instead of lightly caressing them, the tip rubbing against her entrance. Shirley doesn't know why, but somehow, the teasing touch there is much more pleasurable than the penetration from earlier. Slowly, it lights up Shirley's opening, making her walls more interested in being touched than they were before.

"Katarina," she whines when she can't stand it anymore. She needs more, she needs… "Inside!"

Katarina obeys, moving her flower so the pistil is angled correctly to penetrate Shirley, and thrusts inside of her. She does it slowly, incrementally, going a little deeper with each thrust. It only takes a few seconds before Shirley groans, an intense orgasm taking her over. Katarina keeps thrusting, making the orgasm last longer, until Shirley whines and tries to push her away, over-stimulation making the thrusts too much to bear.

When Katarina pulls her flower away, it's ruined, the petals soaked and flopping pitifully.

"Oh! I'm sorry… Your flower…" Shirley starts, feeling bad for hurting such a beautiful part of Katarina.

Unaware of Shirley's feelings, Katarina just picks the flower from her branch and discards it.

"What for?" she asks, confused. When Shirley gestures to the ruined flower on the ground, Katarina waves the concern away. "Don't worry. I've got many of those. More than enough to satisfy you as many times as you want." She winks.

The words make Shirley's heart swoop, and she almost asks for another round right now. She decides against it, though. At the moment, what she wants the most is to feel the comfort of Katarina's gentle embrace.

"Later," Shirley promises.

Determined, she reaches with both roots and branches to hold Katarina close. It takes some shimmying closer and stretching her limbs past their usual limits, but she's able to circle Katarina's trunk fully and hold all of Katarina's biggest roots firmly. Only after she's had a moment to feel proud about her accomplishment does she remember to be shy about her desires.

"Is this okay?" she mumbles, hiding her face against Katarina's trunk.

Katarina's face appears directly in front of her. Maybe this wasn't the smartest hiding place.

"Of course it is," Katarina replies, pecking Shirley on the lips.

When Shirley attempts to jump back in surprise, she finds that Katarina is thoroughly returning her embrace. She can't move away.

She takes advantage of the situation to get more kisses.

From the shiver that runs through her when Katarina reciprocates with a happy hum, "later" will come sooner than Shirley had expected.

GOOD MEMORIES

Taliesin Owens

blow job, consensual non-consent, fantasy, frottage, macro/micro, masochist, master/servant, merperson, nb/nb, non-binary, one-night stand, orgasm delay, present tense, roleplaying: predator/prey, size difference, third person limited (alternating) point of view, violence (non-graphic descriptions)

At first, the sea serpent does not take any particular note of the crimson-tailed mer.

The sea serpent is a Great One of the Waters who has seen seven on seven on seven summers. It is the twelfth in the line of Jade Serpents, known variously to the humans across its territory as The Ravager of the Seven Coasts, Sinker of Ten Thousand Ships, as a god of The Great Waves That Follow The Mountain Fire, or generally as It's-That-Fucking-Green-Bastard-Say-Your-Prayers to most sailors. To itself and its own kind, it goes by the name of Kepetios. It is not an *overly* prideful creature, merely a suitably self-important one. The mers come and go, and Kepetios has never interested itself in their individual personalities.

So when a pod arrives, grouped up for protection as they migrate to new waters, it notices the especially striking color of one mer's tail but pays xem no further mind.

Kepetios has just begun its spring shed and relishes the fresh hands helping to peel and pick all the dead scales and skin off its body. The mer with the crimson tail and short, wavy, dark hair does seem to have a particular knack for noticing Kepetios's most sensitive spots and crevices, and xie attacks the particularly stubborn clumps of barnacles, seaweed, and other debris with thorough concentration—never too harsh in xer touch but never too hesitant, either. Kepetios can always feel the difference where xie has been cleaning, flexing itself in appreciation of how much more freely it can move afterward. Still, this is not so remarkable. Plenty of mers grow especially skilled with their cleaning over the seasons, out of long habit, or because they find satisfaction in the work, or in hopes the serpent might favor them with choice prey.

When the crimson-tailed mer chooses to stay after the first winter, when most of the pod it arrived with moves on, Kepetios still does not think much of it. This, also, is not so unusual. The pod is moving farther south and east; perhaps this mer prefers the colder waters or has an unpleasant history with one of the Gold Serpents. Xie remains along with three or four other mers, and within a few weeks, another pod arrives, seeking fresh territory and a serpent to protect them.

Over the next year, Kepetios notices that the crimson-tailed mer's cleaning becomes especially pleasurable indeed. Not only that, but xie starts adding friendly scratches and massaging Kepetios's most sensitive spots while working, causing its whole body to shiver with pleasure. It has never been one to show favoritism among the mers—while some serpents find causing competition between the mers amusing, Kepetios has never seen much point to it—but exceptional care deserves a reward, so it keeps an eye on that bright crimson tail during feedings and snaps threateningly at any mer who would compete with xem for prey until its position is clear. The crimson-tailed mer bows in gratitude, and xer touches only grow more attentive.

Then, on a rainy summer day, after Kepetios has sunk a great warship and sated itself for the next month on the sinking bodies of the many humans on board, the crimson-tailed mer first brings it a Memory.

Kepetios has only a vague understanding of the mers and their

Memories. It knows the mers pull them from people and objects alike and that they use them as food. It also knows they trade them, though it has never bothered to learn the social particulars of which Memories get traded to whom and why. It has never, in its many scores of seasons, had a mer try to offer *it* a Memory.

But there the crimson-tailed mer is, floating cautiously in front of Kepetios's face, holding out cupped hands with the little silver light of a Memory nestled in them. Kepetios glances up to where the rest of the mers are still gleefully darting around the wreckage of the ship, dragging Memories out of hammocks and cannons and the splintered walls of the ship. It looks back down to the crimson mer, xer arms outstretched, waiting.

You are... offering this Memory... to me?

Kepetios cannot remember a time when its thoughts have been so uncertain. The mer grins wide, showing all xer serrated teeth, and whistles back in the mer language.

"If it pleases you, Great One."

Kepetios, still uncertain what it is even meant to do with such a thing but curious and indulgent regardless, inclines its head. The mer lifts xer hands and presses the Memory in between Kepetios's eyes.

It sees the ocean from the perspective of a creature significantly smaller than itself: a little human, standing on the deck of one of their fragile wooden crafts. The human watches, full of awe and horror, as a green sea serpent breaks the surface of the water miles away, almost at the horizon, its figure too massive and majestic to mistake at any distance.

Kepetios is looking at itself.

In the distance, this past Kepetios takes down another boat, sparing the human to whom this Memory belonged. All over the deck, other humans fall to their knees in relief. This human, though—this Memory—is full of awe, full of a kind of terrified quiver at the power and beauty of what he had just witnessed. There is something hungry in that memory, a yearning for danger that wars against the human's own self-preservation and sends adrenaline pouring through his veins. The Memory is saturated in exhilaration, in a high unlike any the human experienced before or after in his life—except, perhaps, at the very moment that Kepetios devoured him.

Kepetios blinks and returns to the present, where the mer is waiting in front of it, head bowed.

Do you have a name, little mer?

The mer lifts xer head. Xer smile has grown even brighter, and xer eyes shine with something frenzied, something awed, something *hungry*.

"I am called Laku, Great One."

Laku. Kepetios twists, curling its whole body underneath itself and the mer. *You have pleased me indeed.*

Laku brings Kepetios Memories often, after that. It's rare that xie finds one quite so personal and delectable as that first one, but that was a high bar, a suitably impressive first offering to catch a Great One's attention, and now that its attention is caught, Kepetios is intrigued to see what else xie wishes to bring it. The Memories vary in their content. Some are so land-based, so full of humans, that Kepetios understands little of what is actually happening. The emotions, though, still translate. Every Memory that Laku brings it is beautiful, electrified with awe or fear or reverence, and soaked in that same kind of hunger.

Kepetios has been guarding against any other mer's attempt to snatch Laku's prey from xem, but now, compelled by a fascination with the Memories and a strong desire not to alienate those fingers that are so good at finding just the right spot to scratch, it begins to capture especially interesting looking humans or objects and offer them to Laku. Laku accepts the gifts with bows, and demure words, and deliberately stolen looks that let Kepetios see the bright craving in xer eyes.

Kepetios also begins to pay attention to how the other mers trade Memories. It finds it isn't surprised to see they are frequently exchanged before mers copulate.

It ponders its options. It has heard of serpents that ask the mers to massage their private areas, but to fuck one in earnest would be another matter. It fears breaking the poor creature. On the other hand, Laku seems unafraid of the possibility—and the Memories xie brings Kepetios are only becoming hungrier. They are tinged with Laku's scent, desire bleeding out of xer fingertips and coloring the Memories with appetites that yawn as deep and wide as an ocean trench. Perhaps the Memories are affecting Kepetios's own wants, or perhaps it has been too many

seasons since its last coupling, or perhaps the bold curve of Laku's smile as xie makes Kepetios shudder in contentment under xer fingertips is simply too alluring to ignore, but Kepetios finds itself restless, thinking more and more of mating with the mer.

The next problem, however, comes with showing xem xer interest is reciprocated. To simply say so seems uncouth, when xie has made so many delectable offerings. Kepetios cannot extract Memories like a mer. If Laku were a serpent, Kepetios would nip at xem, provoking xem to playful fights, stealing choice prey, and preening in front of xem as a challenge. A mer could never compete in a fight against a Great One, and to steal xer prey would only seem like a reversal of Kepetios's favor toward xem.

Time rolls forward and winter passes its peak, the days elongating and growing warmer. Kepetios finds itself unhappy at the thought that Laku might depart for other waters before it has shown xem it returns xer interest. Swallowing some of its pride, it makes an offer the next time Laku brings it a Memory.

If you were a Great One, I would chase you the length of the Seven Coasts to couple with you.

Laku pauses, the first time Kepetios has seen genuine hesitation in xer movements.

"But because I am not a Great One, you will not?" xie asks in a soft trill.

No. Because you are not a Great One, I cannot fight you, or chase you, or do anything I would normally do to show you my own interest.

Xer eyes dart up to meet Kepetios's, and they glitter with so much naked desire that Kepetios nearly throws away the rest of its pride to pin xem to the sea floor and fuck xem then and there. It restrains itself and watches Laku reach up to the chain of Memories that circle xer upper arm and pluck one free. Xie holds it out slowly, cautious as xie has not been since the first time.

"If you will permit me, Great One, I would like to offer you a second Memory today."

Kepetios inclines its head, and Laku presses the Memory into its forehead.

It sees two naked human women. One of them is struggling to escape the other's grasp, twisting back and forth.

"No," she gasps. "Let me go!"

"You know the rules," the one holding her says. "Naughty girls get spanked."

"I said, let me *go*!"

She twists free but makes no serious attempt to flee. Instead, she gets recaptured almost immediately, and this time, the other woman seizes a rope and binds her arms together. She grips the bound woman's ass, giving it a squeeze.

"That's another five strokes," she murmurs. "Get on your knees now if you don't want it to be more."

The bound woman nods, suddenly meek. "Yes, Mistress." Her pupils are blown so wide that the brown in her eyes has all but disappeared behind them. The Memory—her Memory—has no taste of fear—only lust, excitement, and that shared hunger. Hunger for the ropes to be just a little tighter, for her Mistress to hit her just a little harder, for the punishment to last a few strokes more.

Kepetios blinks back into the present to find Laku grinning at it.

"I cannot be your equal in a fight, Great One," xie says. "But perhaps it would please you if I was a particularly feisty piece of prey?"

The serpent finds Laku chained to a rock on shore, as arranged. The humans xie found to set xem up had been confused but helpful, happy enough to take a mer's promise that no siren song would ever lure them as a fair exchange. Xer wrists are locked above xer head, manacled to an overhang from the cliff. The sea slaps in frothy bursts against the jagged rock xie sits on. The water is still deep here, so only a few meters of the serpent's body rise out of the surf, gleaming eyes considering Laku.

A pretty little sacrifice, waiting here so sweetly for me.

Laku thrashes against the chains, breaths starting to come quickly. The serpent is rising fully out of the water, and xie really has not appreciated just how entirely massive it is before. Xie inhales sharply through xer nose and calls up, voice sing-song sweet above the water.

"Stop! Stay away from me!" The words feel awkward, distantly embarrassing, but Laku curls xer fingers around the chains and thrills at the reminder of the binding. "Great One, I would be a poor meal. Leave me

be! I—I am frightened; please, stay away!" The part about being frightened is not entirely a lie. How easy would it be for the great serpent to break any agreement, to devour Laku or tear xem to pieces, to ignore any genuine request to stop, or even just to leave xem here, chained to a rock, until the humans come back and find a pretty little mer trussed up for the taking and do much worse than simply devour xem?

But xie has chosen well in trusting this Great One. It leans down, teeth inches from Laku's face and throat, and sniffs at xem.

No amount of pleading will save you now, little mer.

Its teeth hook through the chains and tear them free, sending the metal scattering into the waves. Before Laku can attempt to dive away from it, the serpent catches xem in a coil and takes off into the water.

The serpent's speed, even with its body knotted around a mer, is disorienting. Laku almost inhales with lungs rather than gills as xie is plunged into the sea. By the time xie has xer wits back, xie already isn't sure which direction the shoreline is in. They are deep into a quiet, empty stretch of the open ocean. The surface sparkles far above them. Laku is wrapped tightly in the serpent's body, hardly able to move, water rushing through xer ears as xie is whipped back and forth with the motion of the serpent's swimming. The serpent doesn't stop even as xie starts to thrash and struggle. When xie kicks xer tail out, trying to wriggle down and slip out the bottom, the coil only tightens farther, almost crushing xer ribs.

Xie struggles against the coil of muscle with all xer strength. Xie claws at the serpent, but the scales fit with a deceptive perfection, tightly overlapped and snug against its body, especially fresh off its shed. There isn't so much as a fingernail's worth of gap for Laku to try to use—in *almost* every spot.

Xie takes as deep a breath as xie can with xer body constricted, trying to calm xer racing heart, to stop the sound of blood pounding in xer ears long enough to concentrate. Xie traces the curve of the serpent's body with xer fingers, light enough that xie hopes the serpent can't feel the touch, and finds what xie is looking for. There, yes, a gap, a miniscule one, just where the curve is most pronounced, on the inside of the coil. Xie can barely get an angle on it, having to draw xer arm in close against xer own shoulder and reach awkwardly down, at an angle that strains xer wrist.

There's one advantage of the fresh shed: the skin beneath the serpent's scales is as soft and vulnerable as a newborn babe.

Laku jabs the longest, sharpest claw xie has into the infinitesimal gap between the serpent's scales.

The serpent shrieks, a shockwave that rolls through the water, causing a burst of whitecaps above them and every fish in the vicinity to flee. Laku's teeth rattle in xer head. The serpent is furious.

But the coil holding Laku loosens ever so slightly.

Xie takes advantage of the moment and drives the claw in just a little bit deeper, setting xer palm against the coil and pushing as xie does, so that the serpent jerks away instinctively. Xie kicks xer tail violently, and suddenly, xie finds xemself dislodged from the serpent's grip.

Xie wastes no time, shooting straight downward while the serpent writhes above xem, looking for where xie has gone. Xie pours every last bit of adrenaline and urgency into xer tail, fleeing the serpent, heart pounding, veins singing, gills fluttering in a desperate attempt to keep up with the exertion. The scent of blood is acrid in the water, still trailing off the tip of Laku's claw.

Instinct screams an alarm at the sudden absence of sunlight. Xie glances up and sees the serpent swimming parallel directly above xem. Fear twists in xer gut. How angry is it?

That was bold, little mer. It sounds amused. *I never expected you to actually draw blood.*

Laku flips over, slowing down. Xie can't outrun the serpent in open water, not without a head start. The shadow of it is immense, a long column of darkness that envelops Laku completely. Xer gills continue to flutter at double-speed.

"Are you going to"—xie blinks, feeling light-headed as xie tries to take in the full size of the serpent drifting down toward them—"are you going to hurt me?"

Blood for blood only seems fair.

The serpent is quick, but Laku is quicker. Xie dodges the curl of its tail with a back-breaking twist, xer tail aching in protest of the continuous exertion. The serpent hisses in annoyance as xie plummets deeper into the water. Xer eyes dart back and forth—there. A jagged edge of sea floor, full of crevices and places to hide. Xie hurls xemself toward it. The serpent follows, but xie manages to lose it in the shadows and broken crags, even as it continues to circle, searching for xem. Xie darts into a

cave and stays there, trembling, listening for the serpent's approach. Xie is sore and exhausted from the chase, however, and, after a few moments, slumps onto the cave floor, catching xer breath.

You still have my blood on your finger, sweetheart.

Laku starts up, heart thundering in xer chest.

The serpent's eye alone takes up the whole front of the cave, luminous and terrifying.

Xie bears xer teeth. "And how are you going to get me out?" xie asks.

The serpent considers it for a long moment.

Well. You will get hungry before I do. Although waiting for you at the front of this cave seems terribly dull for both of us. The serpent's eye swivels around the cave before returning to Laku, and there's a tremor that feels like teasing as it asks, *Why don't you try to escape past me before you are exhausted from hunger?*

Laku bares xer teeth, but the serpent has a point.

I'll even give you a head start.

The serpent withdraws from the front of the cave. Rather than allow it to get into whatever position it's planning to snag xem from, Laku hurtles forward immediately, aiming to charge farther down into the twisted caverns where the serpent cannot follow. This time, though, the serpent is faster. Laku is caught, wrapped in three coils around xer shoulders, waist, and the top of xer tail fin, and the serpent is carrying xem away from xer refuge.

"Not much of a head start," Laku scoffs.

You didn't give me a chance to say how long it would be. The serpent sounds amused.

Laku squirms, annoyed, but xie is truly immobilized this time.

When they are back in open water, the serpent slows and unwinds two of the coils from around Laku's body. Laku thrashes, trying to free xemself, and the serpent makes a quelling rumble that shakes Laku's entire body.

Blood for blood, little one, the serpent reminds xem.

Laku stills, just for a moment. This is one part they need to be careful not to fuck up, or the Great One might inadvertently injure Laku far more seriously than it intends to, or even kill xem. The danger of it zings pleasantly up Laku's spine, even as xie holds xemself still for the descending teeth.

It barely grazes xer arm—honestly, it could have gone a *little* deeper, Laku pouts—but blood blooms out from the cut, and the venom spreads with a rapidity Laku isn't quite prepared for. Xie had meant to twist itself away from the serpent one last time, but instead xer tail goes numb, and xie drops in the water like a stone. The serpent catches xem, coiling around xem firmly but carefully, pinning xer arms to xer sides this time. Laku's head lolls. The venom is substantially less effective on mers, symbiotic with the serpents as they are, than on humans or other sea creatures. It won't fully paralyze Laku, and it will last at most ten or fifteen minutes before it begins to wear off. It does, however, make all of Laku's muscles go weak and loose, leaving xem at the serpent's mercy. That's precisely why xie wanted to try it, of course.

Laku manages to roll xer head back to look up at the serpent's massive emerald eye, watching xem closely. Slurring xer sounds through a slack jaw and numb lips, xie trill in the back of xer throat, signaling surrender.

"I yield!" xie says. "Mercy, great and powerful serpent. Please. I don't wish to be eaten!"

A vibration scrapes the sides of Laku's brain, something old and terrifying. It takes xem a moment to realize that the serpent is laughing.

Who said I was going to eat you, little mer? the serpent asks. It lifts Laku up close to its mouth, and Laku sees a tongue as large as Laku's entire body darting out to taste the water that's full of xer fear and adrenaline. *Not like that, anyway*, the serpent says, and Laku groans. Even if xie wasn't too weak with the venom for another escape attempt, xie is far too impatient for what is coming next to keep up that part of the game any longer.

"What are you going to do to me, then?"

Anything I wish.

Laku shudders, lax muscles twitching in time with xer rapid heartbeat. The serpent's eye fills xer vision again.

Although, since you have been so very feisty, perhaps I shall start with a little reminder of your place.

The serpent's mouth opens, and before Laku can object or question, xie is being lifted up and into it, the coils of the serpent's body passing xem into the coils of its tongue. Laku yelps, trying to squirm but mostly flopping back and forth as the mouth closes around xem. Then xie is in a sudden and terrible darkness, limp against a massive, powerful tongue.

Xie lays there, panting, gills fluttering, fingers twitching. The serpent is moving—where, Laku doesn't know—but it isn't swallowing xem. It's only holding xem, the end of its tongue curled over the end of Laku's numb tail, keeping xem in place. The tongue undulates, gently and slowly, beneath xem, and Laku groans. Even with the venom in xer system, the slit at the top of xer tail is beginning to unfurl, scales sliding back into each other.

The tongue rolls and, this time, it hits the now-exposed nub of pleasure nerves.

Laku would howl, but xer vocal cords are still slack and numb, so the best xie manages is another trilling surrender sound. Weakly, xie thrusts xer hips into the tongue, unable to prevent xemself from chasing the sensation as the tongue shifts beneath xem. The nub is hardening, growing erect, a little bulb made of nothing but sensation and pleasure sitting at the top of Laku's slit, which is growing wider and longer by the second. With floppy, undignified movements, Laku manages to wrap xer arms around the tongue, holding onto it even as the tongue tightens its grip on xer tail. Laku jerks back and forth against the tongue with what meager strength xie has. If xie were human, xie would be weeping.

What do you think, little mer? Are you truly ready to submit now?

Laku whines, high and thin, and presses a submissive kiss to the serpent's tongue.

Good pet.

All at once, the mouth is opening, the rush of water and oxygen and light making Laku even dizzier. The serpent's tongue dumps xem out onto a sandy stretch of ocean floor, and xie lies there, panting and whimpering, as the serpent surrounds xem in a wall of coils. It stops, looking down, considering Laku, who has managed to roll onto xer back.

"Please," Laku manages to whistle. "Please."

Please?

The serpent leans down and licks Laku head to toe, making xem cry out and shudder. The serpent lowers its head even farther, brushing its teeth like a loving caress over Laku's cheek. Laku's gills are fluttering so fast they're stirring up the sand beneath xem.

You are an easy little thing, the serpent observes. Laku trills again, tail smacking weakly against the sand as xie strains to push xer hips upward. Xer slit is still wide open, the nub of pleasure protruding from the top.

The serpent makes a show of eyeing it and then pulls its head back. Laku would start begging if xie could make xer lips behave. *You will get your pleasure*, the serpent chides, *but I think it is my turn.*

About three quarters of the way down the serpent's massive body, its hemipenes have emerged from its scales. Laku licks xer lips in anticipation, unable to keep the naked desire from shuddering up and down xer body. The serpent bares its teeth again, though not from quite so close this time.

So eager to serve me.

Laku isn't sure if the venom is wearing off or if it is xer sheer arousal that gives xem the ability to nod this frantically. The serpent makes that ancient terrible sound of laughter again, and it vibrates straight through Laku's bones.

That's only proper. I am a Great One of the seas. All things should wish to serve me.

"Yes, Great One." Laku doesn't think xie could have moved even if the venom hadn't still lingered in xer veins. Xie is pinned by the serpent's glowing jade eyes, hypnotic in their beauty and overwhelming power.

Then come. The serpent wraps the bottom of its tail around Laku's torso, tugging xem up and toward itself. *Come and take me in your mouth.*

The hemipenes are squat, almost square, and barbed. Each one is as big as both of Laku's fists, and xie can't hope to get all of either in xer mouth. Xie leans forward, bottom half held in place by the serpent's tail, and wraps xer mouth around as much of one of the cocks as xie can fit. The barbs are inflexible but blunt, pressing into Laku's tongue with a delectable pressure. Laku kisses and sucks, trying to move xer mouth to each part of the cock in turn. After another minute or two, xie finally has enough control of xer arms again to add them to the endeavor, reaching up and massaging what can't fit in xer mouth. Xer fingers stroke along the barbs, learning this last piece of The Great One that xie has not yet touched. Xie hears its rumble of pleasure and redoubles xer efforts.

Keep going. The serpent lifts Laku's body as xie keeps obligingly suckling on its cock. Xie is shifted and turned until xer slit is lined up to take the other cock. Laku stills. Xer slit is large but deeper than it is wide, and with those barbs… The serpent doesn't wait for xem. Before Laku can even think of pulling xer mouth free, the serpent shifts, and the other cock shoves its way inside Laku's slit.

A shrill sound scrapes the back of Laku's throat. The pressure is immense. It pushes xem wider and wider with its cock, the barbs catching and hooking in Laku's walls, so that xie couldn't pull away even if xie wanted to. Wider and wider still, its cock spreads the opening of xer slit, and—there. Laku feels xer hips meet the serpent's body; it must be sheathed all the way inside xem now. Xer gills flutter frantically. The distance between the hemipenes is just wide enough for this position to work without demanding too much contortion from Laku, although xie is now bent over the cock in xer mouth. Xie starts to move, to try to adjust, but the serpent's voice rumbles through their head with the force of a thunderstorm.

I told you to keep going.

Fear and adrenaline race up Laku's spine, and xie immediately pushes xer mouth back down onto the cock, trying to open xer mouth wider to take in even a little bit more. Another barb manages to slip inside, pressing hard at the left corner of xer mouth. Xie whines around it, sucking on the cock as much for comfort and distraction from the massive pressure in xer lower half as for pleasure.

Xer tail flutters and jerks, control returning slowly, and as xie rocks forward, xie manages to push xer own hard nub of a cock into the unyielding scales of the serpent's body. Xie moans, a more guttural sound than xie has made so far, something drawn from deep inside xer throat. Xie is overwhelmed with sensation: the lingering venom turning xer muscles fuzzy, the electric bolts of pleasure sparking through xem, the pressure in xer slit and mouth, the barbs pressing into xem like a brutal massage, a pain that pushes its way past discomfort and into slack-jawed euphoria—all of it threatens to turn xer mind to mush. Xie cups the bottom of the hemipene already in xer mouth with both hands and squeezes it with every bit of concentration left to xem. Xie rubs xer thumb up and over a particularly wide barb, letting xer nail catch the skin, providing just enough of a scratch for the serpent to feel.

Such an eager little pet. The serpent's thoughts have a pleased strain that thrills through Laku's body. Xie did that. *Don't you regret your resistance now?*

Laku whines, licking at the serpent's cock in needy, apologetic little touches.

I'll forgive you, the serpent says, *if you can make me come before you succumb to your own pleasure.*

That, Laku thinks dimly—still occupied with sucking and with the massive pressure splitting open xer lower half and the delicious rough edge of a scale rubbing xer cock *just* right—that's a bit of an unfair ask on the serpent's part. Xie is doing all xie can, truly. Laku lifts xemself up, saliva thick in xer mouth, diffusing into the water as xer jaw hangs loose and open.

Xer words come out slowly, the whistles half-formed and pitched too low, but xie manages to plead, "Show me how to please you, Great One."

The serpent rumbles its approval.

I know how clever those fingers are, it says. *Put them to use. Focus on the barbs.*

Laku doesn't feel that any part of xem is particularly clever right now, but xie does as instructed. Xie lowers xer face back to the cock but focuses less on xer mouth and more on xer fingers. Xie strokes, massages, and then scratches—first gently, and then harder and harder, claws digging into the barb just shy of puncturing skin.

Yes. The word feels like it presses in on Laku with the weight of the deepest ocean, reverberating its way into xer very bones. *That's good, little mer. Just like that. Just—there—*

The serpent's climax is like an earthquake, the entire ocean shaking around them. Laku's teeth rattle in xer head, and xie thrashes involuntarily as the cock stuffed in xer slit swells, pressing the barbs in farther and deeper. Xie loses xer grip on the other hemipene, but it doesn't matter. The serpent is tensing and arcing in pleasure. It wraps itself in tightening coils around Laku, and xie gasps, scrabbles weakly at its scales, and then topples over the edge xemself. Xer orgasm is blinding, an intensity of sensation that whites out the rest of the world for an impossibly endless moment. The serpent's scales undulate across Laku's body in a caress, massaging xem through it.

When xie blinks back into awareness, its cock is still embedded deep in xer slit, barbs hooked into oversensitive skin. Xie moves xer hips but hisses at the way the barbs catch, still holding xem in place. Xie looks up to meet the serpent's massive jade eyes. It shows its teeth.

You didn't think we were done, did you, little pet?

Laku whimpers, trills in the back of xer throat, and, with a rush of hunger, reaches out to grasp the second cock again.

Laku sleeps for a full day after the hours-long copulation finally ends. Kepetios settles xer limp body on its own coils and rests in warm, shallow waters, pleasantly spent and satisfied. It dozes, nesting in the soft sand, coils protectively encircling the curve of its body where the mer rests. Laku's lips are upturned in xer sleep. A smile, Kepetios knows—a sign of happiness and pleasure. That smile brings Kepetios a deep contentment.

When it feels Laku stirring, it lowers its head to meet xer eyes. Xie moves slowly as xie wakes, carefully stretching and shaking out xer tail, massaging the sore edges of xer slit. But xie meets Kepetios's gaze with a ferocious grin.

It was not too much for you, I trust?

Laku laughs, the sound as bright and sparkling as xer tail is in the morning sunlight.

"It was more than I dared dream." Xie caresses Kepetios's scales for a moment, the touch gentle and sure, and then bows xer head. "I am honored by your attentions, Great One. I hope I pleased you."

It has been too many summers since I last had an acceptable mate. Your boldness has charmed me, and your body has brought me much delight—both yesterday and in all the time you have served me. Laku. I shall remember you.

Laku bows lower and then reaches up to xer forehead. With a single finger, xie withdraws a shining, silver shard of light from between xer eyes. With a few twists, xie fashions it into a bracelet that xie loops around xer wrist.

"I will be moving on to new seas this summer," Laku says. "I have seen too many Memories of the same lands and can linger no longer. But this Memory"—xie caresses it, and Kepetios can almost feel the touch along its own skin—"I shall carry this Memory with me and cherish it always."

Kepetios shifts, using the thin end of a tail fin to lift Laku's chin until they are eye to eye again.

Travel safely and far, it says, *and if one day you return, I would be pleased to see what new Memories you bring.*

Laku smiles, leans forward, and kisses the delicate fin.

"I shall see you at the other end of the earth, Great One."

Lovespun

Lyonel Loy

ableism (internalized), aftercare, alien, bipoc, bondage, established relationship, friends, illness, insectoid, kissing, m/nb, m/m/nb/nb (mentions of), overstimulation, polyamory, present tense, purity-focused indoctrination, science fiction, self-esteem issues, service top, spaceship, third person limited (alternating) point of view

"I do hope I'm not being a bother," Zakri says, as they always do, standing by the threshold of Jianlei's open door with all four claspers wringing nervously and their adorable little wings all a-flutter.

" 'Course you aren't," Jianlei says, and kisses them.

Zakri squeals into his lips, a tiny little *ee-eee!* that's the sweetest sound Jianlei's ever heard. They clutch at Jianlei with all four of their claspers, turning their head this way and that, offering every inch of their blunt mandibles to be kissed. The best part of kissing Zakri, in Jianlei's view, is how much and how openly they delight in it.

"I'm full," Zakri tells him shyly, ducking to hide their face against

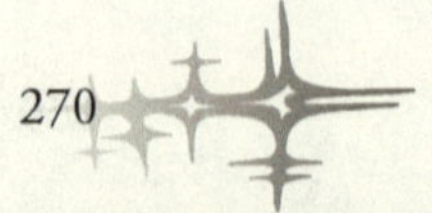

Jianlei's chest; Jianlei drops a final, fond kiss to the soft chitin just above the topmost row of their iridescent eyes. "I'm ready, please. I've been good."

"You're always good, sweetheart, full or not." There's a terrifying amount to unpack in Zakri's desperate need to be always ready for harvesting. But Jianlei's no shrink; he's just the hazardous materials specialist who loves them. "Shall we? Got your favorite chair set up."

Jianlei bought the armchair specially for Zakri, although he's never told them so—worth every cred he spent to see Zakri nestled in its overstuffed cushions, chirping in contentment with their silk-swollen abdomen propped up comfortably between their legs.

Jianlei hooks his stool in place with a foot and adjusts the automated spooler. "Ready?"

"Oh! Yes." All sixteen of Zakri's eyes sparkle an excited green-gold. "And—and can you—?"

They swipe at their nervously wriggling mandibles with their upper claspers.

Jianlei waits.

"Can you start me off with—?" they finally manage, tremulous and shy, "I mean, can you—can you kiss—?"

They trail off, little wings buzzing with embarrassment, hiding their face in their claspers.

" 'Course I'll kiss you." Jianlei drops a kiss to the blunt tip of Zakri's stinger, just past the midline of their abdomen above the throbbing swell of their eager spinnerets. "Here?"

Zakri is click-chittering in laughter, swiping at their mandibles in denial. "No!" they squeak, eyes glinting bright. It wasn't too long ago that they didn't dare to say *no*—it warms Jianlei's heart every time they do. "On my— Below that. My spinnerets, please? Only if you don't mind?"

"I'll kiss you any time you want, lovebug. Anywhere."

The pulsing glands that ring Zakri's spinnerets are warm beneath Jianlei's lips, a sharp contrast to the coolness of their chitin. Their valve is already open, the tubular filaments within it extruding to brush at Jianlei's cheeks. Jianlei sneaks a kiss there too, darting his tongue between the frills, and Zakri squeals. Their spinnerets wave and leak astringent, lethally toxic pre-silk fluid—but Jianlei's hazmat for a reason.

The nanites that have colonized his body for as long he can remember flood his lips and tongue and throat, squirming and feasting just under his skin.

Jianlei licks and suckles at the trembling frills just as greedily. His nanites report chemical makeup as disconnected bursts of taste and smell; Zakri's pre-silk lubricant is the smokey-sweetness of the burnt ends of pork cracklings, accompanied by a distant fragrance of pomelo that grows stronger with Zakri's every shudder and squeal, until—

Jianlei, with the ease of long practice, jerks back, catches the burst of silk strands, and tosses them in a loop around the automated spooler.

"Oh," Zakri chitters, slender legs kicking, claspers rubbing over their waving mandibles. "It's good. I'm sorry! It's so good, I don't mean to—"

Harvesting's supposed to feel good, or so Jianlei's been told by every other Ixian he's ever asked. Very good.

The religious hive-cult of Zakri's hatching apparently disagreed.

"I like when you feel good, lovebug. Everyone deserves to feel good." There are probably better responses to the tangled mess of Zakri-and-pleasure, but again—Jianlei's not a shrink. Any shrink willing to take on the clusterfuck crew of the ISS Redline would have to be a head-case themself. "Your spinnerets look so pretty like this. All swollen and fluttering." He massages at Zakri's gland-ring and the base of their spinnerets, careful not to interrupt the steady flow of glistening silk. "*You're* so pretty."

Zakri squeaks and waggles their mandibles in denial, but their iridescent eyes are tinting green in shy delight. Just a year ago any praise at all made them cry. They couldn't even bear to look at their own silk-swollen abdomen and spinnerets when Jianlei first met them. Now Zakri's sneaking timid glances—more at Jianlei's hand than at their own body, but progress is progress. Not bad for just a *year*…

Shit. Ah, shit.

How has it already been a year?

Zakri's silk sacs are empty. That is a sin. A spinner's purpose is to be harvested; to be empty of silk is to be without purpose. There is no place in a hive for purposelessness.

But the ISS Redline is a ship and not a hive.

It's perfectly fine to be empty here—Jianlei told Zakri that, and so it must be true. It's also fine to want things, Jianlei always says, and right now, Zakri wants very badly to be kissed.

All they have to do is ask. Jianlei will kiss them. Maybe Zakri will get more than just kisses—the crew of the Redline are free and open with affection, even affection of the most dreadfully sinful sort, the sort that leads to pleasure. Jianlei is particularly generous with both kisses and affection, even when Zakri's silk sacs are useless and empty.

To ask, all Zakri has to do is go up to him. But Jianlei is sitting in the crew's rest lounge…and talking to the dead drone Jedou.

Zakri had never spoken to one of the inglorious, purposeless dead before they fled their hive for the Redline.

Zakri's empty silk sacs do not always defy their purpose; Zakri's sacs will refill, with time, until they are harvested and made sinful again. The dead drone Jedou is sleek and strong and stern—so very unlike Zakri—but they lost their soldier-sharp stinger and all but one half of their hooked and curving mandibles in some terrible long-ago battle. What is a drone without their weapons of war? Jedou can never regain their purpose. All that is left for them is death.

Yet they bravely linger on.

Perhaps one day Zakri will find the same courage.

For now, they are barely brave enough to scuttle into the lounge with their uselessly stubby wings pulled tight against their back.

Halfway there, they almost lose their nerve. What if Jianlei and Jedou's conversation is about something more important than kisses? Like the Gobi Cable run—Zakri has heard the rest of the crew worrying about it, even Tseng, the fearless captain of the Redline. Jianlei and Jedou are officers; surely they must be too busy for kisses.

But then Jianlei turns, and sees them, and waves in welcome. Zakri scurries gratefully into his arms.

"Hullo, lovebug," Jianlei laughs.

Jedou buzzes their wounded wings as though Zakri were a sleek drone-sibling who deserved such a greeting, not a purposeless spinner with a grotesquely swollen abdomen. Zakri buzzes their wings, too, feeling terrible shy. Even the remnants of the wings that Jedou also lost in war are longer than Zakri's stunted pair; even a dead drone is above a spinner.

"Hullo," they say. The warm welcome makes them feel almost brave. "I'm terribly sorry to interrupt, but may I please have a kiss?"

" 'Course you can." Jianlei reels them in; Zakri clicks their mandibles in delight. "Wanna sit with us? I'll kiss you while we talk." He scoops Zakri into his lap, abdomen and all, as though their empty sacs and perversely distended spinnerets weren't such terribly shameful things that ought to be hidden away. "We're chatting about courtship. Yours, to be precise. I've been helping with your harvests for a year, lovebug, and that's worth a celebration."

"Oh!" is all Zakri can think to say, scrabbling over their weak mandibles with their even weaker claspers. All their words are tangled in their thorax—Zakri is silkspinner caste, and spinners don't get courted.

But they'd like nothing more.

"Only if you want me to, of course," Jianlei continues. He puts his hand right over Zakri's grotesque spinneret and kneads it so gently, and pleasure that Zakri doesn't deserve tingles wonderfully all the way up their abdomen. "Problem is: I don't have a clue about courtship, and Jedou here doesn't either."

Jedou waggles their half-a-mandible like they're trying to clack in apology.

Zakri buzzes their wings politely—it feels so strange to have a drone apologize to them, even a dead one. Apologies should only flow the other way.

"I—I— Yes, please. I'd love to be courted. But I don't know anything about courting either." Zakri isn't supposed to want to be courted. They're not supposed to have their empty spinnerets petted, either, and Jedou isn't supposed to permit Zakri's greedy sinfulness. But Jedou doesn't look bothered by how shamefully Zakri is behaving, and Jianlei always says that what Zakri wants is more important than what they're supposed or not supposed to be doing.

They hide their face in Jianlei's chest. When Jianlei's close, "not supposed to" seems much less frightening.

"Eh, we'll muddle through." Jianlei wriggles his clever fingers at the twitching valve where the sensitive filaments of Zakri's spinnerets hide. Zakri gasps. All of their empty silk-sacs pulse along their abdomen—and Jedou makes a strange noise.

Zakri looks up in horror. They must have gone too far. Will Jedou demand to punish them now?

But Jedou doesn't look angry, or even disapproving: they are scrubbing at their mandible and eyes with their four strong claspers and fluttering their shredded wings.

Zakri has never seen a drone flutter their wings like a needy spinner begging to be harvested.

"You look very pretty in my lap, Zakri." Jianlei's eyes are expressively eager even though he has only a single pair. "It's making poor Jedou feel very hot and very needy, and they'd very much like Tseng to be touching them just as I'm touching you. That right, Jedou?"

"Tseng's busy," Jedou says softly. Shyly. Zakri can't help goggling. How can a drone be shy? "Gobi Cable."

"We're more than ready. Tseng works too hard." Jianlei tilts Zakri's head toward him, kisses them above the eyes, and winks at them. "I'll touch you if you want—but only, of course, if Zakri here doesn't mind sharing."

"I—I don't mind," Zakri says in a rush. Jedou is always kind even though Zakri is afraid of them; Zakri doesn't want them to be left in need. Even if Zakri doesn't know how a drone could feel needy, nor how they could want to be touched like a lowly spinner.

Zakri wants to learn how.

They want to learn everything, and it's all right to want things.

"You can help me touch them if you like," Jianlei says.

Jedou flexes their mandible in agreement. Their face is still mostly hidden behind their quivering claspers, but Zakri can see the excited green-gold sheen of their eyes as they lift their abdomen—so much smaller and neater than Zakri's own—up onto the sofa.

Below the scarred ruin of their lost stinger lies a twitching little hole, almost like the valve that houses Zakri's filaments but tidier and less engorged. As pretty as Jianlei always says Zakri is, and it mouths at the empty air as Jianlei runs his hand along Jedou's shuddering thorax and down their abdomen…

And Zakri *wants.*

"Just once," Jianlei says conversationally, "I'd like us to run the Gobi Cable without the threat of an explosive decompression."

"That's geopolitics." Tseng's voice is tinny and static-filled through the primitive headset of Jianlei's pressure suit, crackling like the mismatched sensory feedback of Jianlei's over-ramped nanites. "We're not in the geopolitics line."

"So you keep saying. Told you before, I'll back you if you feel like wading into that mess." Nanites swarm through Jianlei's blood, rippling under his skin and over his bones. They taste like sound. *More*, Jianlei tells them. *Go higher. I need more.* If the Redline isn't attacked, he'll have a hell of a time tuning them back down; if she is, he might need more than his body can hold.

Tseng laughs, harsh and rasping and tense. "You might have to, way the galaxy's going." A sharp double-click as he switches from their private channel to main comms, and— "All teams, report."

"Inner hab fully locked down, we're a go."

Zakri is in the inner hab. Zakri will be fine in the inner hab—Jianlei needs to believe that.

"Engineering is go."

"Medical is go."

The security checkpoints report one by one, each grimmer—and closer to the hull—than the last. Above and just ahead of Jianlei, clinging to the low ceiling of the outer shield corridor, Laufrit flicks her proboscis and nods.

"Red team is go," Jedou rasps. They're on the other side of the blast door at Jianlei's back, just a few steps away, and Tseng will be a few paces behind them. Far too close for Jianlei's comfort—he'd rather have them both safe in the inner hab with Zakri.

Jianlei doesn't have a good feeling about the Gobi Cable today. "First line is go," he says anyway, and flicks off the safety on his ion gun. On the other side of the blast door—a world away, if Jianlei does his job right—Tseng is authorizing the bridge crew to begin warp procedures. The Redline's twin engines are rumbling to life, the hull rattling from the strain of the faster-than-light jump.

None of it matters. Nothing matters but the crackling of Jianlei's nanites and the hissing heat of his gun.

"Warping in T-minus-three."

Jianlei's nanites surge inside him, agitated by his tension.
"Two."
The taste of electric yellow floods his tongue.
"*One.*"
And everything goes to hell.

"I do hope everyone's okay," Zakri says, scrubbing fretfully at their mandibles and eyes with a clasper.

The hull has been breached. The blast had rocked the Redline hard enough to be felt even in the protected innermost hab, where Zakri is waiting because they are too useless to fight.

"They are," Koiroi says, and never in Zakri's life have they been as confident as Koiroi is now, with the walls of the Redline rumbling in battle around them both. She pats at their upper arms, burbling reassuringly. "This is a Firestorm-class warship, dearie, and Tseng leads us well—a mere rabble of pirate-rats won't best us."

"Jianlei's first line." Zakri strokes her forelimbs in turn—they love the softness of her slippery skin, and Koiroi adores their chitin; they sit together and pet each other whenever they can.

It's hard for Zakri to enjoy themself properly today. They're too worried.

"So he is, and for good reason! Sol-folk are hard to kill, as a rule, your Jianlei moreso than the rest. And Laufrit will keep him safe." She hums, pulsing the loose skin at her throat. "You are courting, I hear?"

"Oh! We are!" Zakri clatters their mandibles, clutching at her forelimbs in their excitement. It feels so sinfully boastful how much they enjoy talking about Jianlei. But Zakri won't think about sin today. Jianlei kissed them before they parted, and told them not to worry—talking about Jianlei is maybe the only thing that could distract Zakri from their worry. "He's planning to—and I'd love to court him, too, but I haven't worked out how."

"A complicated business," Koiroi agrees. "My folk come equipped with all the necessary parts, thank goodness. All I need to do to win over a nice bull is—"

She puffs up and hums, her throat swelling and swelling until it is as round and wide and large as the rest of her put together. Zakri stares with all of their eyes.

"We call, too," she adds. More boomingly than before, and her throat only deflates a little as she speaks. "I'd demonstrate, but there are decibel limits in this hab by the order of Health and Safety. But for *finding* that nice bull. Well. Tradition gets a little complicated now that we're scattered across the galaxy. My dear mama—and my nana before her—made a rather risqué profile on amphibious-love.io and matched with a handsome bull with similarly straightforward tastes. Each was impressed by the shapeliness of the other's cloaca, so they met in person and impressed each other further with the volume and deep bass tones of their mating cries. They've been spawning happily together since!"

Zakri trills in delight, fluttering their stunted wings—they love a happy ending.

Koiroi beams. "I've been attempting likewise," she confides, deflating all the way, "without the same success. But enough about me! Gift-giving's a part of courtship for most, I hear. Perhaps you could get your Jianlei something nice?"

Zakri fidgets. "Gifts are good, I think," they say. "I asked Davin about it?"

"*Ah*," Koiroi says.

"I don't have," Zakri stutters, worry-wiping at their eyes, "the parts—"

"Ah," Koiroi says. "Yes. Davin's a sweetheart, but he does tend to forget that the rest of us can't just remove our… Well. I'm sure Jianlei doesn't expect your severed member as a courting gift, dearie. Sol-folk don't regrow their genitalia either."

All the segments of Zakri's chitin go slack in relief. "I did like the thought of it," they confess. "Presenting a gift that's such a part of me, I mean. But I've only got my silk, and Jianlei has so much of that already." Zakri's swollen sacs make silk faster than they can give it away, especially now that their silk belongs to them and not their hive. "It doesn't seem like much of a gift to give him more."

Koiroi thrums in thought. "Silk, silk," she hums, and pulls a viewscreen out between them to share. "I have an idea. Sol-folk are very clever with their fibers. So many forms of crafts! And it's all on the 'net."

Thumbnails flood the viewscreen, some so old that the footage is two-dimensional. Zakri leans in close. Even their sixteen eyes aren't

enough—they want to see everything.

"I've always meant to learn crochet." Mercifully, Koiroi picks a video. Zakri wouldn't have known where to begin. "But I keep putting it off. Shall we make a pact to learn together? We can hold each other accountable."

Tseng babbles when he's worried. It's adorable, but misfiring orbital rockets wouldn't drag that little fact out of Jianlei. "…medical's a mess. Biogen tank went over when we got rocked, the goop's everywhere—thank fuck no one was hurt. Starboard engine's mostly toasted, the outer shield corridor is—eh, you saw that. Crew's mostly fine. Davin only lost a couple of claws, which is pretty good by his usual standards, he's planning to regrow them in this gawdawful shade of red…"

The speakers mounted along the walls of the decontamination chamber are top of the line and turned up loud. Tseng's voice still barely cuts through the sensory nightmare of Jianlei's panicked nanites chewing through the radiation in his body.

Pirates with nuclear guns. The galaxy is truly going to hell in a handbasket.

"How's Laufrit?" Jianlei rasps when his mother hen of a captain pauses for breath. "Tell her I owe her one." Stars shine down on solar moths and their radiation-resistant wings—if Laufrit hadn't dived to take the brunt of the blast, Jianlei's bones might have melted before his nanites could do their work.

"She's fine. Surface burns. Nothing her next molt won't fix. She's flying beside the ship until her Geiger counter stops pinging. *And* she says she knew you'd say that, and that you don't."

Jianlei's laughter bubbles past the sludge of trapped radiation rising through his throat. He hacks, retching into the disposal drain; a symphony of discordant chords crawls over his tongue. His ears hear salt and pepper. "And how are *you*?"

"I'm fine," Tseng says, too quickly.

"Like hell you are. When did you last sleep?"

A pause.

"You're in decontamination," Tseng says. Soft and fretful in a way he never is in front of anyone but Jianlei or Jedou—no longer the Redline's untouchable, unflappable captain. Jianlei's best and oldest friend, who's guarded him as he hacked and shuddered through a thousand decontamination sequences, because radiation disposal costs money and hazmat techs come cheap…

"I am," Jianlei agrees. *Wait,* he tells his nanites, and most of them reluctantly do; he needs his voice steady for this. "I'll be in here at least a week. I'm fine. I remember the promise you made me, ge. I trust it." Tseng's captain of their ship now, and he doesn't let his people be vented out the airlocks to save creds on cleanup. "Now hand command over to Koiroi and go rest. Or do I have to sic Jedou on you?"

Tseng's laugh is a wobbly and fragile thing.

"I'm already here," Jedou says through the same comm, plaintive and with a lightness Jianlei knows they're forcing. "I've *been* sic-ing."

"No one's blaming you, Jedou. He's always been a stubborn shit. Go cuddle your lovebug, Tseng." Jianlei's waiting nanites are getting grousy—they hate the acrid taint of radiation. Their anger is black and blue and ocean spray. *Go,* Jianlei tells them, and they surge as one. Their swarming floods his vision with crushed-basil sharpness.

"Ganging up on me," Tseng complains, thready, but Jianlei can hear him giving in. "Sure, boss, I'm going. Your lovebug wants to talk to you, too. You feeling good enough for me to patch them through?"

" 'Course I am. Lock the video feed."

Zakri doesn't need to watch radioactive goop leaking from Jianlei's eyes.

The speakers crackle with the sounds of the handover: Zakri squeaks and tap-taps at their mic; Jedou chivvies Tseng away. Jianlei laughs softly to himself, achingly fond, and blinks dancing nanite-static out of his vision.

"Hello, lovebug," he says.

"Jianlei!" Zakri says, and the sound of their voice bleeds a tight knot of tension out of Jianlei. He'd known, logically, that Zakri would be fine—they'd been with Koiroi, safe in the heart of the Redline. He'd been worried nonetheless.

"I won't be able to help with your next harvest, Zakri. I'm sorry. You'll be good with someone else?"

"I will," Zakri says, so adorably earnest. "Koiroi's offered to help. I'll

miss you so very much, but I'll be all right with her, Jianlei, really. Please don't worry."

"I'll miss you too, lovebug, but you'll be in good hands." He'll have to comm Koiroi a little before the event—when his nanites have cleared enough radiation that he can hold on to a thought without distraction—and go over the technicalities, but Zakri is as safe with her as with anyone else.

Fuck, but Jianlei already misses his bug. It's going to be a long week.

A faint *click-clack-click* that might be nanite-noise or the chittering of Zakri's mandibles; the sound reaches Jianlei through his skin before his ears. Maybe it's both.

"I also thought—" Zakri begins. The next *click! cl-click* is definitely them—they're working their nerve up for something. "That maybe—" Jianlei smiles to himself, shutting his eyes to picture Zakri dancing in place with their cute little wings all a-flutter. "Maybe I could ask Jedou, too, if you don't think they'd mind? I really liked touching them."

"*Of course* they won't mind, lovebug. They really liked you touching them too."

Jianlei knows *exactly* how much Jedou liked Zakri touching them. Tseng had commed the very same night and put Jedou on the line to tell Jianlei just how much they'd loved being spread wide and stroked, and how good it felt to have Jianlei's fingers holding their hole open for Zakri, and how embarrassing it was, and how much it had aroused them to be so embarrassed…

If the radiation didn't currently have his libido zapped to nonexistence, Jianlei would be soaking wet just from the memory. The conversation had taken a while—Jedou kept stuttering and losing their train of thought, because Tseng had his entire damned fist fucking up into the very same hole Zakri'd had such a nice time playing with.

The Redline's captain and chief of security are absolute freaks in bed; Jianlei reaps the benefits.

Zakri *eeees* in delight. "Oh, *oh*, and Koiroi says you have a viewscreen," they say, words tumbling over each other in their excitement. "She can get a live feed hooked out, she says, so that you can watch too! It'll almost be like you're there. And—" Their wings are buzzing loudly enough to be audible even over the overloaded static of Jianlei's nanites. "And until then, can I call you more, like this? Davin taught me how to find old shows on the 'net, and there are so many about courtship—we could watch together?"

"I'd love to, Zakri," Jianlei says, warm with fondness and a small amount of dread. Davin's sense of humor is spectacularly bizarre; his idea of "old shows about courtship" could be anything from ancient telenovelas—because *every damned species* in the galaxy, at some point in their civilization, has produced poorly acted and excessively melodramatic telenovelas—to interstellar anal-probing porn. "Anytime. Even now, if you'd like."

Ee-eee! "Yes! Oh, yes, let's," Zakri gasps with a flurry of tip-tapping noises that are definitely from Zakri's end of the mic, because they reach Jianlei through his ears. "Let's watch—Koiroi, please, can you help me with—"

The viewscreen on the side of the decontamination chamber blinks to life, flickering from the room's ambient radiation.

What the fuck, Jianlei does not say.

"Is that BBC's *Planet Earth*?" He can barely make out the screen through the murmuration of sharply-scented pinpricks that are exploding over his vision, but he'd recognize the music—and voiceover—anywhere.

"Yes, yes! It's the remake, Davin says, from after your folk left your star system, so there's comparison footage from the rest of the galaxy. It's so wonderful. I love the bowerbirds in this episode. Their nests! I love the colors."

Jianlei shuts his scent-aching eyes.

Nanite colors dance across the insides of his eyelids, in every shade of smell and taste and sound. *I wish I could truly be watching this with you now, Zakri. I'm sorry.* He used to watch the original series—the ones long in the public domain—with Tseng, back when they were nothing more than surplus brats huddled over a contraband handheld screen in the dank pits of a mining colony.

His nanites, because they're not *always* asses, offer a splash of smell-sound over his tongue like bowerbird-blue.

"I really like them too, lovebug."

Today will be of surprises: one for Zakri, and another for Jianlei. Not

big ones. Care must be taken with surprises in cross-species relationships, Koiroi had told Zakri, because of the lack of a common cultural context. Better to over-communicate than not.

Zakri already knows most of what to expect today. Jianlei's going to court them, here in the little gallery in the stern of the Redline, overlooking the shimmering arcs of the Cat's Eye Nebula where the Redline is in orbit for repairs. Zakri can hardly take a single eye off the sight—they'd never seen anything so bright or so beautiful before they left their hive. It's almost as exciting as Jianlei setting up safety straps and emergency releases for the courtship, just behind them.

Zakri presses their mandibles and eyes to the viewport.

Laufrit is out there somewhere, dancing amidst the solar winds with freshly molted wings. "This is a hot zone for her folk," Jianlei had told Zakri, "in the spicy sense of the word. Let's hope she finds someone nice."

Zakri hopes very much that Laufrit will find for herself someone as wonderful as Jianlei.

"All done," Jianlei says at last. Zakri jumps—they go much higher than usual, because the Redline's artificial gravity has been reduced for the repairs—and whirls around, all four of their claspers wringing in excitement. Jianlei is holding out a safety line to them and smiling. "Remember how to use this, lovebug?"

"Yes! Oh, yes."

Jianlei's going to turn the gallery's gravity off—it's a tradition of the Redline when courting, or so he said. Jianlei has special boots for maneuvering in zero-g, but Zakri isn't trained to use those. They'll use the safety line instead, clipped around their left leg so that they won't be trapped in the middle of the gallery with nothing to push off.

Safety is very important on the Redline.

Zakri had to attend many classes when they first came onboard, but it's a little hard to focus on regulations as they tighten the thick strap around the uppermost joint of their left leg—it feels so much like being tied up for pleasure, so good and so safe.

They'll be tied up even more today, floating in the gallery with no gravity to weigh their swollen abdomen down.

Zakri can't wait.

They want to dance from foot to foot, but it's important to be standing firm when the gravity goes off—they remember that from the classes. They still wobble when their feet leave the floor, and they clutch at the nearest rail, but they barely have to squeak at all.

Jianlei is waiting in the middle of the gallery, drifting in mid-air as though he was born in zero-g.

Zakri flutters their stunted wings, *click-clacks* their blunt mandibles for courage, and pushes off the rail toward him.

"Well done, lovebug." The outer corners of Jianlei's two eyes are crinkled, which in Sol-folk means happiness. Zakri squeaks in delight and ducks down to be kissed, clinging to Jianlei's shoulders with all of their claspers. "And here's your surprise."

From a little cloth pouch clipped to the side of his belt, Jianlei draws out a rope.

A rope of handspun silk, dyed in bowerbird-blue.

"Oh!" Zakri reaches out with their claspers, so excited that they almost throw themself off-balance. Jianlei catches them around the thorax and shakes the rope out, draping it gently over Zakri's arms. "Oh, it—it's—"

"It's your silk." Jianlei is smiling so wide that his teeth show like many little mandibles. "You like it?"

"I do!" Zakri *loves* the rope. A rope made just for Zakri, spun from the silk that came from their body—a rope for Zakri's pleasure, because Zakri is Jianlei's. "I love it. I love you so much, *oh*—"

They press their mandibles to Jianlei's face and try their best to kiss him.

"Love you too, bug," Jianlei says, voice very soft. He pulls Zakri close and kisses their mandibles and eyes and down to their thorax, and he strokes them so gently all over. Zakri touches him, too, everywhere that they can reach, until they drift together in the middle of the gallery, tangled in each other and the lovely rope of bowerbird-blue silk.

It takes a rather long time to get themselves untangled again. Zakri hardly minds. Untangling is an excuse to continue stroking and being stroked, with the silk rope slithering deliciously across their chitin like a promise.

Already their near-empty silk sacs are pulsing.

They've already practiced tying-up a little, just the two of them in Jianlei's bed, so that Zakri wouldn't be surprised in a bad way during the courting.

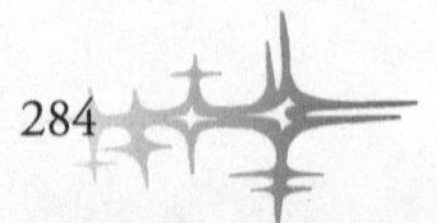

They practiced with Jedou and Tseng, too, on Jedou, with far more straps than Zakri had the courage for themself—so many straps that Jedou couldn't move an inch. All their limbs were splayed out wide, their svelte abdomen thrust up with their tidy little hole on display, and then Tseng and Jianlei had sat on either side of them and taught Zakri how to stroke and stuff them until they shrieked and shook like an overharvested spinner.

Every part of Zakri shivers when they remember Jedou's delightfully pleading cries. They want to be made to squeal just like Jedou, and they want to make Jedou squeal again.

They will have the first today, for their courtship.

Zakri's silk sacs ripple along their abdomen, and their stunted wings flutter. They feel so brave with Jianlei holding them close. So desired and so loved. They even dare to hold all four of their claspers out to Jianlei without being asked: their own eager offering for the day.

Jianlei flashes his pearly not-mandibles, and ties Zakri up.

First their upper pair of arms: a loop of silk around each joint, another over their claspers. More loops to bind each upper limb to its lower counterpart, until Zakri's arms are swathed in the loveliest of blues. They can still wriggle their claspers—Jianlei never binds Zakri as tightly as Jedou likes to be bound—and reach out to pet at Jianlei's face, but already they feel so completely like Jianlei's.

Then Jianlei guides Zakri's body up. They drift through the air, bent almost in half, as Jianlei loops the rope once, twice, around the widest point of their abdomen. They can nibble at their blunt stinger like this, and clutch at it with their bound claspers, but no more. Every joint of their arms is pressed to the swell of their rippling silk sacs.

Their spinneret is engorged and pulsing.

Zakri can see it so clearly—so close to all of their eyes, just beneath their short, blunt stinger, throbbing and on display…all for Jianlei. Their valve is twitching, tense and tight from being held closed so long; the filaments within it are dancing and wriggly in their eagerness, longing to be freed.

But Zakri doesn't want to reveal their filaments yet. They want to be bloomed by the touch of Jianlei's fingers and lips.

"Look at you," Jianlei says, quietly tender. He flips himself upside down, his special boots clinging to the gallery's vaulted ceiling like the feet of the little geckos Zakri learned about on *Planet Earth*, and presses a kiss to the quivering glands closest to the edge of the clenching rim of Zakri's valve.

Zakri squeaks. Jianlei's face is half hidden by the curve of their abdomen, but Zakri feels the shape of his smile against their swollen body.

Zakri wants more: Jianlei's smile, his kisses, his touch.

They want to let their filaments loose, but they also want to wait.

Jianlei kisses them and kisses them. His lips and tongue roam in a deliciously torturous ring around Zakri's quivering valve; his hands find and massage the most swollen of Zakri's silk sacs and tweak at the desperate throbbing of the glands awoken by his kisses.

Every touch makes Zakri warble as though they were being harvested. It takes all of their strength to hold their valve closed.

How much longer can their valve stay closed?

It is almost like a challenge. Spinners are not allowed to offer challenges; spinners only give themselves up as they are told. But this is not the hive. This is the Redline, and Zakri is Jianlei's. They can keep their valve squeezed tightly closed if they wish, and they do. They want to shake and shudder and feel all the segments of their chitin flex from the effort of holding themself closed; they want to be kissed and caressed until their helpless body blooms and opens—for Jianlei. All for Jianlei.

Jianlei's hands are running over the edges of Zakri's chitin, teasing at the gaps. Zakri had never been touched in those places before they became Jianlei's. It is only chitin. How can such a simple touch feel so wonderful? How can they be driven almost to opening just from being petted over their disgracefully soft chitin? Jianlei only has two hands, yet it feels as though he touches Zakri everywhere.

Zakri's overwrought valve is throbbing in time with their gasping breaths. They can see each twitch with every one of their sixteen eyes—and Jianlei is watching too. Jianlei is watching them watch themself.

It is being watched, at last, that overwhelms them.

Zakri tries, they try so hard—they keen and wail and scrabble at their blunt stinger with all of their claspers. It feels so wonderful to struggle like this, to clench in futility and feel their body ripple and spasm out of their control. It feels like falling.

They'd hated that falling-feeling once, but that was before Jianlei. Jianlei is here now, and Jianlei will always catch them.

Their valve twitches. The longest of their filaments escapes; the tip of it peeks out of the pulsating squeeze of Zakri's disobedient valve, already thick with eagerness and shiny-slick with pre-silk fluids. Zakri squeaks at the sight and clenches harder yet; the little protruding tip of their errant filament is swollen by the grip of Zakri's own valve.

Jianlei is watching.

Jianlei is smiling, all his many mandible-teeth flashing pearly and sharp in his predator-red mouth.

Jianlei leans down and kisses the swollen filament-tip, and Zakri screams and *screams* and opens.

Their filaments are waving, dancing, dribbling and trying to weave—their silk-sacs wants so badly to produce for Jianlei. Zakri is much too empty. What little silk lingers in their deflated sacs will not weave cleanly into strong and even strands; their silk will be wasted, and that is a sin.

But what does sin matter here?

Here, they are more than just a spinner. Here, they are Zakri, and they are being courted.

Here, Zakri can be brave like Jedou, who has found for themself a life beyond the death of their drone-purpose. Jedou is a drone who lets themself be bound and spread and fondled, even by a lowly spinner like Zakri. Jedou is not afraid to shriek and shake and surrender to the basest wants of their tight and eager hole.

Zakri can be a spinner who lets themself waste their silk.

Jianlei has not touched their released filaments yet. Jianlei is always so careful with their silk, because Zakri has always been so fretful about waste.

Not today. Today they are being courted.

Today they will be careless.

"Jianlei," Zakri says. They try to focus every one of their eyes on Jianlei's pair. "My love. Don't harvest me today, please. Use me like you taught me to use Jedou."

Both of Jianlei's eyes go wide. "Zakri," he says. His voice is so very soft, but his eyes are glinting bright. "My heart. I am yours to command," and he presses his fingers into Zakri's valve.

Zakri thinks that they shriek. All of their body spasms; their arms strain against the silk rope and their unbound legs kick; their silk sacs ripple. Jianlei's fingers cannot go far—his hand will not fit in Zakri's body in the way Zakri's clasper filled Jedou's, because Zakri's valve is stuffed too full with their own thickly squirming filaments. Jianlei's cleverly nimble fingers instead push amidst the dancing filaments, stroking and caressing and kneading at each swollen strand, stuffing Zakri's valve twice as full. His hand is already coated to the knuckles with shiny fluids and the first glinting threads of tangled silk. The first threads of waste.

The waste looks so beautiful on Jianlei's hand.

Spinners are claimed. Spinners are not allowed to claim. The threads of unwoven silk glimmer on Jianlei's skin. *You are mine*, the threads say, *just as I am yours*, and Zakri wants.

"More," they gasp. "Jianlei, please, more," and of course Jianlei gives them more. Zakri squeals and kicks, helpless and braver than they've been in all their life. Clumps of wonderfully wasted silk burst from their overwrought, overused spinnerets, drifting like dancing dust-motes around their intertwined bodies and catching in Jianlei's hair; the wetness of Zakri's fluids catches all the colors of the Cat's Eye Nebula that lights up the viewport behind them.

Zakri's body is swathed in bowerbird-blue, because they are Jianlei's.

Jianlei strokes them, fondles them, and every touch feels like an offering and a claim. Jianlei nips gently at the engorged glands of Zakri's spinnerets with teeth that are so much smaller and sharper than Zakri's mandibles, sending bright sparks of delicious pleasure pulsing through Zakri's abdomen; his clever fingers are nestled deep in the writhing bundle of Zakri's filaments, and Zakri never wants to be parted from him.

But there is one last thing that Zakri wants to be brave enough for.

Jedou would squeal and wriggle and shake and sob, and give and give and give…and finally they would say *stop*. Then the touching would cease, and the bindings would come off, and the kissing would begin.

Spinners are not supposed to say *stop*.

Zakri is more than just a spinner. They are Zakri, Zakri of the ISS Redline, and they can be brave.

"Jianlei," they say, when the tingling pleasure in their abdomen has risen up like a flood through their thorax to spark behind their eyes. "I'd like to stop now, please," and of course Jianlei stops.

Of course Jianlei kisses them.

He eases his dripping, silk-coated hand from the wriggling grasp of

Zakri's filaments as he kisses them, and Zakri almost wants to beg for its return. Their valve feels so open, their filaments so bereft of the touch of Jianlei's fingers; their silk-sacs are wrung dry, emptier than empty, yet all of their abdomen is pulsing and eager to give. They want more so badly, but there will be more. Zakri is Jianlei's. They have the rest of their lives together to touch and be touched.

Zakri has been courted. It is time for them to court.

All of their limbs tremble as Jianlei unbinds them. Their claspers shiver over the bowerbird-blue silk, but they do not stop clinging to it—Jianlei made and dyed this rope just for them. Just for their pleasure.

They have made something for Jianlei, too.

The surprise for Jianlei waits, carefully bagged, in the locker at the side of the gallery. Jianlei has to help Zakri glide over. They are so glad for the lack of gravity; they could not possibly hold their body up otherwise, not after so much pleasure.

Jianlei kicks himself a little distance away when Zakri has a firm grip on the locker door, and waits patiently as Zakri fumbles with key and door and bag. They are shaking more from nerves than exhausted pleasure as they work their surprise from the bag.

It is almost more frightening than being tied up and fondled, but all Zakri has to do is be brave.

Bravery gets easier every time they try.

Zakri turns and places the crocheted silk blanket into Jianlei's hands.

"Do you like it?" they ask, and they cannot keep the hope out of their voice. This blanket is made of silk from Zakri's own body, crocheted by the labor of their own claspers; it is them, and it is their heart.

Jianlei swings the blanket over his shoulders like a cape. He gathers the drafting, trailing ends to his chest and caresses it just as tenderly as he always touches Zakri.

"I love it, Zakri," he says, and his smile is brighter and more beautiful than the Cat's Eye Nebula. "I love it as much as I love you."

Hands-On Learning

Annika Sage Ellis

blow job, bondage, clitoral fingering, cunnilingus, double penetration in one hole (vaginal), exhibitionism, f/m, fantasy, forced orgasm, free use, hand job, m/nb/nb, m/nb/nb/nb, multiple orgasms, nb/nb, nipple play, non-binary, orgy, overstimulation, past tense, penis in vagina sex, piercings, possessive behavior, snake person, spit roasting, third person limited point of view, trans man, trans woman, vaginal fingering, voyeurism, xenophilia

The sun shone in spectacular rays over the city, a sure sign that spring was here to stay. With the trees and flowers coming back to life, it was no surprise that the citizens were up and about too. Creatures big and small took advantage of the perfect day, and Kieran was about to celebrate the change in the season with an opportunity he'd been waiting years for.

"Are you *positive* I look okay?" Utethi asked for the dozenth time as she slithered up the porch to their destination. Her black and red scales glittered, accented by creamy-white stripes running from the end of her snout to the tip of her tail.

"Yes, I'm *still* sure," Kieran replied. "You just shed last week. You're practically glowing."

"Of course *you'd* say that."

"That's what I'm here for, right? I'm your emotional-support mammal."

She laughed, a jumping hiss. "Don't say it like *that*."

"It's a little true."

"Not if anybody asks."

"Deal."

Utethi coiled up on the front step and knocked on the door of their host's den, tongue flicking at an anxious pace. Kieran stood next to her, folding his hands behind his back to keep from fidgeting. When she'd asked, he'd been happy to attend as a plus-one to her very first mating ball, but he couldn't deny he had his own selfish reasons.

The door flung, Mara springing out of the foyer and onto the front step. It was like seeing double, both nagas displaying the same pattern, but Mara sported a hood of black scales over her head and darker, mature reds dappled her long body.

"Utethi, happy spring!" she cheered, pulling Utethi into a hug. "I hope you had a lovely sleep this winter, and I'm *so* happy you decided to attend this year!"

"Thanks. Happy spring," Utethi said, returning her embrace stiffly. "Did we...miss anything?"

"You're right on time. The party's barely started." She flicked her tongue, the dark appendage curving toward Kieran. "And this must be our special guest?"

"Uh, yes!" Utethi presented him with an awkward gesture. "Here he is!"

"Hi, it's nice to meet you," Kieran said. "And thank you again for letting me tag along, I know I'm not really supposed to be here."

"It's unconventional," Mara said, "but I'm happy to break tradition for the sake of a friend. I let everyone attending know a human would be joining us, so there shouldn't be any problems." She slithered to the side. "Come in, please!"

With her back rigid and hands curled into fists, Utethi slithered into the den and Kieran followed. The first thing he noticed was how warm it was in Mara's den—*balmy* compared to outside. Kieran was glad he'd skipped on a binder and hoped he wouldn't regret wearing jeans.

It was hard to dress for a "casual event" when none of the usual attendees wore clothes. The way Utethi explained it, a mating ball was a once-a-year celebration of the end of brumation and the beginning of their breeding season, but it was a low-key kind of party. It was rare for nagas who paired off at a mating ball to see each other a second time, much less mate for life, so the only real dress-code—if it could even be called that—was to meet your own standard for attractiveness and hope someone else agreed.

Still, Kieran played it safe. Paired with his jeans, he wore a simple star-patterned button-up. He might not have been able to flaunt a perfect shed of his sandy beige skin or tone down his violet shag cut, but he combed it out of his face, made sure his earrings and nostril piercings were matching silver hoops. He almost shaved the whisper of a mustache on his lip, but after two years on testosterone, those faint hairs were the longest he'd *ever* grown. No way was he was giving *that* up.

Not that he was *planning* on hooking up with someone while he was here for moral support, but he couldn't deny that he accepted Utethi's invitation out of more than the kindness of his own heart. Mating balls weren't public, but every spring, they popped up around the city, and every spring, Kieran hoped at least *one* would have more lax invitation restrictions. Every year had disappointed him, until now—and he wasn't going to waste the opportunity.

Mara's den was crowded with guests. Tails and scales draped over every surface in reds, blacks, blues, yellows, and whites. Scaly faces turned as they entered, conversations paused, tongues flicked in their direction. Some of the distracted stares were *specifically* at Kirean. Excitement bubbled up in his chest.

As any good host would, Mara showed the two of them around. The upper den was for socializing: food, drinks, meeting people, and relaxing. There was a long table on the end of the wall, laden with naga-appropriate snacks—Kieran politely declined her offer of a chilled rat. On the other end of the room was a wide set of double doors with a friendly paper sign pasted across one. Doodled with hearts and flowers, it read *MATING BALL IN PROGRESS*!

"The lower den is where the actual *mating* part of the mating ball takes place," Mara explained. "If you meet someone you like up here, you can head down there to make it official." She looked at Utethi pointedly. "Or

more than one."

"Th-that's okay!" Utethi hissed. She scooted back so far that her tail bunched up against the wall. "I'll hang out up here for, um, a while. I think."

Mara laughed, waving a hand. "I'm teasing! You can stay in the upper den the whole time if you want. Not everyone's pheromones match up, after all."

Kieran had no idea what that meant, but nudged Utethi with an elbow. "See? No pressure."

She nodded stiffly. "Totally."

Mara folded her hands on her smooth chest. "Any questions?"

He raised his hand a little. "Can we head down *without* meeting someone first?"

Her cheerful demeanor flipped. She glanced at the doors, tongue flicking inscrutably. He worried he had somehow offended her until she spoke again.

"Utethi can, but I wouldn't recommend *you* going down by yourself. Mating balls can get…*ambitious*. It's part of the celebration."

"That's okay. I've been to more than a couple parties like this."

Utethi nodded. "He's got more experience than me."

Mara hissed a little. "It's—*different* at a mating ball. I don't want anyone getting hurt, so please don't go down to the lower den unless you have someone who can keep an eye on you."

He put on a smile, but deflated inside. "Gotcha. No problem."

Their tour ended when the doorbell rang, and Mara excused herself to welcome her new guests. Utethi and Kieran were abandoned in the middle of the upper den's crowd.

"Can we go this way?" Utethi asked, nearly a whisper.

"Of course," he replied, following behind as she slipped away.

She led him to the corner by the snack table, coiled tight around herself, and hissed in distress. "What should I *do*?"

"What do you mean?" Kieran gestured at the party. "Talk to someone. I don't really get what Mara was saying about pheromones, but there has to be someone here that's your type."

She glanced around, as if someone would overhear. "Some people pick partners based on how their pheromones smell." Her tongue flicks curved dramatically toward the crowd. Kieran would have assumed it was nerves, but after *that* explanation…

"What about *you*?"

"Wh-what?"

He waggled his eyebrows. "*Who* are you smelling so intently right now?"

"I'm not!" Utethi insisted, even as her tongue snuck out in faster and faster intervals. "It's— *Everyone's* pheromones are going nuts right now."

"*And…*?"

Her upper body scrunched into an accordion. "Kieran, *come on*!"

"I'll back you up! Who is it?" He craned his neck, trying to guess which of the nagas in the room would have the best-smelling pheromones.

Utethi yanked his arm desperately. "Don't make it obvious, please!"

"Okay, okay." He cupped his palm around his ear and tilted his head. "Just whisper it to me."

She squirmed, long body rippling all the way to the twitchy end of her tail. Her eyes pointed in a single direction as she hissed quietly into his ear, "The dark-red one, kind of left of center."

Kieran followed her gaze and picked out a naga from the crowd, engaged in conversation with another guest. They were almost maroon, rich red scales forming the base for their pattern instead of the accent. A pale-orange stripe ran down their back and two more ran on either side. The color matched their eyes perfectly.

"Nice pick," he praised.

"What should I do?" Utethi pleaded.

"Go talk to them."

"But what do I *say*?"

"I don't know—tell them they smell nice?"

She hissed sharply. "No way!"

The other naga flicked their tongue. Kieran *swore* it curved in their direction. "Hey—hey, look!"

"What?" Utethi shot up, apparently not worried about making a scene anymore.

"Check out the flicks. I think they're into you."

"Really?"

After a few seconds of intense staring, the other naga noticed. They turned their head and looked right at Utethi. Then they started to move, politely ending their conversation and weaving through the crowd.

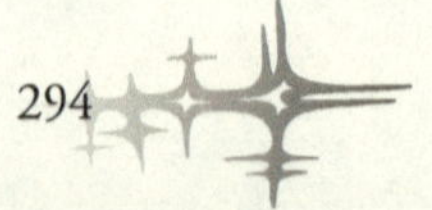

Kieran turned to Utethi to hype her up, but it turned out he didn't need to.

Like magnets, her eyes locked onto the dark-red naga. She flicked her tongue slowly, the appendage staying out of her mouth for full seconds at a time. The closer they got, the better Kieran could see the other naga's tongue flicking too—lethargic, almost sensual. Utethi sat up in her coil as the dark-red naga approached, leaning forward out of the pile of her tail. For a moment, they flicked at each other in total silence. Kieran felt like he was interrupting before they said a single word.

"Hi," Utethi finally spoke, and her whole upper body twitched. "I'm Utethi."

"Raxhis," said the other naga, twitching the same way. "Is this your first time?"

"Yeah, actually. But I'm friends with Mara."

Kieran let them talk, in the process of trying to keep his face neutral. He'd *never* seen Utethi start a conversation so smoothly. He'd never seen her this *fidgety* before, either. She flicked her tail or tongue when she was nervous, but not her *whole head*. Her arms, too. From her waist to her snout, she flinched every few seconds, and Raxhis did the same. Kieran stayed quiet, confused but fascinated. The longer he watched, the more convinced he was they were twitching *toward* each other.

"Have you been to the lower den yet?" Raxhis asked, a very obvious opening.

"Not yet," she answered. "My friend and I just got here about— Oh!" Suddenly back to her old self, Utethi swerved around to take Kieran by the shoulders. "I'm so sorry, this is my friend, Kieran. He's here with me. Since it's my first time and all."

Raxhis flicked their tongue, this time disappointed. "Right, the human."

"Yep, I sure am," Kieran said, and plucked Utethi off him. "Don't mind me. I'm probably not heading down today."

"Oh, really?" All their attention was back on Utethi.

She shrugged, a little flinch in her arms. "Well, yeah. Mara said he shouldn't go to the lower den unless someone invited him."

"Has anyone invited *you*?"

Kieran bit the inside of his cheek to keep from ruining the moment. He eyed Utethi, willing her to take the bait.

"No," she said, tongue sneaking out. "Unless *you* are?"

"I can be."

Raxhis held out one of their scaled hands, long fingers and a creamy-white palm. Utethi raised her own, hesitating just long enough to give Kieran a worried look.

"Go, go!" he insisted, shooing her away.

"Okay!" she hissed happily, and nearly sprung on Raxhis in her excitement. The two of them slithered off together, tails curling snugly around each other as they went, all the way down to the twitchy ends. Kieran watched them go, thrilled for Utethi and more than a little shocked. So much for being the emotional-support mammal! Was this what Mara meant by "ambitious"? He definitely needed to grill Utethi about that later.

Until then, though? Kieran leaned against the wall and took a casual glance around the writhing throng of nagas. Stripes and spots and tails and scales as far as the eye could see. Guests slithered, twisted, and stretched around and over each other. He chewed on his lip, wondering if he could go over and talk to someone. It would be nice to kill time in a *fun* way, if anyone here happened to have a thing for humans.

Mara had explained the basics of a mating ball to them as first-timers, but Kieran got the gist of it before she even opened her mouth. It was a sex party. Even if it was primarily to shake the breeding season urges loose, it ended up the same. He'd been to plenty before, and he wasn't a stranger to being one of the only humans present. It was his favorite kind of party to attend—maybe it was vain, but he liked being a novelty. The bullseye of not only being the only human, but the only *mammal* in attendance was like a dream come true. But his ability to participate relied on a chaperone.

He had to wonder what Mara's warning could have possibly been for. The same full-body twitches that Utethi and Raxhis had shared sprung up all over the room, paired with long, slow tongue flicks. Some nagas rested their chins on others shoulders and backs, which only intensified the twitching response. From there, it was an immediate move to the lower den, tails intertwining the whole way. It was interesting, seeing how flirting was done in a wholly naga space, but Kieran hardly felt out of his depth.

A bright-colored pair of nagas caught his eye, slithering from the

other side of the den with tails wrapped. One was short and slender, jet black with thin, sky-blue stripes running down its back and sides, and as a solid color on its belly. The other was larger in every way, including in their presentation. Their scales were electric blue and fiery red, with a bit of black peeking out between the thick stripes of color. They were a stunning couple, even from a human perspective…and getting closer?

Those nagas were coming right for him, eyes and tongue-flicks locked, moving in unison with their tangled tails.

He waited until they were in earshot to greet them. "Hi."

"Hello there," said the tall one. They slipped their tail away from their partner and coiled up. "You're the human that got invited, right?"

"Yeah, I'm Kieran."

"Ishtha." They nudged the short naga at their side. "This is Khali."

"Hey," it said. It flicked its tongue.

"Cool. Nice to meet you." Kieran glanced between them. "How can I help you?"

"That depends," Khali replied, trading a look with Ishtha. "We weren't sure *exactly* how to go about this, but you're…a mammal."

Ishtha hissed out a sigh. "We're both *really* curious about what warm-blooded creatures are like, and wanted to ask you about…*you*."

"About your body. Specifically that."

Kieran raised his brows. Khali wasn't as subtle as Ishtha, but both of their heads flinched. Their tongues flicked at a pace that he might have mistook for curiosity if he hadn't seen Utethi do it. Nagas wanted to ask him about his *body* at a *mating ball.* His stomach flipped over.

"Sure," Kieran answered. "Would you mind if I asked you a few things too?"

They glanced at each other and shrugged. "I don't mind," Ishtha said.

"Me neither," Khali agreed.

It was almost too good to be true. "Okay, sweet. You two first, ask away."

Ishtha jumped at the opportunity. "What does it *feel like* to have hair?"

"It doesn't really *feel* like anything." Kieran combed his hair with his fingers, more aware of it than he'd been in hours. "It's lightweight unless you grow a lot of it. Most of the time, it's just there to look pretty."

"Is it that color naturally?" Khali asked.

He laughed, shaking his head to make his waves bounce. "No, but I wish! I have to dye it every so often. It's kind of a hassle." He held out his arm, pointing out the dark-brown fuzz there. "My *actual* hair color is more like this."

"Told you," Ishtha muttered.

Khali hissed at them.

They'd been talking about him? Kieran hoped he didn't look too giddy. "My turn." He ran through a dozen questions before forcing himself to pick one. "What do pheromones smell like?"

Both nagas stared with their pupils widened to discs.

"You can't smell them?" Ishtha asked.

"No, not at all."

"Oh." They glanced at Khali baffled. "That explains a lot."

"Why? What does it smell like for you two?"

"It reeks like sex," Khali answered flatly. Ishtha nudged it. "What? It does!"

"It smells *musky*," they corrected.

"Which is what sex smells like."

"What does that explain about me?" Kieran interrupted. "Isn't it supposed to smell like that?"

"It is," Ishtha said, "but it's not all the *same smell*, it's..." They drew a long, slow tongue flick. "It's like you can smell everyone's *personal* desire. Each is a little different."

"And you smell nice," Khali finished.

They full-on shoved it that time.

Kieran barely noticed over his rapid heartbeat. "I do?"

It shrugged a little. "Nice enough both of us wanted to get over here before someone else snapped you up."

Kieran flushed thinking of all the heads he'd turned walking into the room. The glances he'd been getting since he showed up. How many of those stares meant more than they let on? How many of the nagas in here had "opinions" about him?

"Your turn," he said.

"Aren't you warm," Khali asked, "wearing clothes in here?"

"I am, yeah." Kieran shrugged nonchalantly, even as his face went hot. "I almost feel like taking them off."

Ishtha rippled, a stationary slither chasing their long body all the way

down their thick coils. Khali darted closer, and Kieran put his hand out instinctively, flat to the blue scales of its chest. Its forked tongue hung out of its half-open mouth, black at the very ends, and a bright candy red down the rest of its length. Cool, smooth muscles shifted under his palm. He released a shaky breath, trailing his fingers across the open expanse of its chest.

"My turn?" he asked.

Neither naga replied, but both flinched. He shuddered from the thrill of being pursed so intently.

"What is all the twitching for?" he asked, glancing between them both. He wanted to hear it from someone who knew *exactly* what it meant. And who it was for.

Khali laughed, chest jumping against his hand. "That's easy."

It swerved around him lighting fast. Scaly fingers took his shoulders. Ishtha took its place in front of him, slithering out of their coil to tower above them both.

"It means," they said, a low hiss, "that we want you."

"Oh, good," Kieran breathed, heart fluttering. "I was hoping that's what it meant."

"Then why don't we all head to the lower den?"

He looked over his shoulder at Khali and got a friendly tongue flick. Ishtha held their hand out, fingers twitching at the end. Kieran had *two* people willing to "keep an eye" on him—which meant the fun could begin.

He put his hand in theirs, excitement spilling over into a wide smile. "Lead the way."

Khali shoved him forward, Ishtha caught him on their back when he stumbled, and the two of them had wrapped tails before he figured out what he was sitting on. Riding on Ishtha and with fingers laced with Khali's, they made a beeline for the lower den's doors.

"One more question for our game," Ishtha said, pushing the double doors open. Beyond the threshold was a long hallway, lined with warm colored lamps on the walls.

"Ask away," he said.

"Do you know *why* it's called a mating ball?"

That one threw him. He wracked his brain trying to remember if Utethi or Mara had mentioned it. The floor sloped as they descended, giving way to a muffled crowd in the distance. Gradually, the soft noise became a dull roar of voices.

"I *don't* know," he admitted, "but if I had to guess, I'd say it's because it's…a big social event for mating? Like a 'ball' for 'mating'?"

They both laughed, jumping hisses filling his ears almost as loudly as the cacophony ahead. It was too much to pick out a single sound, but it was clear *what* they were. Moans, groans, and cries of ecstasy, with an undercurrent of excited hissing. Kieran nearly choked on the scent—a powerful, bitter musk filled his nose and mouth.

"That's not quite it," Ishtha said.

"Not even close," Khali added.

"Then why…?" he asked, but trailed off.

The answer spoke for itself.

At the bottom of the sloping hallway, the lower den opened into a large room, twice as large as the upper den. Several dome-shaped hides were lined up against the walls, but that was all that was visible of the room itself. The rest of it was overrun by a pile of writhing, squirming, *fucking* nagas. Limbs and bodies tangled into an unpickable knot, tails locked together at the ends where it was clear the real action was happening. It wasn't clear where one body ended and another began—the only constant was flurries of scales and slithering bodies.

It was one big *mating ball.*

A single corner of space had room enough for three. Khali shoved a path through the crowd, and Ishtha slithered over it to claim a spot. Kieran flipped over to sit with his back to their chest, and his stomach jumped again. Both nagas watched him with eager eyes and open mouths.

"How should we start?" Ishtha asked, fingers curling around his waist.

"This is my first mating ball," Kieran said, kicking off his shoes. "So—show me how it's done?"

"With *pleasure.*"

Blue-scaled fingers tugged at his clothes, theirs on his shirt and Khali's on the waistband of his pants. Ishtha flung open his button-up, letting it slip off his arms to the floor. Kieran gasped as their cool hands wandered over his chest.

"What are these?" they asked, seizing one of his tits. The soft fat squished between their fingers, more than filling their palm.

"Boobs?" he offered breathily. "They're, uh, for human babies most of the time, but—" Their other hand pinched his nipple curiously, and he whimpered, the small bud hard and sensitive already.

"But I can play with them?"

Kieran nodded and arched. "Please."

While they made him squirm, Khali triumphantly ripped off his pants. It tossed them aside and rushed in, taking him under the knees and spreading his legs wide apart. Kieran shuddered, wiggling his hips as it eyed the thick bush between his legs.

It hissed lowly, sliding closer. "You smell even better up close."

Kieran tried to thank it, but its tongue flicked against the swollen end of his t-dick. That light brush drew a soft moan from his lips, hips twitching toward its mouth.

Ishtha hissed in his ear. "That was *lovely*."

"How did I do that?" Khali asked.

Kieran fumbled a hand down and pulled back his folds. His t-dick ached for attention, thumb-sized erection throbbing. Khali flicked its tongue again with purpose, brushing more of its length over him. He moaned and watched it twitch—his t-dick and Khali's entire body, both jolting with need. It licked him again, and again, and it didn't stop, forks dancing over the sensitive head. Kieran arched his back as it teased him, moans turning to gasps, hips bucking fruitlessly in its hold.

Ishtha leaned over his shoulder, pinching his nipples hard. Their tongue wasn't long enough to reach his t-dick when they flicked it, but he whimpered anyway. His cunt dripped at the thought of both of them licking him at once.

"I want a turn," they demanded.

"I'm not done yet," Khali shot back.

"Can you hurry up, then?"

"*Fine*."

Khali rose and wrapped itself around Ishtha. It twisted its body from the waist down, around and around, entangling their long torsos in a spiral embrace. When it only had a few feet left, Khali swept its tail forward and let Kieran see what was underneath.

At the end of its body was a long vent, a slit in its bright-blue scales that separated the end of its body from its short tail. It leaked droplets of something clear and viscous, almost like pre-cum, with a prominent bulge pushing against the slit. Two short, thick, pinkish cylinders of flesh popped free, pointing outward into the air. Small bumps dotted the sides from top to bottom, slick and dribbling the same clear fluid.

Naga cocks.

"Two," Kieran observed, dizzy from the implication alone.

Khali laughed. "Let's start with one."

It maneuvered its tail until the base of the vent pressed against his crotch, both cocks resting against his inner thighs. Khali hissed and angled its tail until the slick tip of one cool cock pressed against his cunt, the other resting against his leg. He shivered as both cocks slowly warmed against his body, feverish with lust.

Ishtha massaged his tits and hissed in delight as Khali pushed inside.

Kieran choked. The cock wasn't long enough to fill him completely, but its girth stretched his cunt *more* than enough to make up for it. The very end of Khali's tail curled around his upper thigh, gripping with as much strength as its hands.

"*Wow*, fuck," it moaned.

He nodded, struggling to find language. "*Move, please*."

Ishtha pinched and rolled his nipples. "You heard him."

It didn't need to be told twice. Using the grip of its tail as leverage, Khali pulled out of his cunt and yanked itself back in. Kieran threw his head back and moaned into Ishtha's arm. They teased his chest as he got fucked, two tiny peaks of pleasure that jolted down his spine, but their eyes were trained on watching Khali's cock slide in and out.

Each tiny bump along the shaft rubbed his walls and entrance, a textured thrust that drew countless whimpers out of him. Its second cock bounced against his thigh with heavy, wet slaps. Both of them burned as hot as the rest of him, absorbing his heat and giving back in every hard rut into his cunt. The loose cock squirted that clear, thick wetness over his hip and onto his stomach, and he gasped. Khali let out a long, deep hiss, clenching his legs and slamming in hard. Kieran saw stars, voice breaking around another moan.

"You're making me jealous," Ishtha teased, fingers still working his nipples.

Breathing heavy, Khali hissed, "He's got hands, doesn't he?"

They took the suggestion, sweeping the end of their body around. The very tip of their tail lifted Kieran's hand, sliding him down to the

entrance of their slippery vent.

"Stick your fingers in there, please," Ishtha said, the first time he'd ever heard a snake purr.

Kieran struggled to get his bearings, but pressed his fingers into the slit. "L-like this?"

They writhed underneath him. "Deeper."

Still at Khali's mercy, he pushed his shaky hand farther in. The cool, soft walls warmed at his touch as he pressed against random spots, experimenting. He kept going until their vent swallowed his hand up to the wrist and a small, fleshy nub throbbed against his fingers.

"*There!*" Ishtha cried, tightening around his bicep. "*Right there.*"

Kieran flicked the nub, and they moaned. It felt like a clitoris, so he treated it like one, rubbing and stroking it. When he spread his hand wide inside them, he found a second one on the other wall. They moaned even louder when he played with them both, pinky and thumb stretched as far apart as he could get them.

"Hey!"

A third naga approached, black with thin white stripes. Khali stopped mid-thrust, buried as deep inside Kieran as it could get. He stopped short of begging it to continue when he noticed Ishtha had gone quiet too.

"Is that the human Mara invited?" the third naga asked, flicking hir tongue at him.

"Yeah," Khali answered warily.

"*Awesome!* I didn't know we were mating with him. That's—"

"*We* aren't," Ishtha corrected, a hiss in their tone.

Khali agreed, "Go get your own human."

The third naga folded hir arms. "Does it *look like* I have a ton of humans lying around?"

"That sounds like a you problem."

Kieran raised a weak hand. "Hey, guys?"

All three nagas looked at him, expressions surprisingly heated. Mara's warning crept back into his lust-addled brain, but his body cried for attention *much* louder.

"If you're going to argue," he suggested, "can it be a little more…*fun*?"

Khali and Ishtha glanced at each other for a second. It was one second too long.

The new addition struck forward in a blur. Khali hissed in surprise, knocked aside and cock popping free. Kieran kicked out from the shock, then yelped as he was rudely grabbed out of position. Ishtha made a spitting noise when his hand slipped out.

"Thanks for that," said the third naga, ignoring how furious the other two were. "I'm Eya."

"K-Kieran," he stuttered, struggling to get his bearings.

"What's your *problem*?" Khali demanded.

"That I'm an opportunist, and *you're* too slow."

Kieran scrabbled to hang on as Eya shifted. He threw his arms around hir chest as the wave of scales between his legs shifted, dangling freely on either side. Ze looped the rest of hirself behind him, so hir vent pressed against his ass, leaving the very end of hir tail to circle his waist. Hir arms crept over his shoulders, and ze bent down to hiss in his ear.

"We can make this quick," ze whispered. Two wet, soft cocks popped out of hir vent, splatting on his hot skin. Kieran shivered head to toe.

"*Excuse* me," Ishtha demanded. Their tail thrashed, and Khali didn't look happier. "What makes you think you're sticking around *at all*?"

"Because I have the nerve to take what I want."

Khali hissed. "You've got *some nerve* all right. You can't just—"

Kieran interrupted the argument with a soft moan as Eya pushed inside him. All three of them stopped to watch. Khali and Ishtha flicked their tongues as he crumbled in pleasure again; Eya smoothed hir hands down his back. Ze squeezed his waist tight to hold him in a perfect, fuckable position, and used hir tail for leverage to thrust. While one cock slid smoothly in and out of his pre-fucked hole—Eya hissed loudly with every easy, wet thrust—hir second one rubbed between his ass cheeks. The bumps felt just as good on the outside as they did on the inside, rubbing against his hole in a delicious tease. Ze dripped down his ass and thighs, joining the mess that he and Khali made.

And speaking of, it didn't take long for the bickering to restart.

"You really think we're going to sit here and *watch*?" Khali asked, darting forward to get in Eya's face. Ze didn't even slow down.

"I don't care what you do, just leave *us* alone."

Ishtha hissed, tongue curling out of their open mouth in a threatening display. "*Absolutely* not."

They grabbed one of Kieran's arms and yanked. He gasped, Eya

interrupted mid-thrust, but thanks to hir hold on his waist, he didn't go very far. Undeterred, Khali grabbed his *other* arm. Eya spat an equally furious hiss at the both of them, burying hir cock hard as ze tried to pull him away. Kieran tensed everything as they tugged him from both sides, a prick of worry worming into his hazy mind. He'd rather *not* be split in half by horny nagas tonight—not like *this*, at least.

"Guys," he breathed, opening and closing his hands in Khali and Ishtha's faces. "Give me—"

Eya didn't let him finish—on purpose, if he had to guess—thrusting hard enough to break his voice. By some miracle, they understood what he meant and let go, twisting and coiling to lift their tails into his hands. Khali's throbbing cocks were still out, and Ishtha dripped from their vent as much as he leaked from his cunt. Kieran stuck his wet hand back inside them and guided one of Khali's cocks into his mouth with the other. Both of them hissed long, satisfied sighs, argument forgotten.

He ran his tongue along the thick shaft, the strong, bitter musk flooding his mouth. It was an odd taste, but he was already enjoying it. He circled the bumpy ridges with his tongue and rubbed another with his thumb. Khali moaned as he traced them, and Kieran answered in kind, pressing whimper after whimper into its cock. Stretching his jaw wide, he took the very end of it into his mouth and sucked, drawing a deep, rattling hiss out of its mouth.

Inside Ishtha, he found their clits and went back to finger-fucking them. He massaged circles into one, pressed his fingers against it hard, pinched it, flicked it, then switched sides to fuck the other. They gasped and writhed, ripples cascading down their long body.

"None of this means we're *done* here," Ishtha warned though their pleasure.

"I'm deciding when *I'm* done," Eya shot back.

Kieran could have rolled his eyes. So much for that.

The three of them bickered over his head while they fucked him, so he tuned them out. The argument faded into the background of countless voices in the lower den, the thumps of other nagas writhing on the floor and against each other. Kieran let himself get carried away. Every thrust, every lick, every rub he gave to the soft, wet clits against his fingers—all of it tangled together, overwhelming in the best way.

Climax rushed to meet him faster than expected, egged on by so much stimulation. Kieran moaned urgently, whole body tight with the promise of release. He squirmed desperately, cries climbing higher and higher in his throat. All three nagas paused their fight to watch him intently. Eya's tongue flicked his cheek, and ze hissed.

He clenched every muscle and came *hard*, a broken moan crushed from his mouth by the sheer strength of his orgasm. The room went blurry as wave after wave of ecstasy washed over him.

"Fucking *wow*," Eya said, hir voice sounding a million miles away. "Is that—?"

"Is that a *human*?"

All three nagas snapped around to face the owner of the unfamiliar voice. Kieran's hand popped out of Ishtha's vent, Khali's cock left his face, and he slid down Eya's body when ze twisted around. He used the opportunity to rest, still stuffed full and legs trembling from aftershocks. The pads of his fingers were wrinkled and sticky.

"—got here first, so get in line," Eya's voice floated in.

"That's so dumb," the newcomer complained, "you might land the mating plug *right now*!"

"For your information, I *was* about to, so—"

"Since when was *that* decided?" Khali interrupted.

"You already had your turn!"

Kieran shut his eyes to ignore them—*again*. It was enticing to be fought over, but this was getting ridiculous. It seemed like every naga in the room wanted him all to themselves. His spent body shivered.

Eya's cock slowly slid out, leaving with a *pop*! He flinched and whimpered at the loss, but sighed when cool fingers caressed his back. For a moment, he enjoyed the mystery hands, until they slid him off Eya's body. Kieran jolted up, but he was already on a collision course with the floor.

A long body of black and olive-green scales snapped him out of the air. Before he could *try* to struggle, the naga trapped him in a coil, lifting him so high his feet dangled. Ring after ring of powerful muscle bound his arms to his sides, a snug embrace to hold him still.

"Hi there," said a soft voice in his ear.

"Hi?" he replied.

The new naga nuzzled his cheek, running a scaly hand through his messy hair. "Sorry for stealing you away, but you smelled so *good*. When

the others started fighting, I couldn't help myself."

Kieran craned his neck and found Khali, Ishtha, Eya, and a *different* stranger staring at them, shocked. His captor was a *fifth* person.

The end of a tail brushed between his legs, tickling his puffy folds. Kieran breathed sharply, looking down as far as he could over the loops of his scaly prison. The constriction stopped at his hips, leaving his legs free, and the rest of her body was dedicated to holding herself upright. More importantly, to be able to press her vent between Kieran's legs.

"I'm Ankhat, by the way," the naga said, vent already damp, the ends of her cocks poking out.

"Kieran," he answered, more of a whimper.

"Can I be inside you?"

"G-go for it."

Ankhat popped her cocks free and sank him down onto her coil. Kieran gasped, and his eyes blew wide when he felt *both* of them fight to fit inside his cunt. They were thinner than Eya's or Khali's, but *fuck* it wasn't easy. Kieran groaned as Ankhat stretched him out, going limp to try and help her fit—

"Hold the *fuck* on!" Eya cried. The other four weren't far behind, all in various stages of upset.

Ankhat shrugged. "He said it was fine."

"*Okay*, but what about *us*?"

After a moment, Ankhat shifted her coils. She left gaps just large enough for Kieran to wiggle his arm free up to the elbows. His tits peeked through a hole in her embrace, squished.

"There," she said. "Shareable."

All five nagas eyed each other suspiciously, then agreed that this was the only way to make everyone happy. Kieran's head rushed. He wasn't going to get another break for a while.

Eya and the newcomer were first to use his hands, taking advantage of one loose fist to slide a cock through and his pliable fingers to stick down a vent. They gave his nipples curious flicks and tugs while they were there, making him wish he could squirm. While they took his hands, Ankhat bounced him up and down on her coils to fuck him on her cocks. He wanted to *scream* at how good it felt to be so used and stuffed and massaged from the inside by those *perfect* little bumps, but he was too exhausted to do more than sob in pleasure.

Ishtha and Khali gave up fighting for a spot and fucked each other, tails entwined and meeting at the vent. Khali pinned Ishtha down and thrusted aggressively, and they slapped their tail against it for an even harder fuck. Kieran drooled watching them thrash in delight.

Eya was the first naga to come, cocks shooting a whiteish-tan fluid over Kieran's hand and onto Ankhat's coils. It didn't even have time to dry before another naga took hir place in his hand.

Word had spread to the rest of the mating ball that the sole human attendee was free to fuck, use, and tease. They swarmed him, coming in his hands, on his tits, and Ankhat even came inside him but didn't stop fucking him. Some nagas stuck their heads underneath him, licking his t-dick and the cum streaming down his thighs.

Kieran came twice while he was trapped there, cunt aching and throbbing and abused. His body trembled, exhausted but given no reprieve. Hot, overwhelmed tears pricked the corners of his eyes. He knew he should stop, but he felt so incredible. He wasn't just a novelty here, he was a prize—and he *never* wanted to stop.

Underneath him, Ishtha and Khali finally got their turns, coiled up and licking his t-dick together. Kieran squirmed and moaned for their delicate tongues while he bounced, inches away from another orgasm. As if they could tell, they both backed off and shifted position. Khali uncoiled and muscled in to sit in front of Kieran, grabbing his thighs. Ishtha ducked below and reached underneath him. Kieran braced himself for more, a helpless noise already crawling up his throat.

Ishtha yanked Ankhat out of his cunt, pulling her tail down and pinning it to the floor. She gasped, indignant, but it was too late. Khali took her place, ramming its cocks inside him and shooting something thick and viscous deep in his cunt. It filled him to the very brim and solidified, keeping his hole stretched wide.

Shocked, Kieran froze in a silent scream of pleasure and agony. He came explosively, kicking and thrashing in Ankhat's hold like an animal fighting for its life. But nothing gushed down his legs, not his wetness nor any of the cum inside him. The viscous stuff clumped up and blocked any escape.

Khali slithered out from under Ankhat and announced, "That's the mating plug, folks. Show's over."

The crowd dispersed with some hissing and mild complaints. Ankhat

gently lowered Kieran to the ground but didn't miss a chance to hiss at Khali as she passed. Ishtha put themself between her and Khali as it gathered Kieran onto its back. It whisked him off, the mating ball passing by in a slow blur.

"Feeling okay?" it asked.

He nodded against its body-warmed scales, but the thing filling his cunt still hadn't gone away. Kieran reached down between his legs and his fingers brushed a ball of hardened gunk. "Wha's a matin' plug?" he slurred.

"If we're putting it in 'breeding season' terms, it blocks anyone else from getting a chance to compete with me. If we're putting it in *sexy* terms?" It looked back over its shoulder, flicking its tongue cheekily. "It means I get the last word about coming inside you."

"Oh." It sounded hot in theory, but it *felt* like having a lumpy ball the size of a fist shoved inside him. "Does it…stay?"

"Nah, it's just mucus. It should go away after a day or so. Hot baths help." It got apologetic, adding, "Hope you don't mind I did it without warning, but you looked like you needed a break. It's basically the *only* way to stop the arguing about who gets who and for how long—blah-blah, you saw it down there."

He sure had. Kieran wasn't coherent enough to feel one way or the other about it, which was definitely a sign Khali was right. "'S okay. Tired."

It laughed. "I'll bet. But the fun kind of tired, right?"

"Mhmm."

"Good. Same here."

It pushed open a door and suddenly it was *very* bright. Kieran squinted around until he could tell they were in the upper den, still crowded with guests. Khali rolled him off its tail and against the wall. He shifted around—sitting on the mating ball felt *very* strange.

"You rest up," Khali told him. "Ishtha's down there looking for your clothes. We'll come back to check on you."

It left him alone there, body sore and fuzzy warm. He smiled to himself, naked and a complete mess. There was no way he wouldn't be sore tomorrow, but today was a success.

"Kieran! Oh Gods, are you okay?"

He knew *that* panicked voice anywhere. Utethi raced up to him,

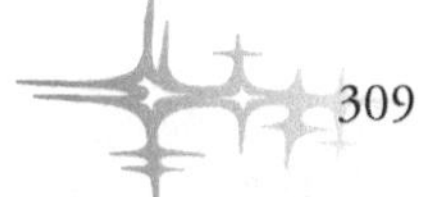

pupils so thin they almost disappeared. She dragged her tail behind her, heavy with a misshapen lump. She had a mating plug too.

"I'm so sorry. I tried to find you down there when I—well, when I smelled the human pheromones, but it was so crowded I couldn't get to—"

Kirean put out his hands weakly. "Slow. Calm."

"What *happened* to you?"

Lacking in energy and brain power, Kieran grinned lazily. "I learned a lot about mating balls."

INDEX

ABOUT THE AUTHORS

Jaye Anderson

Jaye Anderson, fandom name MsWhich, writes original works and fanfiction and has been posting them on the internet since the olden days of mailing lists and Yahoo groups. She supports her writing habit by managing metadata at a day job where, she is fairly sure, her coworkers don't realize she's spending her spare time writing erotic tentacle fiction. She participates in a lot of different fandoms, although she tends to be a late arrival to most of them, as evidenced by the fact that she recently spent a year writing a novel-length story in the *2001: a Space Odyssey* fandom. (She has a HAL 9000 enamel pin on her backpack. When asked about it, she just says that she thinks he's really misunderstood.) She lives in the Midwestern US with her long-term partner, who really gets her and also beta reads most of her work.

Katia Anyway

Hi! I'm Katia_Anyway (they/them). I'm a fanfiction writer who dreams of publishing all the original stories swirling in their brain one day. I love participating in zines and anthologies, they're great occasions to meet new amazing artists and writers! If you check out my AO3,

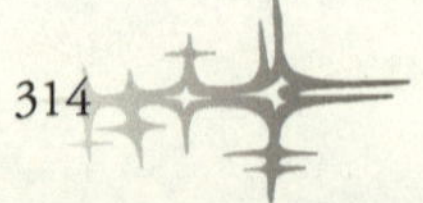

you'll find a lot of *One Piece* fanfics but I'm in many other fandoms, I just haven't had time to write for them all yet.

I. A. Ashcroft

A writer and web developer, I. A. Ashcroft journeys through life alongside their constant feline companion, Potato. Ashcroft has published two original sci-fi/fantasy novels, some short stories, and has been writing for fandoms for over a decade, loving tales that emphasize unlikely bonds, mythology, magic, and hope in the darkness. In between storytelling efforts, he enjoys cooking, fiddling with technology projects, and rolling dice with friends while wearing funny hats.

E. M. Beka

Mx Beka dwells in Australia, in a small pond with an internet connection that does not respond well to rain. Their greatest literary achievements to date involve writing mildly popular fanfiction. They adore their husband, two small children, and semi-feral lucky bamboo. A classic underachiever, they have a yellow belt in karate, a degree in linguistics, and were in a band until they lost their singer to competitive jive dancing.

Nicole Doen

Nicole Doen lives in Western Washington with her family and her mischievous herd of cats (who are also family, but deserve special recognition). She has been a fan writer for over ten years and discovered fandom well before then thanks to watching *Sailor Moon* as a child. She enjoys stories featuring intrigues, complicated romantic entanglements, and unexpected mixes of genres. Though writing is her primary interest, she also likes knitting, zines, solo rpgs, and sitting by the water.

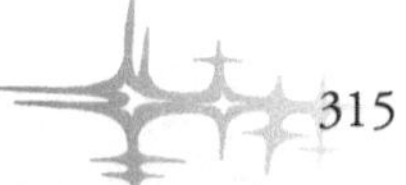

Annika Sage Ellis

Annika Sage Ellis (he/she) is a life-long creative with a passion for telling queer stories. In the scarce moments he didn't have his nose in a book, he could be found immersed in the worlds of his favorite video games or creating his own tales to tell to friends and family alike.

Growing up and discovering the queer community just gave her more to tell—countless stories about people whose narratives are sidelined or silenced. Now, he explores the fantastic in the mundane and the mundane in the fantastic, with a focus on queerness, sexuality, and the radical act of changing ourselves and our world for the better.

Annika has been featured in her self-published collection of flash fiction, *Escapism*. He maintains an online readership for his Magnet Monday poetry series, and for all the various fictional and fandom projects on her roster. When not writing, he can be found dancing, baking, gaming, or reading.

Ivy L. James

Ivy L. James wrote her first story on Post-It notes as a child. Since then, she has graduated to regular paper and enjoys writing inclusive romance, short fiction, and poetry. Her poetry chapbooks include *The Orange and Pink Sunset* and *A Necklace of Teeth* (Dogleech Books). Her work has appeared in *The Stygian Collection* (Stygian Society), *Seers and Sybils* (Brigids Gate Press), *Horns* (Bullshit Lit), HerStry, Snowflake Magazine, and Scavengers Literary Magazine, among others. Ivy lives in Maryland with her pets. You can connect with her at www.authorivyljames.com.

MJ Kiwiana

MJ (he/him) has been kicking around fandom for over two decades—primarily writing fic, though he's also been known to subject people to his accent via podfic from time to time. He's probably best known in the fandom circles he inhabits for writing kink exploration and really fun, sometimes off-the-wall smut, but every once in a while, he'll drop a

surprise angst bomb just to keep people on their toes.

Kitty Lee

Kitty Lee is a quiet woman in her 30s, living happily with her wife and cat. From the reliable stability of her day-to-day life, one would never guess the sumptuous sickness of her inner fantasies. She invites you to be joyfully depraved in your fiction choices, to feast on forbidden flesh so long as the flesh is into that, and to please support your local libraries.

Lyonel Loy

Lifelong maladaptive daydreamer, finally working up the courage to write those daydreams down. Spends time cosplaying as a Responsible Adult With A Job.

Cedar D. McCafferty-Svec

Cedar D. McCafferty-Svec has over two decades of writing experience, a bachelor's degree focusing in English and theater, and a passionate love for telling stories. He is fascinated by fantasy and sci-fi and grew up adamantly wanting to be a dragon. Cedar enjoys experimental writing, attempting shorter works, and has an unfortunate knack for stumbling on stories that could be entire sagas. He lives happily with his life partners and menagerie of animals in the Midwest, and hopes to share his writing far and wide. He has been previously published with Duck Prints Press and is featured in *Many Hands*, along with having published various short stories such as *Glass Slipper* and *sweet static*.

Taliesin Owens

Taliesin is a queer author who grew up bouncing around Europe and the US and currently calls Chicago home. They've been writing stories since they had to pester their mom to help them transcribe their words on the family desktop computer. They work as a stage manager and dog walker, and hold a master's degree in Humanities, with a focus in literature. No amount of school or chaotic array of part-time jobs has yet managed to stop them from reading and writing voraciously. They can also occasionally be found doing calligraphy, baking, or getting really excited about Shakespeare. They have previously contributed stories to the anthologies *Many Hands* and *A Truth Universally Acknowledged*, also from Duck Prints Press.

Ambra Rossi

Ambra is a scientist by day and, more often than not, also a scientist by night. When she manages to escape the clutches of academia, she enjoys making art, writing, and figure skating. She has been active in fandom for almost two decades.

T. L. Sly

A native of the Eastern Seaboard, T. L. Sly lives with their autistic teenage son, loving partner, younger brother and sister, three cats, and a dog. When not writing, Sly enjoys swimming in the ocean, hiking, stargazing, crafting, costuming, and making clothes for their 18" doll collection. They love to read historical and supernatural romance novels, listen to music, and watch horror movies. Sly has dedicated nearly 25 years to writing for fandom and is thrilled to be sharing their original writing at long last. A romantic at heart, Sly believes in hope, true love, and that there's nothing in the world quite like a good thunderstorm.

Teddy Sweet

In theory Teddy writes LGBT+ romance novels. In practice they manage a menagerie of 12 pets (including 8 snakes) and sneak away from them to frantically type as much as humanly possible before their laptop is nudged out of the way in favour of a dog or cat demanding long-overdue adoration. If not wrangling a beloved animal or writing, Teddy can be found under a pile of blankets, knitting another one. On a rainy day they enjoy avoiding the delights of classic British weather by gaming, getting especially engrossed in choice-based endings.

Previous works include contributions to *Gender Euphoria* and a stint as a resident author at a short story subscription service.

Dei Walker

Dei Walker (she/her) is a queer New Englander abroad, having spent almost half her life overseas. She currently lives with her family in Beijing, China. When she isn't writing, she can be found knitting, scuba diving, or playing games (video or tabletop).

Premium Backers List

Our Top-Tier Patreon Backers

Anonymous
Sam Brown
Alex Gruendl
Tina Houck
jumblejen
Aria L.
A Taylor
Karen Welborn

Our Premium Kickstarter Supporters

T.A. Blackstone
Sandra Brabender
Lady Hannah
JefforyGamerGirl
Leo Otherland
Alex "Satyr" P.
seelieAce
Kit Stubbs, Ph.D.
Kiri Thorn
Rachael L. Young

About Duck Prints Press, LLC

Duck Prints Press LLC is an independent publisher based in New York State. Our founding vision is to help fanwork creators navigate the complex process of bringing their original works from first draft to print, culminating in publishing their work under our imprint. We are particularly dedicated to working with queer creators and publishing stories and artwork featuring characters from across the LGBTQIA+ spectrum.

Become a Duck Prints Press Patron by backing us on Patreon!

Find us online at our website, **duckprintspress.com**, or on social media:
Bluesky: duckprintspress
Dreamwidth: duckprintspress.dreamwidth.org
Instagram: duckprintspress
Mastodon: @dppunforth@fandom.ink
Patreon: duckprintspress
Pillowfort: duckprintspress
TikTok: @duckprintspress
Tumblr: duckprintspress

Goodreads: https://www.goodreads.com/user/show/129902473-duck-prints-press-llc
Storygraph: https://app.thestorygraph.com/profile/unforth

www.ingramcontent.com/pod-product-compliance
Lightning Source LLC
LaVergne TN
LVHW041113080826
845145LV00007B/1799

* 9 7 8 1 9 6 2 4 8 8 4 5 7 *